Henry Seton Merriman

With Edged Tools

Henry Seton Merriman

With Edged Tools

ISBN/EAN: 9783337031398

Printed in Europe, USA, Canada, Australia, Japan

Cover: Foto ©Andreas Hilbeck / pixelio.de

More available books at **www.hansebooks.com**

[See p. 13

SHE LAID HER HAND ON HIS ARM, AND FOR A MOMENT
HIS FINGERS PRESSED HERS

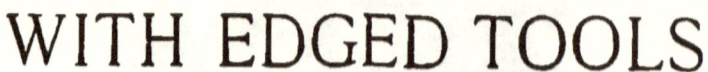

WITH EDGED TOOLS

A NOVEL

BY

HENRY SETON MERRIMAN

ILLUSTRATED

HARPER & BROTHERS PUBLISHERS

NEW YORK AND LONDON

CONTENTS

WITH EDGED TOOLS

CHAPTER I

TWO GENERATIONS

"Why, all delights are vain, but that most vain
Which with pain purchased doth inherit pain."

"My dear—madam—what you call heart does not come into the question at all."

Sir John Meredith was sitting slightly behind Lady Cantourne, leaning towards her with a somewhat stiffened replica of his former grace. But he was not looking at her —and she knew it.

They were both watching a group at the other side of the great ball-room.

"Sir John Meredith on Heart," said the old lady, with a depth of significance in her voice."

"And why not?"

"Yes, indeed. Why not?"

Sir John smiled with that well-bred cynicism which a new school has not yet succeeded in imitating. They both belonged to the old school, these two; and their worldliness, their cynicism, their conversational attitude belonged to a by-gone period. It was a cleaner period in some ways—a period devoid of slums. Ours, on the contrary, is an age of slums, wherein we all dabble to the detriment of our hands —mental, literary, and theological.

Sir John moved slightly in his chair, leaning one hand

on one knee. His back was very flat, his clothes were perfect, his hair was not his own, nor yet his teeth. But his manners were entirely his own. His face was eighty years old, and yet he smiled his keen society smile with the best of them. There was not a young man in the room of whom he was afraid, conversationally.

"No, Lady Cantourne," he repeated. "Your charming niece is heartless. She will get on."

Lady Cantourne smiled and drew the glove farther up her stout and motherly right arm.

"She will get on," she admitted. "As to the other, it is early to give an opinion."

"She has had the best of trainings—" he murmured. And Lady Cantourne turned on him with a twinkle amid the wrinkles.

"For which?" she asked.

"*Choisissez!*" he answered, with a bow.

One sees a veteran swordsman take up the foil with a tentative turn of the wrist, lunging at thin air. His zest for the game has gone; but the skill lingers, and at times he is tempted to show the younger blades a pass or two. These were veteran fencers with a skill of their own which they loved to display at times. The zest was that of remembrance; the sword-play of words was above the head of a younger generation given to slang and music-hall airs; and so these two had little bouts for their own edification, and enjoyed the glitter of it vastly.

Sir John's face relaxed into the only repose he ever allowed it; for he had a habit of twitching and moving his lips such as some old men have. And occasionally, in an access of further senility, he fumbled with his fingers at his mouth. He was clean shaven, and even in his old age he was handsome beyond other men — standing an upright six feet two.

The object of his attention was the belle of that ball, Miss Millicent Chyne, who was hemmed into a corner by a group of eager dancers anxious to insert their names in some corner of her card. She was the fashion at that time. And she probably did not know that at least half of the men crowded round because the other half were there. Nothing succeeds like the success that knows how to draw a crowd.

She received the ovation self - possessedly enough, but without that hauteur affected by belles of balls—in books. She seemed to have a fresh smile for each new applicant— a smile which conveyed to each in turn the fact that she had been attempting all along to get her programme safely into his hands. A halting masculine pen will not be expected to explain how she compassed this, beyond a gentle intimation that masculine vanity had a good deal to do with her success.

"She is having an excellent time," said Sir John, weighing on the modern phrase with a subtle sarcasm. He was addicted to the use of modern phraseology, spiced with a cynicism of his own.

"Yes; I cannot help sympathizing with her — a little," answered the lady.

"Nor I. It will not last."

"Well, she is only gathering the rose-buds."

"Wisely so, your ladyship. They at least *look* as if they were going to last. The full-blown roses do not."

Lady Cantourne gave a little sigh. This was the difference between them. She could not watch without an occasional thought for a time that was no more. The man seemed to be content that the past had been lived through and would never renew itself.

"After all," she said, "she is my sister's child. The sympathy may only be a matter of blood. Perhaps I was like that myself once. Was I? You can tell me."

She looked slowly round the room and his face hardened. He knew that she was reflecting that there was no one else who could tell her; and he did not like it.

"No," he answered, readily.

"And what was the difference?"

She looked straight in front of her with a strange old-fashioned demureness.

"Their name is legion, for they are many."

"Name a few. Was I as good-looking as that, for instance?"

He smiled—a wise, old, woman-searching smile.

"You were better - looking than that," he said, with a glance beneath his lashless lids. "Moreover, there was more of the grand lady about you. You behaved better. There was less shaking hands with your partners, less nodding and becking, and none of that modern forwardness which is called, I believe, *camaraderie*."

"Thank you, Sir John," she answered, looking at him frankly with a pleasant smile. "But it is probable that we had the faults of our age."

He fumbled at his lips, having reasons of his own for disliking too close a scrutiny of his face.

"That is more than probable," he answered, rather indistinctly.

"Then," she said, tapping the back of his gloved hand with her fan, "we ought to be merciful to the faults of a succeeding generation. Tell me, who is that young man with the long stride who is getting himself introduced now?"

"That," answered Sir John, who prided himself upon knowing every one—knowing who they were and who they were not—"is young Oscard."

"Son of the eccentric Oscard?"

"Son of the eccentric Oscard."

"And where did he get that brown face?"

"He got that in Africa, where he has been shooting. He forms part of some one else's bag at the present moment."

"What do you mean?"

"He has been apportioned a dance. Your fair niece has bagged him."

If he had only known it, Guy Oscard won the privilege of a waltz by the same brown face which Lady Cantourne had so promptly noted. Coupled with a sturdy upright-ness of carriage, this raised him at a bound above the pallid habitués of ball-room and pavement. It was, perhaps, only natural that Millicent Chyne should have noted this man as soon as he crossed the threshold. He was as remarkable as some free and dignified denizen of the forest in the midst of domestic animals. She mentally put him down for a waltz, and before five minutes had elapsed he was bowing before her while a mutual friend murmured his name. One does not know how young ladies manage these little affairs, but the fact remains that they are managed. Moreover, it is a singular thing that the young persons who succeed in the ball-room rarely succeed on the larger and rougher floor of life. Your belle of the ball, like your Senior Wrangler, never seems to do much afterwards — and Afterwards is Life.

The other young men rather fell back before Guy Oscard —scared, perhaps, by his long stride, and afraid that he might crush their puny toes. This enabled Miss Chyne to give him the very next dance, of which the music was com-mencing.

"I feel rather out of all this," said Oscard, as they moved away together. "You must excuse uncouthness."

"I see no signs of it," laughed Millicent. "You are be-having very nicely. You cannot help being larger and stronger than—the others. I should say it was an advan-tage and something to be proud of."

"Oh, it is not that," replied Oscard; "it is a feeling of unkemptness and want of smartness among these men who look so clean and correct. Shall we dance?"

He looked down at her with an admiration which almost amounted to awe, as if afraid of entering the throng with

such a dainty and wonderful charge upon his powers of
steering.   Millicent Chyne saw the glance and liked it.
It was different from the others, quite devoid of criticism,
rather simple and full of honest admiration.   She was so
beautiful that she could hardly be expected to be unaware
of the fact.   She had merely to make comparisons, to look
in the mirror and see that her hair was fairer and softer,
that her complexion was more delicately perfect, that her
slight, rounded figure was more graceful than any around
her.   Added to this she knew that she had more to say
than other girls—a larger stock of those little frivolous,
advice-seeking, aid-demanding nothings than her compeers
seemed to possess.

She knew that in saying them she could look brighter
and prettier and more intelligent than her competitors.

"Yes," she said, "let us dance by all means."

Here also she knew her own proficiency, and in a few
seconds she found that her partner was worthy of her skill.

"Where have you been?" she asked, presently.   "I am
sure you have been away somewhere, exploring or something."

"I have only been in Africa, shooting."

"Oh, how interesting!   You must tell me all about it!"

"I am afraid," replied Guy Oscard, with a somewhat shy
laugh, "that that would *not* be interesting.   Besides, I could
not tell you now."

"No, but some other time.   I suppose you are not going
back to Africa to-morrow, Mr. Oscard?"

"Not quite.   And perhaps we may meet somewhere
else."

"I hope so," replied Miss Chyne.   "Besides, you know
my aunt, Lady Cantourne.   I live with her, you know."

"I know her slightly."

"Then take an opportunity of improving the acquaint-
anceship.   She is sitting under the ragged banner over
there."

Millicent Chyne indicated the direction with a nod of
the head, and while he looked she took the opportunity of
glancing hastily round the room. She was seeking some
one.

"Yes," said Oscard, "I see her, talking to an old gentleman who looks like Voltaire. I shall give her a chance of
recognizing me before the evening is out. I don't mind
being snubbed if—"

He paused, and steered neatly through a narrow place.

"If what?" she asked, when they were in swing again.

"If it means seeing you again," he answered, bluntly—
more bluntly than she was accustomed to. But she liked
it. It was a novelty after the smaller change of ball-room
compliments.

She was watching the door all the while.

Presently the music ceased, and they made their way
back to the spot whence he had taken her. She led the
way thither by an almost imperceptible pressure of her
fingers on his arm. There were several men waiting there,
and one or two more entering the room and looking lan-
guidly round.

"There comes the favored one," Lady Cantourne muttered, with a veiled glance towards her companion.

Sir John's gray eyes followed the direction of her glance.

"My bright boy?" he inquired, with a wealth of sarcasm
on the adjective.

"Your bright boy." She replied.

"I hope not," he said, curtly.

They were watching a tall fair man in the doorway who
seemed to know everybody, so slow was his progress into
the room. The most remarkable thing about this man was
a certain grace of movement. He seemed to be specially
constructed to live in narrow, hampered places. He was
above six feet; but, being of slight build, he moved with a
certain languidness which saved him from that unwieldiness
usually associated with large men in a drawing-room.

Such was Jack Meredith, one of the best-known figures
in London society.   He had hitherto succeeded in moving
through the mazes of that coterie, as he now moved through
this room, without jarring any one.

CHAPTER II

OVER THE OLD GROUND

" A man who never makes mistakes never makes anything else either."

Miss Millicent Chyne was vaguely conscious of success—and such a consciousness is apt to make the best of
us a trifle elated.   It was certainly one of the best balls of
the season, and Miss Chyne's dress was, without doubt, one
of the most successful articles of its sort there.

Jack Meredith saw that fact, and noted it as soon as he
came into the room.   Moreover, it pleased him, and he was
pleased to reflect that he was no mean critic in such matters.   There could be no doubt about it, because he *knew*
as well as any woman there.   He knew that Millicent Chyne
was dressed in the latest fashion — no furbished-up gown
from the hands of her maid, but a unique creation from
Bond Street.

" Well," she asked, in a low voice as she handed him her
programme, " are you pleased with it ?"

" Eminently so."

She glanced down at her own dress.   It was not the
nervous glance of the *débutante*, but the practised flash of
experienced eyes which see without appearing to look.

" I am glad," she murmured.

He handed her back the card with the orthodox smile
and bow of gratitude, but there was something more in his
eyes.

"Is that what you did it for?" he inquired.

"Of course," with a glance half coquettish, half humble.

She took the card, and allowed it to drop pendent from her fan without looking at it. He had written nothing on it. This was all a form. The dances that were his had been inscribed on the engagement-card long before by smaller fingers than his.

She turned to take her attendant partner's arm with a little flaunt — a little movement of the hips to bring her dress, and possibly herself, more prominently beneath Jack Meredith's notice. His eyes followed her with that incomparably pleasant society smile which he had no doubt inherited from his father. Then he turned and mingled with the well-dressed throng, bowing where he ought to bow — asking with fervor for dances in plain but influential quarters where dances were to be easily obtained.

And all the while his father and Lady Cantourne watched.

"Yes, I *think*," the lady was saying, "that that is the favored one."

"I fear so."

"I notice," observed Lady Cantourne, "that he asked for a dance."

"And apparently got one—or more."

"Apparently so, Sir John."

"Moreover—"

Lady Cantourne turned on him with her usual vivacity.

"Moreover?" she repeated.

"He did not need to write it down on the card; it was written there already."

She closed her fan with a faint smile.

"I sometimes wonder," she said, "whether, in our young days, you were so preternaturally observant as you are now."

"No," he answered, "I was not. I affected scales of the very opaquest description, like the rest of my kind."

In the meantime this man's son was going about his business with a leisurely *savoir-faire* which few could rival. Jack Meredith was the beau-ideal of the society man in the best acceptation of the word. One met him wherever the best people congregated, and he invariably seemed to know what to do and how to do it better than his compeers. If it was dancing in the season, Jack Meredith danced, and no man rivalled him. If it was grouse-shooting, Jack Meredith held his gun as straight as any man. All the polite accomplishments in their season seemed to come to him without effort; but there was in all the same lack of heart — that utter want of enthusiasm which imparted to his presence a subtle suggestion of boredom. The truth was that he was over-educated. Sir John had taught him how to live and move and have his being with so minute a care, so keen an insight, that existence seemed to be nothing but an habitual observance of set rules.

Sir John called him sarcastically his "bright boy," his "hopeful offspring," the "pride of his old age;" but somewhere in his shrivelled old heart there nestled an unbounded love and admiration for his son. Jack had assimilated his teaching with a wonderful aptitude. He had as nearly as possible realized Sir John Meredith's idea of what an English gentleman should be, and the old aristocrat's standard was uncompromisingly high. Public school, university, and two years on the Continent had produced a finished man, educated to the finger-tips, deeply read, clever, bright, and occasionally witty ; but Jack Meredith was at this time nothing more than a brilliant conglomerate of possibilities. He had obeyed his father to the letter with a conscientiousness bred of admiration. He had always felt that his father knew best. And now he seemed to be waiting—possibly for further orders. He was suggestive of a perfect piece of mechanism standing idle for want of work delicate enough to be manipulated by its delicate craft. Sir John had impressed upon him the desirability of being independent, and he had promptly cultivated that excellent quality, taking kindly enough to rooms of his own in a fashionable quarter. But upon the principle of taking a horse to the water and being unable to make him drink, Sir John had not hitherto succeeded in making Jack take the initiative. He had turned out such a finished and polished English gentleman as his soul delighted in, and now he waited in cynical silence for Jack Meredith to take his life into his own hands and do something brilliant with it. All that he had done up to now had been to prove that he could attain to a greater social popularity than any other man of his age and station; but this was not exactly the success that Sir John Meredith coveted for his son. He had tasted of this success himself, and knew its thinness of flavor—its fleeting value.

Behind his keen old eyes such thoughts as these were passing while he watched Jack go up and claim his dance at the hands of Miss Millicent Chyne. He could almost guess what they said; for Jack was grave, and she smiled demurely. They began dancing at once, and as soon as the floor became crowded they disappeared.

Jack Meredith was an adept at such matters. He knew a seat at the end of a long passage where they could sit, the beheld of all beholders who happened to pass; but no one could possibly overhear their conversation—no one could surprise them. It was essentially a strategical position.

"Well," inquired Jack, with a peculiar breathlessness, when they were seated, "have you thought about it?"

She gave a little nod.

They seemed to be taking up some conversation at a point where it had been dropped on a previous occasion.

"And?" he inquired, suavely. The society polish was very thickly coated over the man, but his eyes had a hungry look.

By way of reply her gloved hand crept out towards his, which rested on the chair at his side.

"Jack!" she whispered; and that was all.

It was very prettily done, and quite naturally. He was a judge of such matters, and appreciated the girlish simplicity of the action fully.

He took the small gloved hand and pressed it lovingly. The thoroughness of his social training prevented any further display of affection.

"Thank Heaven!" he murmured.

They were essentially of the nineteenth century—these two. At a previous dance he had asked her to marry him; she had deferred her answer, and now she had given it. These little matters are all a question of taste. We do not kneel nowadays, either physically or morally. If we are a trifle off-hand, it is the women who are to blame. They should not write in magazines of a doubtful reputation in language devoid of the benefit of the doubt. They are equal to us. *Bien!* One does not kneel to an equal. A better writer than any of us says that men serve women kneeling, and when they get to their feet they go away. We are being hauled up to our feet now.

"But—" began the girl, and went no further.

"But what?"

"There will be difficulties."

"No doubt," he answered, with quiet mockery. "There always are. I will see to them. Difficulties are not without a certain advantage. They keep one on the alert."

"Your father," said the girl. "Sir John—he will object."

Jack Meredith reflected for a moment, lazily, with that leisureliness which gave a sense of repose to his presence.

"Possibly," he admitted, gravely.

"He dislikes me," said the girl. "He is one of my failures."

"I did not know you had any. Have you tried? I cannot quite admit the possibility of failure."

Millicent Chyne smiled. He had emphasized the last remark with lover-like glance and tone. She was young enough; her own beauty was new enough to herself to blind her to the possibility mentioned. She had not even got to the stage of classifying as dull all men who did not fall in love with her at first sight. It was her first season, one must remember.

"I have not tried very hard," she said; "but I don't see why I should not fail."

"That is easily explained."

"Why?"

"No looking-glass about."

She gave a little pout, but she liked it.

The music of the next dance was beginning, and, remembering their social obligations, they both rose. She laid her hand on his arm, and for a moment his fingers pressed hers. He smiled down into her upturned eyes with love, but without passion. He never for a second risked the "gentleman" and showed the "man." He was suggestive of a forest pool with a smiling, rippled surface. There might be depth, but nothing had yet reached beyond the surface.

"Shall we go now," he said, "and say a few words in passing to my redoubtable father? It might be effective."

"Yes, if you like," she answered, promptly. There is no more confident being on earth than a pretty girl in a successful dress.

They met Sir John at the entrance of the ball-room. He was wandering about, taking in a vast deal of detail.

"Well, young lady," he said, with an Old-World bow, "are you having a successful evening?"

Millicent laughed. She never knew quite how to take Sir John.

"Yes, I think so, thank you," she answered, with a pretty smile. "I am enjoying myself very much."

There was just the least suggestion of shyness in her manner, and it is just possible that this softened the old cynic's heart, for his manner was kinder, and almost fatherly when he spoke again.

"Ah!" he said, "at your time of life you do not want

much — plenty of partners and a few ices.   Both easily
obtainable."

The last words were turned into a compliment by the
courtly inclination of the head that accompanied them.

The exigencies of the moment forced the young people
to go with the stream.

"Jack," said Sir John, as they passed on, "when you
have been deprived of Miss Chyne's society, come and con-
sole yourself with a glass of sherry."

The dutiful son nodded a semi-indifferent acquiescence
and disappeared.

"Wonderful thing, sherry!" observed Sir John Meredith,
for his own edification.

He waited there until Jack returned, and then they set
off in search of refreshment.   The son seemed to know his
whereabouts better than the father.

"This way," he said—"through the conservatory."

Amid the palms and tropical ferns Sir John paused.
A great deal of care had been devoted to this conservatory.
Half hidden among languorous scented flowers were a
thousand tiny lights, while overhead in the gloom towered
graceful palms and bananas.   A fountain murmured pleasantly amid a cluster of maidenhairs.   The music from the
ball-room fell softly over all.

Sir John Meredith and his son stood in silence, looking
around them.   Finally their eyes met.

"Are you in earnest with that girl?" asked Sir John,
abruptly.

"I am," replied Jack.   He was smiling pleasantly.

"And you think there is a chance of her marrying you
— unless, of course, something better turns up?"

"With all due modesty I do."

Sir John's hand was at his mouth.   He stood up his full
six feet two and looked hard at his son, whose eyes were
level with his own.   They were ideal representatives of
their school.

"And what do you propose marrying upon? She, I understand, has about eight hundred a year. I respect you too much to suspect any foolish notions of love in a cottage."

Jack Meredith made no reply. He was entirely dependent upon his father.

"Of course," said Sir John, "when I die you will be a baronet, and there will be enough to live on like a gentleman. You had better tell Miss Chyne that. She may not know it. Girls are so innocent. But I am not dead yet, and I shall take especial care to live some time."

"In order to prevent my marriage?" suggested Jack. He was still smiling, and somehow Sir John felt a little uneasy. He did not understand that smile.

"Precisely so," he said, rather indistinctly.

"What is your objection?" inquired Jack Meredith, after a little pause.

"I object to the girl."

"Upon what grounds?"

"I should prefer you to marry a woman of heart."

"Heart?" repeated Jack, with a suspicion of hereditary cynicism. "I do not think heart is of much consequence. Besides, in this case, surely that is my province; you would not have her wear it on her sleeve?"

"She could not do that: not enough sleeve."

Sir John Meredith had his own views on ladies' dress.

"But," he added, "we will not quarrel. Arrange matters with the young lady as best you can. I shall never approve of such a match, and without my approval you cannot well marry."

"I do not admit that."

"Indeed?"

"Your approval means money," explained this dutiful son politely. "I might manage to make the money for myself."

Sir John moved away.

"You might," he admitted, looking back. "I should be very glad to see you doing so. It is an excellent thing—money."

And he walked leisurely away.

CHAPTER III

A FAREWELL

"Since called
The Paradise of Fools, to few unknown."

HAVING been taught to take all the chances and changes of life with a well-bred calmness of demeanor, Jack Meredith turned the teaching against the instructor. He pursued the course of his social duties without appearing to devote so much as a thought to the quarrel which had taken place in the conservatory. His smile was as ready as ever, his sight as keen where an elderly lady looked hungry, his laughter as near the surface as society demands. It is probable that Sir John suffered more, though he betrayed nothing. Youth has the upperhand in these cases, for life is a larger thing when we are young. As we get on in years, our eggs, to use a homely simile, have a way of accumulating into one basket.

At eleven o'clock the next morning Sir John Meredith's valet intimated to his master that Mr. Meredith was waiting in the breakfast-room. Sir John was in the midst of his toilet—a complicated affair, which, like other works of art, would not bear contemplation when incomplete.

"Tell him," said the uncompromising old gentleman, "that I will come down when I am ready."

He made a more careful toilet than usual, and finally came down in a gay tweed suit, of which the general effect was distinctly heightened by a pair of white gaiters. He was upright, trim, and perfectly determined. Jack noted that his clothes looked a little emptier than usual—that was all.

"Well," said the father, "I suppose we both made fools of ourselves last night."

"I have not yet seen you do that," replied the son, laying aside the morning paper which he had been reading.

Sir John smiled grimly. He hoped that Jack was right.

"Well," he added, "let us call it a difference of opinion."

"Yes."

Something in the monosyllable made the old gentleman's lips twitch nervously.

"I may mention," he said, with a dangerous suavity, "that I still hold to my opinion."

Jack Meredith rose, without haste. This, like the interview of the previous night, was conducted upon strictly high-bred and gentlemanly lines.

"And I to mine," he said. "That is why I took the liberty of calling at this early hour. I thought that perhaps we might effect some sort of a compromise."

"It is very good of you to make the proposal." Sir John kept his fingers away from his lips by an obvious exercise of self-control. "I am not partial to compromises; they savor of commerce."

Jack gave a queer, curt nod, and moved towards the door. Sir John extended his unsteady hand and rang the bell.

"Good-morning," he said.

"Garle," he added, to the servant who stood in the doorway, "when you have closed the door behind Mr. Meredith, bring up breakfast, if you please."

On the door-step Jack Meredith looked at his watch. He had an appointment with Millicent Chyne at half-past eleven —an hour when Lady Cantourne might reasonably be expected to be absent at the weekly meeting of a society which, under the guise and nomenclature of friendship, busied itself in making servant-girls discontented with their situations.

It was only eleven o'clock. Jack turned to the left, out of the quiet but fashionable street, and a few steps took him to Piccadilly. He went into the first jeweller's shop he saw, and bought a plain diamond ring. Then he walked on to keep his appointment with his affianced wife.

Miss Millicent Chyne was waiting for him with that mixture of maidenly feelings of which the discreet novelist only details a selection. It is not customary to dwell upon thoughts of vague regret at the approaching withdrawal of a universal admiration—at the future necessity for discreet and humdrum behavior quite devoid of the excitement that lurks in a double meaning. Let it, therefore, be ours to note the outward signs of a very natural emotion. Miss Chyne noted them herself with care, and not without a few deft touches to hair and dress. When Jack Meredith entered the room she was standing near the window, holding back the curtain with one hand and watching, half shyly, for his advent.

What struck her at once was his gravity; and he must have seen the droop in her eyes, for he immediately assumed the pleasant, half-reckless smile which the world of London society had learned to associate with his name.

He played the lover rather well, with that finish and absence of self-consciousness which only comes from sincerity; and when Miss Chyne found opportunity to look at him a second time she was fully convinced that she loved him. She was, perhaps, carried off her feet a little—metaphorically speaking, of course — by his evident sincerity. At that moment she would have done anything that he had asked her. The pleasure of society, the social amenities of aristocratic life, seemed to have vanished suddenly into thin air, and only love was left. She had always known that Jack Meredith was superior in a thousand ways to all her admirers. More gentlemanly, more truthful, honester, nobler, more worthy of love. Beyond that he was cleverer, despite a certain laziness of disposition—more brilliant and more amusing. He had always been to a great extent the

chosen one; and yet it was with a certain surprise and
sense of unreality that she found what she had drifted into.
She saw the diamond ring, and looked upon it with the
beautiful emotions aroused by those small stones in the
female breast; but she did not seem to recognize her own
finger within the golden hoop.

It was at this moment—while she dwelt in this new un-
real world—that he elected to tell her of his quarrel with
his father. And when one walks through a maze of un-
realities nothing seems to come amiss or to cause surprise.
He detailed the very words they had used, and to Millicent
Chyne it did not sound like a real quarrel such as might
affect two lives to their very end. It was not important.
It did not come into her life; for at that moment she did
not know what her life was.

"And so," said Jack Meredith, finishing his story, "we
have begun badly—as badly as the most romantic might
desire."

"Yes, theoretically it is consoling. But I am sorry,
Jack, very sorry. I hate quarrelling with anybody."

"So do I. I haven't time, as a rule. But the old gentleman is so easy to quarrel with, he takes all the trouble."

"Jack," she said, with pretty determination. "You
must go and say you are sorry. Go now! I wish I could
go with you."

But Meredith did not move. He was smiling at her in
evident admiration. She looked very pretty with that determined little pout of the lips, and perhaps she knew it.
Moreover, he did not seem to attach so much importance
to the thought as to the result—to the mind as to the lips.

"Ah!" he said, "you do not know the old gentleman.
That is not our way of doing things. We are not expansive."

His face was grave again, and she noticed it with a sudden throb of misgiving. She did not want to begin taking
life seriously so soon. It was like going back to school in
the middle of the holidays.

"But it will be all right in a day or two, will it not? It is not serious," she said.

"I am afraid it is serious, Millicent."

He took her hand with a gravity which made matters worse.

"What a pity!" she exclaimed; and somehow both the words and the speaker rang shallow. She did not seem to grasp the situation, which was perhaps beyond her reach. But she did the next best thing. She looked puzzled, pretty, and helpless.

"What is to be done, Jack?" she said, laying her two hands on his breast and looking up pleadingly.

There was something in the man's clear-cut face—something beyond aristocratic repose—as he looked down into her eyes—something which Sir John Meredith might perhaps have liked to see there. To all men comes, soon or late, the moment wherein their lives are suddenly thrust into their own hands to shape or spoil, to make or mar. It seemed that where a clever man had failed, this light-hearted girl was about to succeed. Two small clinging hands on Jack Meredith's breast had apparently wrought more than all Sir John's care and foresight. At last the light of energy gleamed in Jack Meredith's lazy eyes. At last he faced the "initiative," and seemed in nowise abashed.

"There are two things," he answered: "a small choice."

"Yes."

"The first, and the simplest," he went on in the tone of voice which she had never quite fathomed—half cynical, half amused—"is to pretend that last night—never was."

He waited for her verdict.

"We will not do that," she replied, softly; "we will take the other alternative, whatever it is."

She glanced up half shyly beneath her lashes, and he felt that no difficulty could affright him.

"The other is generally supposed to be very difficult," he said. "It means—waiting."

"Oh," she answered, cheerfully, "there is no hurry. I do not want to be married yet."

"Waiting perhaps for years," he added—and he saw her face drop.

"Why?"

"Because I am dependent on my father for everything. We could not marry without his consent."

A peculiar, hard look crept into her eyes, and in some subtle way it made her look older. After a little pause she said:

"But we can surely get that—between us?"

"I propose doing without it."

She looked up—past him—out of the window. All the youthfulness seemed to have left her face, but he did not appear to see that.

"How can you do so?"

"Well, I can work. I suppose I must be good for something—a bountiful Providence must surely have seen to that. The difficulty is to find out what it intends me for. We are not called in the night nowadays to a special mission—we have to find it out for ourselves."

"Do you know what I should like you to be?" she said, with a bright smile and one of those sudden descents into shallowness which he appeared to like.

"What?"

"A politician."

"Then I shall be a politician," he answered, with lover-like promptness.

"That would be very nice," she said; and the castles she at once began to build were not entirely aerial in their structure.

This was not a new idea. They had talked of politics before as a possible career for himself. They had moved in a circle where politics and politicians held a first place—a circle removed above the glamour of art, and wherein Bohemianism was not reckoned an attraction. She knew that

behind his listlessness of manner he possessed a certain
steady energy, perfect self-command, and that combination
of self-confidence and indifference which usually attains success in the world. She was ambitious not only for herself,
but for him, and she was shrewd enough to know that the
only safe outlet for a woman's ambition is the channel of a
husband's career.

"But," he said, "it will mean waiting."

He paused, and then the worldly wisdom which he had
learned from his father — that worldly wisdom which is
sometimes called cynicism—prompted him to lay the matter before her in its worst light.

"It will mean waiting for a couple of years at least. And
for you it will mean the dulness of a long engagement, and
the anomalous position of an engaged girl without her right-
ful protector. It will mean that your position in society
will be quite different — that half the world will pity you,
while the other half thinks you — well, a fool for your
pains."

"I don't care," she answered.

"Of course," he went on, "I must go away. That is the
only way to get on in politics in these days. I must go
away and get a specialty. I must know more about some
country than any other man ; and when I come back I must
keep that country ever before the eye of the intelligent
British workman who reads the half-penny evening paper.
That is fame—those are politics."

She laughed. There seemed to be no fear of her taking
life too seriously yet. And, truth to tell, he did not appear
to wish her to do so.

"But you must not go very far," she said, sweetly.

"Africa."

"Africa? That does not sound interesting."

"It is interesting ; moreover, it is the coming country. I
may be able to make money out there, and money is a necessity at present."

"I do not like it, Jack," she said, in a foreboding voice. "When do you go?"

"At once—in fact, I came to say good-bye. It is better to do these things very promptly—to disappear before the onlookers have quite understood what is happening. When they begin to understand, they begin to interfere. They cannot help it. I will write to Lady Cantourne if you like."

"No, I will tell her."

So he bade her good-bye, and those things that lovers say were duly said; but they are not for us to chronicle. Such words are better left to be remembered or forgotten as time and circumstance and result may decree. For one may never tell what words will do when they are laid within the years like the little morsel of leaven that leaveneth the whole.

CHAPTER IV

A TRAGEDY

"Who knows? the man is proven by the hour."

In his stately bedroom on the second floor of the quietest house in Russell Square Mr. Thomas Oscard—the eccentric Oscard—lay, perhaps, a-dying.

Thomas Oscard had written the finest history of an extinct people that had ever been penned; and it has been decreed that he who writes a fine history and paints a fine picture can hardly be too eccentric. Our business, however, does not lie in the life of this historian—a life which certain grave wiseacres from the West (End) had shaken their heads over a few hours before we find him lying prone on a four-poster, counting for the thousandth time the number of tassels fringing the roof of it. In bold contradiction of the medical opinion, the nurse was, however, hopeful.

Whether this comforting condition of mind arose from long experience of the ways of doctors, or from an acquired philosophy, it is not our place to inquire. But that her opinion was sincere is not to be doubted. She had, as a matter of fact, gone to the pantomime, leaving the patient under the immediate eye of his son, Guy Oscard.

The temporary nurse was sitting in a cretonne - covered arm-chair, with a book of travel on his knee, and thoughts of Millicent Chyne in his mind. The astute have no doubt discovered ere this that the mind of Mr. Guy Oscard was a piece of mental mechanism more noticeable for solidity of structure than brilliancy or rapidity of execution. Thoughts and ideas and principles had a strange way of getting mixed up with the machinery, and sticking there. Guy Oscard had, for instance, concluded some years before that the Winchester rifle was, as he termed it, "no go;" and, if the Pope of Rome and the patentee of the fire-arm in question had crossed Europe upon their bended knees to persuade him to use a Winchester rifle, he would have received them with a pleasant smile and an offer of refreshment. He would have listened to their arguments with that patience of manner which characterizes men of large stature, and for the rest of his days he would have continued to follow big game with an "Express" double - barrelled rifle as heretofore. Men who decide such smaller matters as these for themselves, after mature and somewhat slow consideration, have a way of also deciding the larger issues of life without pausing to consider either expediency or the experience of their neighbors.

During the last forty-eight hours Guy Oscard had made the decision that life without Millicent Chyne would not be worth having, and in the hush of the great house he was pondering over this new feature in his existence. Like all deliberate men, he was placidly sanguine. Something in the life of a savage sport that he had led had no doubt taught him to rely upon his own nerve and capacity more

than most men do. It is the in-door atmosphere that con-
tains the germ of pessimism.

His thoughts cannot have been disturbing, for presently
his eyes closed and he appeared to be slumbering. If it
was sleep, it was the light unconsciousness of the traveller;
for a sound so small that waking ears could scarce have
heard it caused him to lift his lashes cautiously. It was
the sound of bare feet on carpet.

Through his lashes Guy Oscard saw his father standing
on the hearth-rug within two yards of him. There was
something strange, something unnatural and disturbing,
about the movements of the man that made Guy keep
quite still—watching him.

Upon the mantel - piece the medicine bottles were arranged in a row, and the "eccentric Oscard" was studying
the labels with a feverish haste. One bottle—a blue one—
bore two labels; the smaller one, of brilliant orange color,
with the word " Poison " in startling simplicity. He took
this up and slowly drew the cork. It was a liniment for
neuralgic pains in an overwrought head—belladonna. He
poured some into a medicine-glass, carefully measuring two
table-spoonfuls.

Then Guy Oscard sprang up and wrenched the glass
away from him, throwing the contents into the fire, which
flared up. Quick as thought, the bottle was at the sick
man's lips. He was a heavily built man with powerful limbs.
Guy seized his arm, closed with him, and for a moment
there was a deadly struggle, while the pungent odor of the
poison filled the atmosphere. At last Guy fell back on art;
he tripped his father cleverly, and they both rolled on the
floor.

The sick man still gripped the bottle, but he could not
get it to his lips. He poured some of the stuff over his
son's face, but fortunately missed his eyes. They struggled
on the floor in the dim light, panting and gasping, but
speaking no word. The strength of the elder man was un-

natural — it frightened the younger and stronger com-
batant.

At last Guy Oscard got his knee on his father's neck,
and bent his wrist back until he was forced to let go his
hold on the bottle.

"Get back to bed!" said the son, breathlessly. "Get back
to bed!"

Thomas Oscard suddenly changed his tactics. He whined
and cringed to his own offspring, and begged him to give
him the bottle. He dragged across the floor on his knees
—three thousand pounds a year on its knees to Guy Oscard,
who wanted that money because he knew that he would
never get Millicent Chyne without it.

"Get back to bed!" repeated Guy, sternly, and at last the
man crept sullenly between the rumpled sheets.

Guy put things straight in a simple, manlike way.   The
doctor's instructions were quite clear.   If any sign of excitement or mental unrest manifested itself, the sleeping-
draught contained in a small bottle on the mantel-piece was
to be administered at once, or the consequences would be
fatal.   But Thomas Oscard refused to take it.   He seemed
determined to kill himself.   The son stood over him and
tried threats, persuasion, prayers; and all the while there
was in his heart the knowledge that, unless his father could
be made to sleep, the reputed three thousand a year would
be his before the morning.

It was worse than the actual physical struggle on the
floor.   The temptation was almost too strong.

After a while the sick man became quieter, but he still
refused to take the opiate.   He closed his eyes and made
no answer to Guy's repeated supplication.   Finally he ceased
shaking his head in negation, and at last breathed regularly
like a child asleep.

Afterwards Guy Oscard reproached himself for suspecting nothing.   But he knew nothing of brain diseases—
those strange maladies that kill the human in the human

being. He knew, however, why his father had tried to kill himself. It was not the first time. It was panic. He was afraid of going mad, of dying mad like his father before him. People called him eccentric. Some said that he was mad. But it was not so. It was only fear of madness. He was still asleep when the nurse came back from the pantomime in a cab, and Guy crept softly down-stairs to let her in.

They stood in the hall for some time while Guy told her in whispers about the belladonna liniment. Then they went up-stairs together and found Thomas Oscard—the great historian—dead on the floor. The liniment bottle, which Guy had left on the mantel-piece, was in his hand—empty. He had feigned sleep in order to carry out his purpose. He had preferred death, of which the meaning was unknown to him, to the possibility of that living death in which his father had lingered for many years. And who shall say that his thoughts were entirely selfish? There may have been a father's love somewhere in this action. Thomas Oscard, the eccentric savant, had always been a strong man, independent of the world's opinion. He had done this thing deliberately, of mature thought, going straight to his Creator with his poor human brain full of argument and reason to prove himself right before the Judge.

They picked him up and laid him reverently on the bed, and then Guy went for the doctor.

"I could," said the attendant of Death, when he had heard the whole story—"I could give you a certificate. I could reconcile it, I mean, with my professional conscience and my—other conscience. He could not have lived thirty hours—there was an abscess on his brain. But I should advise you to face the inquest. It might be "—he paused, looking keenly into the young fellow's face—"it *might* be that at some future date, when you are quite an old man, you may feel inclined to tell this story."

Again the doctor paused, glancing with a vague smile

towards the woman who stood beside them. "Or even nurse—" he added, not troubling to finish his sentence. "We all have our moments of expansiveness. And it is a story that might easily be—discredited."

So the "eccentric Oscard" finished his earthly career in the intellectual atmosphere of a coroner's jury. And the world rather liked it than otherwise. The world, one finds, does like novelty, even in death. Some day an American will invent a new funeral, and, if he can only get the patent, will make a fortune.

The world was, morever, pleased to pity Guy Oscard with that pure and simple sympathy which is ever accorded to the wealthy in affliction. Every one knew that Thomas Oscard had enjoyed affluence during his lifetime, and there was no reason to suppose that Guy would not step into very comfortably lined shoes. It was unfortunate that he should lose his father in such a tragic way, and the keen eye of the world saw the weak point in his story at once. But the coroner's jury was respectful, and the rest of society never so much as hinted at the possibility that Guy had not tried his best to keep his father alive.

Among the letters of sympathy the young fellow received a note from Lady Cantourne, whose acquaintance he had successfully renewed, and in due course he called at her house in Vere Gardens to express somewhat lamely his gratitude.

Her ladyship was at home, and in due course Guy Oscard was ushered into her presence. He looked round the room with a half-suppressed gleam of searching which was not overlooked by Millicent Chyne's aunt.

"It is very good of you to call," she said, "so soon after your poor father's death. You must have had a great deal of trouble and worry. Millicent and I have often talked of you and sympathized with you. She is out at the moment, but I expect her back almost at once. Will you sit down?"

"Thanks," he said; and, after he had drawn forward a

chair, he repeated the word vaguely and comprehensively—
"thanks"—as if to cover as many demands for gratitude
as she could make.

"I knew your father very well," continued the lady,
"when we were young. Great things were expected of
him. Perhaps he expected them himself. That may have
accounted for a tone of pessimism that always seemed to
pervade his life. Now, you are quite different. You are
not a pessimist—eh?"

Guy gravely examined the back of his gloved hand.
"Well, I am afraid I have not given much thought to the
question."

Lady Cantourne gave him the benefit of a very wise
smile. She was unrivalled in the art of turning a young
man's mind inside out and shaking it.

"No, you need not apologize. I am glad you have given
no thought to it. Thought is the beginning of pessimism,
especially with young men; for if they think at all, they
naturally think of themselves."

"Well, I suppose I think as much of myself as other
people."

"Possibly, but I doubt it. Would you ring the bell?
We will have some tea."

He obeyed, and she watched him with approval. For
some reason—possibly because he had not sought it—Lady
Cantourne had bestowed her entire approval on this young
man. She had been duly informed, a few weeks before
this visit, that Miss Millicent Chyne had engaged herself to
be married to Jack Meredith whenever that youth should
find himself in a position to claim the fulfilment of her
promise. She said nothing against her choice or her decision, merely observing that she was sorry that Jack had
quarrelled with his father. By way of counsel she advised
strongly that the engagement be kept as much in the background as possible. She did not, she said, want Millicent
to be a sort of red rag to Sir John, and there was no neces-

sity to publish abroad the lamentable fact that a quarrel had resulted from a very natural and convenient attachment. Sir John was a faddist, and, like the rest of his kind, eminently pig-headed. It was more than likely that in a few months he would recall his son, and, in the meantime, it never did a girl any good to be quarrelled over.

Lady Cantourne was too clever a woman to object to the engagement. On the contrary, she allowed it to be understood that such a match was in many ways entirely satisfactory. At the same time, however, she encouraged Guy Oscard to come to the house, knowing quite well that he was entirely unaware of the existence of Jack Meredith.

"I am," she was in the habit of saying, "a great advocate for allowing young people to manage their affairs themselves. One young man, if he be the right one, has more influence with a girl than a thousand old women; and it is just possible that he knows better than they do what is for her happiness. It is the interference that makes mischief."

So she did not interfere. She merely invited Guy Oschard to stay to tea.

CHAPTER V

WITH EDGED TOOLS

> "Do not give dalliance
> Too much the rein; the strongest oaths are straw
> To the fire i' the blood."

"AND what do you intend to do with yourself?" asked Lady Cantourne when she had poured out tea. "You surely do not intend to mope in that dismal house in Russell Square?"

"No, I shall let that if I can."

"Oh, you will have no difficulty in doing that. People

live in Russell Square again now, and try to make one believe that it is a fashionable quarter. Your father stayed
on there because the carpets fitted the rooms, and on account of other ancestral conveniences.   He did not live
there—he knew nothing of his immediate environments.
He lived in Phœnicia."

"Then," continued Guy Oscard, "I shall go abroad."

"Ah! Will you have a second cup? Why will you go
abroad?"

Guy Oscard paused for a moment. "I know an old
hippopotamus in a certain African river who has twice
upset me.   I want to go back and shoot him."

"Don't go at once; that would be running away from it
—not from the hippopotamus—from the inquest.   It does
not matter being upset in an African river; but you must
not be upset in London by—an inquest."

"I did not propose going at once," replied Guy Oscard,
with a peculiar smile which Lady Cantourne thought she
understood.   "It will take me some time to set my affairs
in order—the will, and all that."

Lady Cantourne waited with perfectly suppressed curiosity, and while she was waiting Millicent Chyne came into
the room.   The girl was dressed with her habitual perfect
taste and success, and she came forward with a smile of
genuine pleasure, holding out a small hand neatly gloved in
Suède.   Her ladyship was looking, not at Millicent, but at
Guy Oscard.

Millicent was glad that he had called, and said so.   She
did not add that during the three months that had elapsed
since Jack Meredith's sudden departure she had gradually
recognized the approaching ebb of a very full tide of popularity.   It was rather dull at times, when Jack's letters
arrived at intervals of two and sometimes of three weeks—
when her girl friends allowed her to see somewhat plainly
that she was no longer to be counted as one of themselves.
An engagement sits as it were on a young lady like a

weak heart on a school-boy, setting her apart in work and play, debarring her from participation in that game of life which is ever going forward where young folks do congregate.

Moreover, she liked Guy Oscard. He aroused her curiosity. There was something in him—something which she vaguely suspected to be connected with herself—which she wanted to drag out and examine. She possessed more than the usual allowance of curiosity—which is saying a good deal; for one may take it that the beginning of all things in the feminine mind is curiosity. They want to know what is inside Love before they love. Guy Oscard was a new specimen of the genus *homo;* and while remaining perfectly faithful to Jack, Miss Millicent Chyne saw no reason why she should not pass the time by studying him, merely, of course, in a safe and innocent manner. She was one of those intelligent young ladies who think deeply—about young men. And such thinking usually takes the form of speculation as to how the various specimens selected will act under specified circumstances. The circumstances need hardly be mentioned. Young men are only interesting to young women in circumstances strictly personal to and bearing upon themselves. In a word, maidens of a speculative mind are always desirous of finding out how different men will act when they are in love; and we all know and cannot fail to applaud the assiduity with which they pursue their studies.

"Ah!" said Miss Chyne, "it is very good of you to take pity upon two lone females. I was afraid that you had gone off to the wilds of America or somewhere in search of big game. Do you know, Mr. Oscard, you are quite a celebrity? I heard you called the 'big-game man' the other day, also the 'travelling fellow.'"

The specimen smiled happily under this delicate handling.

"It is not," he said, modestly, "a very lofty fame. Anybody could let off a rifle."

"I am afraid I could not," replied Millicent, with a pretty little shudder, "if anything growled."

"Mr. Oscard has just been telling me," interposed Lady Cantourne, conversationally, "that he is thinking of going off to the wilds again."

"Then it is very disappointing of him," said Millicent, with a little droop of the eyelids which went home. "It seems to be only the uninteresting people who stay at home and live humdrum lives of enormous duration."

"He seems to think that his friends are going to cast him off because his poor father died without the assistance of a medical man," continued the old lady, meaningly.

"No—I never said that, Lady Cantourne."

"But you implied it."

Guy Oscard shook his head. "I hate being a notoriety," he said. "I like to pass through with the crowd. If I go away for a little while I shall return a nonentity."

At this moment another visitor was announced, and presently made his appearance. He was an old gentleman of no personality whatever, who was nevertheless welcomed effusively, because two people in the room had a distinct use for him. Lady Cantourne was exceedingly gracious. She remembered instantly that horticulture was among his somewhat antiquated accomplishments, and she was immediately consumed with a desire to show him the conservatory which she had had built outside the drawing-room window. She took a genuine interest in this abode of flowers, and watered the plants herself with much enthusiasm—when she remembered.

Added to a number of positive virtues the old gentleman possessed that of abstaining from tea, which enabled the two horticulturists to repair to the conservatory at once, leaving the young people alone at the other end of the drawing-room.

Millicent smoothed her gloves with downcast eyes and that demure air by which the talented fair imply the consciousness of being alone and out of others' ear-shot with an interesting member of the stronger sex.

Guy sat and watched the Suède gloves with a certain sense of placid enjoyment. Then suddenly he spoke, continuing his remarks where they had been broken off by the advent of the useful old gentleman.

"You see," he said, "it is only natural that a great many people should give me the cold shoulder. My story was a little lame. There is no reason why they should believe in me."

"I believe in you," she answered.

"Thank you."

He looked at her in a strange way, as if he liked her terse creed, and would fain have heard it a second time. Then suddenly he leaned back with his head against a corner of the piano. The fronds of a maidenhair fern hanging in delicate profusion almost hid his face. He was essentially muscular in his thoughts, and did not make the most of his dramatic effects. The next remark was make by a pair of long legs ending off with patent-leather boots which were not quite new. The rest of him was invisible.

"It was a very unpleasant business," he said, in a jerky, self-conscious voice. "I didn't know that I was that sort of fellow. The temptation was very great. I nearly gave in and let him do it. He was a stronger man than I. You know —we did not get on well together. He always hoped that I would turn out a literary sort of fellow, and I suppose he was disappointed. I tried at one time, but I found it was no good. From indifference it turned almost to hatred. He disliked me intensely, and I am afraid I did not care for him very much."

She nodded her head, and he went on. Perhaps he could see her through the maidenhair fern. She was getting more and more interested in this man. He obviously disliked talking of himself—a pleasant change which aroused her curiosity. He was so unlike other men, and his life seemed to be different from the lives of the men whom she had known—stronger, more intense, and of greater variety of incident.

"Of course," he went on, "his death was really of enormous advantage to me. They say that I shall have two or three thousand a year, instead of five hundred, paid quarterly at Cox's. He could not prevent it coming to me. It was my mother's money. He would have done so if he could, for we never disguised our antipathy for each other. Yet we lived together, and—and I had the nursing of him."

Millicent was listening gravely without interrupting—like a man. She had the gift of adapting herself to her environments in a marked degree.

"And," he added, curtly, "no one knows how much I wanted that three thousand a year."

The girl moved uneasily and glanced towards the conservatory.

"He was not an old man," Guy Oscard went on. "He was only forty-nine. He might have lived another thirty years."

She nodded, understanding the significance of his tone.

"There," he said, with an awkward laugh, "do you still believe in me?"

"Yes," she answered, still looking into the conservatory.

There was a little pause. They were both sitting forward in their chairs looking towards the conservatory.

"It was not the money that tempted me," said Guy, very deliberately; "it was you."

She rose from her chair as if to join her aunt and the horticultural old gentleman.

"You must not say that," she said, in little more than a whisper, and without looking round she went towards Lady Cantourne. Her eyes were gleaming with a singular suppressed excitement, such as one sees in the eyes of a man fresh from a mad run across country.

Guy Oscard rose also and followed more deliberately. There was nothing for him to do but to take his leave.

"But," said Lady Cantourne, graciously, "if you are determined to go away, you must at least come and say good-bye before you leave."

"Thanks; I should like to do so, if I may."

"We shall be deeply disappointed if you forget," said Millicent, holding out her hand, with a smile full of light-heartedness and innocent girlish friendship.

CHAPTER VI

UNDER THE LINE

"Enough of simpering and grimace,
Enough of vacuity trimmed with lace."

"CURSE this country! Curse it—curse it!" The man spoke aloud, but there was no one near to hear. He shook his skinny yellow fist out over the broad river that crept greasily down to the equatorial sea.

All around him the vegetable kingdom had asserted its sovereignty. At his back loomed a dense forest, impenetrable to the foot of man, defying his puny hand armed with axe or saw. The trees were not high, few of them being above twenty feet, but from their branches creepers and parasites hung in tangled profusion, interlaced, joining tree to tree for acres, nay for miles.

As far as the eye cold reach either bank of the slow river was thus covered with rank vegetation — mile after mile without variety, without hope. The glassy surface of the water was broken here and there by certain black forms floating like logs half hidden beneath the wave. These were crocodiles. The river was the Ogowe, and the man who cursed it was Victor Durnovo, employé of the Loango Trading Association, whose business it was at that season to travel into the interior of Africa to buy, barter, or steal ivory for his masters.

He was a small-faced man, with a squarely aquiline nose and a black mustache which hung like a valance over his mouth. From the growth of that curtain-like mustache Victor Durnovo's worldly prosperity might have been said to date. No one seeing his mouth had before that time been prevailed upon to trust him. Nature has a way of hanging out signs and then covering them up so that the casual fail to see. He was a man of medium height, with abnormally long arms and a somewhat truculent way of walking, as if his foot was ever ready to kick anything or any person who might come in his way.

His movements were nervous and restless, although he was tired out and half-starved. The irritability of Africa was upon him—had hold over him—gripped him remorselessly. No one knows what it is, but it is there, and sometimes it is responsible for murder. It makes honorable European gentleman commit crimes of which they blush to think in after-days. The Powers may draw up treaties and sign the same, but there will never be a peaceful division of the great wasted land so near to Southern Europe. There may be peace in Berlin, or Brussels, or London, but because the atmosphere of Africa is not the same as that of the great cities there will be no peace beneath the equator. From the West Coast of Africa to the East men will fight and quarrel and bicker so long as human nerves are human nerves. The irritability lurks in the shades of boundless forests, where men may starve for want of animal sustenance; it hovers over the broad bosoms of a hundred slow rivers, haunted by the mysterious crocodile, the weird hippopotamus. It is everywhere, and by reason of it men quarrel over trifles, and descend to brutal passion over a futile discussion,

Victor Durnovo had sent his boatmen into the forest to find a few dates, a few handfuls of firewood, and while they were absent he gave vent to that wild unreasoning passion which is inhaled into the white man's lungs with the air of equatorial Africa.   For there are moral microbes in the atmosphere of different countries, and we must not judge one land by the laws of another.   There is the fatalism of India, the restlessness of New York, the fear of the Arctic, the irritability of Africa.

"Curse this country!" he shouted; "curse it—curse it! River and tree—man and beast!"

He rose and slouched down to his boat, which lay moored to a snag alongside the bank, trodden hard to the consistency of asphalt by a hundred bare feet.   He stepped over the gunwale, and made his way aft with a practised balancing step.   The after-part of the canoe was decked in and closed with lock and key.   The key hung at his watch-chain—a large chain with square links and a suggestive doubtfulness of color.   It might have been gold, but the man who wore it somehow imparted to it a suggestion of baser metal.

He opened the locker and took from it a small chest. From this he selected a bottle, and, rummaging in the recesses of the locker, he found an unwashed tumbler.   Into half a glass of water he dropped a minute quantity from the bottle and drank off the mixture.   The passion had left him now, and quite suddenly he looked yellow and very weak.   He was treating himself scientifically for the irritability to which he had given way.   Then he returned to the bank and laid down at full length.   The skin of his face must have been giving him great pain, for it was scarlet in places and exuding from sun-blisters.   He had long ago given up wiping the perspiration from his brow, and evidently did not dare to wash his face.

Presently a peacefulness seemed to come over him, for his eyes lost their glitter and his heavy lids drooped.   His arms were crossed behind his head—before him lay the river,

Suddenly he sat upright, all eagerness and attention. Not a leaf stirred. It was about five o'clock in the evening, the stillest hour of the twenty-four. In such a silence the least sound would travel almost any distance, and there was a sound travelling over the water to him. It was nothing but a thud repeated with singular regularity; but to his practised ears it conveyed much. He knew that a boat was approaching, as yet hidden by some distant curve in the river. The thud was caused by the contact of six paddles with the gunwale of the canoe as the paddlers withdrew them from the water.

Victor Durnovo rose again and brought from the boat a second rifle, which he laid beside the double-barrelled Reilly which was never more than a yard away from him, waking or sleeping. Then he waited. He knew that no boat could reach the bank without his full permission, for every rower could be killed before they got within a hundred yards of his rifle. He was probably the best rifle-shot but one in that country—and the other, the very best, happened to be in the approaching canoe.

After the space of ten minutes the boat came in sight— a long black form on the still waters. It was too far away for him to distinguish anything beyond the fact that it was a native boat.

"Eight hundred yards," muttered Durnovo over the sight of his rifle.

He looked upon this river as his own, and he knew the native of equatorial Africa. Therefore he dropped a bullet into the water, under the bow of the canoe, at eight hundred yards.

A moment later there was a sound which can only be written "P-ttt" between his legs, and he had to wipe a shower of dust from his eyes. A puff of blue smoke rose slowly over the boat and a sharp report broke the silence a second time.

Then Victor Durnovo leaped to his feet and waved his hat

in the air. From the canoe there was an answering greeting, and the man on the bank went to the water's edge, still carrying the rifle from which he was never parted.

Durnovo was the first to speak when the boat came within hail.

"Very sorry," he shouted. "Thought you were a native boat. Must establish a funk — get in the first shot, you know."

"All right," replied one of the Europeans in the approaching craft, with a courteous wave of the hand; "no harm done."

There were two white men and six blacks in the long and clumsy boat. One of the Europeans lay in the bow while the other was stretched at his ease in the stern, reclining on the canvas of a neatly-folded tent. The last-named was evidently the leader of the little expedition, while the manner and attitude of the man in the bow suggested the servitude of a disciplined soldier slightly relaxed by abnormal circumstances.

"Who fired that shot?" inquired Durnovo, when there was no longer any necessity to shout.

"Joseph," replied the man in the stern of the boat, indicating his companion. "Was it a near thing?"

"About as near as I care about—it threw up the dust between my legs."

The man called Joseph grinned. Nature had given him liberally of the wherewithal for indulgence in that relaxation, and Durnovo smiled rather constrainedly. Joseph was grabbing at the long reedy grass, bringing the canoe to a stand-still, and it was some moments before his extensive mouth submitted to control.

"I presume you are Mr. Durnovo?" said the man in the stern of the boat, rising leisurely from his recumbent position and speaking with a courteous *savoir-faire* which seemed slightly out of place in the wilds of Central Africa. He was a tall man with a small aristocratic head and a re-

fined face, which somehow suggested an aristocrat of old
France.

"Yes," answered Durnovo.

The tall man stepped ashore and held out his hand.

"I am glad we have met you," he said.   "I have a letter
of introduction to you from Maurice Gordon, of Loango."

Victor Durnovo's dark face changed slightly ; his eyes—
bilious, fever-shot, unhealthy—took a new light.

"Ah !" he answered; "are you a friend of Maurice
Gordon's ?"

There was another question in this, an unasked one ; and
Victor Durnovo was watching for the answer.   But the
face he watched was like a delicately carved piece of brown
marble, with a courteous, impenetrable smile.

"I met him again the other day at Loango.   He is an
old Etonian like myself."

This conveyed nothing to Durnovo, who belonged to a
different world, whose education was, like other things
about him, an unknown quantity.

"My name," continued the tall man, "is Meredith—John
Meredith—sometimes called Jack."

They were walking up the bank towards the dusky and
uninviting tent.

"And the other fellow ?" inquired Durnovo, with a backward jerk of the head.

"Oh—he is my servant."

Durnovo raised his eyebrows in somewhat contemptuous
amusement, and proceeded to open the letter which Meredith had handed him.

"Not many fellows," he said, "on this coast can afford
to keep a European servant."

Jack Meredith bowed and ignored the irony.

"But," he said, courteously, "I suppose you find these
colored chaps just as good when they have once got into
your ways?"

"Oh yes," muttered Durnovo.   He was reading the letter. "Maurice Gordon," he continued, "says you are travelling for pleasure—just looking about you. What do you think of it?"

He indicated the dismal prospect with a harsh laugh.

"A bit suggestive of hell," he went on, "eh? How does it strike you?"

"Finer timber, I should think," suggested Jack Meredith, and Durnovo laughed more pleasantly.

"The truth is," he explained, "that it strikes one as a bit absurd that any man should travel up here for pleasure. If you take my advice you will come down-stream again with me to-morrow."

He evidently distrusted him; and the sidelong, furtive glance suggested vaguely that Victor Durnovo had something farther up this river which he wished to keep concealed.

"I understand," answered Meredith, with a half-suppressed yawn, "that the country gets finer farther up—more mountainous—less suggestive of—hell."

The proprietors of very dark eyes would do well to remember that it is dangerous to glance furtively to one side or the other. The attention of dark eyes is more easily felt than the glances of gray or blue orbs.

Jack Meredith's suspicions were aroused by the suspicious manner of his interlocutor.

"There is no white man knows this river as I do, and I do not recommend it. Look at me — on the verge of jaundice; look at this wound on my arm — it began with a scratch and has never healed. All that comes from a month up this cursed river. Take my advice, try somewhere else."

"I certainly shall," replied Meredith. "We will discuss it after dinner. My chap is a first-rate cook. Have you got anything to add to the menu?"

"Not a thing. I've been living on plantains and dried elephant-meat for the last fortnight."

"Doesn't sound nourishing. Well, we are pretty well provided, so perhaps you will give me the pleasure of your company to dinner? Come as you are: no ceremony. I think I will wash, though. It is as well to keep up these old customs."

With a pleasant smile he went towards the tent which had just been erected. Joseph was very busy, and his admonishing voice was heard at times.

"Here, Johnny, hammer in that peg. Now, old Cups-and-Saucers, stop that grinning and fetch me some water. None of your frogs and creepy-crawly things this time, my blond beauty, but clean water—comprenny?"

With these and similar lightsome turns of speech was Joseph in the habit of keeping his men up to the mark. The method was eminently successful. His colored compeers crowded round him "all of a grin," as he himself described it, and eager to do his slightest behest. From the throne to the back-kitchen the secret of success is the art of managing men—and women.

CHAPTER VII

THE SECRET OF THE SIMIACINE

"Surtout, messieurs, pas de zèle."

SUCH was the meeting of Victor Durnovo and Jack Meredith. Two men with absolutely nothing in common — no taste, no past, no kinship — nothing but the future. Such men as Fate loves to bring together for her own strange purposes. What these purposes are none of us can tell. Some hold that Fate is wise. She is not so yet, but she cannot fail to acquire wisdom some day, because she experiments so industriously. She is ever bringing about

new combinations, and one can only trust that she, the ex-
perimenter, is as keenly disappointed in the result as are
we, the experimented upon.

To Jack Meredith Victor Durnovo conveyed the impression of little surprise and a slight local interest. He was a
man who was not quite a gentleman ; but for himself Jack
did not give great heed to this. He had associated with
many such ; for, as has been previously intimated, he had
moved in London society where there are many men who
are not quite gentlemen. The difference of a good coat
and that veiled insolence which passes in some circles for
the ease of good-breeding had no weight with the keen son
of Sir John Meredith, and Victor Durnovo fared no worse
in his companion's estimation because he wore a rough coat
and gave small attention to his manners. He attracted
and held Jack's attention by a certain open-air manliness
which was in keeping with the situation and with his life.
Sportsmen, explorers, and wanderers were not new to Jack ;
for nowadays one may never know what manner of man is
inside a faultless dress-suit. It is an age of disappearing,
via Charing Cross station in a first-class carriage, to a life
of backwooding, living from hand to mouth, starving in
desert, prairie, pampas, or arctic wild, with, all the while, a
big balance at Cox's. And most of us come back again,
and put on the dress-suit and the white tie with a certain
sense of restfulness and comfort.

Jack Meredith had known many such. He had, in a
small way, done the same himself. But he had never met
one of the men who do not go home — who possess no
dress-coat and no use for it — whose business it is to go
about with a rifle in one hand and their life in the other —
who risk their lives because it is their trade and not their
pleasure.

Durnovo could not understand the new-comer at all. He
saw at once that this was one of those British aristocrats
who do strange things in a very strange way. In a degree

Meredith reminded him of Maurice Gordon, the man whose letter of introduction was at that moment serving to light the camp fire. But it was Maurice Gordon without that semi-sensual weakness of purpose which made him the boon companion of Tom, Dick, or Harry, provided that one of those was only with him long enough. There was a vast depth of reserve—of indefinable possibilities—which puzzled Durnovo, and in some subtle way inspired fear.

In that part of Africa which lies within touch of the equator life is essentially a struggle. There is hunger about, and where hunger is the emotions will be found also. Now, Jack Meredith was a past-master in the concealment of these, and, as such, came to Victor Durnovo in the guise of a new creation. He had lived the latter and the larger part of his life among men who said, in action if not in words, I am hungry, or I am thirsty; I want this, or I want that; and if you are not strong enough to keep it, I will take it from you.

This man was different; and Victor Durnovo did not know—could not find out—*what* he wanted.

He had at first been inclined to laugh at him. What struck him most forcibly was Joseph, the servant. The idea of a man swaggering up an African river with a European man-servant was so preposterous that it could only be met with ridicule; but the thing seemed so natural to Jack Meredith, he accepted the servitude of Joseph so much as a matter of course, that after a time Durnovo accepted him also as part and parcel of Meredith.

Moreover, he immediately began to realize the benefit of being waited upon by an intelligent European, for Joseph took off his coat, turned up his sleeves, and proceeded to cook such a dinner as Durnovo had not tasted for many months. There was wine also, and afterwards a cigar of such quality as appealed strongly to Durnovo's West-Indian palate.

The night settled down over the land while they sat there,

and before them the great yellow equatorial moon rose slowly over the trees. With the darkness came a greater silence, for the myriad insect life was still. This great silence of Central Africa is wonderfully characteristic. The country is made for silence, the natives are created to steal, spirit-ridden, devil-haunted, through vast tracts of lifeless forest where Nature is oppressive in her grandeur. Here man is put into his right place—a puny, insignificant, helpless being in a world that is too large for him.

"So," said Durnovo, returning to the subject which had never really left his thoughts, "you have come out here for pleasure?"

"Not exactly. I came chiefly to make money, partly to dispel some of the illusions of my youth, and I am getting on very well. Picture-book illusions they were. The man who drew the pictures had never seen Africa."

"This is no country for illusions. Things go naked here —damned naked."

"And only language is adorned?"

Durnovo laughed. He had to be alert to keep up with Jack Meredith—to understand his speech; and he rather liked the necessity, which was a change after the tropic indolence in which he had moved.

"Swearing, you mean," he replied. "Hope you don't mind it?"

"Not a bit! Do it myself."

At this moment Joseph, the servant, brought coffee served up in tin cups.

"First-class dinner," said Durnovo. "The best dinner I have had for years. Clever chap, your man!"

The last remark was made as much for the servant's edification as for the master's, and it was accompanied by an inviting smile directed towards Joseph. Of this the man took no notice whatever. He came from a world where masters and masters' guests knew their place and kept it, even after a good dinner.

The evening had turned out so very differently from what he had expected that Durnovo was a little carried off his equilibrium. Things were so sociable and pleasant in comparison with the habitual loneliness of his life. The fire crackled so cheerily, the moon shone down on the river so grandly, the subdued chatter of the boatmen imparted such a feeling of safety and comfort to the scene, that he gave way to that impulse of expansiveness which ever lurks in West-Indian blood.

" I say," he said, " when you told me that you wanted to make money, were you in earnest ?"

" In the deadliest earnest," replied Jack Meredith, in the half-mocking tone which he never wholly learned to lay aside.

" Then I think I can put you in the way of it. Oh, I know it seems a bit premature—not known you long enough, and all that. But in this country we don't hold much by the formalities. I like you. I liked the look of you when you got out of that boat—so damned cool and self-possessed. You're the right sort, Mr. Meredith."

" Possibly — for some things. For sitting about and smoking first-class cigars and thinking second-class thoughts I am exactly the right sort. But for making money, for hard work and steady work, I am afraid, Mr. Durnovo, that I am distinctly the wrong sort."

" Now you're chaffing again. Do you always chaff ?"

" Mostly ; it lubricates things, doesn't it ?"

There was a little pause. Durnovo looked round as if to make sure that Joseph and the boatmen were out of ear-shot.

" Can you keep a secret ?" he asked, suddenly.

Jack Meredith turned and looked at the questioner with a smile. His hat had slipped to the back of his head, the light of the great yellow moon fell full upon his clean-cut sphinx-like face. The eyes alone seemed living.

" Yes ! I can do that."

He was only amused, and the words were spoken half-mockingly; but his face said more than his lips. It said that even in chaff this was no vain boast that he was uttering. Even before he had set foot on African soil he had been asked to keep so many secrets of a commercial nature. So many had begun by imparting half a secret, to pass on in due course to the statement that only money was required—say, a thousand pounds. And, in the meantime, twenty-five would be very useful, and, if not that—well, ten shillings. Jack Meredith had met all that before.

But there was something different about Durnovo. He was not suitably got up. Your bar-room prospective millionaire is usually a jolly fellow, quite prepared to quench any man's thirst for liquor or information so long as credit and credulity will last. There was nothing jolly or sanguine about Durnovo. Beneath his broad-brimmed hat his dark eyes flashed in a fierce excitement. His hand was unsteady. He had allowed the excellent cigar to go out. The man was full of quinine and fever, in deadly earnest.

"I can see you're a gentleman," he said; "I'll trust you. I want a man to join me in making a fortune. I have got my hand on it at last. But I'm afraid of this country. I'm getting shaky: look at that hand. I've been looking for it too long. I take you into my confidence, the first-comer, you'll think. But there are not many men like you in this country, and I'm beastly afraid of dying. I'm in a damned funk. I want to get out of this for a bit, but I dare not leave until I set things going."

"Take your time," said Meredith, quietly and soothingly; "light that cigar again and lie down. There is no hurry."

Durnovo obeyed him meekly.

"Tell me," he said, "have you ever heard of Simiacine?"

"I cannot say that I have," replied Jack. "What is it for, brown boots or spasms."

"It is a drug, the most expensive drug in the market. And they must have it, they cannot do without it, and they cannot find a substitute. It is the leaf of a shrub, and your hatful is worth a thousand pounds."

"Where is it to be found?" asked Jack Meredith. "I should like some—in a sack."

"Ah, you may laugh now, but you won't when you hear all about it. The scientific chaps called it Simiacine, because of an old African legend which, like all those things, has a grain of truth in it. The legend is, that the monkeys first found out the properties of the leaf, and it is because they live on it that they are so strong. Do you know that a gorilla's arm is not half so thick as yours, and yet he would take you and snap your backbone across his knee; he would bend a gun-barrel as you would bend a cane, merely by the turn of his wrist? That is Simiacine. He can hang on to a tree with one leg and tackle a leopard with his bare hands—that's Simiacine. At home, in England and in Germany, they are only just beginning to find out its properties; it seems that it can bring a man back to life when he is more than half dead. There is no knowing what children that are brought up on it may turn out to be; it may double the power of the human brain—some think it will."

Jack Meredith was leaning forward, watching with a certain sense of fascination the wild, disease-stricken face, listening to the man's breathless periods. It seemed that the fear of death, which had gotten hold of him, gave Victor Durnovo no time to pause for breath.

"Yes," said the Englishman—"yes, go on."

"There is practically no limit to the demand that there is for it. At present the only way of obtaining it is through the natives, and you know their manner of trading. They send a little packet down from the interior, and it very often takes two months and more to reach the buyer's hands. The money is sent back the same way, and each man who fingers it keeps a little. The natives find the leaf in the forests by the aid of trained monkeys, and only in very small quantities. Do you follow me?"

"Yes, I follow you."

Victor Durnovo leaned forward until his face was within three inches of Meredith's, and the dark, wild eyes flashed and glared into the Englishman's steady glance.

"What," he hissed—"what if I know where Simiacine grows like a weed? What if I could supply the world with Simiacine at my own price? Eh—h—h! What of that, Mr. Meredith?"

He threw himself suddenly back and wiped his dripping face. There was a silence, the great African silence that drives educated men mad and fills the imagination of the poor heathen with wild tales of devils and spirits.

Then Jack Meredith spoke, without moving.

"I'm your man," he said, "with a few more details."

Victor Durnovo was lying back at full length on the hard, dry mud, his arms beneath his head. Without altering his position, he gave the details, speaking slowly and much more quietly. It seemed as if he spoke the result of long-pent-up thought.

"We shall want," he said, "two thousand pounds to start it. For we must have an armed force of our own. We have to penetrate through a cannibal country of the fiercest devils in Africa. It is a plateau, a little plateau of two square miles, and the niggers think that it is haunted by an evil spirit. When we get there we shall have to hold it by force of arms, and when we send the stuff down to the coast we must have an escort of picked men. The bushes grow up there as thick as gooseberry-bushes in a garden at home. With a little cultivation they will yield twice as much as they do now. We shall want another partner. I know a man, a soldierly fellow, full of fight, who knows the natives and the country. I will undertake to lead you there, but you will have to take great care of me. You will have to have me carried most of the way. I am weak, devilish weak, and I am afraid of dying; but I know the way there, and no other man can say as much! It is in my head here;

it is not written down. It is only in my head, and no one can get it out of there."

"No," said Meredith, in his quiet, refined voice—"no, no one can get it out. Come, let us turn in. To-morrow I will go down the river with you. I will turn back, and we can talk it over as we go down-stream."

CHAPTER VIII

A RECRUIT

"Said the Engine from the East,
   'They who work best talk the least.'"

It is not, of course, for a poor limited masculine mind to utter heresies regarding the great question of woman's rights. But as things stand at present, as in fact the fore-named rights are to-day situated, women have not found comprehension of the dual life. The dual life is led solely by men, and until women have found out its full compass and meaning, they can never lead in the world. There is the public life and the private; and the men who are most successful in the former are the most exclusive in the latter. Women have only learned to lead one life; they must be all public or all private; there is no medium. Those who give up the private life for which Providence destined them to assume the public existence to which their own conceit urges them have their own reward. They taste all the bitterness of fame, and never know its sweets, because the bitterness is public and the sweets are private.

Women cannot understand that part of a man's life which brings him into daily contact with men whom he does not bring home to dinner. One woman does not know another without bringing her in to meals and showing her her new hat. It is merely a matter of custom. Men are in the habit of associating in daily, almost hourly, intercourse with others who are never really their friends, and are always held at a distance. It is useless attempting to explain it, for we are merely reprimanded for unfriendliness, stiffness, and stupid pride. *Soit!* Let it go. Some of us, perhaps, know our own business best. And there are, thank Heaven! amidst a multitude of female doctors, female professors, female wranglers, a few female women left.

Jack Meredith knew quite well what he was about when he listened with a favorable ear to Durnovo's scheme. He knew that this man was not a gentleman, but his own position was so assured that he could afford to associate with any one. Here, again, men are safer. A woman is too delicate a social flower to be independent of environments. She takes the tone of her surroundings. It is, one notices, only the ladies who protest that the barmaid married in haste and, repented of at leisure, can raise herself to her husband's level. The husband's friends keep silence, and perhaps, like the mariner's bird, they meditate all the more.

What Meredith proposed to do was to enter into a partnership with Victor Durnovo, and, when the purpose of it was accomplished, to let each man go his way. Such partnerships are entered into every day. Men have carried through a brilliant campaign—a world-affecting scheme—side by side, working with one mind and one heart ; and when the result has been attained they drop out of each other's lives forever. They are created so—for a very good purpose, no doubt. But sometimes Providence steps in and turns the little point of contact into the leaven that leaveneth the whole lump. Providence, it seems—or let us call it Fate—was hovering over that lone African river, where two men, sitting in the stern of a native canoe, took it upon themselves to prearrange their lives.

A month later Victor Durnovo was in London. He left

behind him in Africa Jack Meredith, whose capacities for organization were developing very quickly.

There was plenty of work for each to do. In Africa Meredith had undertaken to get together men and boats, while Durnovo went home to Europe for a threefold purpose. Firstly, a visit to Europe was absolutely necessary for his health, shattered as it was by too long a sojourn in the fever-ridden river-beds of the West Coast. Secondly, there were rifles, ammunition, and stores to be purchased, and packed in suitable cases. And, lastly, he was to find and enlist the third man, "the soldierly fellow, full of fight," who knew the natives and the country.

This, indeed, was his first care on reaching London, and before his eyes and brain were accustomed to the roar of the street life he took a cab to Russell Square, giving the number affixed to the door of a gloomy house in the least-frequented corner of the stately quadrangle.

"Is Mr. Guy Oscard at home?" he inquired of the grave man-servant.

"He is, sir," replied the butler, stepping aside.

Victor Durnovo thought that a momentary hesitation on the part of the butler was caused by a very natural and proper feeling of admiration for the new clothes and hat which he had purchased out of the money advanced by Jack Meredith for the outfit of the expedition. In reality the man was waiting for the visitor to throw away his cigar before crossing the threshold. But he waited in vain, and Durnovo waited, cigar in mouth, in the dining-room until Guy Oscard came to him.

At first Oscard did not recognize him, and conveyed this fact by a distant bow and an expectant silence.

"You do not seem to recognize me," said Durnovo, with a laugh which lasted until the servant had closed the door. "Victor Durnovo!"

"Oh—yes—how are you?"

Oscard came forward and shook hands. His manner was

not exactly effusive. The truth was that their acquaintance-
ship in Africa had been of the slightest, dating from some
trivial services which Durnovo had been able and very eager
to render to the sportsman.

"I'm all right, thanks," replied Durnovo. "I only landed
at Liverpool yesterday. I'm home on business. I'm buying rifles and stores."

Guy Oscard's honest face lighted up at once — the curse
of Ishmael was on him in its full force. He was destined
to be a wanderer on God's earth, and all things appertain-
ing to the wild life of the forests were music in his ears.

Durnovo was no mean diplomatist. He had learned to
know man, within a white or colored skin. The effect of
his words was patent to him.

"You remember the Simiacine?" he said, abruptly.

"Yes."

"I've found it."

"The devil you have! Sit down."

Durnovo took the chair indicated.

"Yes, sir," he said, "I've got it. I've laid my hand on
it at last. I've always been on its track. That has been
my little game all the time. I did not tell you when we
met out there, because I was afraid I should never find it,
and because I wanted to keep quiet about it."

Guy Oscard was looking out of the window across to the
dull houses and chimneys that formed his horizon, and in
his eyes there was the longing for a vaster horizon, a larger
life.

"I have got a partner," continued Durnovo, "a good man
—Jack Meredith, son of Sir John Meredith. You have,
perhaps, met him."

"No," answered Oscard; "but I have heard his name,
and I have met Sir John—the father—once or twice."

"He is out there," went on Durnovo, "getting things together quietly. I have come home to buy rifles, ammunition, and stores."

He paused, watching the eager, simple face.

"We want to know," he said, quietly, "if you will organize and lead the fighting men."

Guy Oscard drew a deep breath. There are some Englishmen left, thank Heaven! who love fighting for its own sake, and not only for the gain of it. Such men as this lived in the old days of chivalry, at which modern puny carpet-knights make bold to laugh, while inwardly thanking their stars that they live in the peaceful age of the policeman. Such men as this ran their thick simple heads against many a windmill, couched lance over many a far-fetched insult, and swung a sword in honor of many a worthless maid; but they made England, my masters. Let us remember that they made England.

"Then there is to be fighting?"

"Yes," said Durnovo, "there will be fighting. We must fight our way there, and we must hold it when we get there. But so far as the world is concerned, we are only a private expedition exploring the source of the Ogowe."

"The Ogowe?" and again Guy Oscard's eyes lighted up.

"Yes, I do not mind telling you that much. To begin with, I trust you; secondly, no one could get there without me to lead the way."

Guy Oscard looked at him with some admiration, and that sympathy which exists between the sons of Ishmael. Durnovo looked quite fit for the task he set himself. He had regained his strength on the voyage, and with returning muscular force his moral tone was higher, his influence over men greater. Amid the pallid sons of the pavement, among whom Guy Oscard had moved of late, this African traveller was a man apart—a being much more after his own heart. The brown of the man's face and hands appealed to him—the dark flashing eyes, the energetic carriage of the head and shoulders. Among men of a fairer skin the taint that was in Victor Durnovo's blood became

more apparent—the shadow on his finger-nails, the deep
olive of his neck against the snowy collar, and the blue tint
in the whites of his eyes.

But none of these things militated against him in Oscard's eyes. They only made him fitter for the work he
had undertaken.

"How long will it take?" asked Guy.

Durnovo tugged at his strange, curtain-like mustache.
His mouth was hidden; it was quite impossible to divine
his thoughts.

"Three months to get there," he answered at length.
"One month to pick the leaf, and then you can bring the
first crop down to the coast and home, while Meredith and
I stay on at the plateau."

"I could be home again in eight months?"

"Certainly! We thought that you might work the sale
of the stuff in London, and in a couple of years or so, when
the thing is in swing, Meredith will come home. We can
safely leave the cultivation in native hands when once we
have established ourselves up there, and made ourselves respected among the tribes."

A significance in his tone made Guy Oscard look up in-
quiringly.

"How?"

"You know my way with the natives," answered Durnovo, with a cruel smile. "It is the only way. There are
no laws in Central Africa except the laws of necessity."

Oscard was nothing if not outspoken.

"I do not like your way with the natives," he said, with
a pleasant smile.

"That is because you do not know them. But in this
affair you are to be the leader of the fighting column.
You will, of course, have *carte blanche*."

Oscard nodded.

"I suppose," he said, after a pause, "that there is the
question of money?"

"Yes; Meredith and I have talked that over. The plan we fixed upon was that you and he each put a thousand pounds into it; I put five hundred. For the first two years we share the profits equally. After that we must come to some fresh arrangement, should you or Meredith wish to give up an active part in the affair. I presume you would not object to coming up at the end of the year, with a handy squad of men to bring down the crop under escort?"

"No," replied Oscard, after a moment's reflection. "I should probably be able to do that."

"I reckon," continued the other, "that the journey down could be accomplished in two months, and each time you do the trip you will reduce your time."

"Yes."

"Of course," Durnovo went on, with the details which he knew were music in Oscard's ears—"of course we shall be a clumsy party going up. We shall have heavy loads of provisions, ammunition, and seeds for cultivating the land up there."

"Yes," replied Guy Oscard, absently. In his ears there rang already the steady plash of the paddle, the weird melancholy song of the boatmen, the music of the wind amid the forest trees.

Durnovo rose briskly.

"Then," he said, "you will join us? I may telegraph out to Meredith that you will join us?"

"Yes," replied Oscard, simply. "You may do that."

"There is no time to be lost," Durnovo went on. "Every moment wasted adds to the risk of our being superseded. I sail for Loango in a fortnight; will you come with me?"

"Yes."

"Shall I take a passage for you?"

"Yes."

Durnovo held out his hand.

"Good-bye," he said. "Shall I always find you here when I want you?"

"Yes—stay, though! I shall be going away for a few days. Come to-morrow to luncheon, and we will settle the preliminaries."

"Right—one o'clock?"

"One o'clock."

When Durnovo had gone Guy sat down and wrote to Lady Cantourne accepting her invitation to spend a few days at Cantourne Place, on the Solent. He explained that his visit would be in the nature of a farewell, as he was about to leave for Africa for a little big-game hunting.

CHAPTER IX

TO PASS THE TIME

"Quand on n'a pas ce que l'on aime, il faut aimer ce que l'on a."

"Your energy, my dear lady, is not the least of many attributes."

Lady Cantourne looked up from her writing-desk with her brightest smile. Sir John Meredith was standing by the open window, leaning against the jamb thereof with a grace that had lost its youthful repose. He was looking out, across a sloping lawn, over the Solent, and for that purpose he had caused himself to be clad in a suit of blue serge. He looked the veteran yachtsman to perfection—he could look anything in its season; but he did his yachting from the shore — by preference from the drawing-room window.

"One must keep up with the times, John," replied the lady, daintily dipping her quill.

"And 'the times' fills its house from roof to cellar with

people who behave as if they were in a hotel. Some of them—say number five on the first floor, number eleven on the second, or some of the atticated relatives—announce at breakfast that they will not be home to lunch. Another says he cannot possibly be home to dinner at half-past seven, and so on. 'The times' expects a great deal for its money, and does not even allow one to keep the small change of civility."

Lady Cantourne was blotting vigorously.

"I admit," she answered, "that the reaction is rather strong; reactions are always stronger than they intend to be. In our early days the formalities were made too much of; now they are——"

"Made into a social hash," he suggested, when she paused for a word, "where the prevailing flavor is the commor onion of commerce! Now, I'll wager any sum that that is an invitation to some one you do not care a screw about."

"It is. But, Sir John, the hash must be kept moving; cold hash is not palatable. I will tell you at once; I am inviting young Scmoor to fill the vacancy caused by Mr. Oscard's departure."

"Ah! Mr. Oscard proposes depriving us of his — society."

"He leaves to-morrow. He only came to say good-bye."

"He moves on—to some other hostlery?"

"No! He is going to——"

She paused, so that Sir John was forced to turn in courteous inquiry and look her in the face.

"Africa!" she added, sharply, never taking her bright eyes from his face.

She saw the twitching of the aged lips before his hand got there to hide them. She saw his eyes fall before her steady gaze, and she pitied him while she admired his uncompromising pride.

"Indeed!" he said. "I have reason to believe," he added,

turning to the window again, "that there is a great future
before that country; all the intellect of Great Britain seems
to be converging in its direction."

Since his departure Jack's name had never been mentioned, even between these two whose friendship dated back
a generation. Once or twice Sir John had made a subtle
passing reference to him, such as perhaps no other woman
but Lady Cantourne could have understood; but Africa
was, so to speak, blotted out of Sir John Meredith's map of
the world. It was there that he kept his skeleton—the son
who had been his greatest pride and his deepest humiliation—his highest hope in life—almost the only failure of
his career.

He stood there by the window, looking out with that
well-bred interest in details of sport and pastime which was
part of his creed. He braved it out even before the woman
who had been a better friend to him than his dead wife.
Not even to her would he confess that any event of existence could reach him through the impenetrable mask he
wore before the world. Not even she must know that
aught in his life could breathe of failure or disappointment.
As it is given to the best of women to want to take their
sorrows to another, so the strongest men instinctively deny
their desire for sympathy.

Lady Cantourne, pretending to select another sheet of
note-paper, glanced at him with a pathetic little smile. Although they had never been anything to each other, these
two people had passed through many of the trials to which
humanity is heir almost side by side. But neither had ever
broken down. Each acted as a sort of mental tonic on the
other. They had tacitly agreed, years before, to laugh at
most things. She saw, more distinctly than any, the singular emptiness of his clothes, as if the man were shrinking,
and she knew that the emptiness was of the heart.

Sir John Meredith had taught his son that Self, and Self
alone, reigns in the world. He had taught him that the

thing called Love, with a capital L, is nearly all self, and
that it finally dies in the arms of Self. He had told him
that a father's love, or a son's, or a mother's, is merely a
matter of convenience, and vanishes when Self asserts itself.

Upon this principle they were both acting now, with a
strikingly suggestive similarity of method. Neither was
willing to admit to the world in general, and to the other
in particular, that a cynical theory could possibly be erroneous.

"I am sorry that our young friend is going to leave us,"
said Sir John, taking up and unfolding the morning paper.
" He is honest and candid, if he is nothing else."

This meant that Guy Oscard's admiration for Millicent
Chyne had never been concealed for a moment, and Lady
Cantourne knew it.

"He interests me," went on the old aristocrat, studying
the newspaper; and his hearer knew the inner significance
of the remark.

At times she was secretly ashamed of her niece, but that
esprit de corps which binds women together prompted her
always to defend Millicent. The only defence at the moment was silence, and an assumed density which did not
deceive Sir John—even she could not do that.

In the meantime Miss Millicent Chyne was walking on
the sea-wall at the end of the garden with Guy Oscard.
One of the necessary acquirements of a modern educational
outfit is the power of looking perfectly at home in a score
of different costumes during the year, and, needless to say,
Miss Chyne was perfectly finished in this art. The manner
in which she wore her sailor-hat, her blue serge, and her neat
brown shoes conveyed to the onlooker, and especially the
male of that species (we cannot in conscience call them observers), the impression that she was a yachtswoman born
and bred. Her delicate complexion was enhanced by the
faintest suspicion of sunburn and a few exceedingly becoming freckles. There was a freedom in her movements which

had not been observed in London drawing-rooms. This was
Diana-like and in perfect keeping with the dainty sailor outfit; moreover, nine men out of ten would fail to attribute
the difference to sundry cunning strings within the (London) skirt.

"It is sad," Millicent was saying, "to think that we shall
have no more chances of sailing. The wind has quite
dropped, that horrid tide is running, and — this is your last
day."

She ended with a little laugh, knowing full well that there
was little sentiment in the big man by her side.

"Really," she went on, "I think I should be able to manage a boat in time, don't you think so? Please encourage
me. I am sure I have tried to learn."

But he remained persistently grave. She did not like
that gravity; she had met it before in the course of her experiments. One of the grievances harbored by Miss Millicent Chyne against the opposite sex was that they could
not settle down into a harmless, honest flirtation. Of course,
this could be nothing but a flirtation of the lightest and
most evanescent description. She was engaged to Jack
Meredith — poor Jack, who was working for her, ever so
hard, somewhere near the equator — and if Guy Oscard did
not know this he had only himself to blame. There were
plenty of people ready to tell him. He had only to ask.

Millicent Chyne, like Guy, was hampered at the outset of
life by theories upon it. Experience, the fashionable novel,
and modern cynicism had taught her to expect little from
human nature—a dangerous lesson, for it eases responsibility,
and responsibility is the ten commandments rolled into a
compact whole, suitable for the pocket.

She expected of no man—not even of Jack—that perfect
faithfulness in every word and thought which is read of in
books. And it is one of the theories of the day that what
one does not expect one is not called upon to give. Jack,
she reflected, was too much a man of the world to expect

her to sit and mope alone. She was apparently incapable of seeing the difference between that pastime and sitting on the sea-wall behind a large, flowering currant-tree with a man who did not pretend to hide the fact that he was in love with her. Some women are thus.

"I do not know if you have learned much," he answered; "but I have."

"What have you learned?" she asked, in a low voice, half-fascinated by the danger into which she knew that she was running.

"That I love you," he answered, standing squarely in front of her, and announcing the fact with a deliberate honesty which was rather startling. "I was not sure of it before, so I stayed away from you for three weeks; but now I know for certain."

"Oh, you mustn't say that!"

She rose hastily and turned away from him. There was in her heart a sudden feeling of regret. It was the feeling that the keenest sportsman sometimes has when some majestic monarch of the forest falls before his merciless rifle—a sudden passing desire that it might be undone.

"Why not?" he asked. He was desperately in earnest, and that which made him a good sportsman—an unmatched big-game hunter, calm and self-possessed in any strait—gave him a strange deliberation now, which Millicent Chyne could not understand. "Why not?"

"I do not know—because you mustn't."

And in her heart she wanted him to say it again.

"I am not ashamed of it," he said, "and I do not see why I should not say it to you—or to any one else, so far as that goes."

"No, never!" she cried, really frightened. "To me it does not matter so much. But to no one else—no, never! Aunt Marian must not know it—nor Sir John."

"I cannot see that it is any business of Sir John's. Of course, Lady Cantourne would have liked you to marry a

title; but if you cared for me she would be ready to listen
to reason."

In which judgment of the good lady he was no doubt
right—especially if reason spoke with the voice of three
thousand pounds per annum.

"Do you care for me?" he asked, coming a little closer.

There was a whole world of gratified vanity and ungrati-
fied curiosity for her in the presence of this strong man at
her elbow. It was one of the supreme triumphs of her life,
because he was different from the rest. He was for her
what his first tiger had been for him. The danger that he
might come still nearer had for her a sense of keen pleasure. She was thoroughly enjoying herself, and the nearest
approach that men can experience to the joy that was hers
is the joy of battle.

"I cannot answer that—not now."

And the little half-shrinking glance over her shoulder was
a low-minded, unmaidenly invitation. But he was in earnest, and he was, above all, a gentleman. He stood his
ground a yard away from her.

"Then when," he asked—"when will you answer me?"

She stood with her back turned towards him, looking out
over the smooth waters of the Solent, where one or two
yachts and a heavy black schooner were creeping up on the
tide before the morning breeze. She drummed reflectively
with her fingers on the low stone wall. Beneath them a
few gulls whirled and screamed over a shoal of little fish.
One of the birds had a singular cry, as if it were laughing
to itself.

"You said just now," Millicent answered at length, "that
you were not sure yourself—not at first—and, therefore, you
cannot expect me to know all at once."

"You would know at once," he argued, gravely, "if it
were going to be 'No.' If you do not say 'No' now, I can
only think that it may be 'Yes' some day. And"—he came
closer—he took the hand that hung at her side—conven-

iently near—"and I don't want you to say 'No' now. Don't say 'No'! I will wait as long as you like for 'Yes.' Millicent, I would rather go on waiting and thinking that it is going to be 'Yes,' even if it is 'No' after all."

She said nothing, but she left her hand in his.

"May I go on thinking that it will be 'Yes' until I come back?"

"I cannot prevent your thinking, can I?" she whispered, with a tender look in her eyes.

"And may I write to you?"

She shook her head.

"Well—I—I— Now and then," he pleaded. "Not often. Just to remind you of my existence."

She gave a little laugh, which he liked exceedingly and remembered afterwards.

"If you like," she answered.

At this moment Lady Cantourne's voice was heard in the distance, calling them.

"There!" exclaimed Millicent. "We must go at once. And no one—no one, mind—must know of this."

"No one shall know of it," he answered.

CHAPTER X

LOANGO

"Faithful and hopeful, wise in charity,
Strong in grave peace, in pity circumspect."

THOSE who for their sins have been to Loango will scarcely care to have its beauties recalled to memory. And to such as have not visited the spot one can only earnestly recommend a careful avoidance.

Suffice it to say, therefore, that there is such a place, and the curious may find it marked in larger type than it deserves on the map of Africa, on the west coast of that country, and within an inch or so of the equator.

Loango has a bar, and outside of that mysterious and somewhat suggestive nautical hinderance the coasting steamers anchor, while the smaller local fry find harbor nearer to the land. The passenger is not recommended to go ashore—indeed, many difficulties are placed in his way, and he usually stays on board while the steamer receives or discharges a scanty cargo, rolling ceaselessly in the Atlantic swell. The roar of the surf may be heard, and at times some weird cry or song. There is nothing to tempt even the most adventurous through that surf. A moderately large white building attracts the eye, and usually brings upon itself a contemptuous stare, for it seems to be the town of Loango, marked so bravely on the map. As a matter of fact the town is five miles inland, and the white building is only a factory or trading establishment.

Loango is the reverse of cheerful. To begin with, it is usually raining there. The roar of the surf—than which there are few sadder sounds on earth—fills the atmosphere with a never-ceasing melancholy. The country is overwooded; the tropical vegetation, the huge tangled African trees, stand almost in the surf; and inland the red serrated hills mount guard in gloomy array. For Europeans this country is accursed. From the mysterious forest-land there creeps down a subtle, tainted air that poisons the white man's blood, and either strikes him down in a fever or terrifies him by strange unknown symptoms and sudden disfiguring disease. The Almighty speaks very plainly sometimes and in some places—nowhere more plainly than on the West Coast of Africa, which land He evidently wants for the black man. We, of the fairer skin, have Australia now; we are taking America, we are dominant in Asia; but somehow we don't get on in Africa. The Umpire is there, and He insists on fair play.

"This is not cheery," Jack Meredith observed to his servant, as they found themselves deposited on the beach within a stone's-throw of the French factory.

"No, sir, not cheery, sir," replied Joseph. He was very busy attending to the landing of their personal effects, and had only time to be respectful. It was Joseph's way to do only one thing at a time, on the principle, no doubt, that enough for the moment is the evil thereof. His manner implied that, when those colored gentlemen had got the baggage safely conveyed out of the boats onto the beach, it would be time enough to think about Loango.

Moreover, Joseph was, in his way, rather a dauntless person. He held that there were few difficulties which he and his master, each in his respective capacity, were unable to meet. This African mode of life was certainly not one for which he had bargained when taking service; but he rather enjoyed it than otherwise, and he was consoled by the reflection that what was good enough for his master was good enough for him. Beneath the impenetrable mask of a dignified servitude he knew that this was "all along of that Chyne girl," and rightly conjectured that it would not last forever. He had an immense respect for Sir John, whom he tersely described as a "game one," but his knowledge of the world went towards the supposition that headstrong age would finally bow before headstrong youth. He did not, however, devote much consideration to these matters, being a young man, although an old soldier, and taking a lively interest in the present.

It had been arranged by letter that Jack Meredith should put up, as his host expressed it, at the small bungalow occupied by Maurice Gordon and his sister. Gordon was the local head of a large trading association somewhat after the style of the old East India Company, and his duties partook more of the glory of a governor than of the routine of a trader.

Of Maurice Gordon's past Meredith knew nothing beyond

the fact that they were school-fellows strangely brought together again on the deck of a coasting steamer.   Maurice Gordon was not a reserved person, and it was rather from a lack of opportunity than from an excess of caution that he allowed his new-found friend to go up the Ogowe River knowing so little of himself—Maurice Gordon, of Loango.

There were plenty of willing guides and porters on the beach ; for in this part of Africa there is no such thing as continued and methodical labor.   The entire population consider the lilies of the fields to obvious purpose.

Joseph presently organized a considerable portion of this population into a procession, headed triumphantly by an old white-woolled negro whose son cleaned Maurice Gordon's boots.   This man Joseph selected—not without one or two jokes of a somewhat personal nature—as a fitting guide to the Gordons' house.   As they neared the little settlement on the outskirts of the black town where the mission and other European residences are situated, the veteran guide sent on couriers to announce the arrival of the great gentleman, who had for body-servant the father of laughter.

On finally reaching the bungalow Meredith was pleasantly surprised.   It was pretty and homelike—surrounded by a garden wherein grew a strange profusion of homely English vegetables and tropical flowers.

Joseph happened to be in front, and, as he neared the veranda, he suddenly stopped at the salute ; moreover, he began to wonder in which trunk he had packed his master's dress-clothes.

An English lady was coming out of the drawing-room window to meet the travellers—a lady whose presence diffused that sense of refinement and peace into the atmosphere which has done as much towards the expansion of our piecemeal empire as ever did the strong right arm of Thomas Atkins.   It is because—sooner or later—these ladies come with us that we have learned to mingle peace with war—to make friends of whilom enemies.

She nodded in answer to the servant's salutation, and passed on to greet the master.

"My brother has been called away suddenly," she said. "One of his sub-agents has been getting into trouble with the natives. Of course you are Mr. Meredith?"

"I am," replied Jack, taking the hand she held out; it was a small white hand—small without being frail or diaphanous. "And you are Miss Gordon, I suppose? I am sorry Gordon is away, but no doubt we shall be able to find somewhere to put up."

"You need not do that," she said, quietly. "This is Africa, you know. You can quite well stay with us, although Maurice is away until to-morrow."

"Sure?" he asked.

"Quite!" she answered.

She was tall and fair, with a certain stateliness of carriage which harmonized wonderfully with a thoughtful and pale face. She was not exactly pretty, but gracious and womanly, with honest blue eyes that looked on men and women alike. She was probably twenty-eight years of age; her manner was that of a woman rather than that of a girl—of one who was in life and not on the outskirts.

"We rather pride ourselves," she said, leading the way into the drawing-room, "upon having the best house in Loango. You will, I think, be more comfortable here than anywhere."

She turned and looked at him with a slow, grave smile. She was noticing that, of the men who had been in this drawing-room, none had seemed so entirely at his ease as this one.

"I must ask you to believe that I was thinking of your comfort and not of my own."

"Yes, I know you were," she answered. "Our circle is rather limited, as you will find, and very few of the neighbors have time to think of their houses. Most of them are missionaries, and they are so busy; they have a large field, you see."

"Very—and a weedy one, I should think."

He was looking round, noting with well-trained glance the thousand little indescribable touches that make a charming room. He knew his ground. He knew the date and the meaning of every little ornament—the title and the writer of each book—the very material with which the chairs were covered; and he knew that all was good—all arranged with that art which is the difference between ignorance and knowledge.

"I see you have all the new books."

"Yes, we have books and magazines; but, of course, we live quite out of the world."

She paused, leaving the conversation with him as in the hands of one who knows his business.

"I," he said, filling up the pause, "have hitherto lived in the world—right in it. There is a lot of dust and commotion; the dust gets into people's eyes and blinds them; the commotion wears them out; and perhaps, after all, Loango is better!"

He spoke with the easy independence of the man of the world, accustomed to feel his way in strange places—not heeding what opinion he might raise—what criticism he might brave. He was glancing round him all the while, noting things, and wondering for whose benefit this pretty room had been evolved in the heart of a savage country. Perhaps he had assimilated erroneous notions of womankind in the world of which he spoke; perhaps he had never met any of those women whose natural refinement urges them to surround themselves, even in solitude, with pretty things, and prompts them to dress as neatly and becomingly as their circumstances allow for the edification of no man.

"I never abuse Loango," she answered; "such abuse is apt to recoil. To call a place dull is often a confession of dulness."

He laughed—still in that somewhat unnatural manner, as

if desirous of filling up time. He had spent the latter year of his life in doing nothing else. The man's method was so different to what Jocelyn Gordon had met with in Loango, where men were all in deadly earnest, pursuing souls or wealth, that it struck her forcibly, and she remembered it long after Meredith had forgotten its use.

"I have no idea," she continued, "how the place strikes the passing traveller; he usually passes by on the other side; but I am afraid there is nothing to arouse the smallest interest."

"But, Miss Gordon, I am not the passing traveller."

She looked up with a sudden interest.

"Indeed! I understood from Maurice that you were travelling down the coast without any particular object."

"I have an object—estimable, if not quite original."

"Yes?"

"I want to make some money. I have never made any yet, so there is a certain novelty in the thought which is pleasant."

She smiled with the faintest suspicion of incredulity.

"I know what you are thinking," he said; "that I am too neat and tidy — too namby-pamby to do anything in this country. That my boots are too narrow in the toe, my hair too short, and my face too clean. I cannot help it. It is the fault of the individual you saw outside—Joseph. He insists on a strict observance of the social duties."

"We are rougher here," she answered.

"I left England," he explained, "in rather a hurry. I had no time to buy uncomfortable boots, or anything like that. I know it was wrong. The ordinary young man of society who goes morally to the dogs and physically to the colonies always has an outfit. His friends buy him an outfit, and certain enterprising haberdashers make a study of such things. I came as I am."

While he was speaking she had been watching him—studying him more closely than she had hitherto been able to do.

"I once met a Sir John Meredith," she said, suddenly.

"My father."

He paused, drawing in his legs, and apparently studying the neat brown boots of which there had been question.

"Should you meet him again," he went on, "it would not be advisable to mention my name. He might not care to hear it. We have had a slight difference of opinion. With me it is different. I am always glad to hear about him. I have an immense respect for him."

She listened gravely, with a sympathy that did not attempt to express itself in words. On such a short acquaintance she had not learned to expect a certain lightness of conversational touch which he always assumed when speaking of himself, as if his own thoughts and feelings were matters for ridicule.

"Of course," he went on, "I was in the wrong. I know that. But it sometimes happens that a man is not in a position to admit that he is in the wrong—when, for instance, another person would suffer by such an admission."

"Yes," answered Jocelyn—"I understand."

At this moment a servant came in with lamps, and proceeded to close the windows. She was quite an old woman —an Englishwoman; and as she placed the lamps upon the table she scrutinized the guest after the manner of a privileged servitor. When she had departed Jack Meredith continued his narrative with a sort of deliberation which was explained later on.

"And," he said, "that is why I came to Africa—that is why I want to make money. I do not mind confessing to a low greed of gain, because I think I have the best motive that a man can have for wanting to make money."

He said this meaningly, and watched her face all the while.

"A motive which any lady ought to approve of."

She smiled sympathetically.

"I approve and I admire your spirit."

She rose as she spoke, and moved towards a side-table, where two lighted candles had been placed.

"My motive for talking so barefacedly about myself," he said, as they moved towards the door together, "was to let you know exactly who I am and why I am here. It was only due to you on accepting your hospitality. .I might have been a criminal, or an escaped embezzler. There were two on board the steamer coming out, and several other shady characters."

"Yes," said the girl, "I saw your motive."

They were now in the hall, and the aged servant was waiting to show him his room.

CHAPTER XI

A COMPACT

"Drifting, slow drifting down a wizard stream."

"No one knows," Victor Durnovo was in the habit of saying, "what is going on in the middle of Africa."

And on this principle he acted.

"Ten miles above the camping-ground where we first met," he had told Meredith, "you will find a village where I have my headquarters. There is quite a respectable house there, with—a—a woman to look after your wants. When you have fixed things up at Loango, and have arranged for the dhows to meet my steamer, take up all your men to this village — Msala is the name — and send the boats back. Wait there till we come."

In due time the telegram came, *via* St. Paul de Loanda, announcing the fact that Oscard had agreed to join the expedition, and that Durnovo and he might be expected at Msala in one month from that time. It was not without a

vague feeling of regret that Jack Meredith read this telegram. To be at Msala in a month with forty men and a
vast load of provisions meant leaving Loango almost at
once. And, strange though it may seem, he had become
somewhat attached to the dreary East African town. The
singular cosmopolitan society was entirely new to him; the
life, taken as a life, almost unique. He knew that he had
not outstayed his welcome. Maurice Gordon had taken
care to assure him of that in his boisterous, hearty manner,
savoring more of Harrow than of Eton, every morning at
breakfast.

"Confound Durnovo!" he cried, when the telegram had
been read aloud. "Confound him, with his energy and his
business-like habits! That means that you will have to
leave us before long; and somehow it has got to be quite
natural to see you come lounging in ten minutes late for
most things, with an apology for Jocelyn, but none for me.
We shall miss you, old chap."

"Yes," added Jocelyn, "we shall."

She was busy with the cups, and spoke rather indifferently.

"So you've got Oscard?" continued Maurice. "I imagine
he is a good man—tip-top shot, and all that. I've never
met him, but I have heard of him."

"He is a gentleman, at all events," said Meredith, quietly;
"I know that."

Jocelyn was looking at him between the hibiscus flowers
decorating the table.

"Is Mr. Durnovo going to be leader of the expedition?"
she inquired, casually, after a few moments' silence; and
Jack, looking up with a queer smile, met her glance for a
moment.

"No," he answered.

Maurice Gordon's hearty laugh interrupted.

"Ha, ha!" he cried. "I wonder where the dickens you
men are going to?"

"Up the Ogowe River," replied Jack.

"No doubt. But what for? There is something mysterious about that river. Durnovo keeps his poor relations there, or something of that kind."

"We are not going to look for them."

"I suppose," said Maurice, helping himself to marmalade, "that he has dropped upon some large deposit of ivory; that will turn out to be the solution of the mystery. It is the solution of most mysteries in this country. I wish I could solve the mysteries of ways and means, and drop upon a large deposit of ivory, or spice, or precious stones. We should soon be out of this country, should we not, old girl?"

"I do not think we have much to complain of," answered Jocelyn.

"No; you never do. Moreover, I do not suppose you would do so if you had the excuse."

"Oh yes, I should, if I thought it would do any good."

"Ah!" put in Meredith; "there speaks Philosophy—jam, please."

"Or resignation—that is strawberry and this is black currant."

"Thanks, black currant. No—Philosophy. Resignation is the most loathsome of the virtues."

"I can't say I care for any of them very much," put in Maurice.

"No; I thought you seemed to shun them," said Jack, like a flash.

"Sharp! very sharp! Jocelyn, do you know what we called him at school?—the French nail; he was so very long and thin and sharp! I might add polished and strong, but we were not so polite in those days. Poor old Jack! he gave as good as he got. But I must be off—the commerce of Eastern Africa awaits me. You'll be round at the office presently, I suppose, Jack?"

"Yes; I have an appointment there with a colored person who is a liar by nature and a cook by trade."

Maurice Gordon usually went off like this — at a mo. ment's notice.   IIe was one of those loud - speaking, quick-actioned men, who often get a reputation for energy and capacity without fully deserving it.

Jack, of a more meditative habit, rarely followed his host with the same obvious haste.   He finished his breakfast calmly, and then asked Jocelyn whether she was coming out onto the veranda.   It was a habit they had unconsciously dropped into.   The veranda was a very important feature of the house, thickly overhung as it was with palms, bananas, and other tropical verdure.   Africa is the land of creepers, and all around this veranda, over the trellis-work, around the supports, hanging in festoons from the roof, were a thousand different creeping flowers.   The legend of the house — for, as in India, almost every bungalow on the West Coast has its tale—was that one of the early missionaries had built it, and, to beguile the long months of the rainy season, had carefully collected these creepers to beautify the place against the arrival of his young wife.   She never came.   A telegram stopped her.   A snake interrupted his labor of love.

Jack took a seat at once, and began to search for his cigar-case in the pocket of his jacket.   In this land of flies and moths, men need not ask permission before they smoke. Jocelyn did not sit down at once.   She went to the front of the veranda and watched her brother mount his horse. She was a year older than Maurice Gordon, and exercised a larger influence over his life than either of them suspected.

Presently he rode past the veranda, waving his hand cheerily.   He was one of those large, hearty Englishmen who seem to be all appetite and laughter — men who may be said to be manly, and beyond that, nothing.   Their manliness is so overpowering that it swallows up many other qualities which are not out of place in men, such as tact and thoughtfulness, and *perhaps* intellectuality, and the power to take some interest in those gentler things that interest women.

When Jocelyn came to the back of the veranda she was thinking about her brother Maurice, and it never suggested itself to her that she should not speak her thoughts to Meredith, whom she had not seen until three weeks ago. She had never spoken of Maurice behind his back to any man before.

"Does it ever strike you," she said, "that Maurice is the sort of man to be led astray by evil influence?"

"Yes; or to be led straight by a good influence, such as yours."

He did not meet her thoughtful gaze. He was apparently watching the retreating form of the horse through the tangle of flower and leaf and tendril.

"I am afraid," said the girl, "that my influence is not of much account."

"Do you really believe that?" asked Meredith, turning upon her with a half-cynical smile.

"Yes," she answered, simply.

Before speaking again he took a pull at his cigar.

"Your influence," he said, "appears to me to be the making of Maurice Gordon. I frequently see serious flaws in the policy of Providence; but I suppose there is wisdom in making the strongest influence that which is unconscious of its power."

"I am glad you think I have some power over him," said Jocelyn; "but, at the same time, it makes me uneasy, because it only confirms my conviction that he is very easily led. And suppose my influence—such as it is—was withdrawn? Suppose that I were to die, or, what appears to be more likely, suppose that he should marry?"

"Then let us hope that he will marry the right person. People sometimes do, you know."

She smiled with a strange little flicker of the eyelids. They had grown wonderfully accustomed to each other dur-

ing the last three weeks. Here, it would appear, was one
of those friendships between man and woman that occasionally set the world agog with curiosity and scepticism.
But there seemed to be no doubt about it. He was over
thirty, she verging on that prosaic age. Both had lived
and moved in the world; to both life was an open book,
and they had probably discovered, as most of us do, that
the larger number of the leaves are blank. He had almost
told her that he was engaged to be married, and she had
quite understood. There could not possibly be any misap-
prehension; there was no room for one of those little mistakes about which people write novels and foldly hope that
some youthful· reader may be carried away by a very faint
resemblance to that which they hold to be life. Moreover,
at thirty, one leaves the first romance of youth behind.

There was something in her smile that suggested that
she did not quite believe in his cynicism.

"Also," she said, gravely, "some stronger influence might
appear—an influence which I could not counteract."

Jack Meredith turned in his long chair and looked at her
searchingly.

"I have a vague idea," he said, "that you are thinking
of Durnovo."

"I am," she admitted, with some surprise. "I wonder
how you knew? I am afraid of him."

"I can reassure you on that score," said Meredith. "For
the next two years or so Durnovo will be in daily intercourse with me. He will be under my immediate eye. I
did not anticipate much pleasure from his society, but now
I do."

"Why?" she asked, rather mystified.

"Because I shall have the daily satisfaction of knowing
that I am relieving you of an anxiety."

"It is very kind of you to put it in that way," said
Jocelyn. "But I should not like you to sacrifice yourself
to what may be a foolish prejudice on my part."

"It is not a foolish prejudice. Durnovo is not a gentleman, either by birth or inclination. He is not fit to associate with you."

To this Jocelyn answered nothing. Victor Durnovo was one of her brother's closest friends—a friend of his own choosing.

"Miss Gordon," said Meredith, suddenly, with a gravity that was rare, "will you do me a favor?"

"I think I should like to."

"You admit that you are afraid of Durnovo now; if at any time you have reason to be more afraid, will you make use of me? Will you write or come to me and ask my help?"

"Thank you," she said, hesitatingly.

"You see," he went on in a lighter tone, "I am not afraid of Durnovo. I have met Durnovo before. You may have observed that my locks no longer resemble the raven's wing. There is a little gray—just here—above the temple. I am getting on in life, and I know how to deal with Durnovos."

"Thank you," said the girl, with a little sigh of relief. "The feeling that I have some one to turn to will be a great relief. You see how I am placed here. The missionaries are very kind and well-meaning, but there are some things which they do not quite understand. They may be gentlemen—some of them are; but they are not men of the world. I have no definite thought or fear, and very good persons, one finds, are occasionally a little dense. Unless things are very definite, they do not understand."

"On the other hand," pursued Jack, in the same reflective tone, as if taking up her thought, "persons who are not good have a perception of the indefinite. I did not think of it in that light before."

Jocelyn Gordon laughed softly, without attempting to meet his lighter vein.

"Do you know," she said, after a little silence, "that I

was actually thinking of warning you against Mr. Durnovo? Now I stand aghast at my own presumption."

"It was kind of you to give the matter any thought whatever."

He rose and threw away the end of his cigar. Joseph was already before the door, leading the horse which Maurice Gordon had placed at his visitor's disposal.

"I will lay the warning to heart," he said, standing in front of Jocelyn, and looking down at her as she lay back in the deep basket-chair. She was simply dressed in white —as was her wont, for it must be remembered that they were beneath the equator—a fair English maiden, whose thoughts were hidden behind a certain gracious, impenetrable reserve. "I will lay it to heart, although you have not uttered it. But I have always known with what sort of man I was dealing. We serve each other's purpose, that is all; and he knows that as well as I do."

"I am glad Mr. Oscard is going with you," she answered, guardedly.

He waited a moment. It seemed as if she had not done speaking—as if there was another thought near the surface. But she did not give voice to it, and he turned away. The sound of the horse's feet on the gravel did not arouse her from a reverie into which she had fallen; and long after it had died away, leaving only the hum of insect life and the distant ceaseless song of the surf, Jocelyn Gordon sat apparently watching the dancing shadows on the floor as the creepers waved in the breeze.

CHAPTER XII

A MEETING

"No one can be more wise than destiny."

THE short equatorial twilight was drawing to an end, and all Nature stood in silence, while Night crept up to claim the land where her reign is more autocratic than elsewhere on earth. There is a black night above the trees, and a blacker beneath. In an hour it would be dark, and, in the meantime, the lowering clouds were tinged with a pink glow that filtered through from above. There was rain coming, and probably thunder. Moreover, the trees seemed to know it, for there was a limpness in their attitude, as if they were tucking their heads into their shoulders in anticipation of the worst. The insects were certainly possessed of a premonition. They had crept away.

It was distinctly an unlikely evening for the sportsman. The stillness was so complete that the faintest rustle could be heard at a great distance. Moreover, it was the sort of evening when Nature herself seems to be glancing over her shoulder with timorous restlessness.

Nevertheless, a sportsman was abroad. He was creeping up the right-hand bank of a stream, his only chance lying in the noise of the waters which might serve to deaden the sound of broken twig or rustling leaf.

This sportsman was Jack Meredith, and it was evident that he was bringing to bear upon the matter in hand that intelligence and keenness of perception which had made him a person of some prominence in other scenes where Nature has a less assured place.

It would appear that he was not so much at home in the

tangle of an African forest as in the crooked paths of
London society; for his clothes were torn in more than one
place; a mosquito, done to sudden death, adhered san-
guinarily to the side of his aristocratic nose, while heat and
mental distress had drawn damp stripes down his coun-
tenance. His hands were scratched and inclined to bleed,
and one leg had apparently been in a morass. Added to
these physical drawbacks there was no visible sign of success, which was probably the worst part of Jack Meredith's
plight.

Since sunset he had been crawling, scrambling, stumbling
up the bank of this stream in relentless pursuit of some
large animal which persistently kept hidden in the tangle
across the bed of the river. The strange part of it was that
when he stopped to peep through the branches the animal
stopped too, and he found no way of discovering its whereabouts. More than once they stopped thus for nearly five
minutes, peering at each other through the heavy leafage.
It was distinctly unpleasant, for Meredith felt that the
animal was not afraid of him, and did not fully understand
the situation. The respective positions of hunter and hunted
were imperfectly defined. He had hitherto confined his
attentions to such game as showed a sporting readiness to
run away, and there was a striking novelty in this unseen
beast of the forest, fresh, as it were, from the hands of its
Creator, that entered into the fun of the thing from a
totally mistaken standpoint.

Once Meredith was able to decide approximately the
whereabouts of his prey by the momentary shaking of a
twig. He raised his rifle and covered that twig steadily;
his forefinger played tentatively on the trigger, but on
second thoughts he refrained. He was keenly conscious of
the fact that the beast was doing its work with skill superior
to his own. In comparison to his, its movements were
almost noiseless. Jack Meredith was too clever a man to
be conceited in the wrong place, which is the habit of

fools. He recognized very plainly that he was not distinguishing himself in this new field of glory; he was not yet an accomplished big-game hunter.

Twice he raised his rifle with the intention of firing at random into the underwood on the remote chance of bringing his enemy into the open. But the fascination of this duel of cunning was too strong, and he crept onward with bated breath.

It was terrifically hot, and all the while Night was stalking westward on the summits of the trees with stealthy tread.

While absorbed in the intricacies of pursuit — while anathematizing tendrils and condemning thorns to summary judgment—Jack Meredith was not losing sight of his chance of getting back to the little village of Msala. He knew that he had only to follow the course of the stream downward, retracing his steps until a junction with the Ogowe River was effected. In the meantime his lips were parted breathlessly, and there was a light in the quiet eyes which might have startled some of his well-bred friends could they have seen it.

At last he came to an open space made by a slip of the land into the bed of the river. When Jack Meredith came to this he stepped out of the thicket and stood in the open, awaiting the approach of his stealthy prey. The sound of its footfall was just perceptible, slowly diminishing the distance that divided them. Then the trees were parted, and a tall, fair man stepped forward onto the opposite bank.

Jack Meredith bowed gravely, and the other sportsman, seeing the absurdity of the situation, burst into hearty laughter. In a moment or two he had leaped from rock to rock and come to Meredith.

" It seems," he said, " that we have been wasting a considerable amount of time."

" I very nearly wasted powder and shot," replied Jack, significantly indicating his rifle.

" I saw you twice, and raised my rifle ; your breeches are

just the color of a young doe.   Are you Meredith?   My
name is Oscard."

"Ah! Yes, I am Meredith.   I am glad to see you."

They shook hands.   There was a twinkle in Jack Meredith's eyes, but Oscard was quite grave.   His sense of humor
was not very keen, and he was before all things a sportsman.

" I left the canoes a mile below Msala and landed to shoot
a deer we saw drinking, but I never saw him afterwards.
Then I heard you, and I have been stalking you ever since."

" But I never expected you so soon ; you were not due
till—look !" Jack whispered, suddenly.

Oscard turned on his heel, and the next instant their two
rifles rang out through the forest stillness in one sharp
crack.   Across the stream, ten yards behind the spot where
Oscard had emerged from the brush, a leopard sprang into
the air, five feet from the ground, with head thrown back
and paws clawing at the thinness of space with grand free
sweeps.   The beast fell with a thud, and lay still—dead.

The two men clambered across the rocks again, side by
side.   While they stood over the prostrate form of the
leopard—beautiful, incomparably graceful and sleek even
in death—Guy Oscard stole a sidelong glance at his companion.   He was a modest man, and yet he knew that he
was reckoned among the big-game hunters of the age.   This
man had fired as quickly as himself, and there were two
small trickling holes in the animal's head.

While he was being quietly scrutinized Jack Meredith
stooped down, and, taking the leopard beneath the shoulders,
lifted it bodily back from the pool of blood.

" Pity to spoil the skin," he explained, as he put a fresh
cartridge into his rifle.

Oscar nodded in an approving way.   He knew the weight
of a full-grown male leopard, all muscle and bone, and he
was one of those old-fashioned persons mentioned in the
Scriptures as taking a delight in a man's legs—or his arms,
so long as they were strong.

"I suppose," he said, quietly, "we had better skin him here."

As he spoke he drew a long hunting-knife, and, slashing down a bunch of the maidenhair fern that grew like nettles around them, he wiped the blood gently, almost affectionately, from the leopard's cat-like face.

There was about these two men a strict attention to the matter in hand, a mutual and common respect for all things pertaining to sport, a quiet sense of settling down without delay to the regulation of necessary detail that promised well for any future interest they might have in common.

So these highly-educated young gentlemen turned up their sleeves and steeped themselves to the elbow in gore. Moreover, they did it with a certain technical skill and a distinct sense of enjoyment. Truly, the modern English gentleman is a strange being. There is nothing his soul takes so much delight in as the process of getting hot and very dirty, and, if convenient, somewhat sanguinary. You cannot educate the manliness out of him, try as you will; and for such blessings let us in all humbleness give thanks to Heaven.

This was the bringing together of Jack Meredith and Guy Oscard—two men who loved the same woman. They knelt side by side, and Jack Meredith—the older man, the accomplished, gifted gentleman of the world, who stood second to none in that varied knowledge required nowadays of the successful societarian—Jack Meredith, be it noted, humbly dragged the skin away from the body while Guy Oscard cut the clinging integuments with a delicate touch and finished skill.

They laid the skin out on the trampled maidenhair and contemplated it with silent satisfaction. In the course of their inspection they both arrived at the head at the same moment. The two holes in the hide, just above the eyes, came under their notice at the same moment, and they turned and smiled gravely at each other, thinking the same thought—the sort of thought that Englishmen rarely put into intelligible English.

"I'm glad we did that," said Guy Oscard at length; suddenly, "Whatever comes of this expedition of ours—if we fight like hell, as we probably shall, before it is finished —if we hate each other ever afterwards, that skin ought to remind us that we are much of a muchness."

It might have been put into better English; it might almost have sounded like poetry had Guy Oscard been possessed of the poetic soul. But this, fortunately, was not his; and all that might have been said was left to the imagination of Meredith. What he really felt was that there need be no rivalry, and that he for one had no thought of such; that in the quest which they were about to undertake there need be no question of first and last; that they were merely two men, good or bad, competent or incompetent, but through all equal.

Neither of them suspected that the friendship thus strangely inaugurated at the rifle's mouth was to run through a longer period than the few months required to reach the plateau—that it was, in fact, to extend through that long expedition over a strange country that we call Life, and that it was to stand the greatest test that friendship has to meet with here on earth.

It was almost dark when at last they turned to go, Jack Meredith carrying the skin over his shoulder and leading the way. There was no opportunity for conversation, as their progress was necessarily very difficult. Only by the prattle of the stream were they able to make sure of keeping in the right direction. Each had a thousand questions to ask the other. They were total strangers; but it is not, one finds, by conversation that men get to know each other. A common danger, a common pleasure, a common pursuit— these are the touches of nature by which men are drawn together into the kinship of mutual esteem.

Once they gained the banks of the Ogowe their progress

was quicker, and by nine o'clock they reached the camp at
Msala.   Victor Durnovo was still at work superintending
the discharge of the baggage and stores from the large
trading-canoes.   They heard the shouting and chattering
before coming in sight of the camp, and one voice raised
angrily above the others.

"Is that Durnovo's voice?" asked Meredith.

"Yes," answered his companion, curtly.

It was a new voice, which Meredith had not heard before.   When they shouted to announce their arrival it was
suddenly hushed, and presently Durnovo came forward to
greet them.

Meredith hardly knew him, he was so much stronger and
healthier in appearance.   Durnovo shook hands heartily.

"No need to introduce you two," he said, looking from
one to the other.

"No; after one mistake we discovered each other's iden-
tity in the forest," answered Meredith.

Durnovo smiled; but there was something behind the
smile.   He did not seem to approve of their meeting without his intervention.

CHAPTER XIII

IN BLACK AND WHITE

"A little lurking secret of the blood,
A little serpent secret rankling keen."

THE three men walked up towards the house together.
It was a fair-sized house, with a heavy thatched roof that
overhung the walls like the crown of a mushroom.   The
walls were only mud, and the thatching was nothing else
than banana leaves; but there was evidence of European

taste in the garden surrounding the structure, and in the glazed windows and wooden door.

As they approached the open doorway three little children, clad in very little more than their native modesty, ran gleefully out, and proceeded to engage seats on Jack Meredith's boots, looking upon him as a mere public conveyance. They took hardly any notice of him, but chattered and quarrelled among themselves, sometimes in baby English, sometimes in a dialect unknown to Oscard and Meredith.

"These," said the latter, when they were seated, and clinging with their little dusky arms round his legs, "are the very rummest little kids I ever came across."

Durnovo gave an impatient laugh, and went on towards the house. But Guy Oscard stopped, and walked more slowly beside Meredith, as he labored along heavy-footed.

"They are the jolliest little souls imaginable," continued Jack Meredith. "There," he said to them when they had reached the door - step, "run away to your mother—very fine ride—no! no more to-night! I'm aweary—you understand—aweary!"

"Aweary—awe-e-e-ary!" repeated the little things, standing before him in infantile nude rotundity, looking up with bright eyes.

"Aweary—that is it. Good-night, Epaminondas—good-night, Xantippe! Give ye good hap, most stout Nestorius!"

He stooped and gravely shook hands with each one in turn, and, after forcing a like ceremonial upon Guy Oscard, they reluctantly withdrew.

"They have not joined us, I suppose?" said Oscard, as he followed his companion into the house.

"Not yet. They live in this place. Nestorius, I understand, takes care of his mother, who in her turn takes care of this house. He is one and a half."

Guy Oscard seemed to have inherited the mind inquisitive from his learned father. He asked another question later on.

"Who is that woman?" he said, during dinner, with a little nod towards the doorway, through which the object of his curiosity had passed with some plates.

"That is the mother of the stout Nestorius," answered Jack—"Durnovo's house-keeper."

He spoke quietly, looking straight in front of him; and Joseph, who was drawing a cork at the back of the room, was watching his face.

There was a little pause, during which Durnovo drank slowly. Then Guy Oscard spoke again.

"If she cooked the dinner," he said, "she knows her business."

"Yes," answered Durnovo, "she is a good cook—if she is nothing else."

It did not sound as if further inquiries would be welcome, and so the subject was dropped with a silent tribute to the culinary powers of Durnovo's house-keeper at the Msala Station.

The woman had only appeared for a moment, bringing in some dishes for Joseph — a tall, stately woman, with great dark eyes, in which the patience of motherhood had succeeded to the soft fire of West-Indian love and youth. She had the graceful, slow carriage of the Creole, although her skin was darker than that of those dangerous sirens. That Spanish blood ran in her veins could be seen by the intelligence of her eyes; for there is an intelligence in Spanish eyes which stands apart. In the men it seems to refer to the past or the future, for their incorrigible leisureliness prevents the present rendering of a full justice to their powers. In the women it belongs essentially to the present; for there is no time like the present for love and other things.

"They call me," she had said to Jack Meredith, in her soft, mumbled English, a fortnight earlier—"they call me Marie."

The children he had named after his own fantasy, and

when she had once seen him with them there was a notable
change in her manner. Her eyes rested on him with a sort
of wondering attention, and when she cooked his meals or
touched anything that was his, there was something in her
attitude that denoted a special care.

Joseph called her "Missis," with a sort of friendliness in
his voice, which never rose to badinage nor descended to
familiarity.

"Seems to me, missis," he said, on the third evening
after the arrival of the advance column, "that the guv'nor
takes uncommon kindly to them little uns of yours."

They were washing up together after dinner in a part of
the garden which was used for a scullery, and Joseph was
enjoying a postprandial pipe.

"Yes," she said, simply, following the direction of
Joseph's glance. Jack Meredith was engaged in teaching
Epaminondas the intellectual game of bowls with a rounded
pebble and a beer-bottle. Nestorius, whose person seemed
more distended than usual, stood gravely by, engaged in
dental endeavors on a cork, while Xantippe joined noisily
in the game. Their lack of dress was essentially native to
the country, while their mother affected a simple European
style of costume.

"And," added Joseph, on politeness bent, "it don't surprise me. I'm wonderfully fond of the little nig — nippers
already. I am — straight."

The truth was that the position of this grave and still
comely woman was ambiguous. Neither Joseph nor his
master called her by the name she had offered for their use.
Joseph compromised by the universal and elastic "Missis";
his master simply avoided all names.

Ambiguity is one of those intangible nothings that get
into the atmosphere and have a trick of remaining there.
Marie seemed in some subtle way to pervade the atmosphere
of Msala. It would seem that Guy Oscard, in his thick-
headed way, was conscious of this mystery in the air; for

he had not been two hours in Msala before he asked, "Who is that woman?" and received the reply which has been recorded.

After dinner they had passed out onto the little terrace overlooking the river, and it was here that the great Simiacine scheme was pieced together. It was here, beneath the vast palm-trees that stood like two beacons towering over the surrounding forest, that three men deliberately staked their own lives and the lives of others against a fortune. Nature has a strange way of hiding her gifts. Many of the most precious have lain unheeded for hundreds of years in barren plains, on inaccessible mountains, or beneath the wave, while others are thrown at the feet of savages who know no use for them.

The man who had found the Simiacine was eager, restless, full of suspicion. To the others the scheme obviously presented itself in a different light. Jack Meredith was *dilettante*, light-hearted, and unsatisfactory. It was impossible to arouse any enthusiasm in him — to make him take it seriously. Guy Oscard was gravely indifferent. He wanted to get rid of a certain space of time, and the African forest, containing as it did the only excitement that his large heart knew, was as good a place as any. The Simiacine was, in his mind, relegated to a distant place behind weeks of sport and adventure such as his soul loved. He scarcely took Victor Durnovo *au pied de la lettre*. Perhaps he knew too much about him for that. Certain it is that neither of the two realized at that moment the importance of the step that they were taking.

"You men," said Durnovo, eagerly, "don't seem to take the thing seriously."

"I," answered Meredith, "intend, at all events, to take the profits very seriously. When they begin to come in, J. Meredith will be at the above address, and trusts by a careful attention to business to merit a continuance of your kind patronage."

Durnovo laughed somewhat nervously. Oscard did not seem to hear.

"It is all very well for you," said the half-caste, in a lower voice. "You have not so much at stake. It is likely that the happiness of my whole life depends upon this venture."

A curious smile passed across Jack Meredith's face. Without turning his head, he glanced sideways into Durnovo's face through the gloom. But he said nothing, and it was Oscard who broke the silence by saying, simply:

"The same may possibly apply to me."

There was a little pause, during which he lighted his pipe.

"To a certain extent," he said, in emendation. "Of course, my real object, as you no doubt know, is to get away from England until my father's death has been forgotten. My own conscience is quite clear, but—"

Jack Meredith drew in his legs and leaned forward.

"But," he said, interrupting, and yet not interrupting—"but the public mind is an unclean sink. Everything that goes into it comes out tainted. Therefore, it is best only to let the public mind have the scourings, as it were, of one's existence. If they get anything better — anything more important—it is better to skedaddle until it has run through and been swept away by a flow of social garbage."

Guy Oscard grunted with his pipe between his teeth, after the manner of the stoic American Indian — a grunt that seemed to say, "My pale-faced brother has spoken well; he expresses my feelings." Then he gave further vent to the deliberate expansiveness which was his.

"What I cannot stand," he said, "are the nudges and the nods and the surreptitious glances of the silly women who think that one cannot see them looking. I hate being pointed out."

"Together with the latest skirt-dancing girl and the last female society-detective, with the blushing honors of the witness-box thick upon her," suggested Jack Meredith.

"Yes," muttered Guy. He turned with a sort of simple wonder, and looked at Meredith curiously. He had never been understood so quickly before. He had never met man or woman possessing in so marked a degree that subtle power of going right inside the mind of another and feeling the things that are there—the greatest power of all—the power that rules the world; and it is only called Sympathy.

"Well," said the voice of Durnovo through the darkness, "I don't mind admitting that all I want is the money. I want to get out of this confounded country, but I don't want to leave till I have made a fortune."

The subtle influence that Meredith wielded seemed to have reached him too, warming into expansiveness his hot Spanish blood. His voice was full of confidence.

"Very right and proper," said Meredith. "Got a grudge against the country; make the country pay for it, in cash."

"That's what I intend to do; and it shall pay heavily. Then, when I've got the money, I'll know what to do with it. I know where to look, and I do not think that I shall look in vain."

Guy Oscard shuffled uneasily in his camp-chair. He had an Englishman's horror of putting into speech those things which we all think, while only Frenchmen and Italians say them. The Spaniards are not so bad, and Victor Durnovo had enough of their blood in him to say no more.

It did not seem to occur to any of them that the only person whose individuality was still veiled happened to be Jack Meredith. He alone had said nothing, had imparted no confidence. He it was who spake first, after a proper period of silence. He was too much of an adept to betray haste, and thus admit his debt of mutual confidence.

"It seems to me," he said, "that we have all the technicalities arranged now. So far as the working of the expedition is concerned, we know our places, and the difficulties will be met as they present themselves. But there is one thing which I think we should set in order now. I have been thinking about it while I have been waiting here alone."

The glow of Victor Durnovo's cigar died away as if in his attention he was forgetting to smoke; but he said nothing.

"It seems to me," Jack went on, "that before we leave here we should draw up and sign a sort of deed of partnership. Of course, we trust each other perfectly—there is no question of that. But life is an uncertain thing, as some earlier philosopher said before me; and one never knows what may happen. I have drawn up a paper in triplicate. If you have a match, I will read it to you."

Oscard produced a match, and, striking it on his boot, sheltered it with the hollow of his hand while Jack read:

"We, the undersigned, hereby enter into partnership to search for and sell, to our mutual profit, the herb known as Simiacine, the profits to be divided into three equal portions, after the deduction of one-hundredth part to be handed to the servant, Joseph Atkinson. Any further expenses that may be incurred to be borne in the same proportion as the original expense of fitting out the expedition—namely, two-fifths to be paid by Guy Cravener Oscard, two-fifths by John Meredith, one-fifth by Victor Durnovo.

"The sum of fifty pounds per month to be paid to Victor Durnovo, wherewith he may pay the thirty special men taken from his estate and headquarters at Msala to cultivate the Simiacine, and such corn and vegetables as may be required for the sustenance of the expedition; these men to act as porters until the plateau be reached.

"The opinion of two of the three leaders against one to be accepted unconditionally in all questions where controversy may arise. In case of death each of us undertakes hereby to hand over to the executor of the dead partner or partners such moneys as shall belong to him or them."

At this juncture there was a little pause, while Guy Oscard lighted a second match.

"And," continued Jack, " we hereby undertake severally, on oath, to hold the secret of the whereabouts of the Simiacine a strict secret, which secret may not be revealed by any one of us to whomsoever it may be without the sanction, in writing, of the other two partners."

"There," concluded Jack Meredith, " I am rather pleased with that literary production ; it is forcible and yet devoid of violence. I feel that in me the commerce of the century has lost an ornament. Moreover, I am ready to swear to the terms of the agreement."

There was a little pause. Guy Oscard took his pipe from his mouth, and while he knocked the ashes out against the leg of his chair he mumbled, " I swear to hold to that agreement."

Victor Durnovo took off his hat with a sweep and a flourish, and, raising his bared brow to the stars, he said : " I swear to hold to that agreement. If I fail, may God strike me dead !"

CHAPTER XIV

PANIC-STRICKEN

"Is this reason? Is this humanity? Alas! it is man."

THE next morning Jack Meredith was awakened by his servant Joseph before it was fully light. It would appear as if Joseph had taken no means of awakening him, for Meredith awoke quite quietly to find Joseph standing by his bed.

" Holloa !" exclaimed the master, fully awake at once, as townsmen are.

Joseph stood at attention by the bedside.

" Woke you before yer time, sir," he said. " There's something wrong among these 'ere darky fellers, sir."

"Wrong! What do you mean?"

Meredith was already lacing his shoes.

"Not rebellion?" he said, curtly, looking towards his fire-arms.

"No, sir, not that. It's some mortual sickness. I don't know what it is. I've been up half the night with them. It's spreading, too."

"Sickness! what does it seem like? Just give me that jacket. Not that sleeping sickness?"

"No, sir. It's not that. Missis Marie was telling me about that — awful scourge that, sir. No, the poor chaps are wide awake enough. Groanin', and off their heads too, mostly."

"Have you called Mr. Oscard?"

"No, sir."

"Call him and Mr. Durnovo."

"Met Mr. Durnovo, sir, goin' out as I came in."

In a few moments Jack joined Durnovo and Oscard, who were talking together on the terrace in front of the house. Guy Oscard was still in his pyjamas, which he had tucked into top-boots. He also wore a sun-helmet, which added a finish to his costume. They got quite accustomed to this get-up during the next three days, for he never had time to change it; and, somehow, it ceased to be humorous long before the end of that time.

"Oh, it's nothing," Durnovo was saying, with a singular eagerness. "I know these chaps. They have been paid in advance. They are probably shamming, and if they are not they are only suffering from the effects of a farewell glorification. They want to delay our start. That is their little game. It will give them a better chance of deserting."

"At any rate, we had better go and see them," suggested Jack.

"No, don't!" cried Durnovo, eagerly, detaining him with both hands. "Take my advice, and don't. Just have breakfast in the ordinary way, and pretend there is nothing wrong. Then afterwards you can lounge casually into the camp."

"All right," said Jack, rather unwillingly.

"It has been of some use — this scare," said Durnovo, turning and looking towards the river. "It has reminded me of something. We have not nearly enough quinine. I will just take a quick canoe, and run down to Loango to fetch some."

He turned quite away from them, and stooped to attach the lace of his boot.

"I can travel night and day, and be back here in three days," he added. "In the meantime you can be getting on with the loading of the canoes, and we will start as soon as I get back."

He stood upright and looked around with weather-wise, furtive eyes.

"Seems to me," he said, "there's thunder coming. I think I had better be off at once."

In the course of his inspection of the lowering clouds which hung, black as ink, just above the trees, his eyes lighted on Joseph, standing within the door of the cottage, watching him with a singular half-suppressed smile.

"Yes," he said, hurriedly, "I will start at once. I can eat some sort of a breakfast when we are under way."

He looked beneath his lashes quickly from Jack to Guy and back again. Their silent acquiescence was not quite satisfactory. Then he called his own men, and spoke to them in a tongue unknown to the Englishmen. He hurried forward their preparations with a feverish irritability which made Jack Meredith think of the first time he had ever seen Durnovo—a few miles farther down the river—all palpitating and trembling with climatic nervousness. His face was quite yellow, and there was a line drawn diagonally from the nostrils down each cheek, to lose itself ultimately in the heavy black mustache.

Before he stepped into his canoe the thunder was rumbling in the distance, and the air was still as death. Breathing was an effort; the inhaled air did not satisfy the lungs, and seemed powerless to expand them.

Overhead the clouds, of a blue-black intensity, seemed almost to touch the trees; the river was of ink. The rowers said nothing, but they lingered on the bank and watched Durnovo's face anxiously. When he took his seat in the canoe they looked protestingly up to the sky. Durnovo said something to them rapidly, and they laid their paddles to the water.

Scarcely had the boat disappeared in the bend of the river before the rain broke. It came with the rush of an express train—the trees bending before the squall like reeds. The face of the river was tormented into a white fury by the drops which splashed up again a foot in height. The lashing of the water on the bare backs of the negroes was distinctly audible to Victor Durnovo.

Then the black clouds split up like a rent cloth, and showed behind them, not heaven, but the living fire of hell. The thunder crashed out in sharp reports like file-firing at a review, and with one accord the men ceased rowing and crouched down in the canoe.

Durnovo shouted to them, his face livid with fury. But for some moments his voice was quite lost. The lightning ran over the face of the river like will-o'-the-wisps; the whole heaven was streaked continuously with it.

Suddenly the negroes leaped to their paddles and rowed with bent backs and wild, staring eyes, as if possessed. They were covered by the muzzle of Durnovo's revolver.

Behind the evil-looking barrel of blue steel the half-caste's dripping face looked forth, peering into the terrific storm. There was no question of fending off such torrents of rain, nor did he attempt it. Indeed, he seemed to court its downfall. He held out his arms and stretched forth his legs, giving free play to the water which ran off him in a continual stream, washing his thin khaki clothing on his limbs. He raised his face to the sky, and let the water beat upon his brow and hair.

The roar of the thunder, which could be *felt*, so great was the vibration of the laden air, seemed to have no fear for him. The lightning, ever shooting athwart the sky, made him blink as if dazzled, but he looked upon it without emotion.

He knew that behind him he had left a greater danger than this, and he stretched out his limbs to the cleansing torrent with an exulting relief to be washed from the dread infection. Small-pox had laid its hand on the camp at Msala; and from the curse of it Victor Durnovo was flying in a mad, chattering panic through all the anger of the tropic elements, holding Death over his half-stunned crew, not daring to look behind him or pause in his coward's flight.

It is still said on the Ogowe River that no man travels like Victor Durnovo. Certain it is that, in twenty-seven hours from the time that he left Msala on the morning of the great storm, he presented himself before Maurice Gordon in his office at the factory at Loango.

"Ah!" cried Gordon, hardly noticing the washed-out, harassed appearance of his visitor; "here you are again. I heard that the great expedition had started."

"So it has, but I have come back to get one or two things we have forgotten. Got any sherry handy?"

"Of course," replied Gordon, with perfect adhesion to the truth.

He laid aside his pen, and, turning in his chair, drew a decanter from a small cupboard, which stood on the ground at his side.

"Here you are," he continued, pouring out a full glass with practised, but slightly unsteady, hand.

Durnovo drank the wine at one gulp and set the glass down.

"Ah!" he said, "that does a chap good."

"Does it now?" exclaimed Maurice Gordon, with mock surprise. "Well, I'll just try."

The manner in which he emptied his glass was quite different, with a long, slow drawing-out of the enjoyment, full of significance for the initiated.

"Will you be at home to-night?" asked Durnovo, gently pushing aside the hospitable decanter. "I have got a lot of work to do to-day, but I should like to run in and see you this evening."

"Yes, come and dine."

Durnovo shook his head and looked down at his wrinkled and draggled clothing.

"No, I can't do that, old man. Not in this trim."

"Bosh! What matter? Jocelyn doesn't mind."

"No, but I do."

It was obvious that he wanted to accept the invitation, although the objection he raised was probably honest. For that taint in the blood that cometh from the subtle tar-brush brings with it a vanity that has its equal in no white man's heart.

"Well, I'll lend you a black coat! Seven o'clock sharp!"

Durnovo hurried away with a gleam of excitement in his dark eyes.

Maurice Gordon did not resume his work at once. He sat for some time idly drumming with his fingers on the desk.

"If I can only get her to be civil to him," he reflected aloud, "I'll get into this business yet."

At seven o'clock Durnovo appeared at the Gordons' house. He had managed to borrow a dress-suit, and wore an orchid in his button-hole. It was probably the first time that Jocelyn had seen him in this garb of civilization, which is at the same time the most becoming and the most trying variety of costume left to sensible men in these days. A dress-suit finds a man out sooner than anything except speech.

Jocelyn was civil in her reception — more so, indeed, than

Maurice Gordon had hoped for. She seemed almost glad to see Durnovo, and evinced quite a kindly interest in his movements. Durnovo attributed this to the dress-suit, while Maurice concluded that his obvious hints, thrown out before dinner, had fallen on fruitful ground.

At dinner Victor Durnovo was quite charmed with the interest that Jocelyn took in the expedition, of which, he gave it to be understood, he was the chief. So also was Maurice, because Durnovo's evident admiration of Jocelyn somewhat overcame his natural secrecy of character.

" You'll hear of me, Miss Gordon, never fear, before three months are past," said Durnovo, in reply to a vague suggestion that his absence might extend to several months. " I am not the sort of man to come to grief by a foolish mistake or any unnecessary risk."

To which sentiment two men at Msala bore generous testimony later on.

The simple dinner was almost at an end, and it was at this time that Jocelyn Gordon began once more to dislike Durnovo. At first she had felt drawn towards him. Although he wore the dress-clothes rather awkwardly, there was something in his manner which reminded her vaguely of a gentleman. It was not that he was exactly gentlemanly, but there was the reflection of good-breeding in his bearing. Dark-skinned people, be it noted, have usually the imitative faculty. As the dinner and the wine warmed his heart, so by degrees he drew on his old self like a glove. He grew bolder and less guarded. His own opinion of himself rose momentarily, and with it a certain gleam in his eyes increased as they rested on Jocelyn.

It was not long before she noted this, and quite suddenly her ancient dislike of the man was up in arms with a new intensity gathered she knew not whence.

" And," said Maurice, when Jocelyn had left them, " I suppose you'll be a millionaire in about six months ?"

He gently pushed the wine towards him at the same time.

Durnovo had not slept for forty hours. The excitement of his escape from the plague-ridden camp had scarcely subsided. The glitter of the silver on the table, the shaded candles, the subtle sensuality of refinement and daintiness appealed to his hot-blooded nature. He was a little off his feet perhaps. He took the decanter and put it to the worst use he could have selected.

"Not so soon as that," he said; "but in time—in time."

"Lucky beggar!" muttered Maurice Gordon, with a little sigh.

"I don't mind telling you," said Durnovo, with a sudden confidence begotten of Madeira, "that it's Simiacine—that's what it is. I can't tell you more."

"Simiacine," repeated Gordon, fingering the stem of his wineglass and looking at him keenly between the candle-shades. "Yes. You've always been on its track, haven't you?"

"In six months your go-downs will be full of it—my Simiacine, my Simiacine."

"By God, I wish I had a hand in it!"

Maurice Gordon pushed the decanter again—gently, almost surreptitiously.

"And so you may, some day. You help me and I'll help you—that is my ticket. Reciprocity—reciprocity, my dear Maurice."

"Yes, but how?"

"Can't tell you now, but I will in good time—in my own time. Come, let's join the ladies—eh? ha, ha!"

But at this moment the servant brought in coffee, saying in his master's ear that Miss Jocelyn had gone to bed with a slight headache.

CHAPTER XV

"The spirits
Of coming things stride on before their issues."

THERE is nothing that brings men so close to each other
as a common grievance or a common danger. Men who
find pleasure in the same game or the same pursuit are
drawn together by a common taste; but in the indulgence
of it there is sure to arise, sooner or later, a spirit of competition. Now, this spirit, which is in most human affairs, is
a new bond of union when men are fighting side by side
against a common foe.

During the three days that followed Durnovo's departure
from Msala, Jack Meredith and Oscard learned to know each
other. These three days were as severe a test as could well
be found; for courage, humanity, tenderness, loyalty, were
by turns called forth by circumstance. Small-pox rages in
Africa as it rages nowhere else in these days. The natives
fight it or bow before it as before an ancient and deeply-
dreaded foe. It was nothing new to them; and it would
have been easy enough for Jack and Oscard to prove to their
own satisfaction that the presence of three white men at
Msala was a danger to themselves and no advantage to the
natives. It would have been very simple to abandon the
river station, leaving there such men as were stricken down
to care for each other. But such a thought never seemed
to suggest itself.

The camp was moved across the river, where all who
seemed strong and healthy were placed under canvas, awaiting further developments.

The infected were carried to a special camp set apart and guarded, and this work was executed almost entirely by the three Englishmen, aided by a few natives who had had the disease.

For three days these men went about with their lives literally in their hands, tending the sick, cheering the despondent, frightening the cowards into some semblance of self-respect and dignity. And during these three days, wherein they never took an organized meal or three consecutive hours of rest, Joseph, Meredith, and Oscard rose together to that height of manhood where master and servant, educated man and common soldier, stand equal before their Maker.

Owing to the promptness with which measures had been taken for isolating the affected, the terrible sickness did not spread. In all eleven men were stricken, and of these ten died within three days. The eleventh recovered, but eventually remained at Msala.

It was only on the evening of the third day that Jack and Guy found time to talk of the future. They had never left Durnovo's house, and on this third day they found time to dine together.

"Do you think," Oscard asked, bluntly, when they were left alone to smoke, "that Durnovo spotted what was the matter?"

"I am afraid that I have not the slightest doubt of it," replied Jack, lightly.

"And bolted?" suggested Oscard.

"And bolted."

Guy Oscard gave a contemptuous little laugh, which had a deeper insult in it than he could have put into words.

"And what is to be done?" he inquired.

"Nothing. People in books would mount on a very high pinnacle of virtue and cast off Mr. Durnovo and all his works; but it is much more practical to make what use we can of him. That is a worldly-wise, nineteenth-century way of looking at it; we cannot do without him."

The contemplativeness of nicotine was upon Guy Oscard.

"Umph!" he grunted. "It is rather disgusting," he said, after a pause; "I hate dealing with cowards."

"And I with fools. For every-day use, give me a coward by preference."

"Yes, there is something in that. Still, I'd throw up the whole thing if—"

"So would I," said Jack, turning sharply in his chair, "if—"

Oscard laughed curtly and waited.

"If," continued Jack, "I could. But I am more or less bound to go on now. Such chances as this do not turn up every day; I cannot afford to let it go by. Truth is, I told —some one who shall be nameless—that I would make money to keep her in that state of life wherein her godfathers, etc., have placed her; and make that money I must."

"That's about my size, too," said Guy Oscard, somewhat indistinctly, owing to the fact that he habitually smoked a thick-stemmed pipe.

"Is it? I'm glad of that. It gives us something in common to work for."

"Yes." Guy paused, and made a huge effort, finally conquering that taciturnity which was almost an affliction to him. "The reason I gave the other night to you and that chap Durnovo was honest enough, but I have another. I want to lie low for a few months, but I also want to make money. I'm as good as engaged to be married, and I find that I am not so well off as I thought I was. People told me that I should have three thousand a year when the guv'nor died, but I find that people know less of my affairs than I thought."

"They invariably do," put in Jack, encouragingly.

"It is barely two thousand, and—and she has been brought up to something better than that."

"Um! they mostly are. Mine has been brought up to something better than that, too. That is the worst of it."

Jack Meredith leaned back in his folding-chair, and gazed practically up into the heavens.

"Of course," Guy went on, doggedly expansive now that he had once plunged, "two thousand a year sounds pretty good, and it is not bad to start upon. But there is no chance of its increasing; in fact, the lawyer fellows say it may diminish. I know of no other way to make money—had no sort of training for it. I'm not of a commercial turn of mind. Fellows go into the City and brew beer or float companies, whatever that may be."

"It means they sink other people's funds," explained Jack.

"Yes, I suppose it does. The guv'nor, y' know, never taught me how to make a livelihood; wouldn't let me be a soldier; sent me to college, and all that; wanted me to be a *littérateur*. Now, I'm not literary."

"No, I shouldn't think you were."

"Remains Africa. I am not a clever chap like you, Meredith."

"For which you may thank a gracious Providence," interposed Jack. "Chaps like me are what some people call 'fools' in their uncouth way."

"But I know a little about Africa, and I know something about Durnovo. That man has got a mania, and it is called Simiacine. He is quite straight upon that point, whatever he may be upon others. He knows this country, and he is not making any mistake about the Simiacine, whatever—"

"His powers of sick-nursing may be," suggested Jack.

"Yes, that's it. We'll put it that way if you like."

"Thanks, I do prefer it. Any fool could call a spade a spade. The natural ambition would be to find something more flowery and yet equally descriptive."

Guy Oscard subsided into a monosyllabic sound.

"I believe implicitly in this scheme," he went on, after a pause. "It is a certain fact that the men who can supply pure Simiacine have only to name their price for it. They will make a fortune, and I believe that Durnovo knows where it is growing in quantities."

"I cannot see how it would pay him to deceive us in the matter. That is the best way of looking at it," murmured Jack, reflectively. "When I first met him the man thought he was dying, and for the time I really believe that he was honest. Some men are honest when they feel unwell. There was so little doubt in my mind that I went into the thing at once."

"If you will go on with it I will stand by you," said Oscard, shortly.

"All right; I think we two together are as good as any half-bred sharper on this coast, to put it gracefully."

Jack Meredith lighted a fresh cigarette, and leaned back with the somewhat exaggerated grace of movement which was in reality partly attributable to natural litheness. For some time they smoked in silence, subject to the influence of the dreamy tropic night. Across the river some belated bird was calling continuously and cautiously for its mate. At times the splashing movements of a crocodile broke the smooth silence of the water. Overhead the air was luminous with that night-glow which never speaks to the senses in latitudes above the teens.

There is something in man's nature that inclines him sympathetically — almost respectfully — towards a mental inferior. Moreover, the feeling, whatever it may be, is rarely, if ever, found in women. A man does not openly triumph in victory, as do women. One sees an easy victor —at lawn-tennis, for instance—go to his vanquished foe, wiping vigorously a brow that is scarcely damp, and explaining more or less lamely how it came about. But the same rarely happens in the "ladies' singles." What, to quote another instance, is more profound than the contempt bestowed by the girl with the good figure upon her who has no figure at all? Without claiming the virtue of a greater generosity for the sex, one may, perhaps, assume that men learn by experience the danger of despising any man. The girl with the good figure is sometimes—nay, often—found blooming alone in her superiority, while the despised competitor is a happy mother of children. And all this to explain that Jack Meredith felt drawn towards his great hulking companion by something that was not a mere respect of mind for matter.

As love is inexplicable, so is friendship. No man can explain why Saul held Jonathan in such high esteem. Between men it would appear that admiration is no part of friendship. And such as have the patience to follow the lives of the two Englishmen thus brought together by a series of chances will perhaps be able to discover in this record of a great scheme the reason why Jack Meredith, the brilliant, the gifted, should bestow upon Guy Oscard such a wealth of love and esteem as he never received in return.

During the silence Jack was apparently meditating over the debt of confidence which he still owed to his companion; for he spoke first, and spoke seriously, about himself, which was somewhat against his habit.

"I dare say you have heard," he said, "that I had a—a disagreement with my father."

"Yes. Heard something about it," replied Oscard, in a tone which seemed to imply that the "something" was quite sufficient for his requirements.

"It was about my engagement," Jack went on, deliberately. "I do not know how it was, but they did not hit it off together. She was too honest to throw herself at his head, I suppose; for I imagine a pretty girl can usually do what she likes with an old man if she takes the trouble."

"Not with him, I think. Seemed to be rather down on girls in general," said Oscard, coolly.

"Then you know him?"

"Yes, a little. I have met him once or twice, out, you know. I don't suppose he would know me again if he saw me."

Which last remark does not redound to the credit of Guy's powers of observation.

They paused. It is wonderful how near we may stand to the brink and look far away beyond the chasm. Years afterwards they remembered this conversation, and it is possible that Jack Meredith wondered then what instinct it was that made him change the direction of their thoughts.

"If it is agreeable to you," he said, "I think it would be wise for me to go down to Loango, and gently intimate to Durnovo that we should be glad of his services."

"Certainly."

"He cannot be buying quinine all this time, you know. He said he would travel night and day."

Oscard nodded gravely.

"How will you put it?" he asked.

"I thought I would simply say that his non-arrival caused us some anxiety, and that I had come down to see if anything was wrong."

Jack rose and threw away the end of his cigarette. It was quite late, and across the river the gleam of the moonlight on fixed bayonets told that only the sentries were astir.

"And what about the small-pox?" pursued Oscard, more with the desire to learn than to amend.

"Don't think I shall say anything about that. The man wants careful handling."

"You will have to tell him that we have got it under."

"Yes, I'll do that. Good-night, old fellow; I shall be off by daylight."

By seven o'clock the next morning the canoe was ready, with its swarthy rowers in their places. The two Englishmen breakfasted together, and then walked down to the landing-stage side by side.

It was raining steadily, and the atmosphere had that singular feeling of total relaxation and limpness which is only to be felt in the rain-ridden districts of Central Africa.

"Take care of yourself," said Oscard, gruffly, as Jack stepped into the canoe.

"All right."

"And bring back Durnovo with you."

Jack Meredith looked up with a vague smile.

"That man," he said, lightly, "is going to the plateau if I have to drag him there by the scruff of the neck."

And he believed that he was thinking of the expedition only.

CHAPTER XVI

WAR

"Who, when they slash and cut to pieces,
Do so with civilest addresses."

THERE is no power so subtle and so strong as that of association. We have learned to associate mustard with beef, and therefore mustard shall be eaten with beef until the day wherein the lion shall lie down with the lamb.

Miss Millicent Chyne became aware, as the year advanced towards the sere and yellow age, that in opposing her wayward will in single combat against a simple little association in the public mind she was undertaking a somewhat herculean task.

Society — itself an association — is the slave of a word, and society had acquired the habit of coupling the names of Sir John Meredith and Lady Cantourne. They belonged to the same generation; they had similar tastes; they were both of some considerable power in the world of leisured pleasure; and, lastly, they amused each other. The result

is not far to seek. Wherever the one was invited, the other
was considered to be in demand; and Millicent found herself face to face with a huge difficulty.

Sir John was distinctly in the way. He had a keener eye
than the majority of young men, and occasionally exercised
the old man's privilege of saying outright things which, despite theory, are better left unsaid. Moreover, the situation
was ill-defined, and an ill-defined situation does not improve
in the keeping. Sir John said sharp things—too sharp even
for Millicent—and, in addition to the original grudge begotten of his quarrel with Jack and its result, the girl nour-
ished an ever-present feeling of resentment at a persistency
in misunderstanding her, of which she shrewdly suspected
the existence.

Perhaps the worst of it was that Sir John never said anything which could be construed into direct disapproval. He
merely indicated, in passing, the possession of a keen eyesight coupled with the embarrassing faculty of adding together correctly two small numerals.

When, therefore, Millicent allowed herself to be assisted
from the carriage at the door of a large midland country-
house by an eager and lively little French baron of her acquaintance, she was disgusted but not surprised to see a
well-known figure leaning gracefully on a billiard-cue in the
hall.

"I wish I could think that this pleasure was mutual,"
said Sir John with his courtliest smile, as he bowed over
Millicent's hand.

"It might be," with a coquettish glance.

"If—"

"If I were not afraid of you."

Sir John turned, smiling, to greet Lady Cantourne. He
did not appear to have heard, but in reality the remark had
made a distinct impression on him. It signalized a new departure—the attack at a fresh quarter. Millicent had tried
most methods—and she possessed many—hitherto in vain.

She had attempted to coax him with a filial playfulness of demeanor, to dazzle him by a brilliancy which had that effect upon the majority of men in her train, to win him by respectful affection; but the result had been failure. She was now bringing her last reserve up to the front; and there are few things more dangerous, even to an old campaigner, than a confession of fear from the lips of a pretty girl.

Sir John Meredith gave himself a little jerk—a throw back of the shoulders which was habitual—which might have been a tribute either to Millicent behind, or to Lady Cantourne in front.

The pleasantest part of existence in a large country-house full of visitors is the facility with which one may avoid those among the guests for whom one has no sympathy. Millicent managed very well to avoid Sir John Meredith. The baron was her slave—at least, he said so—and she easily kept him at her beck and call during the first evening.

It would seem that that strange hollow energy of old age had laid its hand upon Sir John Meredith, for he was the first to appear in the breakfast-room the next morning. He went straight to the sideboard, where the letters and newspapers lay in an orderly heap. It is a question whether he had not come down early on purpose to look for a letter. Perhaps he could not stay in his bed with the knowledge that the postman had called. He was possibly afraid to ask his old servant to go down and fetch his letters.

His bent and knotted hands fumbled among the correspondence, and suddenly his twitching lips were still. A strange stillness indeed overcame his whole face, turning it to stone. The letter was there; it had come, but it was not addressed to him.   .

Sir John Meredith took up the missive; he looked at the back, turned it, and examined the handwriting of his own son. There was a whole volume—filled with pride and love and unquenchable resolve—written on his face. He threw the letter down among its fellows, and his hand went fumbling weakly at his lips. He gazed, blinking his lashless lids, at the heap of letters, and the corner of another envelope presently arrested his attention. It was of the same paper, the same shape and hue, as that addressed to Miss Chyne. Sir John drew a deep breath, and reached out his hand. The letter had come at last. At last, thank God! And how weakly ready he was to grasp at the olive-branch held out to him across a continent!

He took the letter; he made a step with it towards the door, seeking solitude ; then, as an after-thought, he looked at the superscription. It was addressed to the same person, Miss Chyne, but in a different handwriting — the handwriting of a man well educated, but little used to wielding the pen.

"The other," mumbled Sir John — "the other man, by God!"

And, with a smile that sat singularly on his withered face, he took up a newspaper and went towards the fireplace, where he sat stiffly in an arm-chair, taking an enormous interest in the morning's news. He read a single piece of news three times over, and a fourth time in a whisper, so as to rivet his attention upon it. He would not admit that he was worsted — would not humble his pride even before the ornaments on the mantel-piece.

Before Millicent came down, looking very fresh and pretty in her tweed dress, the butler had sorted the letters. There were only two upon her plate—the twin envelopes addressed by different hands. Sir John was talking with a certain labored lightness to Lady Cantourne when that lady's niece came into the room. He was watching keenly. There was a certain amount of interest in the question of those two envelopes, as to which she would open first. She looked at each in turn, glanced furtively towards Sir John, made a suitable reply to some remark addressed to her by the baron, and tore open Jack's envelope. There was a

gravity—a concentrated gravity—about her lips as she unfolded the thin paper; and Sir John, who knew the world
and the little all-important trifles thereof, gave an impatient
sigh. It is the little trifle that betrays the man, and not
the larger issues of life in which we usually follow precedent. It was that passing gravity (of the lips only) that
told Sir John more about Millicent Chyne than she herself
knew, and what he had learned did not seem to be to his
liking.

There is nothing so disquieting as the unknown motive,
which disquietude was Sir John's soon after breakfast.
The other men dispersed to put on gaiters and cartridge-
bags, and the old aristocrat took his newspaper onto the
terrace.

Millicent followed him almost at once.

"Sir John," she said, "I have had a letter from Africa."

Did she take it for granted that he knew this already?
Was this spontaneous? Had Jack told her to do it?

These questions flashed through the old man's mind as
his eyes rested on her pretty face.

He was beginning to be afraid of this girl; which
showed his wisdom. For the maiden beautiful is a stronger
power in the world than the strong man. The proof of
which is that she gets her own way more often than the
strong man gets his.

"From Africa?" repeated Sir John Meredith, with a
twitching lip. "And from whom is your letter, my dear
young lady?"

His face was quite still, his old eyes steady, as he waited
for the answer.

"From Jack."

Sir John winced inwardly. Outwardly he smiled and
folded his newspaper upon his knees.

"Ah, from my brilliant son. That is interesting."

"Have you had one?" she asked, in prompt payment of
his sarcasm.

Sir John Meredith looked up with a queer little smile. He admired the girl's spirit. It was the smile of the fencer on touching worthy steel.

"No, my dear young lady, I have not. Mr. John Meredith does not find time to write to me—but he draws his allowance from the bank with a filial regularity."

Millicent had the letter in her hand. She made it crinkle in her fingers within a foot of the old gentleman's face. A faint odor of the scent she used reached his nostrils. He drew back a little as if he disliked it. His feeling for her almost amounted to a repugnance.

"I thought you might like to hear that he is well," she said, gently. She was reading the address on the envelope, and again he saw that look of concentrated gravity which made him feel uneasy for reasons of his own.

"It is very kind of you to throw me even that crumb from your richly-stored intellectual table. I am very glad to hear that he is well. A whole long letter from him must be a treat indeed."

She thought of a proverb relating to the grapes that are out of reach, but said nothing.

It was the fashion that year to wear little flyaway jackets with a coquettish pocket on each side. Millicent was wearing one of them, and she now became aware that Sir John had glanced more than once with a certain significance towards her left hand, which happened to be in that pocket. It, moreover, happened that Guy Oscard's letter was in the same receptacle.

She withdrew the hand, and changed color slightly as she became conscious that the corner of the envelope was protruding.

"I suppose that by this time," said Sir John, pleasantly, "you are quite an authority upon African matters?"

His manner was so extremely conversational and innocent that she did not think it necessary to look for an inner meaning. She was relieved to find that the two men, having actually met, spoke of each other frankly. It was evident that Guy Oscard could be trusted to keep his promise, and Jack Meredith was not the man to force or repose a confidence.

"He does not tell me much about Africa," she replied, determined to hold her ground. She was engaged to be married to Jack Meredith, and, whether Sir John chose to ignore the fact or not, she did not mean to admit that the subject should be tabooed.

" No—I suppose he has plenty to tell you about himself and his prospects?"

"Yes, he has.   His prospects are not so hopeless as you think."

"My dear Miss Chyne," protested Sir John, " I know nothing about his prospects beyond the fact that, when I am removed from this sphere of activity, he will come into possession of my title, such as it is, and my means, such as they are."

"Then you attach no importance to the work he is inaugurating in Africa?"

"Not the least. I did not even know that he was endeavoring to work. I only trust it is not manual labor— it is so injurious to the finger-nails. I have no sympathy with a gentleman who imagines that manual labor is compatible with his position, provided that he does not put his hand to the plough in England. Is not there something in the Scriptures about a man putting his hand to the plough and looking back? If Jack undertakes any work of that description I trust that he will recognize the fact that he forfeits his position by doing so."

" It is not manual labor—I can assure you of that."

"I am glad to hear it. He probably sells printed cottons to the natives, or exchanges wrought metal for ivory— an intellectual craft. But he is gaining experience, and I suppose he thinks he is going to make a fortune."

It happened that this was precisely the thought expressed by Jack Meredith in the letter in Millicent's hand.

"He is sanguine," she admitted.

"Of course. Quite right. Pray do not discourage him—if you find time to write. But, between you and me, my dear Miss Chyne, fortunes are not made in Africa. I am an old man, and I have some experience of the world. That part of it which is called Africa is not the place where fortunes are made. It is as different from India as chalk is from cheese, if you will permit so vulgar a simile."

Millicent's face dropped.

"But *some* people have made fortunes there."

"Yes—in slaves! But that interesting commerce is at an end. However, so long as my son does not suffer in health, I suppose we must be thankful that he is creditably employed."

He rose as he spoke.

"I see," he went on, "your amiable friend the baron approaching with lawn-tennis necessaries. It is wonderful that our neighbors never learn to keep their enthusiasm for lawn-tennis in bounds until the afternoon."

With that he left her, and the baron came to the conclusion, before very long, that something had "contraried" the charming Miss Chyne. The truth was that Millicent was bitterly disappointed. The idea of failure had never entered her head since Jack's letters, full of life and energy, had begun to arrive. Sir John Meredith was a man whose words commanded respect—partly because he was an old man whose powers of perception had as yet apparently retained their full force, and the vast experience of life which was his could hardly be overrated. Man's prime is that period when the widest experience and the keenest perception meet.

Millicent Chyne had lulled herself into a false security. She had taken it for granted that Jack would succeed, and would return rich and prosperous within a few months. Upon this pleasant certainty Sir John had cast a doubt, and she could hardly treat his words with contempt. She

had almost forgotten Guy Oscard's letter.   Across a hemisphere Jack Meredith was a stronger influence in her life
than Oscard.

While she sat on the terrace and flirted with the baron
she reflected hurriedly over the situation.   She was, she
argued to herself, not in any way engaged to Guy Oscard.
If he in an unguarded moment should dare to mention such
a possibility to Jack, it would be quite easy to contradict
the statement with convincing heat.   But in her heart she
was sure of Guy Oscard.   One of the worst traits in the
character of an unfaithful woman is the readiness with
which she trades upon the faithfulness of men.

CHAPTER XVII

UNDERHAND

"The offender never pardons."

VICTOR DURNOVO lingered on at Loango.   He elaborated
and detailed to all interested, and to some whom it did not
concern, many excuses for his delay in returning to his expedition, lying supine and attendant at Msala.   It was by
now an open secret on the coast that a great trading expedition was about to ascend the Ogowe River, with, it was
whispered, a fortune awaiting it in the dim perspective of
Central Africa.

Durnovo had already built up for himself a reputation.
He was known as one of the foremost ivory traders on the
coast—a man capable of standing against those enormous
climatic risks before which his competitors surely fell sooner or later.   His knowledge of the interior was unrivalled,
his power over the natives a household word.   Great things
were therefore expected, and Durnovo found himself looked

up to and respected in Loango with that friendly worship which is only to be acquired by the possession or prospective possession of vast wealth.

It is possible even in Loango to have a fling, but the carouser must be prepared to face, even in the midst of his revelry, the haunting thought that the exercise of the strictest economy in any other part of the world might be a preferable pastime.

During the three days following his arrival Victor Durnovo indulged, according to his lights, in the doubtful pleasure mentioned. He purchased at the best factory the best clothes obtainable; he lived like a fighting cock in the one so-called hotel—a house chiefly affected and supported by ship-captains. He spent freely of money that was not his, and imagined himself to be leading the life of a gentleman. He rode round on a hired horse to call on his friends, and on the afternoon of the sixth day he alighted from this quadruped at the gate of the Gordons' bungalow.

He knew that Maurice Gordon had left that morning on one of his frequent visits to a neighboring sub-factory. Nevertheless, he expressed surprise when the servant gave him the information.

"Miss Gordon," he said, tapping his boot with a riding-whip: "is she in?"

"Yes, sir."

A few minutes later Jocelyn came into the drawing-room, where he was waiting with a brazen face and a sinking heart. Somehow the very room had power to bring him down towards his own level. When he set eyes on Jocelyn, in her fair Saxon beauty, he regained *aplomb*.

She appeared to be rather glad to see him.

"I thought," she said, "that you had gone back to the expedition?"

And Victor Durnovo's boundless conceit substituted "feared" for "thought."

"Not without coming to say good-bye," he answered. "It is not likely."

Just to demonstrate how fully he felt at ease, he took a chair without waiting for an invitation, and sat tapping his boot with his whip, looking her furtively up and down all the while with an appraising eye.

"And when do you go?" she asked, with a subtle change in her tone which did not penetrate through his mental epidermis.

"I suppose in a few days now; but I'll let you know all right, never fear."

Victor Durnovo stretched out his legs and made himself quite at home; but Jocelyn did not sit down. On the contrary, she remained standing, persistently and significantly.

"Maurice gone away?" he inquired.

"Yes."

"And left you all alone," in a tone of light badinage, which fell rather flat, on stony ground.

"I am accustomed to being left," she answered, gravely.

"I don't quite like it, you know."

"*You?*"

She looked at him with a steady surprise which made him feel a trifle uncomfortable.

"Well, you know," he was forced to explain, shuffling the while uneasily in his chair and dropping his whip, "one naturally takes an interest in one's friends' welfare. You and Maurice are the best friends I have in Loango. I often speak to Maurice about it. It isn't as if there was an English garrison, or anything like that. I don't trust these niggers a bit."

"Perhaps you do not understand them?" suggested she, gently.

She moved away from him as far as she could get. Every moment increased her repugnance for his presence.

"I don't think Maurice would endorse that," he said, with a conceited laugh.

She winced at the familiar mention of her brother's name, which was probably intentional, and her old fear of this man came back with renewed force.

"I don't think," he went on, "that Maurice's estimation of my humble self is quite so low as yours."

She gave a nervous little laugh.

"Maurice has always spoken of you with gratitude," she said.

"To deaf ears, eh? Yes, he has reason to be grateful, though perhaps I ought not to say it. I have put him into several very good things on the coast, and it is in my power to get him into this new scheme. It is a big thing; he would be a rich man in no time."

He rose from his seat, and deliberately crossed the room to the sofa where she had sat down, where he reclined, with one arm stretched out along the back of it towards her. In his other hand he held his riding-whip, with which he began to stroke the skirt of her dress, which reached along the floor almost to his feet.

"Would you like him to be in it?" he asked, with a meaning glance beneath his lashes. "It is a pity to throw away a good chance; his position is not so very secure, you know."

She gave a strange little hunted glance round the room. She was wedged into a corner, and could not rise without incurring the risk of his saying something she did not wish to hear. Then she leaned forward and deliberately withdrew her dress from the touch of his whip, which was, in its way, a subtle caress.

"Is he throwing away the chance?" she asked

"No, but you are."

Then she rose from her seat, and, standing in the middle of the room, faced him with a sudden gleam in her eyes.

"I do not see what it has to do with me," she said; "I do not know anything about Maurice's business arrangements, and very little about his business friends."

"Then let me tell you, Jocelyn—well, then, Miss Gordon, if you prefer it—that you will know more about one of his business friends before you have finished with him. I've got Maurice more or less in my power now, and it rests with you—"

At this moment a shadow darkened the floor of the veranda, and an instant later Jack Meredith walked quietly in by the window.

"Enter, young man," he said, dramatically, "by window —centre."

"I am sorry," he went on, in a different tone to Jocelyn, "to come in this unceremonious way, but the servant told me that you were in the veranda with Durnovo, and—"

He turned towards the half-breed, pausing.

"And Durnovo is the man I want," weighing each word.

Durnovo's right hand was in his jacket-pocket. Seeing Meredith's proffered salutation, he slowly withdrew it and shook hands.

The flash of hatred was still in his eyes when Jack Meredith turned upon him with aggravating courtesy. The pleasant, half-cynical glance wandered from Durnovo's dark face very deliberately down to his jacket-pocket, where the stock of a revolver was imperfectly concealed.

"We were getting anxious about you," he explained, "seeing that you did not come back. Of course, we knew that you were capable of taking—care—of yourself."

He was still looking innocently at the tell-tale jacket-pocket, and Durnovo, following the direction of his glance, hastily thrust his hand into it.

"But one can never tell, with a treacherous climate like this, what a day may bring forth. However, I am glad to find you looking—so very fit."

Victor Durnovo gave an awkward little laugh, extremely conscious of the factory clothes.

"Oh yes; I'm all right," he said. "I was going to start this evening."

The girl stood behind them, with a flush slowly fading

from her face. There are some women who become suddenly beautiful—not by the glory of a beautiful thought, not by the exaltation of a lofty virtue, but by the mere practical human flush. Jack Meredith, when he took his eyes from Durnovo's, glancing at Jocelyn, suddenly became aware of the presence of a beautiful woman.

The crisis was past; and if Jack knew it, so also did Jocelyn. She knew that the imperturbable gentlemanliness of the Englishman had conveyed to the more passionate West-Indian the simple, downright fact that in a lady's drawing-room there was to be no raised voice, no itching fingers, no flash of fiery eyes.

"Yes," he said, "that will suit me splendidly. We will travel together."

He turned to Jocelyn.

"I hear your brother is away?"

"Yes, for a few days. He has gone up the coast."

Then there was a silence. They both paused, helping each other as if by prearrangement, and Victor Durnovo suddenly felt that he must go. He rose, and picked up the whip which he had dropped on the matting. There was no help for it—the united wills of these two people were too strong for him.

Jack Meredith passed out of the veranda with him, murmuring something about giving him a leg up. While they were walking round the house, Victor Durnovo made one of those hideous mistakes which one remembers all through life with a sudden rush of warm shame and self-contempt. The very thing that was uppermost in his mind to be avoided suddenly bubbled to his lips, almost, it would seem, in defiance of his own will.

"What about the small—the small-pox?" he asked.

"We have got it under," replied Jack, quietly. "We had a very bad time for three days, but we got all the cases isolated and prevented it from spreading. Of course, we could do little or nothing to save them; they died."

Durnovo had the air of a whipped dog. His mind was a blank. He simply had nothing to say; the humiliation of utter self-contempt was his.

"You need not be afraid to come back now," Jack Meredith went on, with a strange refinement of cruelty.

And that was all he ever said about it.

"Will it be convenient for you to meet me on the beach at four o'clock this afternoon?" he asked, when Durnovo was in the saddle.

"Yes."

"All right, four o'clock."

He turned and deliberately went back to the bungalow.

There are some friendships where the intercourse is only the seed which absence duly germinates. Jocelyn Gordon and Jack had parted as acquaintances; they met as friends. There is no explaining these things, for there is no gauging the depths of the human mind. There is no getting down to the little bond that lies at the bottom of the well—the bond of sympathy. There is no knowing what it is that prompts us to say, "This man, or this woman, of all the millions, shall be my friend."

"I am sorry," he said, "that he should have had a chance of causing you uneasiness again."

Jocelyn remembered that all her life. She remembers still—and Africa has slipped away from her existence forever. It is one of the mental photographs of her memory, standing out clear and strong amid a host of minor recollections.

CHAPTER XVIII

"It surely was my profit had I known,
It would have been my pleasure had I seen."

"Why did he come back?"

Jocelyn had risen as if to intimate that, if he cared to do so, they would sit in the veranda.

"Why did Mr. Durnovo come back?" she repeated; for Jack did not seem to have heard the question. He was drawing forward a cane chair with the leisurely *débonnair* grace that was his, and, before replying, he considered for a moment.

"To get quinine," he answered.

Without looking at her, he seemed to divine that he had made a mistake. He seemed to know that she had flushed suddenly to the roots of her hair, with a distressed look in her eyes. The reason was too trivial. She could only draw one conclusion.

"No," he continued; "to tell you the truth, I think his nerve gave way a little. His health is undermined by the climate. He has been too long in Africa. We have had a bad time at Msala. We have had small-pox in the camp. Oscard and I have been doing doughty deeds. I feel convinced that, if we applied to some society, we should get something or other—a testimonial or a monument—also Joseph."

"I like Joseph," she said, in a low tone.

"So do I. If circumstances had been different—if Joseph had not been my domestic servant—I should have liked him for a friend."

He was looking straight in front of him with a singular fixity. It is possible that he was conscious of the sidelong scrutiny which he was undergoing.

"And you—you have been all right?" she said, lightly.

"Oh yes," with a laugh. "I have not brought the infection down to Loango; you need not be afraid of that."

For a moment she looked as if she were going to explain that she was not "afraid of that." Then she changed her mind and let it pass, as he seemed to believe.

"Joseph constructed a disinfecting - room with a wood-smoke fire, or something of that description, and he has been disinfecting everything, down to Oscard's pipes."

She gave a little laugh, which stopped suddenly.

"Was it very bad?" she asked.

"Oh no. We took it in time, you see. We had eleven deaths. And now we are all right. We are only waiting for Durnovo to join, and then we shall make a start. Of course, somebody else could have come down for the quinine."

"Yes."

He glanced at her beneath his lashes before going on.

"But, as Durnovo's nerves were a little shaken, it — was just as well, don't you know, to get him out of it all."

"I suppose he got himself out of it all?" she said, quietly.

"Well — to a certain extent. With our approval, you understand."

Men have an *esprit de sexe* as well as women. They like to hustle the cowards through with the crowd, unobserved.

"It is a strange thing," said Jocelyn, with a woman's scorn of the man who fears those things of which she herself has no sort of dread—"a very strange thing that Mr. Durnovo said nothing about it down here. It is not known in Loango that you had small-pox in the camp."

"Well, you see, when he left we were not quite sure about it."

"I imagine Mr. Durnovo knows all about small - pox.

We all do on this coast. He could hardly help recognizing it in its earliest stage."

She turned on him with a smile which he remembered afterwards. At the moment he felt rather abashed, as if he had been caught in a very maze of untruths. He did not meet her eyes. It was a matter of pride with him that he was equal to any social emergency that might arise. He had always deemed himself capable of withholding from the whole questioning world anything that he might wish to withhold. But afterwards—later in his life—he remembered that look in Jocelyn Gordon's face.

"Altogether," she said, with a peculiar little contented laugh, "I think you cannot keep it up any longer. He ran away from you, and left you to fight against it alone. All the same, it was — nice — of you to try and screen him— very nice; but I do not think that I could have done it myself. I suppose it was—noble—and women cannot be noble."

"No, it was only expedient. The best way to take the world is to wring it dry — not to try and convert it and make it better, but to turn its vices to account. That method has the double advantage of serving one's purpose at the time, and standing as a warning later. The best way to cure vice is to turn it ruthlessly to one's own account. That is what we are doing with Durnovo. His little idio- syncrasies will turn in witness against him later on."

She shook her head in disbelief.

"Your practice and your theory do not agree," she said.

There was a little pause; then she turned to him, gravely.

"Have you been vaccinated?" she asked.

"In the days of my baptism, wherein I was made—"

"No doubt," she interrupted, impatiently; "but since? Have you had it done lately?"

"Just before I came away from England. My tailor urged it so strongly. He said that he had made outfits for many gents going to Africa, and they had all made their

wills and been vaccinated. For reasons which are too painful to dwell upon in these pages I could not make a will, so
I was enthusiastically vaccinated."

"And have you all the medicines you will require? Did
you really want that quinine?"

There was a practical common-sense anxiety in the way
she asked these questions which made him answer, gravely:

"All, thanks. We did not really want the quinine, but
we can do with it. Oscard is our doctor; he is really very
good. He looks it all up in a book, puts all the negative
symptoms on one side and the positive on the other—adds
them all up; then deducts the smaller from the larger, and
treats what is left of the patient accordingly."

She laughed more with the view of pleasing him than
from a real sense of the ludicrous.

"I do not believe," she said, "that you know the risks
you are running into. Even in the short time that Maurice
and I have been here we have learned to treat the climate
of Western Africa with a proper respect. We have known
so many people who have—succumbed."

"Yes, but I do not mean to do that. In a way, Durnovo's—what shall we call it?—lack of nerve is a great safeguard. He will not run into any danger."

"No, but he might run you into it."

"Not a second time, Miss Gordon. Not if we know it.
Oscard mentioned a desire to wring Durnovo's neck. I am
afraid he will do it one of these days."

"The mistake that most people make," the girl went on,
more lightly, "is a want of care. You cannot be too careful, you know, in Africa."

"I am careful; I have reason to be."

She was looking at him steadily, her blue eyes searching
his.

"Yes?" she said, slowly, and there were a thousand questions in the word.

"It would be very foolish of me to be otherwise," he said.

"I am engaged to be married, and I came out here to make the wherewithal. This expedition is an expedition to seek the wherewithal."

"Yes," she said, "and therefore you must be more careful than any one else. Because, you see, your life is something which does not belong to you, but with which you are trusted. I mean, if there is anything dangerous to be done, let some one else do it. What is she like? What is her name?"

"Her name is Millicent—Millicent Chyne."

"And—what is she like?"

He leaned back, and, interlocking his fingers, stretched his arms out with the palms of his hands outward—a habit of his when asked a question needing consideration.

"She is of medium height; her hair is brown. Her worst enemy admits, I believe, that she is pretty. Of course, I am convinced of it."

"Of course," replied Jocelyn, steadily. "That is as it should be. And I have no doubt that you and her worst enemy are both quite right."

He nodded cheerfully, indicating a great faith in his own judgment on the matter under discussion.

"I am afraid," he said, "that I have not a photograph. That would be the correct thing, would it not? I ought to have one always with me in a locket round my neck, or somewhere. A curiously - wrought locket is the correct thing, I believe. People in books usually carry something of that description—and it is always curiously wrought. I don't know where they buy them."

"I think they are usually inherited," suggested Jocelyn.

"I suppose they are," he went on, in the same semi-serious tone. "And then I ought to have it always ready to clasp in my dying hand, where Joseph would find it and wipe away a furtive tear as he buried me. It is a pity. I am afraid I inherited nothing from my ancestors except a very practical mind."

"I should have liked very much to see a photograph of Miss Chyne," said Jocelyn, who had, apparently, not been listening.

"I hope some day you will see herself, at home in England. For you have no abiding city here."

"Only a few more years now. Has she—are her parents living?"

"No; they are both dead. Indian people they were. Indian people have a tragic way of dying young. Millicent lives with her aunt, Lady Cantourne. And Lady Cantourne ought to have married my respected father."

"Why did she not do so?"

He shrugged his shoulders—paused—sat up, and flicked a large moth off the arm of his chair. Then:

"Goodness only knows," he said. "Goodness, and themselves. I suppose they found it out too late. That is one of the little risks of life."

She answered nothing.

"Do you think," he went on, "that there will be a special hell in the hereafter for parents who have sacrificed their children's lives to their own ambition? I hope there will be."

"I have never given the matter the consideration it deserves," she answered. "Was that the reason? Is Lady Cantourne a more important person than Lady Meredith?"

"Yes."

She gave a little nod of comprehension, as if he had raised a curtain for her to see into his life—into the far perspective of it, reaching back into the dim distance of fifty years before. For our lives do reach back into the lives of our fathers and grandfathers; the beginnings made there come down into our daily existence, shaping our thought and action. That which stood between Sir John Meredith and his son was not so much the present personality of Millicent Chyne as the past shadows of a disappointed life, an unloved wife and an unsympathetic mother. And these things Jocelyn

Gordon knew while she sat, gazing with thoughtful eyes, wherein something lived and burned of which she was almost ignorant—gazing through the tendrils of the creeping flowers that hung around them.

At last Jack Meredith rose briskly, watch in hand, and Jocelyn came back to things of earth with a quick, gasping sigh which took her by surprise.

" Miss Gordon, will you do something for me ?"

" With pleasure."

He tore a leaf from his pocket-book, and, going to the table, he wrote on the paper with a pencil pendent at his watch-chain.

" The last few days," he explained while he wrote, "have awakened me to the lamentable fact that human life is rather an uncertain affair."

He came towards her, holding out the paper.

" If you hear—if anything happens to me, would you be so kind as to write to Millicent and tell her of it ? That is the address."

She took the paper, and read the address with a dull sort of interest.

" Yes," she said. " Yes, if you like. But — nothing must happen to you."

There was a slight unsteadiness in her voice which made her stop suddenly. She did not fold the paper, but continued to read the address.

" No," he said, " nothing will. But would you not despise a man who could not screw up his courage to face the possibility ?"

He wondered what she was thinking about, for she did not seem to hear him.

A clock in the drawing-room behind them struck the half-hour, and the sound seemed to recall her to the present.

" Are you going now ?" she asked.

" Yes," he answered, vaguely puzzled. " Yes, I must go now."

She rose, and for a moment he held her hand. He was distinctly conscious of something left unsaid — of many things. He even paused on the edge of the veranda, trying to think what it was that he had to say. Then he pushed aside the hanging flowers and passed out.

"Good-bye!" he said, over his shoulder.

Her lips moved, but he heard no sound. She turned with a white, drawn face and sat down again. The paper was still in her hand. She consulted it again, reading in a whisper:

"Millicent Chyne—Millicent!"

She turned the paper over and studied the back of it— almost as if she were trying to find what there was behind that name.

Through the trees there rose and fell the music of the distant surf. Somewhere near at hand a water-wheel, slowly irrigating the rice-fields, creaked and groaned after the manner of water-wheels all over Africa. In all there was that subtle sense of unreality — that utter lack of permanency which touches the heart of the white exile in tropic lands, and lets life slip away without allowing the reality of it to be felt.

The girl sat there with the name before her—written on the little slip of paper—the only memento he had left her.

CHAPTER XIX

IVORY

"'Tis one thing to be tempted, Escalus,
Another thing to fall."

ONE of the peculiarities of Africa yet to be explained is the almost supernatural rapidity with which rumor travels. Across the whole breadth of this darkest continent a mere bit of gossip has made its way in a month. A man may divulge a secret, say, at St. Paul de Loanda, take ship to Zanzibar, and there his own secret will be told to him.

Rumor met Maurice Gordon almost at the outset of his journey northward.

"Small-pox is raging on the Ogowe River," they told him. "The English expedition is stricken down with it. The three leaders are dead."

Maurice Gordon had not lived four years on the West African coast in vain. He took this for what it was worth. But if he had acquired scepticism, he had lost his nerve. He put about and sailed back to Loango.

"I wonder," he muttered, as he walked up from the beach to his office that same afternoon—"I wonder if Durnovo is among them?"

And he was conscious of a ray of hope in his mind. He was a kind-hearted man, in his way—this Maurice Gordon, of Loango; but he could not disguise from himself the simple fact that the death of Victor Durnovo would be a distinct convenience and a most desirable relief. Even the best of us—that is to say, the present writer and his reader —have these inconvenient little feelings. There are people who have done us no particular injury, to whom we wish no particular harm, but we feel that it would be very expedient and considerate of them to die.

Thinking these thoughts, Maurice Gordon arrived at the factory and went straight to his own office, where he found the object of them—Victor Durnovo—sitting in consumption of the office sherry.

Gordon saw at once that the rumor was true. There was a hunted, unwholesome look in Durnovo's eyes. He looked shaken, and failed to convey a suggestion of personal dignity.

"Holloa!" exclaimed the proprietor of the decanter. "You look a bit chippy. I've heard you've got small-pox up at Msala."

"So have I. I've just heard it from Meredith."

"Just heard it—is Meredith down here too?"

" Yes, and the fool wants to go back to-night. I have to meet him on the beach at four o'clock."

Maurice Gordon sat down, poured out for himself a glass of sherry, and drank it thoughtfully.

" Do you know, Durnovo," he said, emphatically, " I have my doubts about Meredith being a fool."

" Indeed !" with a derisive laugh.

" Yes."

Maurice Gordon looked over his shoulder to see that the door was shut.

" You'll have to be very careful," he said. " The least slip might let it all out. Meredith has a quiet way of looking at one which disquiets me. He might find out."

" Not he," replied Durnovo confidently, " especially if we succeed ; and we shall succeed—by God, we shall!"

Maurice Gordon made a little movement of the shoulders, as indicating a certain uneasiness ; but he said nothing.

There was a pause of considerable duration, at the end of which Durnovo produced a paper from his pocket and threw it down.

" That's good business," he said.

" Two thousand tusks," murmured Maurice Gordon. "Yes, that's good. Through Akmed, I suppose ?"

" Yes. We can outdo these Arabs at their own trade."

An evil smile lighted up Durnovo's sallow face. When he smiled, his drooping, curtain-like mustache projected in a way that made keen observers of the human face wonder what his mouth was like.

Gordon, who had been handling the paper with the tips of his fingers, as if it were something unclean, threw it down on the table again.

" Ye—es," he said, slowly ; "but it does not seem to dirty black hands as it does white. They know no better."

" Lord !" ejaculated Durnovo. " Don't let us begin the old arguments all over again. I thought we settled that the trade was there ; we couldn't prevent it, and therefore the best thing is to make hay while the sun shines, and then clear out of the country."

"But suppose Meredith finds out?" reiterated Maurice Gordon, with the lamentable hesitation that precedes loss.

"If Meredith finds out, it will be the worse for him."

A certain concentration of tone aroused Maurice Gordon's attention, and he glanced uneasily at his companion.

"No one knows what goes on in the heart of Africa," said Durnovo, darkly. "But we will not trouble about that; Meredith won't find out."

"Where is he now?"

"With your sister, at the bungalow. A lady's man— that is what he is."

Victor Durnovo was smarting under a sense of injury which was annoyingly indefinite. It was true that Jack Meredith had come at a very unpropitious moment; but it was equally clear that the intrusion could only have been the result of accident. It was really a case of the third person who is no company, with aggravated symptoms. Durnovo had vaguely felt in the presence of either a subtle possibility of sympathy between Jocelyn Gordon and Jack Meredith. When he saw them together, for only a few minutes as it happened, the sympathy rose up and buffeted him in the face, and he hated Jack Meredith for it. He hated him for a certain reposeful sense of capability which he had at first set down as conceit, and later on had learned to value as something innate in blood and education which was not conceit. He hated him because his gentlemanliness was so obvious that it showed up the flaws in other men, as the masterpiece upon the wall shows up the weaknesses of the surrounding pictures. But most of all he hated him because Jocelyn Gordon seemed to have something in common with the son of Sir John Meredith—a world above the head of even the most successful trader on the coast — a world in which he, Victor Durnovo, could never live and move at ease.

Beyond this, Victor Durnovo cherished the hatred of the Found Out. He felt instinctively that behind the courteous demeanor of Jack Meredith there was an opinion — a cool, unbiassed criticism — of himself, which Meredith had no intention of divulging.

On hearing that Jack was at the bungalow with Jocelyn, Maurice Gordon glanced at the clock and wondered how he could get away from his present visitor. The atmosphere of Jack Meredith's presence was preferable to that diffused by Victor Durnovo. There was a feeling of personal safety and dignity in the very sound of his voice which set a weak and easily-led man upon his feet.

But Victor Durnovo had something to say to Gordon which circumstances had brought to a crisis.

"Look here," he said, leaning forward and throwing away the cigarette he had been smoking, "this Simiacine scheme is going to be the biggest thing that has ever been run on this coast."

"Yes," said Gordon, with the indifference that comes from non-participation.

"And I'm the only business man in it," significantly.

Gordon nodded his head, awaiting further developments.

"Which means that I could work another man into it. I might find out that we could not get on without him."

The black eyes seemed to probe the good-natured, sensual face of Maurice Gordon, so keen, so searching was their glance.

"And I would be willing to do it — to make that man's fortune — provided — that he was — my brother-in-law."

"What the devil do you mean?" asked Gordon, setting down the glass that was half-raised to his lips.

"I mean that I want to marry — Jocelyn."

And the modern school of realistic, mawkishly foul novelists, who hold that Love excuseth all, would have taken delight in the passionate rendering of the girl's name.

"Want to marry Jocelyn, do you?" answered Maurice,

with a derisive little laugh. On the first impulse of the moment he gave no thought to himself or his own interests, and spoke with undisguised contempt. He might have been speaking to a beggar on the road-side.

Durnovo's eyes flashed dangerously, and his tobacco-stained teeth clinched for a moment over his lower lip.

"That is my desire — and intention."

"Look here, Durnovo," exclaimed Gordon, "don't be a fool! Can't you see that it is quite out of the question?"

He attempted weakly to dismiss the matter by leaning forward on his writing-table, taking up his pen, and busying himself with a number of papers.

Victor Durnovo rose from his chair so hastily that in a flash Maurice Gordon's hand was in the top right-hand drawer of his writing-table. The good-natured blue eyes suddenly became fixed and steady. But Durnovo seemed to make an effort over himself, and walked to the window, where he drew aside the woven-grass blind and looked out into the glaring sunlight. Still standing there, he turned and spoke in a low, concentrated voice :

"No," he said, "I can't see that it is out of the question. On the contrary, it seems only natural that she should marry the man who is her brother's partner in many a little — speculation."

Maurice Gordon, sitting there, staring hopelessly into the half-breed's face, saw it all. He went back in a flash of recollection to many passing details which had been un-noted at the time — details which now fitted into each other like links of a chain — and that chain was around him. He leaped forward in a momentary opening of the future, and saw himself ruined, disgraced, held up to the execration of the whole civilized world. He was utterly in this man's power — bound hand and foot. He could not say him no ; and least of all could he say no to this de-mand, which had roused all the latent chivalry, gentleman-liness, brotherly love that was in him. Maurice Gordon

knew that Victor Durnovo possessed knowledge which Jocelyn would consider cheap at the price of her person.

There was one way out of it. His hand was still on the
handle of the top right-hand drawer. He was a dead-shot.
His finger was within two inches of the stock of a revolver.
One bullet for Victor Durnovo, another for himself. Then
the old training of his school-days—the training that makes
an upright, honest gentleman — asserted itself, and he saw
the cowardice of it. There was time enough for that later,
when the crisis came. In the meantime, if the worst came
to the worst, he could fight to the end.

"I don't think," said Durnovo, who seemed to be following Gordon's thoughts, "that the idea will be so repellent
to your sister as you seem to think."

And a sudden ray of hope shot athwart the future into
which his listener was staring. It might be so. One can
never tell with women. Maurice Gordon had had considerable experience of the world, and, after all, he was only
building up hope upon precedent. He knew, as well as you
or I, that women will dance and flirt with—even marry—
men who are not gentlemen. Not only for the moment,
but as a permanency, something seems to kill their perception of a fact which is patent to every educated man in the
room ; and one never knows what it is. One can only sur-
mise that it is that thirst for admiration which does more
harm in the world than the thirst for alcoholic stimulant
which we fight by societies and guilds, oaths, and little bits
of ribbon.

"The idea never entered my head," said Gordon.

"It has never been out of mine," replied Durnovo, with
a little harsh laugh which was almost pathetic.

"I don't want you to do anything now," he went on,
more gently. It was wonderful how well he knew Maurice Gordon. The suggested delay appealed to one side of
his nature, the softened tone to another. "There is time
enough. When I come back I will speak of it again."

"You have not spoken to her?"

"No, I have not spoken to her."

Maurice Gordon shook his head.

"She is a queer girl," he said, trying to conceal the hope that was in his voice. "She is cleverer than me, you know, and all that. My influence is very small, and would scarcely be considered."

"But your interests would," suggested Durnovo. "Your sister is very fond of you, and—I think I have one or two arguments to put forward which she would recognize as uncommonly strong."

The color which had been returning slowly to Maurice Gordon's face now faded away again. His lips were dry and shrivelled as if he had passed through a sirocco.

"Mind," continued Durnovo, reassuringly, "I don't say I would use them unless I suspected that you were acting in opposition to my wishes."

Gordon said nothing. His heart was throbbing uncomfortably—it seemed to be in his throat.

"I would not bring forward those arguments except as a last resource," went on Victor Durnovo, with the deliberate cruelty of a tyrant. "I would first point out the advantages; a fourth share in the Simiacine scheme would make you a rich man—above suspicion—independent of the gossip of the market-place."

Maurice Gordon winced visibly, and his eyes wavered as if he were about to give way to panic.

"You could retire and go home to England—to a cooler climate. This country might get too hot for your constitution—see?"

Durnovo came back into the centre of the room and stood by the writing-table. His attitude was that of a man holding a whip over a cowering dog.

He took up his hat and riding-whip with a satisfied little laugh, as if the dog had cringingly done his bidding.

"Besides," he said, with a certain defiance of manner, "I may succeed without any of that—eh?"

"Yes," Gordon was obliged to admit with a gulp, as if he were swallowing his pride, and he knew that in saying the word he was degrading his sister—throwing her at this man's feet as the price of his own honor.

With a half-contemptuous nod Victor Durnovo turned and went away to keep his appointment with Meredith.

———

CHAPTER XX

BROUGHT TO THE SCRATCH

"Take heed of still waters; the quick pass away."

GUY OSCARD was sitting on the natural terrace in front of Durnovo's house at Msala, and Marie attended to his simple wants with that patient dignity which suggested the recollection of better times, and appealed strongly to the manhood of her fellow-servant Joseph and her whilom master.

Oscard was not good at the enunciation of those small amenities which are supposed to soothe the feelings of the temporarily debased. He vaguely felt that this woman was not accustomed to menial service, but he knew that any suggestion of sympathy was more than he could compass. So he merely spoke to her more gently than to the men, and perhaps she understood, despite her chocolate-colored skin.

They had inaugurated a strange unequal friendship during the three days that Oscard had been left alone at Msala. Joseph had been promoted to the command of a certain number of the porters, and his domestic duties were laid aside. Thus Marie was called upon to attend to Guy Oscard's daily wants.

"I think I'll take coffee," he was saying to her, in reply to a question. "Yes—coffee, please, Marie."

He was smoking one of his big wooden pipes, staring straight in front of him with a placidity natural to his bulk.

The woman turned away with a little smile. She liked this big man with his halting tongue and quiet ways. She liked his awkward attempts to conciliate the coquette Xantippe—to extract a smile from the grave Nestorius, and she liked his manner towards herself. She liked the poised pipe and the jerky voice as he said, "Yes—coffee, please, Marie."

Women do like these things — they seem to understand them, and to attach some strange, subtle importance of their own to them. For which power some of us who have not the knack of turning a pretty phrase, or throwing off an appropriate pleasantry, may well be thankful.

Presently she returned, bringing the coffee on a rough tray, also a box of matches and Oscard's tobacco-pouch. Noting this gratuitous attention to his comfort, he looked up with a little laugh.

"Er—thank you," he said. "Very kind."

He did not put his pipe back to his lips—keenly alive to the fact that the exigency of the moment demanded a little polite exchange of commonplace.

"Children gone to bed?" he asked, anxiously.

She paused in her slow, deft arrangement of the little table.

"Yes," she answered, quietly.

He nodded as if the news were eminently satisfactory. "Nestorius," he said, adhering to Meredith's pleasantry, "is the jolliest little chap I have met for a long time."

"Yes," she answered, softly. "Yes—but listen!"

He raised his head, listening as she did — both looking down the river into the gathering darkness.

"I hear the sound of paddles," she said. "And you?"

"Not yet. My ears are not so sharp as yours."

"I am accustomed to it," the woman said, with some

emotion in her voice which he did not understand then.
" I am always listening."

Oscard seemed to be struck with this description of herself. It was so very apt—so comprehensive. The woman's
attitude before the world was the attitude of the listener for
some distant sound.

She poured out his coffee, setting the cup at his elbow.
" Now you will hear," she said, standing upright with that
untrammelled dignity of carriage which is found wherever
African blood is in the veins. " They have just come round
Broken Tree Bend. . There are two boats."

He listened, and after a moment heard the regular glug-
glug of the paddles stealing over the waters of the still
tropic river, covering a wonderful distance.

" Yes," he said, " I hear. Mr. Meredith said he would be
back to-night."

She gave a strange little low laugh—almost the laugh of
a happy woman.

" He is like that, Mr. Meredith," she said ; " what he says
he does "—in the pretty English of one who has learned
Spanish first.

" Yes, Marie—he is like that."

She turned, in her strangely subdued way, and went into
the house to prepare some supper for the new-comers.

It was not long before the sound of the paddles was quite
distinct, and then — probably on turning a corner of the
river and coming in sight of the lights of Msala — Jack
Meredith's cheery shout came floating through the night.
Oscard took his pipe from his lips and sent back an answer
that echoed against the trees across the river. He walked
down to the water's edge, where he was presently joined by
Joseph with a lantern.

The two boats came on to the sloping shore with a grat-
ing sound, and by the light of the waving lantern Oscard
saw Durnovo and Jack land from the same boat.

The three men walked up to the house together. Marie

was at the door, and bowed her head gravely in answer to Jack's salutation. Durnovo nodded curtly and said nothing.

In the sitting-room, by the light of the paraffin lamp, the two Englishmen exchanged a long questioning glance, quite different from the quick interrogation of a woman's eyes. There was a smile on Jack Meredith's face.

" All ready to start to-morrow ?" he inquired.

"Yes," replied Oscard.

And that was all they could say. Durnovo never left them alone together that night. He watched their faces with keen, suspicious eyes. Behind the mustache his lips were pursed up in restless anxiety. But he saw nothing— learned nothing. These two men were inscrutable.

At eleven o'clock the next morning the Simiacine seekers left their first unhappy camp at Msala. They had tasted of misfortune at the very beginning, but after the first reverse they returned to their work with that dogged determination which is a better spirit than the wild enthusiasm of departure, where friends shout and flags wave, and an artificial hopefulness throws in its jarring note.

They had left behind them with the artifice of civilization that subtle handicap of a woman's presence; and the little flotilla of canoes that set sail from the terrace at Msala one morning in November, not so many years ago, was essentially masculine in its bearing. The four white men—quiet, self-contained, and intrepid—seemed to work together with a perfect unity, a oneness of thought and action which really lay in the brain of one of them. No man can define a true leader; for one is too autocratic and the next too easily led ; one is too quick-tempered, another too reserved. It would almost seem that the ideal leader is that man who knows how to extract from the brains of his subordinates all that is best and strongest therein — who knows how to suppress his own individuality, and merge it for the time being into that of his fellow-worker—whose influence is from within, and not from without.

The most successful Presidents of Republics have been those who are or pretend to be nonentities, content to be mere pegs, standing still and lifeless, for things to be hung upon. Jack Meredith was, or pretended to be, this. He never assumed the airs of a leader. He never was a leader. He merely smoothed things over, suggested here, laughed there, and seemed to stand by, indifferent all the while.

In less than a week they left the river, hauling their canoes up on the bank, and hiding them in the tangle of the virgin underwood. A depot of provisions, likewise hidden, was duly made, and the long, weary march began.

The daily routine of this need not be followed, for there were weeks of long monotony varied only by a new difficulty, a fresh danger, or a deplorable accident. Twice the whole company had to lay aside the baggage and assume arms, when Guy Oscard proved himself to be a cool and daring leader. Not twice, but two hundred times, the ring of Joseph's unerring rifle sent some naked savage crawling into the brake to die, with a sudden wonder in his half-awakened brain. They could not afford to be merciful; their own safeguard was to pass through this country, leaving a track of blood and fire and dread behind them.

This, however, is no record of travel in Central Africa. There are many such to be had at any circulating library, written by abler and more fantastic pens. Some of us who have wandered in the darkest continent have looked in vain for things seen by former travellers—things which, as the saying is, are neither here nor there. Indeed, there is not much to see in a vast, boundless forest with little life and no variety—nothing but a deadly monotony of twilight tangle. There is nothing new under the sun—even immediately under it in Central Africa. The only novelty is the human heart — Central Man. That is never stale, and there are depths still unexplored, heights still unattained, warm rivers of love, cold streams of hatred, and vast plains where strange motives grow. These are our business.

We have not to deal so much with the finding of the Simiacine as with the finders, and of these the chief at this time was Jack Meredith. It seemed quite natural that one duty after another should devolve upon him, and he invariably had time to do them all, and leisure to comment pleasantly upon it. But his chief care was Victor Durnovo.

As soon as they entered the forest two hundred miles above Msala, the half-breed was a changed man. The strange restlessness asserted itself again — the man was nervous, eager, sincere. His whole being was given up to this search; his whole heart and soul were enveloped in it. At first he worked steadily, like a mariner threading his way through known waters; but gradually his composure left him, and he became incapable of doing other work.

Jack Meredith was at his side always. By day he walked near him as he piloted the column through the trackless forest. At night he slept in the same tent, stretched across the door-way. Despite the enormous fatigue, he slept the light sleep of the townsman, and often he was awakened by Durnovo talking aloud, groaning, tossing on his narrow bed.

When they had been on the march for two months— piloted with marvellous instinct by Durnovo — Meredith made one or two changes in the organization. The caravan naturally moved slowly, owing to the enormous amount of baggage to be carried, and this delay seemed to irritate Victor Durnovo to such an extent that at last it was obvious that the man would go mad unless this enormous tension could be relieved.

"For God's sake," he would shout, "hurry those men on! We haven't done ten miles to-day. Another man down—damn him!"

And more than once he had to be dragged forcibly away from the fallen porter, whom he battered with both fists. Had he had his will he would have allowed no time for meals, and only a few hours' halt for rest. Guy Oscard did not understand it. His denser nerves were incapable of comprehending the state of irritation and unreasoning restlessness into which the climate and excitement had brought Durnovo. But Meredith, in his finer organization, understood the case better. He it was who soothingly explained the necessity for giving the men a longer rest. He alone could persuade Durnovo to lie down at night and cease his perpetual calculations. The man's hands were so unsteady that he could hardly take the sights necessary to determine their position in this sea-like waste. And to Jack alone did Victor Durnovo ever approach the precincts of mutual confidence.

" I can't help it, Meredith," he said one day, with a scared look, after a particularly violent outburst of temper. " I don't know what it is. I sometimes think I'm going mad."

And soon after that the change was made.

An advance column, commanded by Meredith and Durnovo, was selected to push on to the plateau, while Oscard and Joseph followed more leisurely with the baggage and the slower travellers.

One of the strangest journeys in the vast unwritten history of commercial advance was that made by the five men from the camp of the main expedition across the lower slopes of a mountain range—unmarked on any map, unnamed by any geographer — to the mysterious Simiacine Plateau. It almost seemed as if the wild, bloodshot eyes of their guide could pierce the density of the forest where Nature had held unchecked, untrimmed sway for countless generations. Victor Durnovo noted a thousand indications unseen by his four companions. The journey no longer partook of the nature of a carefully calculated progress across a country untrodden by a white man's foot ; it was a wild rush in a straight line through unbroken forest fastness, guided by an instinct that was stronger than knowledge. And the only Englishman in the party—Jack Meredith—had to choose between madness and rest. He knew enough of the human brain to be convinced that the only possible relief to this tension was success.

Victor Durnovo would never know rest now until he reached the spot where the Simiacine should be. If the trees were there, growing, as he said, in solitary state and order, strangely suggestive of human handiwork, then Victor Durnovo was saved. If no such spot was found, madness and death could only follow.

To save his companion's reason, Meredith more than once drugged his food; but when the land began to rise beneath their feet in slight billow-like inequalities—the deposit of a glacial age—Durnovo refused to stop for the preparation of food. Eating dry biscuits and stringy tinned meat as they went along, the four men—three blacks and one white—followed in the footsteps of their mad pilot.

"We're getting to the mountains—we're getting to the mountains! We shall be there to-night! Think of that, Meredith—to-night!" he kept repeating with a sickening monotony. And all the while he stumbled on. The perspiration ran down his face in one continuous stream; at times he paused to wipe it from his eyes with the back of his hands, and as these were torn and bleeding there were smears of blood across his cheeks.

The night fell; the moon rose, red and glorious, and the beasts of this untrodden forest paused in their search for food to watch with wondering, fearless eyes that strange, unknown animal—man.

It was Durnovo who, climbing wildly, first saw the break in the trees ahead. He gave a muffled cry of delight, and in a few minutes they were all rushing, like men possessed, up a bare slope of broken shale.

Durnovo reached the summit first. A faint, pleasant odor was wafted into their faces. They stood on the edge of a vast table-land melting away in the yellow moonlight.

Studded all over, like sheep in a meadow, were a number of little bushes, and no other vegetation.

Victor Durnovo stooped over one of these. He buried his face among the leaves of it, and suddenly he toppled over.

"Yes," he cried, as he fell, "it's Simiacine!"

And he turned over with a groan of satisfaction, and lay like a dead man.

CHAPTER XXI

THE FIRST CONSIGNMENT

"Since all that I can ever do for thee
Is to do nothing, may'st thou never see,
Never divine, the all that nothing costeth me."

ONE morning, three months later, Guy Oscard drew up in line his flying column. He was going back to England with the first consignment of Simiacine. During the twelve weeks that lay behind there had been constant reference made to his little body of picked men, and the leader had selected with a grave deliberation that promised well.

The lost soldier that was in him was all astir in his veins as he reviewed his command in the cool air of early morning. The journey from Msala to the plateau had occupied a busy two months. Oscard expected to reach Msala with his men in forty days. Piled up in neat square cases, such as could be carried in pairs by a man of ordinary strength, was the crop of Simiacine, roughly valued by Victor Durnovo at forty thousand pounds. Ten men could carry the whole of it, and the twenty cases set close together on the ground made a bed for Guy Oscard. Upon this improvised couch he gravely stretched his bulk every night all through the journey that followed.

Over the whole face of the sparsely vegetated table-land the dwarf bushes grew at intervals, each one in a little circle of its own, where no grass grew; for the dead leaves, falling, poisoned the earth. There were no leaves on the bushes now, for they had all been denuded, and the twisted branches stood out nakedly in the morning mist. Some of the bushes had been roughly pruned, to foster, if possible, a more bushy growth and a heavier crop of leaves near to the parent stem.

It was a strange landscape; and any passing traveller, knowing nothing of the Simiacine, must perforce have seen at once that these insignificant little trees were something quite apart in the vegetable kingdom. Each standing within its magic circle, no bird built its nest within the branches—no insect constructed its filmy home—no spider weaved its busy web from twig to twig.

Solitary, mournful, lifeless, the plateau which had nearly cost Victor Durnovo his life lay beneath the face of heaven, far above the surrounding country—the summit of an un-named mountain — a land lying in the heart of a tropic country which was neither tropic, temperate, nor arctic. Fauna had it none, for it produced nothing that could sustain life. Flora it knew not, for the little trees, each with its perennial fortune of brilliant brown - tinted leaves, monopolized vegetable life and slew all comers. It seemed like some stray tract of another planet, where the condition of living things was different. There was a strange sense of having been thrown up—thrown up, as it were, into mid-heaven, there to hang forever—neither this world nor the world to come. The silence of it all was such as would drive men mad if they came to think of it. It was the silence of the stars.

The men who had lived up here for three months did not look quite natural. There was a singular heaviness of the eyelids which all had noticed, though none had spoken of it. A craving for animal food, which could only be stayed by the consumption of abnormal quantities or meat, kept the hunters ever at work on the lower slopes of the mountain. Sleep was broken, and uncanny things happened in the night. Men said that they saw other men like trees, walking abroad with sightless eyes; and Joseph said, "Gammon, my festive darky — gammon!" but he nevertheless glanced somewhat uneasily towards his master whenever the natives said such things.

A clearing had been made on that part of the plateau which was most accessible from below. The Simiacine-trees had been ruthlessly cut away—even the roots were grubbed up and burned—far away on the leeward side of the little kingdom. This was done because there arose at sunset a soft and pleasant odor from the bushes which seemed to affect the nerves and even made the teeth chatter. It was therefore deemed wise that the camp should stand on bare ground.

It was on this ground, in front of the tents, that Guy Oscard drew up his quick-marching column before the sun had sprung up in its fantastic tropical way from the distant line of virgin forest. As he walked along the line, making a suggestion here, pulling on a shoulder-rope there, he looked stanch and strong as any man might wish to be. His face was burned so brown that eyebrows and mustache stood out almost blond, though in reality they were only brown. His eyes did not seem to be suffering from the heaviness noticeable in others; altogether, the climate and the mystic breath of the Simiacine grove did not appear to affect him as it did his companions. This was probably accounted for by the fact that, being chief of the hunters, most of his days had been passed on the lower slopes in search of game.

To him came presently Jack Meredith—the same gentle-mannered man, with an incongruously brown face and quick eyes seeing all. It is not, after all, the life that makes the man. There are gentle backwoodsmen, and ruffians among those who live in drawing-rooms.

"Well?" said Meredith, following the glance of his friend's eye as he surveyed his men.

Oscard took his pipe from his lips and looked gravely at him.

"Don't half like it, you know," he said, in a low voice; for Durnovo was talking with a head-porter a few yards away.

"Don't half like what — the flavor of that pipe? It looks a little strong."

"No, leaving you here," replied Oscard.

"Oh, that's all right, old chap! You can't take me with you, you know. I intended to stick to it when I came away from home, and I am not going to turn back now."

Oscard gave a queer little upward jerk of the head, as if he had just collected further evidence in support of a theory which chronically surprised him. Then he turned away and looked down over the vast untrodden tract of Africa that lay beneath them. He kept his eyes fixed there, after the manner of a man who has no fluency in personal comment.

"You know," he said, jerkily, "I didn't think—I mean you're not the sort of chap I took you for. When I first saw you I thought you were a bit of a dandy and—all that. Not the sort of man for this work. I thought that the thing was bound to be a failure. I knew Durnovo, and had no faith in him. You've got a gentle way about you, and your clothes are so confoundedly neat. But—" Here he paused and pulled down the folds of his Norfolk jacket. "But I liked the way you shot that leopard the day we first met."

"Beastly fluke," put in Meredith, with his pleasant laugh.

Oscard contented himself with a denying shake of the head.

"Of course," he continued, with obvious determination to get it all off his mind, "I know as well as you do that you are the chief of this concern—have been chief since we left Msala—and I never want to work under a better man."

He put his pipe back between his lips and turned round with a contented smile, as much as to say, " There, that is the sort of man I am! When I want to say that sort of thing I can say it with the best of you."

" We have pulled along very comfortably, haven't we?" said Meredith; " thanks to your angelic temper. And you'll deliver that packet of letters to the governor, won't you? I have sent them in one packet, addressed to him, as it is easier to carry. I will let you hear of us somehow within the next six months. Do not go and get married before I get home. I want to be your best man."

Oscard laughed and gave the signal for the men to start, and the long caravan defiled before them. The porters nodded to Meredith with a great display of white teeth, while the neadmen, the captains of tens, stepped out of the ranks and shook hands.

Before they had disappeared over the edge of the plateau Joseph came forward to say good-bye to Oscard.

" And it is understood," said the latter, " that I pay in to your account at Lloyd's Bank your share of the proceeds."

Joseph grinned. " Yes, sir, if you please, presumin' it's a safe bank."

" Safe as houses."

" Cos it's a tolerable big amount," settling himself into his boots in the manner of a millionaire.

" Lots of money—about four hundred pounds! But you can trust me to see to it all right."

" No fear, sir," replied Joseph, grandly. " I'm quite content, I'm sure, that you should have the—fingering o' the dibs."

As he finished—somewhat lamely, perhaps—his rounded periods, he looked very deliberately over Oscard's shoulder towards Durnovo, who was approaching them.

Meredith walked a little way down the slope with Oscard.

"Good-bye, old chap!" he said, when the parting came. "Good-luck, and all that. Hope you will find all right at home. By-the-way," he shouted after him, "give my kind regards to the Gordons at Loango."

And so the first consignment of Simiacine was sent from the plateau to the coast.

Guy Oscard was one of those deceptive men who only do a few things, and do those few very well. In forty-three days he deposited the twenty precious cases in Gordon's godowns at Loango, and paid off the porters, of whom he had not lost one. These duties performed, he turned his steps towards the bungalow. He had refused Gordon's invitation to stay with him until the next day, when the coasting steamer was expected. To tell the truth, he was not very much prepossessed in Maurice's favor, and it was with a doubtful mind that he turned his steps towards the little house in the forest between Loango and the sea.

The room was the first surprise that awaited him, its youthful mistress the second. Guy Oscard was rather afraid of most women. He did not understand them, and probably he despised them. Men who are afraid or ignorant often do.

"And when did you leave them?" asked Jocelyn, after her visitor had explained who he was. He was rather taken aback by so much dainty refinement in remote Africa, and explained rather badly. But she helped him out by intimating that she knew all about him.

"I left them forty-four days ago," he replied.

"And were they well?"

"She is very much interested," reflected Oscard, upon whom her eagerness of manner had not been lost. "Surely, it cannot be that fellow Durnovo?"

"Oh yes," he replied, with unconscious curtness.

"Mr. Durnovo cannot ever remain inland for long without feeling the effect of the climate."

Guy Oscard, with the perspicacity of his sex, gobbled up the bait. " It *is* Durnovo," he reflected.

" Oh, he is all right," he said ; " wonderfully well, and so are the others — Joseph and Meredith. You know Meredith ?"

Jocelyn was busy with a vase of flowers standing on the table at her elbow. One of the flowers had fallen half out, and she was replacing it—very carefully.

" Oh yes," she said, without ceasing her occupation, " we know Mr. Meredith."

The visitor did not speak at once, and she looked up at him, over the flowers, with grave politeness.

" Meredith," he said, " is one of the most remarkable men I have ever met."

It was evident that this ordinarily taciturn man wanted to unburden his mind. He was desirous of talking to some one of Jack Meredith ; and perhaps Jocelyn reflected that she was as good a listener as he would find in Loango.

" Really," she replied, with a kindly interest. " How ?"

He paused, not because he found it difficult to talk to this woman, but because he was thinking of something.

" I have read or heard somewhere of a steel gauntlet beneath a velvet glove."

" Yes."

" That describes Meredith. He is not the man I took him for. He is so wonderfully polite and gentle and pleasant. Not the qualities that make a good leader for an African exploring expedition—eh ?"

Jocelyn gave a strange little laugh, which included, among other things, a subtle intimation that she rather liked Guy Oscard. Women do convey these small meanings sometimes, but one finds that they do not intend them to be acted upon.

" And he has kept well all the time ?" she asked, softly.

" He did not look strong."

" Oh yes. He is much stronger than he looks."

"And you—you have been all right?"

"Yes, thanks."

"Are you going back to—them?"

"No, I leave to-morrow morning early by the Portuguese boat. I am going home to be married."

"Indeed! Then I suppose you will wash your hands of Africa forever?"

"Not quite," he replied. "I told Meredith that I would be prepared to go up to him in case of emergency, but not otherwise. I shall, of course, still be interested in the scheme. I take home the first consignment of Simiacine; we have been very successful, you know. I shall have to stay in London to sell that. I have a house there."

"Are you to be married at once?" inquired Jocelyn, with that frank interest which makes it so much easier for a man to talk of his own affairs to a woman than to one of his own sex.

"As soon as I can arrange it," he answered, with a little laugh. "There is nothing to wait for. We are both orphans, and, fortunately, we are fairly well off."

He was fumbling in his breast-pocket, and presently he rose, crossed the room, and handed her, quite without afterthought or self-consciousness, a photograph in a morocco case.

Explanation was unnecessary, and Jocelyn Gordon looked smilingly upon a smiling, bright young face.

"She is very pretty," she said, honestly.

Whereupon Guy Oscard grunted unintelligibly.

"Millicent," he said, after a little pause—"Millicent is her name."

"Millicent?" repeated Jocelyn—"Millicent *what!*"

"Millicent Chyne."

Jocelyn folded the morocco case together and handed it back to him.

"She is very pretty," she repeated slowly, as if her mind could only reproduce—it was incapable of creation.

Oscard looked puzzled. Having risen, he did not sit down
again, and presently he took his leave, feeling convinced that
Jocelyn was about to faint.

When he was gone the girl sat wearily down.

"Millicent Chyne," she whispered. "What is to be
done?"

"Nothing," she answered to herself after a while. "Nothing. It is not my business. I can do nothing."

She sat there—alone, as she had been all her life—until
the short tropical twilight fell over the forest. Quite suddenly she burst into tears.

"It *is* my business," she sobbed. "It is no good pretending otherwise; but I can do nothing."

CHAPTER XXII

THE SECOND CONSIGNMENT

"Who has lost all hope has also lost all fear."

AMONG others, it was a strange thing that Jocelyn felt no
surprise at meeting the name of Millicent Chyne on the lips
of another man. Women understand these things better
than we do. They understand each other, and they seem
to have a practical way of accepting human nature as it is
which we never learn to apply to our fellow-men. They
never bluster as we do, nor expect impossibilities from the
frail.

Another somewhat singular residue left, as it were, in
Jocelyn's mind when the storm of emotion had subsided was
a certain indefinite tenderness for Millicent Chyne. She felt
sure that Jack Meredith's feeling for her was that feeling
vaguely called the right one, and, as such, unalterable. To
this knowledge the subtle sympathy for Millicent was per-

haps attributable. But navigation with pen and thought among the shoals and depths of a woman's heart is hazardous and uncertain.

Coupled with this—as only a woman could couple contradictions—was an unpardoning abhorrence for the deceit practised. But Jocelyn knew the world well enough to suspect that, if she were ever brought face to face with her meanness, Millicent would be able to bring about her own forgiveness. It is the knowledge of this lamentable fact that undermines the feminine sense of honor.

Lastly, there was a calm acceptance of the fact that Guy Oscard must and would inevitably go to the wall. There could be no comparison between the two men. Millicent Chyne could scarcely hesitate for a moment. That she herself must likewise suffer uncomplainingly, inevitably, seemed to be an equally natural consequence in Jocelyn Gordon's mind.

She could not go to Jack Meredith and say:

"This woman is deceiving you, but I love you, and my love is a nobler, grander thing than hers. It is no passing fancy of a giddy, dazzled girl, but the deep, strong passion of a woman almost in the middle of her life. It is a love so complete, so sufficing, that I know I could make you forget this girl. I could so envelop you with love, so watch over you and care for you, and tend you and understand you, that you *must* be happy. I feel that I could make you happier than any other woman in the world could make you."

Jocelyn Gordon could not do this; and all the advanced females in the world, all the blue-stockings and divided skirts, all the wild women and those who pant for burdens other than children will never bring it to pass that women can say such things.

And precisely because she could not say this Jocelyn felt hot and sick at the very thought that Jack Meredith should learn aught of Millicent Chyne from her. Her own inner motive in divulging what she had learned from Guy Oscard could never for a moment be hidden behind a wish, however sincere, to act for the happiness of two honorable gentlemen.

Jocelyn had no one to consult—no one to whom she could turn, in the maddening difficulty of her position, for advice or sympathy. She had to work it out by herself, steering through the quicksands by that compass that knows no deviation—the compass of her own honor and maidenly reserve.

Just because she was so sure of her own love she felt that she could never betray the falseness of Millicent Chyne. She felt somehow that Millicent's fall in Jack Meredith's estimation would drag down with it the whole of her sex, and consequently herself. She did not dare to betray Millicent, because the honor of her sex must be held up by an exaggerated honor in herself. Thus her love for Jack Meredith tied her hands while she stood idly by to see him wreck his own life by what could only be a miserable union.

With the clear sight of the on-looker Jocelyn Gordon now saw that, by Jack Meredith's own showing, Millicent was quite unworthy of him. But she also remembered words, silences, and hints which demonstrated with lamentable plainness the fact that he loved her. She was old enough and sufficiently experienced to avoid the futile speculation as to what had attracted this love. She knew that men marry women who in the estimation of on-looking relatives are unworthy of them, and live happily ever afterwards without deeming it necessary to explain to those relatives how it comes about.

Now it happened that this woman—Jocelyn Gordon—was not one of those who gracefully betray themselves at the right moment and are immediately covered with a most becoming confusion. She was strong to hold to her purpose, to subdue herself, to keep silent. And this task she set herself, having thought it all carefully out in the little flower-scented veranda, so full of pathetic association. But it must be remembered that she in no wise seemed to see the pathos in her own life. She was unconscious of romance. It was all plain fact, and the plainest was her love for Jack Meredith.

Her daily life was in no perceptible way changed. Maurice Gordon saw no difference. She had never been an hilarious person. Now she went about her household, her kindnesses, and unobtrusive good works with a quieter mien; but, when occasion or social duty demanded, she seemed perhaps a little readier than before to talk of indifferent topics, to laugh at indifferent wit. Those who have ears to hear and eyes wherewith to see learn to distrust the laugh that is too ready, the sympathy that flows in too broad a stream. Happiness is self-absorbed.

Four months elapsed, and the excitement created in the small world of Western Africa by the first dazzling success of the Simiacine Expedition began to subside. The thing took its usual course. At first the experts disbelieved, and then they prophesied that it could not last. Finally, the active period of envy, hatred, and malice gave way to a sullen tolerance not unmixed with an indefinite grudge towards Fortune who had favored the brave once more.

Maurice Gordon was in daily expectation of news from that far-off favored spot they vaguely called the Plateau. And Jocelyn did not pretend to conceal from herself the hope that filled her whole being—the hope that Jack Meredith might bring the news in person.

Instead, came Victor Durnovo.

He came upon her one evening when she was walking slowly home from a mild tea-party at the house of a missionary. Hearing footsteps on the sandy soil, she turned, and found herself face to face with Durnovo.

"Ah!" she exclaimed, and her voice thrilled with some emotion which he did not understand. "Ah, it is you."

"Yes," he said, holding her hand a little longer than was necessary.   "It is I."

His journey from Msala through the more civilized reaches of the lower river, his voyage in the coasting-boat, and his arrival at Loango, had partaken of the nature of a triumphal progress.   Victor Durnovo was elated—like a girl in a new dress.

"I was coming along to see you," he said, and there was a subtle offence in his tone.

She did not trouble to tell him that Maurice was away for ten days.   She felt that he knew that.   There was a certain truculence in his walk which annoyed her, but she was wonderingly conscious of the fact that she was no longer afraid of him.   This feeling had as yet taken no definite shape.   She did not know what she felt, but she knew that there was no fear in her mind.

"Have you been successful?" she asked, with a certain negative kindness of tone bred of this new self-confidence.

"I should think we had.   Why, the lot that Oscard brought down was a fortune in itself.   But you saw Oscard, of course.   Did he stay at the bungalow?"

"No; he stayed at the hotel."

"Did you like him?"

The question was accompanied by a momentary glance of the dark, jealous eyes.

"Yes, very much."

"He is a nice fellow—first-rate fellow.   Of course, he has his faults, but he and I got on splendidly.   He's—engaged, you know."

"So he told me."

Durnovo glanced at her again searchingly, and looked relieved.   He gave an awkward little laugh.

"And I understand," he said, "that Meredith is in the same enviable position."

"Indeed!"

Durnovo indulged in a meaning silence,

" When do you go back?" she asked, carelessly.

" Almost at once," in a tone that apologized for causing her necessary pain. " I must leave to-morrow or the next day. I do not like the idea of Meredith being left too long alone up there with a reduced number of men. Of course, I had to bring a pretty large escort. I brought down sixty thousand pounds' worth of Simiacine."

" Yes," she said; " and you take all the men back to-morrow?"

He did not remember having stated for certain that he was leaving the next day.

" Or the day after," he amended.

" Have you had any more sickness among the men?" she asked at once, in a tone of half-veiled sarcasm which made him wince.

" No," he answered; " they have been quite all right."

" What time do you start?" she asked. " There are letters for Mr. Meredith at the office. Maurice's head-clerk will give them to you."

She knew that these letters were from Millicent. She had actually had them in her hand. She had inhaled the faint, refined scent of the paper and envelopes.

" You will be careful that they are not lost, won't you?" she said, tearing at her own heart with a strange love of the pain. " They may be important."

" Oh, I will deliver them sharp enough," he answered. " I suppose I had better start to-morrow."

" I should think so," she replied quietly, with that gentle mendacity which can scarcely be grudged to women because they are so poorly armed. " I should think so. You know what these men are. Every hour they have in Loango demoralizes them more and more."

They had reached the gate of the bungalow garden. She turned and held out her hand in an undeniable manner. He bade her good-bye and went his way, wondering vaguely what had happened to them both. The conversation had taken quite a different turn to what he had expected and intended. But somehow it had got beyond his control. He had looked forward to a very different ending to the interview. And now he found himself returning somewhat disconsolately to the wretched hotel in Loango—dismissed —sent back.

The next day he actually left the little West African Coast town, turning his face northward with bad grace. Even at that distance he feared Jack Meredith's half-veiled sarcasm. He knew that nothing could be hidden for long from the Englishman's suavely persistent inquiry and deduction. Besides, the natives were no longer safe. Meredith, with the quickness of a cultured linguist, had picked up enough of their language to understand them, while Joseph talked freely with them in that singular mixture of slang and vernacular which follows the redcoat all over the world. Durnovo had only been allowed to come down to the coast under a promise, gracefully veiled but distinct enough, that he should only remain twenty hours in Loango.

Jocelyn avoided seeing him again. She was forced to forego the opportunity of hearing much that she wanted to learn, because Durnovo, the source of the desired knowledge, was unsafe. But the relief from the suspense of the last few months was in itself a consolation. All seemed to be going on well at the plateau. Danger is always discounted at sight, and Jocelyn felt comparatively easy respecting the present welfare of Jack Meredith, living as she did on the edge of danger.

Four days later she was riding through the native town of Loango, accompanied by a lady - friend, when she met Victor Durnovo. The sight of him gave her a distinct shock. She knew that he had left Loango three days before with all his men. There was no doubt about that. Moreover, his air was distinctly furtive—almost scared. It was evident that the chance meeting was as undesired by him as it was surprising to her.

"I thought you had left," she said shortly, pulling up her horse with undeniable decision.

"Yes . . . but I have come back—for, for more men."

She knew he was lying, and he felt that she knew.

"Indeed!" she said. "You are not . . . a good starter."

She turned her horse's head, nodded to her friend, bowed coldly to Durnovo, and trotted towards home. When she had reached the corner of the rambling ill-paved street she touched her horse. The animal responded. It broke into a gentle canter, which made the little children cease their play and stare. In the forest she applied the spur, and beneath the whispering trees, over the silent sand, the girl galloped home as fast as her horse could lay legs to ground.

Jocelyn Gordon was one of those women who rise slowly to the occasion, and the limit of their power seems at times to be only defined by the greatness of the need.

CHAPTER XXIII

MERCURY

"So cowards never use their might
But against such that will not fight."

On nearing the bungalow Jocelyn turned aside into the forest where a little colony of huts nestled in a hollow of the sand-dunes.

"Nâla," she cried, "the paddle-maker. Ask him to come to me."

She spoke in the dialect of the coast to some women who sat together before one of the huts.

"Nâla — yes," they answered. And they raised their strident voices.

In a few moments a man emerged from a shed of banana-leaves.   He was a scraggy man — very lightly clad — and a violent squint handicapped him seriously in the matter of first impressions.   When he saw Jocelyn he dropped his burden of wood and ran towards her.   The African negro does not cringe.   He is a proud man in his way.   If he is properly handled he is not only trustworthy — he is something stronger.   Nàla grinned as he ran towards Jocelyn.

"Nàla," she said, "will you go a journey for me?"

"I will go at once."

"I came to you," said Jocelyn, "because I know that you are an intelligent man and a great traveller."

"I have travelled much," he answered, "when I was younger."

"Before you were married?" said the English girl. "Before little Nàla came?"

The man grinned.

He looked back over his shoulder towards one of the huts where a scraggy infant with a violent squint lay on its stomach on the sand.

"Where do you wish me to go?" asked the proud father.

"To Msala, on the Ogowe River."

"I know the Ogowe.   I have been to Msala," with the grave nod of a great traveller.

"When can you leave?"

He shrugged his shoulders.

"Now."

Jocelyn had her purse in her hand.

"You can hire a dhow," she said; "and on the river you may have as many rowers as you like.   You must go very quickly to Msala.   There you must ask about the Englishman's expedition.   You have heard of it?"

"Yes; the Englishman Durnovo, and the soldier who laughs."

"Yes.   Some of the men are at Msala now.   They were going up-country to join the other Englishman far away — near the mountains.   They have stopped at Msala.   Find

out why they have not gone on, and come back very quickly to tell me. You understand, Nàla?"

"Yes."

"And I can trust you?"

"Yes; because you cured the little one when he had an
evil spirit. Yes, you can trust me."

She gave him money and rode on home. Before she
reached the bungalow the paddle-maker passed her at a trot,
going towards the sea.

She waited for three days, and then Victor Durnovo came
again. Maurice was still away. There was an awful sense
of impending danger in the very air—in the loneliness of her
position. Yet she was not afraid of Durnovo. She had
left that fear behind. She went to the drawing-room to see
him, full of resolution.

"I could not go away," he said, after relinquishing her
hand, "without coming to see you."

Jocelyn said nothing. The scared look which she had
last seen in his face was no longer there; but the eyes were
full of lies.

"Jocelyn," the man went on, "I suppose you know that
I love you? It must have been plain to you for a long
time."

"No," she answered, with a little catch in her breath.
"No, it has not. And I am sorry to hear it now."

"Why?" he asked, with a dull gleam which could not be
dignified by the name of love.

"Because it can only lead to trouble."

Victor Durnovo was standing with his back to the window, while Jocelyn, in the full light of the afternoon, stood
before him. He looked her slowly up and down with a
glance of approval which alarmed and disquieted her.

"Will you marry me?" he asked.

"No!"

His black mustache was pushed forward by some motion of the hidden lips.

" Why ?"

" Do you want the real reason ?" asked Jocelyn.

Victor Durnovo paused for a moment.

" Yes," he said.

" Because I not only do not care for you, but I despise and distrust you."

" You are candid," he said, with an unpleasant little laugh.
" Yes."

He moved a little to one side and drew a chair towards him, half leaning, half sitting on the back of it.

" Then," he said, " I will be candid with you. I intend you to marry me; I have intended it for a long time. I am not going down on my knees to ask you to do it; that is not my way. But, if you drive me to it, I will make your brother Maurice go down on his knees and beg you to marry me."

" I don't think you will do that," answered the girl, steadily. " Whatever your power over Maurice may be, it is not strong enough for that; you overrate it."

" You think so ?" he sneered.

" I am sure of it."

Durnovo glanced hastily round the room in order to make sure that they were not overheard.

" Suppose," he said, in a low, hissing voice, " that I possess knowledge that I have only to mention to one or two people to make this place too hot for Maurice Gordon. If he escaped the fury of the natives, it would be difficult to know where he could go to. England would be too hot for him. They wouldn't have him there; I could see to that. He would be a ruined man — an outcast — execrated by all the civilized world."

He was watching her face all the while. He saw the color leave even her lips, but they were steady and firm. A strange wonder crept into his heart. This woman never flinched. There was some reserved strength within herself upon which she was now drawing. His dealings had all been with half-castes—with impure blood and doubtful descendants of a mixed ancestry. He had never fairly roused a pure-bred English man or woman, and suddenly he began to feel out of his depth.

"What is your knowledge?" asked Jocelyn, in a coldly measured voice.

"I think you had better not ask that; you will be sorry afterwards. I would rather that you thought quietly over what I have told you. Perhaps, on second thoughts, you will see your way to give me some—slight hope. I should really advise it."

"I did not ask your advice. What is your knowledge?"

"You will have it?" he hissed.

"Yes."

He leaned forward, craning his neck, pushing his yellow face and hungering black eyes into hers.

"Then, if you will have it, your brother — Maurice Gordon—is a slave-trader."

She drew back as she might have done from some unclean animal. She knew that he was telling the truth. There might be extenuating circumstances. The real truth might have quite a different sound, spoken in different words; but there was enough of the truth in it, as Victor Durnovo placed it before her, to condemn Maurice before the world.

"Now will you marry me?" he sneered.

"No!"

Quick as thought she had seen the only loop-hole—the only possible way of meeting this terrible accusation.

He laughed; but there was a faint jangle of uneasiness in his laughter.

"Indeed!"

"Supposing," said Jocelyn, "for one moment that there was a grain of truth in your fabrication, who would believe you? Who on this coast would take your word against the word of an English gentleman? Even if the whole story

were true, which it is not, could you prove it? You are a
liar, as well as a coward and traitor! Do you think that
the very servants in the stable would believe you? Do you
think that the incident of the small-pox at Msala is forgotten? Do you think that all Loango, even to the boatmen
on the beach, ignores the fact that you are here in Loango
now because you are afraid to go through a savage country
to the Simiacine Plateau, as you are pledged to do? You
were afraid of the small-pox once; there is something else
that you are afraid of now. I do not know what it is, but
I will find out. Coward! Go! Leave the house at once,
before I call in the stable-boys to turn you out, and never
dare to speak to me again!"

Victor Durnovo recoiled before her, conscious all the
while that she had never been so beautiful as at that moment. But she was something far above him—a different
creation altogether. He never knew what drove him from
that room. It was the fear of something that he did not
understand.

He heard her close the window after him as he walked
away beneath the trees.

She stood watching him — proud, cold, terrible in her
womanly anger. Then she turned, and suddenly sank
down upon the sofa, sobbing.

But fortune decreed that she should have neither time
to weep nor think. She heard the approaching footsteps
of her old servant, and when the door was opened Jocelyn
Gordon was reading a book, with her back turned towards
the window.

"That man Nâla, miss, the paddle-maker, wants to see
you."

"Tell him to go round to the veranda."

Jocelyn went out by the open window, and presently
Nâla came grinning towards her. He was evidently very
much pleased with himself—held himself erect, and squinted
more violently than usual.

"I have been to Msala," he said, with considerable dig-nity of manner.

"Yes, and what news have you ?"

Nâla squatted down on the chunam floor, and proceeded to unfold a leaf. The operation took some time. Within the outer covering there was a second envelope of paper, like-wise secured by a string. Finally the man produced a small note, which showed signs of having been read more than once. This he handed to Jocelyn with an absurd air of importance.

She opened the paper and read :

"To MARIE, AT MSALA,—Send at once to Mr. Durnovo, informing him that the tribes have risen and are rapidly surrounding the Plateau. He must return here at once with as large an armed force as he can raise. But the most important consideration is time. He must not wait for men from elsewhere, but must pick up as many as he can in Loando and on the way up to Msala. I reckon that we can hold out for three months without outside assistance, but after that period we shall be forced to surrender or try and cut our way through *without* the Simiacine. With a larger force we could beat back the tribes, and establish our hold on the Plateau by force of arms. This must be forwarded to Mr. Durnovo at once, wherever he is. The letter is in duplicate, sent by two good messengers, who go by different routes.

"JOHN MEREDITH."

When Jocelyn looked up, dry-lipped, breathless, Nâla was standing before her, beaming with self-importance.

"Who gave you this ?"

"Marie, at Msala."

"Who is she ?"

"Oh, Mr. Durnovo's woman at Msala. She keeps his house."

"But this letter is for Mr. Durnovo!" cried Jocelyn, whose fear made her unreasonably angry. "Why has he not had it ?"

Nâla came nearer, with upraised forefinger and explana-tory palm.

"Marie tell me," he said, "that Mr. Meredith send two letters. Marie give Mr. Durnovo one. This—other letter."

There was a strange glitter in the girl's blue eyes— something steely and unpleasant.

"You are sure of that? You are quite sure that Mr. Durnovo has had a letter like this?" she asked, slowly and carefully, so that there could be no mistake.

"That is true," answered the man.

"Have you any more news from Msala?"

Nâla looked slightly hurt. He evidently thought that he had brought as much news as one man could be expected to carry.

"Marie has heard," he said, "that there is much fighting up in the country."

"She has heard no particulars—nothing more than that?"

"No; nothing."

Jocelyn Gordon rose to this occasion also.

"Can you go," she said, after a moment's thought, "to St. Paul de Loanda for me?"

The man laughed.

"Yes," he answered, simply.

"At once—now?"

"Oh yes," with a sigh.

Already Jocelyn was writing something on a sheet of paper.

"Take this," she said, "to the telegraph - office at St. Paul de Loanda, and send it off at once. Here is money. You understand? I will pay you when you bring back the receipt. If you have been very quick, I will pay you well."

That same evening a second messenger started northward after Maurice Gordon with a letter telling him to come back at once to Loango.

CHAPTER XXIV

NEMESIS

"Take heed of still waters."

DESPITE his assertion to Lady Cantourne, Guy Oscard stayed on in the gloomy house in Russell Square. He had naturally gone thither on his return from Africa, and during the months that followed he did not find time to think much of his own affairs. Millicent Chyne occupied all his thoughts—all his waking moments. It is marvellous how busily an active-minded young lady can keep a man employed.

In the ill-lighted study rendered famous by the great history which had emanated in the manuscript therefrom, Guy Oscard had interviewed sundry great commercial experts, and a check for forty-eight thousand pounds had been handed to him across the table polished bright by his father's studious elbow. The Simiacine was sold, and the first portion of it spent went to buy a diamond aigrette for the dainty head of Miss Millicent Chyne.

Guy Oscard was in the midst of the London season. His wealth and a certain restricted renown had soon made him popular. He had only to choose his society, and the selection was not difficult. Wherever Millicent Chyne went, he went also, and to the lady's credit it must be recorded that no one beyond herself and Guy Oscard had hitherto noticed this fact. Millicent was nothing if not discreet. It was more or less generally known that she was engaged to Jack Meredith, who, although absent on some vaguely romantic quest of a fortune, was not yet forgotten. No word, how-

ever, was popularly whispered connecting her name with
that of any other swain nearer home. Miss Chyne was too
much of a woman of the world to allow that. But, in the
meantime, she rather liked diamond aigrettes and the suppressed devotion of Guy Oscard.

It was the evening of a great ball, and Guy Oscard, having received his orders and instructions, was dining alone
in Russell Square, when a telegram was handed to him. He
opened it and spread the thin paper out upon the table-
cloth. A word from that far, wild country, which seemed
so much fitter a background to his simple bulk and strength
than the cramped ways of London society—a message from
the very heart of the dark continent—to him :

" Meredith surrounded and in danger. Durnovo false. Come at once.
—Jocelyn Gordon."

Guy Oscard pushed back his chair and rose at once, as if
there were somebody waiting in the hall to see him.

" I do not want any more dinner," he said. " I am going to Africa. Come and help me to pack my things."

He studied Bradshaw and wrote a note to Millicent
Chyne. To her he said the same as he had said to the
butler, " I am going to Africa."

There was something refreshingly direct and simple
about this man. He did not enter into long explanations.
He simply went on in the line he had marked out. He rose
from the table and never looked back. His attitude seemed
to say, " I am going to Africa ; kindly get out of my way."

At three minutes to nine—that is to say, in one hour and
a half—Guy Oscard took his seat in the Plymouth Express.
He had ascertained that a Madeira boat was timed to sail
from Dartmouth at eight o'clock that evening. He was
preceded by a telegram to Lloyd's agent at Plymouth :

" Have fastest craft available, steam up, ready to put to sea to
catch the Banyan, African steamer, four o'clock to-morrow morning.
Expense not to be considered."

As the train crept out into the night the butler of the gloomy house in Russell Square, who had finished the port, and was beginning to feel resigned, received a second shock. This came in the form of a carriage and pair, followed by a ring at the bell.

The man opened the door, and his fellow-servitor of an eccentric class and generation stepped back on the door-step to let a young lady pass into the hall.

" Mr. Oscard ?" she said, curtly.

" Left 'ome, miss," replied the butler, stiffly conscious of walnut-peel on his waistcoat.

" How long ago ?"

" A matter of half an hour, miss."

Millicent Chyne, whose face was drawn and white, passed farther into the hall. Seeing the dining-room door ajar, she passed into that stately apartment, followed by the butler.

" Mr. Oscard sent me this note," she said, showing a crumpled paper, " saying that he was leaving for Africa to-night. He gives no explanation. Why has he gone to Africa ?"

" He received a telegram while he was at dinner, miss," replied the butler, whose knowledge of the world indicated the approach of at least a sovereign. " He rose and threw down his napkin, miss. ' I'm goin' to Africa,' he says. ' Come and help me pack.' "

" Did you see the telegram—by any chance ?" asked Miss Chyne.

" Well, miss, I didn't rightly read it."

Millicent had given way to a sudden panic on the receipt of Guy's note. A telegram calling him to Africa — calling with a voice which he obeyed with such alacrity that he had not paused to finish his dinner — could only mean that some disaster had happened—some disaster to Jack Meredith. And quite suddenly Millicent Chyne's world was emptied of all else but Jack Meredith. For a moment she forgot herself. She ran to the room where Lady Cantourne was affixing the family jewelry on her dress, and, showing the letter, said breathlessly that she must see Guy Oscard at once. Lady Cantourne, wise woman of the world that she was, said nothing. She merely finished her toilet, and, when the carriage was ready, they drove round by Russell Square.

" Who was it from?" asked Millicent.

" From a person named Gordon, miss."

" And what did it say?"

" Well, miss, as I said before, I did not rightly see. But it seems that it said, 'Come at once.' I saw that."

" And what else? Be quick, please."

" I think there was mention of somebody bein' surrounded, miss. Some name like Denver, I think. No! Wait a bit : it wasn't that; it was somebody else."

Finishing off the port had also meant beginning it, and the worthy butler's mind was not particularly clear.

" Was there any mention of Mr. Oscard's partner, Mr.—eh—Meredith?" asked Millicent, glancing at the clock.

" Yes, miss, there was that name, but I don't rightly remember in what connection."

" It didn't say that he— " Millicent paused and drew in her breath with a jerk—" was dead, or anything like that?"

" Oh no, miss."

" Thank you. I—am sorry we missed Mr. Oscard."

She turned and went back to Lady Cantourne, who was sitting in the carriage. And while she was dancing the second extra with the first-comer at four o'clock the next morning, Guy Oscard was racing out of Plymouth Sound into the teeth of a fine, driving rain. On the bridge of the trembling tug-boat, by Oscard's side, stood a keen-eyed Channel pilot, who knew the tracks of the steamers up and down Channel as a game-keeper knows the hare-tracks across a stubble-field. Moreover, the tug-boat caught the big steamer pounding down into the gray of the Atlantic Ocean, and in due time Guy Oscard landed on the beach at Loanda.

He had the telegram still in his pocket, and he went, not to Maurice Gordon's office, but to the bungalow.

Jocelyn greeted him with a little inarticulate cry of joy.

"I did not think that you could possibly be here so soon," she said.

"What news have you?" he asked, without pausing to explain. He was one of those men who are silenced by an unlimited capacity for prompt action.

"That," she replied, handing him the note written by Jack Meredith to Marie at Msala.

Guy Oscard read it carefully.

"Dated seven weeks last Monday — nearly two months ago," he muttered, half to himself.

He raised his head and looked out of the window. There were lines of anxiety round his eyes. Jocelyn never took her glance from his face.

"Nearly two months ago," he repeated.

"But you will go?" she said—and something in her voice startled him.

"Of course I will go," he replied. He looked down into her face with a vague question in his quiet eyes; and who knows what he saw there? Perhaps she was off her guard. Perhaps she read this man aright and did not care.

With a certain slow hesitation he laid his hand on her arm. There was something almost paternal in his manner which was in keeping with his stature.

"Moreover," he went on, "I will get there in time. I have an immense respect for Meredith. If he said that he could hold out for four months, I should say that he could hold out for six. There is no one like Meredith, once he makes up his mind to take things seriously."

It was not very well done, and she probably saw through it. She probably knew that he was as anxious as she was herself. But his very presence was full of comfort. It somehow brought a change to the moral atmosphere — a sense of purposeful, direct simplicity which was new to the West African Coast.

"I will send over to the factory for Maurice," said the girl. "He has been hard at work getting together your men. If your telegram had not come he was going up to the Plateau himself."

Oscard looked slightly surprised. That did not sound like Maurice Gordon.

"I believe you are almost capable of going yourself," said the big man, with a slow smile.

"If I had been a man I should have been half-way there by this time."

"Where is Durnovo?" he asked, suddenly.

"I believe he is in Loango. He has not been to this house for more than a fortnight; but Maurice has heard that he is still somewhere in Loango."

Jocelyn paused. There was an expression on Guy Oscard's face which she rather liked, while it alarmed her.

"It is not likely," she went on, "that he will come here. I—I rather lost my temper with him, and said things which, I imagine, hurt his feelings."

Oscar nodded gravely.

"I'm rather afraid of doing that myself," he said; "only it will not be his feelings."

"I do not think," she replied, "that it would be at all expedient to say or do anything at present. He must go with you to the Plateau. Afterwards—perhaps."

Oscard laughed quietly.

"Ah," he said, "that sounds like one of Meredith's propositions. But he does not mean it any more than you do."

"I do mean it," replied Jocelyn, quietly. There is no hatred so complete, so merciless, as the hatred of a woman for one who has wronged the man she loves. At such times women do not pause to give fair play. They make no allowance.

Jocelyn Gordon found a sort of fearful joy in the anger

of this self-contained Englishman. It was an unfathomed mine of possible punishment over which she could in thought hold Victor Durnovo.

"Nothing," she went on, "could be too mean—nothing could be mean enough—to mete out to him in payment of his own treachery and cowardice."

She went to a drawer in her writing-table and took from it an almanac.

"The letter you have in your hand," she said, "was handed to Mr. Durnovo exactly a month ago by the woman at Msala. From that time to this he has done nothing. He has simply abandoned Mr. Meredith."

"He is in Loango?" inquired Oscard, with a premonitory sense of enjoyment in his voice.

"Yes."

"Does he know that you have sent for me?"

"No," replied Jocelyn.

Guy Oscard smiled.

"I think I will go and look for him," he said.

At dusk that same evening there was a singular incident in the bar-room of the only hotel in Loango.

Victor Durnovo was there, surrounded by a few friends of antecedents and blood similar to his own. They were having a convivial time of it, and the consumption of whiskey was greater than might be deemed discreet in such a climate as that of Loango.

Durnovo was in the act of raising his glass to his lips when the open doorway was darkened, and Guy Oscard stood before him. The half-breed's jaw dropped; the glass was set down again rather unsteadily on the zinc-covered counter.

"I want you," said Oscard.

There was a little pause, an ominous silence, and Victor Durnovo slowly followed Oscard out of the room, leaving that ominous silence behind.

"I leave for Msala to-night," said Oscard, when they were outside, "and you are coming with me."

"I'll see you damned first!" replied Durnovo, with a courage born of Irish whiskey.

Guy Oscard said nothing, but he stretched out his right hand suddenly. His fingers closed in the collar of Victor Durnovo's coat, and that parti-colored scion of two races found himself feebly trotting through the one street of Loango.

"Le' go!" he gasped.

But the hand at his neck neither relinquished nor contracted. When they reached the beach the embarkation of the little army was going forward under Maurice Gordon's supervision. Victor looked at Gordon. He reflected over the trump card held in his hand, but he was too skilful to play it then.

CHAPTER XXV

TO THE RESCUE

"I must mix myself with action lest I wither by despair."

JOCELYN had not conveyed to her brother by word or hint the accusation brought against him by Victor Durnovo. But when he returned home it almost seemed as if he were conscious of the knowledge that was hers. She thought she detected a subtle difference in his manner towards herself — something apologetic and humble. This was really the result of Victor Durnovo's threat made in the office of the factory long before.

Maurice Gordon was not the sort of man to carry through the burden of a half-discovered secret. It needs a special temperament for this — one that is able to inspire fear in whomsoever it may be necessary to hold in check — a temperament with sufficient self-reliance and strength to play an open game steadily through to the end. Since Durnovo's plain-spoken threat had been uttered Gordon had thought of little else, and it was well known that Jocelyn's influence was all that prevented him from taking hopelessly to drink. When away from her at the sub-factories it is to be feared that he gave way to the temptation. There is nothing so wearing as a constant suspense, a never-resting fear; and if a man knows that both may be relieved by a slight over-indulgence he must be a strong man indeed if he can turn aside.

Gordon betrayed himself to Jocelyn in a thousand little ways. He consulted her wishes, deferred to her opinion, and sought her advice in a way which never had been his hitherto; and while both were conscious of this difference, both were alike afraid of seeking to explain it.

Jocelyn knew that her repulse of Victor Durnovo was only a temporary advantage; the position could not remain long undecided. Victor Durnovo would have to be met sooner or later. Each day increased the strength of her conviction that her brother was in the power of this man. Whether he had really allowed himself to be dragged into the horrors of even a slight connection with the slave-trade she could not tell; but she knew the world well enough to recognize the fact that Durnovo had only to make the accusation for it to be believed by the million sensation-mongers who are always on the alert for some new horror. She knew that should Durnovo breathe a word of this in the right quarter — that is to say, into the eager journalistic ear — there would hardly be a civilized country in the world where Maurice Gordon of Loango could dwell under his own name. She felt that they were all living on a slumbering volcano. It was one of those rare cases where human life seems no longer sacred ; and this refined, educated, gentle English lady found herself face to face with the fact that Victor Durnovo's life would be cheap at the price of her own.

At this moment Providence, with the wisdom of which

we sometimes catch a glimpse, laid another trouble upon
her shoulders.   While she was half distracted with the
thought of her brother's danger, the news was put into her
hand by the grinning Nâla that Jack Meredith — the man
she openly in her own heart loved — was in an even greater
strait.

Here, at all events, was a peril that could be met, however heavy might be the odds.   Her own danger, the horror of Maurice's crime, the hatred for Victor Durnovo,
were all swallowed up in the sudden call to help Jack
Meredith.   And Jocelyn found at least a saving excitement
in working night and day for the rescue of the man who
was to be Millicent Chyne's husband.

Maurice aided her loyally.   His influence with the natives was great; his knowledge of the country second only
to Durnovo's.   During the fortnight that elapsed between
the despatch of the telegram to Guy Oscard and the arrival
of that resourceful individual at Loango, the whole coast
was astir with preparation and excitement.   Thus it came
about that Guy Oscard found a little army awaiting him,
and to Maurice Gordon was the credit given.   Victor Durnovo simply kept out of the way.   The news that an expedition was being got together to go to the relief of Jack
Meredith never reached him in his retreat.   But after a fortnight spent in idleness in the neighboring interior he could
stand the suspense no longer, and came down into the town,
to be pounced upon at once by Guy Oscard.

As he stood on the beach near to Oscard, watching the
embarkation of the men, his feelings were decidedly mixed.
There was an immense relief from the anxiety of the last
few weeks.   He had stood on the verge of many crimes,
and had been forcibly dragged back therefrom by the strong
arm of Guy Oscard.   It had been Victor Durnovo's intention not only to abandon Jack Meredith to his certain fate,
but to appropriate to his own use the consignment of Simiacine, valued at sixty thousand pounds, which he had brought

down to the coast. The end of it all was, of course, the possession of Jocelyn Gordon. The programme was simple; but, racked as he was by anxiety, weakened by incipient disease, and paralyzed by chronic fear, the difficulties were too great to be overcome. To be a thorough villain one must possess, first of all, good health; secondly, untiring energy; and thirdly, a certain enthusiasm for wrong-doing for its own sake. Criminals of the first standard have always loved crime. Victor Durnovo was not like that. He only made use of crime, and had no desire to cultivate it for its own sake. To be forcibly dragged back, therefore, into the paths of virtue was in some ways a great relief. The presence of Guy Oscard, also, was in itself a comfort. Durnovo felt that no responsibility attached itself to him; he had entire faith in Oscard and had only to obey.

Durnovo was not a person who suffered from too delicate a susceptibility. The shame of his present position did not affect him deeply Indeed, he was one of those men who have no sense of shame before certain persons; and Guy Oscard was one of those. The position was not in itself one to be proud of, but the half-breed accepted it with wonderful equanimity, and presently he began to assist in the embarkation.

It was nearly dark when the little coast steamer secured by Maurice Gordon for the service turned her prow northward and steamed away.

"The truth is," Durnovo took an early opportunity of saying to Oscard, "that my nerve is no longer up to this work. I should not care to undertake this business alone, despite my reputation on the coast. It is a wonderful thing how closely the nerves are allied to the state of one's health."

"Wonderful!" acquiesced Guy Oscard, with a lack of irony which only made the irony keener.

"I've been too long in this damned country," exclaimed Durnovo, "that's the fact. I'm not the man I was."

Guy Oscard smoked for some moments in silence; then he took his pipe from his lips.

"The only pity is," he said, judicially, "that you ever undertook to look for the Simiacine if you were going to funk it when the first difficulty arose."

Without further comment he walked away, and entered into conversation with the captain of the steamer.

"All right," muttered Durnovo between his teeth—"all right, my sarcastic, grand gentlemen. I'll be even with you yet."

The strange part of it was that Guy Oscard never attempted to degrade Durnovo from his post of joint commander. This puzzled the half-breed sorely. It may have been that Oscard knew men better than his indifferent manner would have led the observer to believe. Durnovo's was just one of those natures which in good hands might have been turned to good account. Too much solitude, too much dealing with negro peoples, and, chiefly, too long a sojourn in the demoralizing atmosphere of West Africa, had made a worse man of Victor Durnovo than nature originally intended. He was not wholly bad. Badness is, after all, a matter of comparison, and, in order to draw correctly such a comparison, every allowance must be made for a difference in standard. Victor Durnovo's standard was not a high one; that was all. And in continuing to treat him as an equal and trust him as such, Guy Oscard only showed that he was a cleverer man than the world took him to be.

In due time Msala was reached. As the canoes suitable for up-river traffic were by no means sufficient to transport the whole of the expeditionary force in one journey, a division was made. Durnovo took charge of the advance column, journeying up to the camp from which the long march through the forest was to begin, and sending back the canoes for Oscard and the remainder of the force. With these canoes he sent back word that the hostile tribes were within a few days' march, and that he was fortifying his camp.

This news seemed to furnish Guy Oscard with food for considerable thought, and after some space of time he called Marie.

She came, and, standing before him with her patient dignity of mien, awaited his communication. She never took her eyes off the letter in his hand. Oscard noticed the persistency of her gaze at the time and remembered it again afterwards.

"Marie," he said, "I have had rather serious news from Mr. Durnovo."

"Yes?" rather breathlessly.

"It will not be safe for you to stay at Msala—you must take the children down to Loango."

"Does he say that?" she asked, in her rapid, indistinct English.

"Who?"

"Vic—Mr. Durnovo."

"No," replied Oscard, wondering at the question.

"He does not say anything about me or the children?" persisted Marie.

"No."

"And yet he says there is danger?"

There was a strange, angry look in her great dark eyes which Oscard did not understand.

"He says that the tribes are within two days' march of his camp."

She gave an unpleasant little laugh.

"He does not seem to have thought of us at Msala."

"I suppose," said Oscard, folding the letter and putting it in his pocket, "that he thinks it is my duty to do what is best for Msala. That is why I asked you to speak to me."

Marie did not seem to be listening. She was looking over his head up the river, in the direction from whence the message had come, and there was a singular hopelessness in her eyes.

" I cannot leave until he tells me to," she said, doggedly.

Guy Oscard took the pipe from his lips and examined the bowl of it attentively for a moment.

" Excuse me," he said, gently, " but I insist on your leaving with the children to-morrow. I will send two men down with you, and will give you a letter to Miss Gordon, who will see to your wants at Loango."

She looked at him with a sort of wonder.

" You insist?" she said.

He raised his eyes to meet hers.

" Yes," he answered.

She bowed her head in grave submission, and made a little movement as if to go.

" It is chiefly on account of the children," he added.

Quite suddenly she smiled, and seemed to check a sob in her throat.

" Yes," said she, softly, " I know." And she went into the house.

The next morning brought further rumors of approaching danger, and it seemed certain that this news must have filtered through Durnovo's fortified camp farther up the river. This time the report was more definite. There were Arabs leading the tribes, and rumor further stated that an organized descent on Msala was intended. And yet there was no word from Durnovo—no sign to suggest that he had even thought of securing the safety of his house-keeper and the few aged negroes in charge of Msala. This news only strengthened Oscard's determination to send Marie down to the coast, and he personally superintended their departure before taking his seat in the canoe for the up-river voyage. The men of his division had all preceded him, and no one except his own boatmen knew that Msala was to be abandoned.

There was in Guy Oscard a dogged sense of justice

which sometimes amounted to a cruel mercilessness. When he reached the camp he deliberately withheld from Durnovo the news that the Msala household had left the river station. Moreover, he allowed Victor Durnovo to further inculpate himself. He led him on to discuss the position of affairs, and the half-breed displayed an intimate knowledge of the enemy's doings. There was only one inference to be drawn — namely, that Victor Durnovo had abandoned his people at Msala with the same deliberation which had characterized his cowardly faithlessness to Jack Meredith.

Guy Oscard was a slow-thinking man, although quick in action. He pieced all these things together. The pieces did not seem to fit just then—the construction was decidedly chaotic in its architecture. But later on the corner-stone of knowledge propped up the edifice, and everything slipped into its place.

Despite disquieting rumors, the expedition was allowed to depart from the river-camp unmolested. For two days they marched through the gloomy forest with all speed. On the third day one of the men of Durnovo's division captured a native who had been prowling on their heels in the line of march. Victor Durnovo sent captor and prisoner to the front of the column, with a message to Oscard that he would come presently and see what information was to be abstracted from the captive. At the mid-day halt Durnovo accordingly joined Oscard, and the man was brought before them. He was hardly worthy of the name, so disease-stricken, so miserable, and half-starved was he.

At first Durnovo and he did not seem to be able to get to an understanding at all; but presently they hit upon a dialect in which they possessed a small common knowledge. His news was not reassuring. In dealing with numbers he rarely condescended to the use of less than four figures, and his conception of distance was very vague.

"Ask him," said Oscard, " whether he knows that there

is an Englishman with a large force on the top of a moun‧ tain far to the east."

Durnovo translated, and the man answered with a smile. In reply to some further question the negro launched into a detailed narrative, to which Durnovo listened eagerly.

"He says," said the latter to Oscard, "that the Plateau is in possession of the Masais. It was taken two months ago. The blacks were sold as slaves; the two Englishmen were tortured to death and their bodies burned."

Oscard never moved a muscle.

"Ask him if he is quite sure about it."

"Quite," replied Durnovo, after questioning. "By God! Oscard; what a pity! But I always knew it. I knew it was quite hopeless from the first."

He passed his brown hand nervously over his face, where the perspiration stood in beads.

"Yes," said Oscard, slowly; "but I think we will go on all the same."

"What!" cried Durnovo. "Go on?"

"Yes," replied Guy Oscard; "we will go on, and if I find you trying to desert I'll shoot you down like a rat."

CHAPTER XXVI

IN PERIL

"He made no sign; the fires of hell were round him,
    The pit of hell below."

"ABOUT as bad as they can be, sir. That's how things is." Joseph set down his master's breakfast on the rough table that stood in front of his tent and looked at Jack Meredith.

Meredith had a way of performing most of his toilet out‧

side his tent, and while Joseph made his discouraging report he was engaged in buttoning his waistcoat. He nodded gravely, but his manner was not that of a man who fully realized his position of imminent danger. Some men are like this—they die without getting at all flustered.

"There's not more nor two or three out of the whole lot that I can put any trust in," continued Joseph.

Jack Meredith was putting on his coat.

"I know what a barrack-room mutiny is. I've felt it in the hatmosphere, so to speak, before now, sir."

"And what does it feel like?" inquired Jack Meredith, lightly arranging his watch-chain.

But Joseph did not answer. He stepped backward into the tent and brought two rifles. There was no need of answer; for this came in the sound of many voices, the clang and clatter of varied arms.

"Here they come, sir," said the soldier-servant—respectful, mindful of his place even at this moment.

Jack Meredith merely sat down, behind the little table where his breakfast stood untouched. He leaned his elbow on the table and watched the approach of the disorderly band of blacks. Some ran, some hung back, but all were armed.

In front walked a small, truculent-looking man with broad shoulders and an aggressive head.

He planted himself before Meredith, and turning, with a wave of the hand, to indicate his followers, said in English :

"These men—these friends of me—say they are tired of you. You no good leader. They make me their leader."

He shrugged his shoulders with a hideous grin of deprecation.

"I not want. They make me. We go to join our friends in the valley."

He pointed down into the valley where the enemy was encamped.

"We have agreed to take two hundred pounds for you. Price given by our friends in valley—"

The man stopped suddenly. He was looking into the muzzle of a revolver with a fixed fascination. Jack Meredith exhibited no haste. He did not seem *yet* to have realized the gravity of the situation. He took very careful aim and pulled the trigger. A little puff of white smoke floated over their heads. The broad - shouldered man with the aggressive head looked stupidly surprised. He turned towards his supporters with a pained look of inquiry, as if there was something he did not quite understand, and then he fell on his face and lay quite still.

Jack Meredith looked on the blank faces with a glance of urbane inquiry.

"Has anybody else anything to say to me?" he asked.

There was a dead silence. Some one laughed rather feebly in the background.

"Then I think I will go on with my breakfast."

Which he accordingly proceeded to do.

One or two of the mutineers dropped away and went back to their own quarters.

"Take it away," said Meredith, indicating the body of the dead man with his teaspoon.

"And look here," he cried out after them, "do not let us have any more of this nonsense! It will only lead to unpleasantness."

Some of the men grinned. They were not particularly respectful in their manner of bearing away the mortal remains of their late leader. The feeling had already turned.

Joseph thought fit to clinch matters later on in the day by a few remarks of his own.

"That's the sort o' man," he said, more in resignation than in anger, "that the guv'nor is. He's quiet like and smooth-spoken, but when he does 'it he 'its 'ard, and when he shoots he shoots mortal straight. Now, what I says to you Christy Minstrels is this: We're all in the same box and we all want the same thing, although I admit there's a bit of a difference in our complexions. Some o' you jokers have got a fine richness of color on your physiognomies that I don't pretend to emulate. But no matter. What you wants is to get out of this confounded old Platter, quick time, ain't it now?—to get down to Loango and go out on the bust, eh?"

The "Christy Minstrels" acquiesced.

"Then," said Joseph, "obey orders and be hanged to yer."

It had been apparent to Meredith for some weeks past that the man Nattoo, whom he had just shot, was bent on making trouble. His prompt action had not, therefore, been the result of panic, but the deliberate execution of a foreordained sentence. The only question was how to make the necessary execution most awe-inspiring and exemplary. The moment was well-chosen, and served to strengthen, for the time being, the waning authority of these two Englishmen thus thrown upon their own resources in the heart of Africa.

The position was not a pleasant one. For three months the Plateau had been surrounded by hostile tribes, who made desultory raids from time to time. These the little force on the summit was able to repulse; but a combined attack from, say, two sides at once would certainly have been successful. Meredith had no reason to suppose that his appeal for help had reached Msala, infested as the intervening forests were by cannibal tribes. Provisions were at a low ebb. There seemed to be no hope of outside aid, and disaffection was rife in his small force. Jack Meredith, who was no soldier, found himself called upon to defend a weak position, with unreliable men, for an indefinite period.

Joseph had a rough knowledge of soldiering and a very rudimentary notion of fortification. But he had that which served as well: the unerring eye for covert—of a marksman. He was a dead-shot at any range, and knowing what he could hit he also knew how to screen himself from the rifle of an enemy.

Above all, perhaps, was the quiet influence of a man who never flinched from danger nor seemed to be in the least disconcerted by its presence.

"It seems, sir," said Joseph to his master later in the day, "that you've kinder stumped them. They don't understand you."

"They must be kept in check by fear. There is no other way," replied Meredith, rather wearily. Of late he had felt less and less inclined to exert himself.

"Yes, sir. Those sort o' men."

Meredith made no answer, and after a little pause Joseph repeated the words significantly, if ungrammatically.

"Those sort o' men."

"What do you mean?"

"Slaves," replied Joseph, sharply, touching his hat without knowing why.

"Slaves! What the devil are you talking about?"

The man came a little nearer.

"Those forty men — leastwise thirty-four men — that we brought from Msala—Mr. Durnovo's men that cultivate this 'ere Simiacine, as they call it—they're different from the rest, sir."

"Yes, of course they are. We do not hire them direct —we hire them from Mr. Durnovo and pay their wages to him. They are of a different tribe from the others—not fighting men, but agriculturists."

"Ah—" Joseph paused. "Strange thing, sir, but I've not seen 'em handling any of their pay yet."

"Well, that is their affair."

"Yessir!"

Having unburdened himself of his suspicion, the servant retired, shaking his head ominously. At any other time the words just recorded would have aroused Jack Meredith's attention, but the singular slothfulness that seemed to be creeping over his intellect was already acting as a clog on his mental energy.

The next morning he was unable to leave his bed, and lay all day in a state of semi-somnolence. Joseph explained to the men that the leader was so disgusted with their ungrateful conduct that he would not leave the tent. In the evening there was a slight attack made from the southern side. This Joseph was able to repulse, chiefly by his own long-range firing, assisted by a few picked rifles. But the situation was extremely critical. The roll of the big wardrum could be heard almost incessantly, rising with weird melancholy from the forest land beneath them.

Despite difficulties, the new crop of Simiacine—the second within twelve months — had been picked, dried, and stored in cases. Without, on the Plateau, stood the bare trees, affording no covert for savage warfare — no screen against the deadly bullet. The camp was placed near one edge of the table-land, and on this exposed side the stockade was wisely constructed of double strength, The attacks had hitherto been made only from this side, but Joseph knew that anything in the nature of a combined assault would carry his defence before it. In his rough-and-ready way he doctored his master, making for him such soups and strength-giving food as he could. Once, very late in the night, when it almost seemed that the shadow of death lay over the little tent, he pounded up some of the magic Simiacine leaves and mixed them in the brandy which he administered from time to time.

Before sunrise the next morning the alarm was given again, and the little garrison was called to arms.

When Joseph left his master's tent he was convinced that neither of them had long to live; but he was of that hard material which is found in its very best form in the ranks and on the forecastle — men who die swearing. It may be very reprehensible—no doubt it is— but it is very difficult for a plain-going man to withhold his admiration for such as these. It shows, at all events, that Thomas Atkins and Jack are alike unafraid of meeting their Maker. It *is* their duty to fight either a living enemy or a cruel sea, and if a little profanity helps them to do their duty, who are we that we may condemn them?

So Joseph went out with a rifle in each hand and a fine selection of epithets on his tongue.

"Now, you devils," he said, "we're just going to fight like hell."

And what else he said it booteth little.

He took his station on the roof of a hut in the centre of the little stockade, and from there he directed the fire of his men. Crouching beneath him he had a disabled native who loaded each rifle in turn; and just by way of encouraging the others he picked off the prominent men outside the stockade with a deadly steadiness. By way of relieving the tension he indulged in an occasional pleasantry at the expense of the enemy.

"Now," he would say, "there's a man lookin' over that bush with a green feather on his nut. It's a mistake to wear green feathers; it makes a body so conspicuous."

And the wearer of the obnoxious feather would throw up his arms and topple backward down the hill.

If Joseph detected anything like cowardice or carelessness, he pointed his rifle with a threatening frown towards the culprit, with instant effect. Presently, however, things began to get more serious. This was not the sudden assault of a single chief, but an organized attack. Before long Joseph ceased to smile. By sunrise he was off the roof, running from one weak point to another, encouraging, threatening, fighting, and swearing very hard. More than once the enemy reached the stockade, and — ominous sign —one or two of their dead lay inside the defence.

"Fight, yer devils—fight!" he cried in a hoarse whisper, for his voice had given away. "Hell—give 'em hell!"

He was everywhere at once, urging on his men, kicking them, pushing them, forcing them up to the stockade. But he saw the end. Half dazed, the blacks fought on in silence.

The grim African sun leaped up above the distant line of forest and shone upon one of the finest sights to be seen on earth—a soldier wounded, driven desperate, and not afraid.

In the midst of it a hand was laid on Joseph's shoulder. "There," cried a voice, " *that* corner.   See to it."

Without looking round, Joseph obeyed, and the breached corner was saved.   He only knew that his master, who was almost dead, had come to life again.   There was no time for anything else.

For half an hour it was a question of any moment.   Master and man were for the time being nothing better than madmen, and the fighting frenzy is wildly infectious.

At last there was a pause.   The enemy fell back, and in the momentary silence the sound of distant firing reached the ears of the little band of defenders.

"What's that?" asked Meredith, sharply.   He looked liked one risen from the dead.

"Fighting among themselves," replied Joseph, who was wiping blood and grime from his eyes.

"Then one of them is fighting with an Express rifle."

Joseph listened.

"By God!" he shouted—"by God, Mer—sir, we're saved!"

The enemy had apparently heard the firing, too.   Perhaps they also recognized the peculiar sharp "smack" of the Express rifle amid the others.   There was a fresh attack—an ugly rush of reckless men.   But the news soon spread that there was firing in the valley, and the sound of a white man's rifle.   The little garrison plucked up heart, and the rifles, almost too hot to hold, dealt death around.

They held back the savages until the sound of the firing behind them was quite audible even amid the heavy rattle of the musketry.

Then suddenly the firing ceased—the enemy had divided and fled.   For a few moments there was a strange, tense silence.   Then a voice—an English voice—cried,

"Come on!"

The next moment Guy Oscard stood on the edge of the Plateau. He held up both arms as a signal to those within the stockade to cease firing, and then he came forward, followed by a number of blacks and Durnovo.

The gate was rapidly disencumbered of its rough supports and thrown open.

Jack Meredith stood in the aperture, holding out his hand.

"It's all right; it's—all right," he said.

Oscard did not seem to take so cheerful a view of matters. He scrutinized Meredith's face with visible anxiety.

Then suddenly Jack lurched up against his rescuer, grabbing at him vaguely.

In a minute Oscard was supporting him back towards his tent.

"It's all right, you know," explained Jack Meredith, very gravely; "I am a bit weak—that is all. I am hungry—haven't had anything to eat for some time, you know."

"Oh yes," said Oscard, shortly; "I know all about it."

<hr />

CHAPTER XXVII

OFF DUTY

"Chacun de vous peut-être en son cœur solitaire
Sous des ris passagers étouffe un long regret."

"Good-bye to that damned old Platter—may it be forever!" With this valedictory remark Joseph shook his fist once more at the unmoved mountain and resumed his march.

"William," he continued, gravely, to a native porter who walked at his side and knew no word of English, "there is some money that is not worth the making."

The man grinned from ear to ear and nodded with a
vast appreciation of what experience taught him to take as
a joke.

"Remember that, my black diamond, and just mind the
corner of your mouth don't get hitched over yer ear," said
Joseph, patting him with friendly cheerfulness.

Then he made his way forward to walk by the side of
his master's litter and encourage the carriers with that mixture of light badinage and heavy swearing which composed
his method of dealing with the natives.

Three days after the arrival of the rescuing force at the
Plateau, Guy Oscard had organized a retreating party, commanded by Joseph, to convey Jack Meredith down to the
coast.   He knew enough of medicine to recognize the fact
that this was no passing indisposition, but a thorough breakdown in health.   The work and anxiety of the last year,
added to the strange disquieting breath of the Simiacine
grove, had brought about a serious collapse in the system
which only months of rest and freedom from care could repair.

Before the retreating column was ready to march it was
discovered that the hostile tribes had finally evacuated the
country; which deliverance was brought about not by Oscard's blood-stained track through the forest, not by the
desperate defence of the Plateau, but by the whisper that
Victor Durnovo was with them.   Truly a man's reputation
is a strange thing!

And this man—the mighty warrior whose name was as
good as an army in Central Africa — went down on his
knees one night to Guy Oscard, imploring him to abandon
the Simiacine Plateau, or at all events to allow him to go
down to Loango with Meredith and Joseph.

"No," said Oscard; "Meredith held this place for us
when he could have left it safely.   He has held it for a
year.   It is our turn now.   We will hold it for him.   I am
going to stay, and you have to stay with me."

For Jack Meredith, life was at this time nothing but a constant, never-ceasing fatigue.   When Oscard helped him into the rough litter they had constructed for his comfort, he laid his head on the pillow, overcome with a dead sleep.

"Good-bye, old chap," said Oscard, patting him on the shoulder.

"G'bye;" and Jack Meredith turned over on his side as if he were in bed, drew up the blanket, and closed his eyes. He did not seem to know where he was, and, what was worse, he did not seem to care.   Oscard gave the signal to the bearers, and the march began.   There is something in the spring of human muscles unlike any other motive power; the power of thought may be felt even on the pole of a litter, and one thing that modern invention can never equal is the comfort of being carried on the human shoulder.   The slow swinging movement came to be a part of Jack Meredith's life—indeed, life itself seemed to be nothing but a huge journey thus peacefully accomplished.   Through the flapping curtains an endless procession of trees passed before his half-closed eyes.   The unintelligible gabble of the light-hearted bearers of his litter was all that reached his ears. And ever at his side was Joseph—cheerful, indefatigable, resourceful.   There was in his mind one of the greatest happinesses of life — the sense of something satisfactorily accomplished—the peacefulness that comes when the necessity for effort is past and left behind—that lying down to rest which must surely be something like Death in its kindest form.

The awe inspired by Victor Durnovo's name went before the little caravan like a moral convoy and cleared their path. Thus, guarded by the name of a man whom he hated, Jack Meredith was enabled to pass through a savage country literally cast upon a bed of sickness.

In due course the river was reached, and the gentle swing of the litter was changed for the smoother motion of the canoe.   And it was at this period of the journey—in the forced restfulness of body entailed—that Joseph's mind soared to higher things, and he determined to write a letter to Sir John.

He was, he admitted even to himself, no great penman, and his epistolary style tended, perhaps, more to the forcible than to the finished.

"Somethin'," he reflected, "that'll just curl his back hair for 'im ; that's what I'll write 'im."

Msala had been devastated, and it was within the roofless walls of Durnovo's house that Joseph finally wrote out laboriously the projected capillary invigorator."

"HONORED SIR [he wrote],—Trusting you will excuse the liberty, I take up my pen to advise you respectfully "—while writing this word Joseph closed his left eye—" that my master is taken seriously worse. Having been on the sick-list now for a matter of five weeks, he just lies on his bed as weak as a new-born babe, as the sayin' is, and doesn't take no notice of nothing. I have succeeded in bringing him down to the coast, which we hope to reach to-morrow, and when we get to Loango—a poor sort of place—I shall at once obtain the best advice obtainable—that is to be had. However, I may have to send for it ; but money being no object to either master or me, respectfully I beg to say that every care will be took. Master having kind friends at Loango, I have no anxiety as to the future, but, honored sir, it has been a near touch in the past—just touch and go, so to speak. Not being in a position to form a estimate of what is the matter with master, I can only respectfully mention that I take it to be a general kerlapse of the system, brought on, no doubt, by too long a living in the unhealthy platters of Central Africa. When I gets him to Loango I shall go straight to the house of Mr. and Miss Gordon, where we stayed before, and with no fear but what we will be received with every kindness and the greatest hospitality. Thank God, honored sir, I've kept my health and strength wonderful, and am therefore more able to look after master. When we reach Loango I shall ask Miss Gordon kindly to write to you, sir, seeing as I have no great facility with my pen. I am, honored sir, your respectful servant to command, "JOSEPH ATKINSON,

"Late Corporal 217th Regt."

There were one or two round splashes on the paper suggestive, perhaps, of tears, but not indicative of those useless

tributes. The truth was that it was a ho. evening, and
Joseph had, as he confessed, but little facility with the pen.
"There," said the scribe, with a smile of intense satisfaction. "That will give the old un beans. Not that I don't
respect him—oh no."

He paused, and gazed thoughtfully at the evening-star.

"Strange thing—life," he muttered, "uncommon strange.
Perhaps the old un is right; there's no knowin'. The
ways o' Providence *are* mysterious—onnecessarily mysterious, to my thinkin'."

And he shook his head at the evening-star, as if he were
not quite pleased with it.

With a feeling of considerable satisfaction Joseph approached the bungalow at Loango three days later. The
short sea voyage had somewhat revived Meredith, who had
been desirous of walking up from the beach, but after a
short attempt had been compelled to enter the spring-cart
which Joseph had secured.

Joseph walked by the side of this cart with an erect carriage, and a suppressed importance suggestive of ambulance
duty in the old days.

As the somewhat melancholy cortege approached the
house, Meredith drew back the dusky brown-holland curtain and looked anxiously out. Nor were Joseph's eyes
devoid of expectation. He thought that Jocelyn would
presently emerge from the flower-hung trellis of the veranda;
and he had rehearsed over and over again a neat, respectful
speech, explanatory of his action in bringing a sick man to
the house.

But the hanging fronds of flower and leaf remained motionless, and the cart drove, unchallenged, round to the
principal door.

A black servant—a stranger—held the handle, and stood
back invitingly. Supported by Joseph's arm, Jack Meredith entered. The servant threw open the drawing-room
door; they passed in. The room was empty. On the ta-

ble lay two letters, one addressed to Guy Oscard, the other to Jack Meredith.

Meredith felt suddenly how weak he was, and sat wearily down on the sofa.

"Give me that letter," he said.

Joseph looked at him keenly. There was something forlorn and cold about the room—about the whole house —with the silent, smiling black servants and the shaded windows.

Joseph handed the letter as desired, and then, with quick, practised hands, he poured a small quantity of brandy into the cup of his flask. "Drink this first, sir," he said.

Jack Meredith fumbled rather feebly at the letter. It was distinctly an effort to him to tear the paper.

"My dear Meredith" [he read],—Just a line to tell you that the bungalow and its contents are at your service. Jocelyn and I are off home for two months' change of air. I have been a bit seedy. I leave this at the bungalow, and we shall feel hurt if you do not make the house your home whenever you happen to come down to Loango. I have left a similar note for Oscard, in whose expedition to your relief I have all faith. Yours ever,

"Maurice Gordon."

"Here," said Meredith to his servant, "you may as well read it for yourself."

He handed the letter to Joseph and leaned back with a strange rapidity of movement on the sofa. As he lay there with his eyes closed he looked remarkably like a dead man.

While Joseph was reading the letter the sound of bare feet on the cocoa-leaf matting made him turn round.

A small, rotund white figure of a child, clad in a cotton garment, stood in the doorway, finger in mouth, gazing gravely at the two occupants of the room.

"Nestorius!" exclaimed Joseph, "by all that's holy! Well, I *am* glad to see you, my son. Where's mammy, eh?"

Nestorius turned gravely round and pointed a small dusky finger in the direction of the servants' quarters. Then he

replaced the finger between his lips and came slowly forward
to examine Meredith, who had opened his eyes.

"Well, stout Nestorius! This is a bad case, is it not?"
said the sick man.

"Bad case," repeated Nestorius, mechanically.

At that moment Marie came into the room, dignified,
gentle, self-possessed.

"Ah, missis," said Joseph, "I'm glad to see you. You're
wanted badly, and that's the truth. Mr. Meredith's not at
all well."

Marie bowed gravely. She went to Meredith's side and
looked at him with a smile that was at once critical and encouraging. Nestorius, holding on to her skirt, looked up to
her face, and, seeing the smile, smiled too. He went further.
He turned round and smiled at Joseph as if to make things
pleasant all round.

Marie stooped over the sofa, and her clever dusky fingers
moved the cushions.

"You will be better in bed," she said; "I will get Mr.
Gordon's room made ready for you—yes?"

There are occasions when the mere presence of a woman
supplies a distinct want. She need not be clever, or very
capable; she need have no great learning or experience.
She merely has to be a woman — the more womanly the
better. There are times when a man may actually be afraid
for the want of a woman, but that is usually for the want of
one particular woman. There may be a distinct sense of
fear—a fear of life and its possibilities—which is nothing
else than a want—the want of a certain voice, the desire to
be touched by a certain hand, the carping necessity (which
takes the physical form of a pressure deep town in the
throat) for the sympathy of that one person whose presence is different from the presence of other people. And
failing that particular woman, another can in a certain
degree, by her mere womanliness, stay the pressure of the
want.

This was what Marie did for Jack Meredith by coming into the room and bending over him and touching his cushions with a sort of deftness and *savoir faire.* He did not define his feelings—he was too weak for that; but he had been conscious, for the first time in his life, of a distinct sense of fear when he read Maurice Gordon's letter. Of course he had thought of the possibility of death many times during the last five weeks; but he had no intention of dying. He set the fact plainly before himself that with care he might recover, but that at any moment some symptom could declare itself which would mean death.

But he and Joseph had, without making mention of it to each other, counted entirely on finding the Gordons at home. It was more than a disappointment — very much more for Jack Meredith. But in real life we do not analyze our feelings as do men in books—more especially books of the mawko-religious tenor written by ladies. Jack Meredith only knew that he felt suddenly afraid of dying when he read Maurice Gordon's letter, and that when the half-caste woman came into the room and gently asserted her claim, as it were, to supreme authority in this situation, the fear seemed to be allayed.

Joseph, with something bright glistening in his keen, quick eyes, stood watching her face as if for a verdict.

"You are tired," she said, "after your long journey."

Then she turned to Joseph with that soft, natural way which seems to run through the negro blood, however much it may be diluted.

"Help Mr. Meredith," she said, "to Mr. Gordon's room. I will go at once and see that the bed is got ready."

CHAPTER XXVIII

"We dare not let our tears flow, lest, in truth,
They fall upon our work which must be done."

"They was just in time," said Joseph pleasantly to Marie that same evening, when Jack Meredith had been made comfortable for the night and there was time to spare for supper.

"Ah!" replied the woman, who was busy with the supper-table.

Joseph glanced at her keenly. The exclamation not only displayed a due interest, but contained many questions. He stretched out his legs and wagged his head sapiently.

"And no mistake!" he said. "They timed it almost to the minute. We had sort of beaten them back for the time bein'. Mr. Meredith had woke up sudden, as I told you, and came into the thick of the melêe, as we say in the service. Then we heard the firin' in the distance and the 'splat' of Mr. Oscard's Express rifle. I just turns, like this 'ere, my head over me shoulder, quite confidential, and I says, 'Good Lord, I thank yer.' I'm no hand at tracts and Bible - readin's, but I'm not such a blamed fool, Mistress Marie, as to think that this 'ere rum-go of a world made itself. No, not quite. So I just put in a word, quiet-like, to the Creator."

Marie was setting before him such luxuries as she could command. She nodded encouragingly.

"Go on," she said. "Tell me!"

"Cheddar cheese," he said, parenthetically, with an appreciative sniff. "Haven't seen a bit o' that for a long time. Well, then, up comes Mr. Oscard as cool as a cow-cumber, and Mr. Meredith he gives a sort of a little laugh and says, 'Open that gate.' Quite quiet, yer know. No high falutin' and potry and that. A few minutes before he had been fightin' and cussin' and shoutin', just like any Johnny in the ranks. Then he calms down and wipes the blood off'n his hand on the side of his pants, and says, 'Open that gate.' That's a nice piece of butter you've got there, mistress. Lord! it's strange I never missed all them things."

"Bring your chair to the table," said Marie, "and begin. You are hungry—yes?"

"Hungry ain't quite the word."

"You will have some mutton—yes? And Mr. Durnovo, where was he?"

Joseph bent over his plate, with elbows well out, wielding his knife and fork with a more obvious sense of enjoyment than usually obtains in the politer circles.

"Mr. Durnovo," he said, with one quick glance towards her. "Oh, he was just behind Mr. Oscard. And he fol-lows 'im, and we all shakes hands just as if we was meet-ing in the Row, except that most of our hands was a bit grimy and sticky-like with blood and the grease off'n the car-tridges."

"And," said Marie, in an indirectly interrogative way, as she helped him to a piece of sweet potato, "you were glad to see them, Mr. Oscard and Mr. Durnovo—yes?"

"Glad ain't quite the word," replied Joseph, with his mouth full.

"And they were not hurt or—ill?"

"Oh no!" returned Joseph, with another quick glance. "They were all right. But I don't like sitting here and eatin' while you don't take bit or sup yourself. Won't you chip in, Mistress Marie? Come now, do."

With her deep, patient smile she obeyed him, eating little and carelessly, like a woman in some distress.

"When will they come down to Loango?" she asked suddenly, without looking at him.

"Ah! that I can't tell you. We left quite in a hurry, as one may say, with nothin' arranged. Truth is, I think we all feared that the guv'nor had got his route. He looked very like peggin' out, and that's the truth. Howsomever, I hope for the best now."

Marie said nothing, merely contenting herself with attending to his wants, which were numerous and frequent.

"That God - forsaken place, Msala," said Joseph, presently "has been rather crumbled up by the enemy."

They have destroyed it—yes?"

"That is so. You're right, they 'ave destroyed it.

Marie gave a quick little sigh—one of those sighs which the worldly-wise recognize at once.

"You don't seem over-pleased," said Joseph.

"I was very happy there," she answered.

Joseph leaned back in his chair, fingering reflectively his beer-glass.

"I'm afraid, mistress," he said, half shyly, "that your life can't have been a very happy one. There's some folk that *is* like that—through no fault of their own, too, so far as our mortal vision, so to speak, can reckon it up."

"I have my troubles, like other people," she answered, softly.

Joseph inclined his head to one side and collected his bread-crumbs thoughtfully.

"Always seems to me," he said, "that your married life can't have been so happy-like as—well, as one might say you deserved, missis. But then you've got them clever little kids. I *do* like them little kids wonderful. Not bein' a marrying man myself, I don't know much of such matters. But I've always understood that little uns—especially cunning little souls like yours—go a long way towards makin' up a woman's happiness."

"Yes," she murmured, with her slow smile.

" Been dead long—their pa ?"

" He is not dead."

" Oh—beg pardon."

And Joseph drowned a very proper confusion in bitter beer.

" He has only ceased to care about me—or his children," explained Marie.

Joseph shook his head; but whether denial of such a possibility was intended, or an expression of sympathy, he did not explain.

"I hope," he said, with a somewhat labored change of manner, " that the little ones are in good health."

" Yes, thank you."

Joseph pushed back his chair with considerable vigor, and passed the back of his hand convivially across his mustache.

"A square meal I call that," he said, with a pleasant laugh, " and I thank you kindly."

With a tact which is sometimes found wanting inside a better coat than he possessed, Joseph never again referred to that part of Marie's life which seemed to hang like a shadow over her being. Instead, he set himself the task of driving away the dull sense of care which was hers, and he succeeded so well that Jack Meredith, lying between sleep and death in his bedroom, sometimes heard a new strange laugh.

By daybreak next morning Joseph was at sea again, steaming south in a coasting-boat towards St. Paul de Loanda. He sent off a telegram to Maurice Gordon in England, announcing the success of the Relief Expedition, and then proceeded to secure the entire services of a medical man. With this youthful disciple of Æsculapius he returned forthwith to Loango, and settled down with characteristic energy to nurse his master.

Meredith's progress was lamentably slow, but still it was progress, and in the right direction. The doctor, who was wise in the strange maladies of the West Coast, stayed for two days, and promised to return once a week. He left full instructions, and particularly impressed upon the two nurses the fact that the recovery would necessarily be so slow that their unpractised eyes could hardly expect to trace its progress.

It is just possible that Meredith could at this time have had no better nurse than Joseph. There was a military discipline about the man's method which was worth more than much feminine persuasion.

"Beef tea, sir," he would announce with a face of wood, for the sixth time in one day.

" What, again?   No, hang it! I can't."

" Them's my orders, sir," was Joseph's invariable reply, and he was usually in a position to produce documentary confirmation of his statement.   The two men—master and servant—had grown so accustomed to the military discipline of a besieged garrison that it did not seem to occur to them to question the doctor's orders.

Nestorius—small, stout, and silent—was a frequenter of the sick-room, by desire of the invalid.   After laboriously toiling up the shallow stairs—a work entailing huge effort of limbs and chin—he would stump gravely into the room without any form of salutation.   There are some great minds above such trifles.   His examination of the patient was a matter of some minutes.   Then he would say, "Bad case," with the peculiar mechanical diction that was his— the words that Meredith had taught him on the evening of his arrival.   After making his diagnosis Nestorius usually proceeded to entertain the patient with a display of his treasures for the time being.   These were not in themselves of great value : sundry pebbles, a trouser-button, two shells, and a glass stopper formed, as it were, the basis of his collection, which was increased or diminished according to circumstances.   Some of these he named; others were exhibited with a single adjective, uttered curtly, as between men who required no great tale of words wherewith to understand each other. A few were considered to be of sufficient value and importance to tell their own story and make their way in the world thereupon. He held these out with a face of grave and contemplative patronage.

"Never, Nestorius," Meredith would say, gravely, "in the course of a long and varied experience, have I seen a Worcester-sauce stopper of such transcendent beauty."

Sometimes Nestorius clambered onto the bed, when the mosquito curtains were up, and rested from his labors—a small, curled-up form, looking very comfortable. And then, when his mother's soft voice called him, he was wont to gather up his belongings and take his departure. On the threshold he always paused, finger in mouth, to utter a valedictory "Bad case" before making his way down-stairs with a shadowy, mystic smile.

Kind neighbors called, and well-meaning but mistaken dissenting missionaries left religious works of a morbid nature, eminently suitable to the sick-bed; but Joseph, Marie, and Nestorius were the only three who had free access to the quiet room.

And all the while the rain fell—night and day, morning, noon, and evening—as if the floodgates had been left open by mistake.

"Sloobrious, no doubt," said Joseph, "but blamed depressing."

And he shook his head at the lowering sky with a tolerant smile, which was his way of taking Providence to task.

"Do y' know what I would like, missis?" he asked, briskly, of Marie one evening.

"No."

"Well, I'd like to clap my eyes on Miss Gordon, just a-stepping in at that open door—that's what we want. That sawbones feller is right when he says the progress will be slow. Slow! Slow ain't quite the word. No more ain't progress the word—that's my opinion. He just lies on that bed, and the most he can do is to skylark a bit with Nestorius. He don't take no interest in nothin', least of all in his victuals—and a man's in a bad way when he takes no interest in his victuals. Yes, I'll take another pancake, thankin' you kindly. You've got a rare light hand for pancakes. Rare—rare ain't quite the word."

"But what could Miss Gordon do ?" asked Marie.

"Well, she could kinder interest him in things—don't you see? Him and I we ain't got much in common—except his clothes and that confounded beef-tea and slushin's. And then there's Mr. Gordon—he's a good hearty sort, he is — comes galamphin' into the room, kickin' a couple of footstools and upsettin' things promiscuous. It cheers a invalid up, that sort o' thing."

Marie laughed in an awkward, unwonted way.

"But it do, missis," pursued Joseph, "wonderful; and I can't do it myself. I tried the other day, and master only thought I'd been drinkin'."

"You are impatient," said Marie. "He is better, I know. I can see it. You see it yourself—yes ?"

"A bit—just a bit. But he wants some one of his own station in life, without offence, Mistress Marie. Some one as will talk with him about books and evenin' parties and things. And—" he paused reflectively, "and Miss Gordon would do that."

There was a little silence, during which another pancake met its fate.

"You know," said Joseph, with sudden confidence, "he's goin' to marry a young lady at home, in London; a young lady of fashion, as they say — one of them that's got one smile for men and another for women. Not his sort, as I should have thought myself, knowin' him as I do."

"Then why does he marry her ?" asked Marie.

"Ah !" Joseph rose, and stretched out his arms with a

freedom from restraint learned in the barrack-room. "There you're asking me more than I can tell you. I suppose—it's the old story—I suppose he thinks that she is his sort."

CHAPTER XXIX

A CHANCE ACQUAINTANCE

"The pride that prompts the bitter jest."

A SPACE had with some difficulty been cleared at the upper end of an aristocratic London drawing-room, and with considerable enthusiasm Miss Fitzmannering pranced into the middle of it. Miss Fitzmannering had kindly allowed herself to be persuaded to do "only a few steps" of her celebrated skirt dance. Miss Eline Fitzmannering officiated at the piano, and later on, while they were brushing their hair, they quarrelled because she took the time too quickly.

The aristocratic assembly looked on with mixed feelings, and faces suitable to the same. The girls who could not skirt-dance yawned behind their fans—gauze preferred, because the Fitzmannerings could see through gauze if they could not see through anything else. The gifted products of fashionable Brighton schools, who could in their own way make exhibitions of themselves also, wondered who on earth had taught Miss Fitzmannering; and the servants at the door felt ashamed of themselves without knowing why.

Miss Fitzmannering had practised that skirt-dance—those few steps—religiously for the last month. She had been taught those same contortions by a young lady in *the* profession, whom even Billy Fitzmannering raised his eyebrows at. And every one knows that Billy is not particular. The performance was not graceful, and the gentlemen present who knew more about dancing—skirt or otherwise—

than they cared to admit, pursed up the corners of their mouths and looked straight in front of them—afraid to meet the eye of some person or persons undefined.

But the best face there was that of Sir John Meredith. He was not bored, as were many of his juniors—at least, he did not look it. He was neither shocked nor disgusted, as apparently were some of his contemporaries—at least, his face betrayed neither of those emotions. He was keenly interested—suavely attentive. He followed each spasmodic movement with imperturbably pleasant eyes.

"My dear young lady," he said, with one of his courtliest bows, when at last Miss Fitzmannering had had enough of it, "you have given us a great treat—you have, indeed."

"A most unique performance," he continued, turning gravely to Lady Cantourne, by whose side he had been standing; and, strange to say, her ladyship, made a reproving little movement of the lips, and tapped his elbow surreptitiously, as if he were misbehaving himself.

He offered his arm with a murmur of refreshments, and she accepted.

"Well," he said, when they were alone or nearly so, "do you not admit that it was a most unique performance?"

"Hush!" replied the lady, either because she was a woman or because she was a woman of the world. "The poor girl cannot help it. She is forced into it by the exigencies of society, and her mother. It is not entirely her fault."

"It will be entirely my fault," replied Sir John, "if I see her do it again."

"It does not matter about a man," said Lady Cantourne, after a little pause; "but a woman cannot afford to make a fool of herself. She ought never to run the risk of being laughed at. And yet I am told that they teach that elegant accomplishment at fashionable schools."

"Which proves that the school-mistress is a knave as well as—the other thing."

They passed down the long room together—a pattern,

to the younger generation, of politeness and mutual respect. And that which one or other did not see was not worth comprehension.

"Who," asked Sir John, when they had passed into the other room—"who is the tall fair girl who was sitting near the fireplace?"

He did not seem to think it necessary to ask Lady Cantourne whether she had noticed the object of his curiosity.

"I was just wondering," replied Lady Cantourne, stirring her tea comfortably. "I will find out. She interests me. She is different from the rest."

"And she does not let it be seen—that is what I like," said Sir John. "The great secret of success in the world is to be different from other people and conceal the fact." He stood his full height, and looked round with blinking, cynical eyes. "They are all very like each other, and they fail to conceal that."

"I dislike a person," said Lady Cantourne, in her tolerant way, "who looks out of place anywhere. That girl would never look so."

Sir John was still looking round, seeing all that there was to be seen, and much that was not intended for that purpose.

"Some of them," he said, "will look self-conscious in heaven."

"I hope so," said Lady Cantourne, quietly; "that is the least one may expect."

"I trust there will be no skirt—" Sir John broke off suddenly with a quick smile.

"I was about to be profane," he said, taking her cup. "But I know you do not like it."

She looked up at him with a wan little smile. She was wondering whether he remembered as well as she did that half an ordinary lifetime lay between that moment and the occasion when she had reproved his profanity.

"Come," she said, rising, "take me back to the drawing-room, and I will make somebody introduce me to the girl."

Jocelyn Gordon, sitting near the fire, talking to a white-mustached explorer, and listening good - naturedly to a graphic account of travels which had been put in the background by more recent wanderers, was somewhat astounded when the hostess came up to her a few minutes later, and introduced a stout little lady with twinkling, kindly eyes by the name of Lady Cantourne. She had heard vaguely of Lady Cantourne as a society leader of the old school, but had no clew to this obviously intentional introduction.

"You are wondering," said Lady Cantourne, when she had sent the explorer on his travels elsewhere in order that she might have his seat—"you are wondering why I asked to know you."

She looked into the girl's face with bright, searching eyes.

"I am afraid I was," admitted Jocelyn.

"I have two reasons : one vulgar—the other sentimental. The vulgar reason was curiosity. I like to know people whose appearance prepossesses me. I am an old woman— no, you need not shake your head, my dear ! not with me— I am almost a *very* old woman, but not quite; and all my life I have trusted in appearances. And," she paused, studying the lace of her fan, "I suppose I have not made more mistakes than other people. I have always made a point of trying to get to know people whose appearance I like. That is my vulgar reason. You do not mind my saying so —do you?"

Jocelyn laughed with slightly heightened color, which Lady Cantourne noted with an appreciative little nod.

"My other reason is that, years ago at school, I knew a girl who was very like you. I loved her intensely—for a short time—as girls do at school, you know. Her name was Treseaton—the Honorable Julia Treseaton."

"My mother !" said Jocelyn, eagerly.

"I thought so. I did not think so at first, but when you

spoke I was certain of it. She had a way with her lips. I am afraid she is dead."

" Yes ; she died nearly twenty-five years ago in Africa."

" Africa ? Whereabouts in Africa?"

Then suddenly Jocelyn remembered where she had heard Lady Cantourne's name. It had only been mentioned to her once. And this was the aunt with whom Millicent Chyne lived. This cheery little lady knew Jack Meredith and Guy Oscard ; and Millicent Chyne's daily life was part of her existence.

"The West Coast," she answered, vaguely. She wanted time to think—to arrange things in her mind. She was afraid of the mention of Jack's name in the presence of this woman of the world. She did not mind Maurice or Guy Oscard — but it was different with a woman. She could hardly have said a better thing, because it took Lady Cantourne some seconds to work out in her mind where the West Coast of Africa was.

" That is the unhealthy coast, is it not ?" asked her ladyship.

" Yes."

Jocelyn hardly heard the question. She was looking round with a sudden breathless eagerness. It was probable that Millicent Chyne was in the rooms ; and she never doubted that she would know her face.

" And I suppose you know that part of the world very well ?" said Lady Cantourne, who had detected a change in her companion's manner.

" Oh yes."

" Have you ever heard of a place called Loango ?"

" Oh yes. I live there."

" Indeed, how very interesting ! I am very much interested in Loango just now, I must tell you. But I did not know that anybody lived there."

" No one does by choice," explained Jocelyn. " My father was a judge on the Coast, and since his death my brother Maurice has held an appointment at Loango. We are obliged to live there for eight months in the twelve."

She knew it was coming. But, as chance would have it, it was easier than she could have hoped. For some reason Lady Cantourne looked straight in front of her when she asked the question.

"Then you have, no doubt, met a friend of mine, Mr. Meredith? Indeed, two friends; for I understand that Guy Oscard is associated with him in this wonderful discovery."

"Oh yes," replied Jocelyn, with a carefully modulated interest. "I have met them both. Mr. Oscard lunched with us shortly before we left Africa."

"Ah, that was when he disappeared so suddenly. We never got quite to the base of that affair. He left at a moment's notice on receipt of a telegram or something, only leaving a short and somewhat vague note for my— for us. He wrote from Africa, I believe, but I never heard the details. I imagine Jack Meredith was in some difficulty. But it is a wonderful scheme this, is it not? They are certain to make a fortune, I understand."

"So people say," replied Jocelyn. It was a choice to tell all—to tell as much as she herself knew—or nothing. So she told nothing. She could not say that she had been forced by a sudden breakdown of her brother's health to leave Loango while Jack Meredith's fate was still wrapped in doubt. She could not tell Lady Cantourne that all her world was in Africa—that she was counting the days until she could go back there. She could not lift for a second the veil that hid the aching, restless anxiety in her heart, the life-absorbing desire to know whether Guy Oscard had reached the Plateau in time. Her heart was so sore that she could not even speak of Jack Meredith's danger.

"How strange," said Lady Cantourne, "to think that you are actually living in Loango, and that you are the last person who has spoken to Jack Meredith! There are two people in this house to-night who would like to ask you

questions from now till morning, but neither of them will
do it. Did you see me go through the room just now with
a tall gentleman—rather old?"

"Yes," answered Jocelyn.

"That was Sir John Meredith, Jack's father," said Lady
Cantourne, in a lowered voice. "They have quarrelled, you
know. People say that Sir John does not care—that he is
heartless, and all that sort of thing. The world never says
the other sort of thing, one finds. But—but I think I
know to the contrary. He feels it very deeply. He would
give worlds to hear some news of Jack; but he won't ask
it, you know."

"Yes," said Jocelyn, "I understand."

She saw what was coming, and she desired it intensely,
while still feeling afraid—as if they were walking on some
sacred ground and might at any moment make a false
step.

"I should like Sir John to meet you," said Lady Cantourne, pleasantly. "Will you come to tea some afternoon? Strange to say, he asked who you were not half an
hour ago. It almost seems like instinct, does it not? I do
not believe in mystic things about spirits and souls going
out to each other, and all that nonsense; but I believe in
instinct. Will you come to - morrow? You are here to-
night with Mrs. Sander, are you not? I know her. She
will let you come alone. Five o'clock. You will see my
niece, Millicent. She is engaged to be married to Jack
Meredith, you know. That is why they quarrelled — the
father and son. You will find a little difficulty with her,
too. She is a difficult girl. But I dare say you will manage to tell her what she wants to know."

"Yes," said Jocelyn, quietly — almost too quietly, "I
shall manage."

Lady Cantourne rose, and so did Jocelyn.

"You know," she said, looking up into the girl's face,
"it is a good action. That is why I ask you to do it. It

is not often that one has the opportunity of doing a good action, to which even one's dearest friend cannot attribute an ulterior motive! Who is that man over there?"

"That is my brother."

"I should like to know him; but do not bring him to-morrow. We women are better alone—you understand?"

With a confidential little nod, the great lady went away to attend to other affairs; possibly to carry through some more good actions of a safe nature.

It was plain to Jocelyn that Maurice was looking for some one. He had just come, and was making his way through the crowd. Presently she managed to touch his elbow.

"Oh, there you are!" he exclaimed; "I want you. Come out of this room."

He offered her his arm, and together they made their way out of the crowded room into a smaller apartment where an amateur reciter was hovering disconsolately, await-ing an audience.

"Here," said Maurice, when they were alone, "I have just had this telegram."

He handed her the thin white submarine telegraph-form with its streaks of adhesive text.

"Relief entirely successful. Meredith—Joseph—returned—Loan-go. Meredith bad health."

Jocelyn drew a deep breath.

"So that's all right—eh?" said Maurice, heartily.

"Yes," answered Jocelyn, "that is all right."

CHAPTER XXX

OLD BIRDS

"Angels call it heavenly joy;
 Infernal tortures the devils say;
 And men? They call it—Love."

"BY-THE-WAY, dear," said Lady Cantourne to her niece the next afternoon, "I have asked a Miss Gordon to come to tea this afternoon. I met her last night at the Fitz-mannerings'. She lives in Loango and knows Jack. I thought you might like to know her. She is exceptionally lady-like and rather pretty."

And straightway Miss Millicent Chyne went up-stairs to put on her best dress.

We men cannot expect to understand these small matters —these exigencies, as it were, of female life. But we may be permitted to note feebly *en passant* through existence that there are occasions when women put on their best clothes without the desire to please. And, while Millicent Chyne was actually attiring herself, Jocelyn Gordon, in another house not so far away, was busy with that beautiful hair of hers, patting here, drawing out there, pinning, poking, pressing with all the cunning that her fingers possessed.

When they met a little later in Lady Cantourne's uncompromisingly solid and old-fashioned drawing-room, one may be certain that nothing was lost.

"My aunt tells me," began Millicent at once, with that *dégagé* treatment of certain topics hitherto held sacred which obtains among young folks to-day, "that you know Loango."

"Oh yes—I live there."

"And you know Mr. Meredith?"

"Yes, and Mr. Oscard also."

There was a little pause while two politely smiling pairs of eyes probed each other.

"She knows something—how much?" was behind one pair of eyes.

"She cannot find out—I am not afraid of her," behind the other.

And Lady Cantourne, the proverbial looker-on, slowly rubbed her white hands one over the other.

"Ah, yes," said Millicent, unblushingly—that was her strong point, blushing in the right place, but not in the wrong—"Mr. Oscard; he is associated with Mr. Meredith, is he not, in this hare-brained scheme?"

"I believe they are together in it—the Simiacine, you mean?" said Jocelyn.

"What else could she mean?" reflected the looker-on.

"Yes—the Simiacine. Such a singular name, is it not? I always say they will ruin themselves suddenly. People always do, don't they? But what do you think of it? I *should* like to know."

"I think they certainly will make a fortune," replied Jocelyn—and she noted the light in Millicent's eyes with a sudden feeling of dislike—"unless the risks prove too great and they are forced to abandon it."

"What risks?" asked Millicent, quite forgetting to modulate her voice.

"Well, of course, the Ogowe River is most horribly unhealthy, and there are other risks. The natives in the plains surrounding the Simiacine Plateau are antagonistic. Indeed, the Plateau was surrounded and quite besieged when we left Africa."

It may have hurt Millicent, but it hurt Jocelyn more—for the smile had left her hearer's face. She was off her guard, as she had been once before when Sir John was near,

and Millicent's face betrayed something which Jocelyn saw
at once with a sick heart—something that Sir John knew
from the morning when he had seen Millicent open two
letters — something that Lady Cantourne had known all
along.

"And was Mr. Meredith on the Plateau when it was besieged?" asked Millicent, with a drawn, crooked smile.

"Yes," answered Jocelyn. She could not help seizing
the poor little satisfaction of this punishment; but she felt
all the while that it was nothing to the punishment she was
bearing and would bear all her life. There are few more
contradictory things than the heart of a women who really
loves. For one man it is very tender; for the rest of the
world it is the hardest heart on earth if it is called upon to
defend the object of its love or the love itself.

"But," cried Millicent, "of course, something was done.
They could never leave Mr. Meredith unprotected."

"Yes," answered Jocelyn, quietly, "Mr. Oscard went up
and rescued him. My brother heard yesterday that the relief had been effected."

Millicent smiled again in her light-hearted way.

"That is all right," she said. "What a good thing we
did not know! Just think, auntie dear, what a lot of anxiety we have been spared!"

"In the height of the season, too!" said Jocelyn.

"Ye—es," replied Millicent, rather doubtfully.

Lady Cantourne was puzzled. There was something going
on which she did not understand. Within the sound of the
pleasant conversation there was the *cliquetis* of the foil; behind the polite smile there was the gleam of steel. She was
rather relieved to turn at this moment and see Sir John Meredith entering the room with his usual courtly bow. He
always entered her drawing-room like that. Ah! that little secret of a mutual respect. Some people who are young
now will wish, before they have grown old, that they had
known it,

He shook hands with Lady Cantourne and with Millicent. Then he stood with a deferential half-bow, waiting for the introduction to the girl who was young enough to be his daughter—almost to be his granddaughter. There was something pathetic and yet proud in this old man's uncompromising adherence to the lessons of his youth.

"Sir John Meredith—Miss Gordon."

The beginning—the thin end of the wedge, as the homely saying has it—the end which we introduce almost every day of our lives, little suspecting to what it may broaden out.

"I had the pleasure of seeing you last night," said Sir John at once, "at Lady Fitzmannering's evening party, or 'At Home,' I believe we call them nowadays. Some of the guests read the invitation too much *au pied de la lettre* for my taste. They were so much at home that I, fearing to intrude, left rather early."

"I believe the skirt-dancing frightened you away, Sir John," said Millicent, merrily.

"Even old birds, my dear young lady, may sometimes be alarmed by a scarecrow."

"I missed you quite early in the evening," put in Lady Cantourne, sternly refusing to laugh. She had not had an opportunity of seeing him since her conversation with Jocelyn, and the dangers of the situation were fully appreciated by such an experienced woman of the world.

"They began to clear the upper end of the room," he explained, "and I assisted them in the most practical manner in my power."

He was beginning to wonder why he had been invited—nay, almost commanded—to come, by an imperious little note. And of late, whenever Sir John began to wonder he began also to feel old. His fingers strayed towards his unsteady lips as if he were about to make one of those little movements of senile helplessness to which he sometimes gave way.

For a moment Lady Cantourne hesitated between two

strokes of social diplomacy—but only for a moment. She had heard the bell ring, and trusted that at the other end of the wire there might be one of those fatuous young men who nibbled at that wire like foolish fish round a gilt spoon-bait. Her ladyship decided to carry on the social farce a few minutes longer, instead of offering the explanation which all were awaiting.

"We women," she said, "were not so early deterred from our social duties."

At that moment the door opened, and there entered a complex odor of hair-wash and perfumery—a collar which must have been nearly related to a cuff, and a pair of tight patent-leather boots, all attached to and somewhat over-powering a young man.

"Ah, my dear Mr. Grubb," said Lady Cantourne, "how good of you to call so soon! You will have some tea. Millicent, give Mr. Grubb some tea."

"Not too strong," added Sir John, apparently to himself, under the cover of Mr. Grubb's somewhat scrappy greeting.

Then Lady Cantourne went to the conservatory and left Sir John and Jocelyn at the end of the long room together. There is nothing like a woman's instinct. Jocelyn spoke at once.

"Lady Cantourne," she said, "kindly asked me to meet you to-day on purpose. I live at Loango; I know your son, Mr. Meredith, and we thought you might like to hear about him and about Loango."

She knew that with a man like Sir John any indirect approach to the subject would be courting failure. His veiled old eyes suddenly lighted up, and he turned to glance over his shoulder.

"Yes," he said, with a strange hesitation, "yes—you are kind. Of course I am interested. I wonder," he went on, with a sudden change of manner—"I wonder how much you know."

His unsteady hand was resting on her gloved fingers, and he blinked at it as if wondering how it got there.

Jocelyn did not seem to notice.

"I know," she answered, "that you have had a difference of opinion—but no one else knows! You must not think that Mr. Meredith has spoken of his private affairs to any one else. The circumstances were exceptional, and Mr. Meredith thought that it was due to me to give me an explanation."

Sir John looked a little puzzled, and Jocelyn went on rather hastily to explain :

"My brother and Mr. Meredith were at Eton together. They met somewhere up the Coast, and my brother asked Mr. Meredith to come and stay. It happened that Maurice was away when Mr. Meredith arrived, and I did not know who he was, so he explained."

"I see," said Sir John. "And you and your brother have been kind to my boy."

Somehow he seemed to have forgotten to be cynical. He had never known what it is to have a daughter, and she was ignorant of the pleasant, everyday amenities of a father's love. As there is undoubtedly such a thing as love at first sight, so must there be sympathy at first sight. For Jocelyn it was comprehensible—nay, it was most natural. This was Jack's father. In his manner, in everything about him, there were suggestions of Jack. This seemed to be a creature hewn, as it were, from the same material, moulded on the same lines with slightly divergent tools. And for him—who can tell? The love that was in her heart may have reached out to meet almost as great a love locked up in his proud soul. It may have shown itself to him, openly, fearlessly, recklessly, as love sometimes does when it is strong and pure.

He had carefully selected a seat within the shadow of the curtains ; but Jocelyn saw quite suddenly that he was an older man than she had taken him to be the evening before. She saw through the deception of the piteous wig—the whole art that strove to conceal the sure decay of the body, despite the desperate effort of a mind still fresh and vigorous.

"And I dare say," he said, with a somewhat lame attempt at cynicism, "that you have heard no good of me?"

But Jocelyn would have none of that. She was no child to be abashed by sarcasm; but a woman, completed and perfected by her love.

"Excuse me," she said, sharply; "but that is not the truth, and you know it. You know as well as I do that your son would never say a word against you."

Sir John looked hastily round. Lady Cantourne had come into the room and was talking to the two young people. Millicent was glancing uneasily over Mr. Grubb's brainless cranium towards them. Sir John's stiff, unsteady fingers fumbled for a moment round his lips.

"Yes," he said, "I was wrong."

"He has always spoken of you with the greatest love and respect," said Jocelyn. "More than that, with admiration. But he very rarely spoke of you at all, which I think means more."

Sir John blinked, and suddenly pulled himself together with a backward jerk of the arms which was habitual with him. It almost seemed as if he said to himself, as he squared his shoulders, "Come, no giving way to old age!"

"Has his health been good?" he asked, rather formally.

"I believe so, until quite lately. My brother heard yesterday by telegram that he was at Loango in broken health," replied Jocelyn.

Sir John was looking at her keenly—his hard blue eyes like steel between the lashless lids.

"You disquiet me," he said. "I have a sort of feeling that you have bad news to tell me."

"No," she answered, "not exactly. But it seems to me

that no one realizes what he is doing out in Africa—what risks he is running."

"Tell me," he said, drawing in his chair. "I will not interrupt you. Tell me all you know from beginning to end. I am naturally—somewhat interested."

So Jocelyn told him. And what she said was only a recapitulation of facts known to such as have followed these pages to this point. But the story did not sound quite the same as that related to Millicent. It was fuller, and there were certain details touched upon lightly which had before been emphasized—details of dangers run and risks incurred. Also was it listened to in a different spirit, without shallow comment, with a deeper insight. Suddenly he broke into the narrative. He saw—keen old worldling that he was— a discrepancy.

"But," he said, "there was no one in Loango connected with the scheme who"—he paused, touching her sleeve with a bony finger — "who sent the telegram home to young Oscard—the telegram calling him out to Jack's relief?"

"Oh," she explained, lightly, "I did. My brother was away, so there was no one else to do it, you see!"

"Yes—I see."

And perhaps he did.

Lady Cantourne helped them skilfully. But there came a time when Millicent would stand it no longer, and the amiable Grubb wriggled out of the room, crushed by a too obvious dismissal.

Sir John rose at once, and when Millicent reached them they were talking of the previous evening's entertainment.

Sir John took his leave. He bowed over Jocelyn's hand, and Millicent, watching them keenly, could see nothing— no gleam of a mutual understanding in the politely smiling eyes.

"Perhaps," he said, "I may have the pleasure of meeting you again?"

"I am afraid it is doubtful," she answered, with some. thing that sounded singularly like exultation in her voice. "We are going back to Africa almost at once."

And she, also, took her leave of Lady Cantourne.

CHAPTER XXXI

SEED-TIME

"What Fate does, let Fate answer for."

ONE afternoon Joseph had his wish. Moreover, he had it given to him even as he desired, which does not usually happen. We are given a part, or the whole, so distorted that we fail to recognize it.

Joseph looked up from his work and saw Jocelyn coming into the bungalow garden.

He went out to meet her, putting on his coat as he went.

"How is Mr. Meredith?" she asked at once. Her eyes were very bright, and there was a sort of breathlessness in her manner which Joseph did not understand.

"He is a bit better, miss, thank you kindly. But he don't make the progress I should like. It's the weakness that follows the malarial attack that the doctor has to fight against."

"Where is he?" asked Jocelyn.

"Well, miss, at the moment he is in the drawing-room. We bring him down there for the change of air in the afternoon. Likely as not, he's asleep."

And presently Jack Meredith, lying comfortably somnolent on the outskirts of life, heard light footsteps, but hardly heeded them. He knew that some one came into the room and stood silently by his couch for some seconds. He lazily unclosed his eyelids for a moment, not in order to see

who was there, but with a view of intimating that he was
not asleep. But he was not wholly conscious. To men accustomed to an active, energetic life, a long illness is nothing but a period of complete rest. In his more active moments Jack Meredith sometimes thought that this rest of
his was extending into a dangerously long period, but he
was too weak to feel anxiety about anything.

Jocelyn moved away and busied herself noiselessly with
one or two of those small duties of the sick-room which
women see and men ignore. But she could not keep away.
She came back and stood over him with a silent sense of
possession which made that moment one of the happiest of
her life. She remembered it in after-years, and the complex feelings of utter happiness and complete misery that
filled it.

At last a fluttering moth gave the excuse her heart longed
for, and her fingers rested for a moment, light as the moth
itself, on his hair. There was something in the touch which
made him open his eyes—uncomprehending at first, and
then filled with a sudden life.

"Ah!" he said, "you—you at last!"

He took her hand in both of his. He was weakened by
illness and a great fatigue. Perhaps he was off his guard,
or only half awake.

"I never should have got better if you had not come," he
said. Then, suddenly, he seemed to recall himself, and rose
with an effort from his recumbent position.

"I do not know," he said, with a return of his old half-
humorous manner, "whether to thank you first for your
hospitality or to beg your pardon for making such unscru-
pulous use of it."

She was looking at him closely as he stood before her,
and all her knowledge of human ills as explored on the
West Coast of Africa, all her experience, all her powers of
observation, were on the alert. He did not look very ill.
The brown of a year's sunburn such as he had gone through

on the summit of an equatorial mountain, where there was but little atmosphere between earth and sun, does not bleach off in a couple of months. Physically regarded, he was stronger, broader, heavier-limbed, more robust than when she had last seen him—but her knowledge went deeper than complexion, or the passing effort of a strong will.

"Sit down," she said, quietly. "You are not strong enough to stand about."

He obeyed her with a little laugh.

"You do not know," he said, "how pleasant it is to see you—fresh and English-looking. It is like a tonic. Where is Maurice?"

"He will be here soon," she replied; "he is attending to the landing of the stores. We will soon make you strong and well; for we have come laden with cases of delicacies for your special delectation. Your father chose them himself at Fortnum & Mason's."

He winced at the mention of his father's name, and drew in his legs in a peculiar, decisive way.

"Then you knew I was ill?" he said, almost suspiciously.

"Yes; Joseph telegraphed."

"To whom?" sharply.

"To Maurice."

Jack Meredith nodded his head. It was perhaps just as well that the communicative Joseph was not there at that moment.

"We did not expect you for another ten days," said Meredith after a little pause, as if anxious to change the subject. "Marie said that your brother's leave was not up until the week after next."

Jocelyn turned away, apparently to close the window. She hesitated. She could not tell him what had brought them back sooner—what had demanded of Maurice Gordon the sacrifice of ten days of his holiday.

"We do not always take our full term," she said, vaguely.

And he never saw it. The vanity of man is a strange

thing. It makes him see intentions that were never con-ceived; and without vanity to guide his perception man is as blind a creature as walks upon this earth.

"However," he said, as if to prove his own density, "I am selfishly very glad that you had to come back sooner. Not only on account of the delicacies — I must ask you to believe that. Did my eye brighten at the mention of Fortnum & Mason? I am afraid it did."

She laughed softly. She did not pause to think that it was to be her daily task to tend him and help to make him stronger in order that he might go away without delay. She only knew that every moment of the next few weeks was going to be full of a greater happiness than she had ever tasted. As we get deeper into the slough of life most of us learn to be thankful that the future is hidden—some of us recognize the wisdom and the mercy which decree that even the present be only partly revealed.

"As a matter of fact," she said, lightly, "I suppose that you loathe all food?"

"Loathe it," he replied. He was still looking at her, as if in enjoyment of the Englishness and freshness of which he had spoken. "Simply loathe it. All Joseph's tact and patience are required to make me eat even eleven meals in the day. He would like thirteen."

At this moment Maurice came in — Maurice — hearty, eager, full of life. He blustered in almost as Joseph had prophesied, kicking the furniture, throwing his own vitality into the atmosphere. Jocelyn knew that he liked Jack Meredith — and she knew more. She knew, namely, that Maurice Gordon was a different man when Jack Meredith was in Loango. From Meredith's presence he seemed to gather a sense of security and comfort even as she did — a sense which in herself she understood (for women analyze love), but which in her brother puzzled her.

"Well, old chap," said Maurice, "glad to see you. I *am* glad to see you. Thank Heaven you were bowled over by that confounded malaria, for otherwise we should have missed you."

"That is one way of looking at it," answered Meredith. But he did not go so far as to say that it was a way which had not previously suggested itself to him.

"Of course it is. The best way, I take it. Well—how do you feel? Come, you don't look so bad."

"Oh—much better, thanks. I have got on splendidly the last week, and better still the last five minutes! The worst of it is that I shall be getting well too soon and shall have to be off."

"Home?" inquired Maurice, significantly.

Jocelyn moved uneasily.

"Yes, home."

"We don't often hear people say that they are sorry to leave Loango," said Maurice.

"*I* will oblige you whenever you are taken with the desire," answered Jack, lightly; "Loango has been a very good friend to me. But I am afraid there is no choice. The doctor speaks very plain words about it. Besides, I am bound to go home."

"To sell the Simiacine?" inquired Maurice.

"Yes."

"Have you the second crop with you?"

"Yes."

"And the trees have improved under cultivation?"

"Yes," answered Jack, rather wonderingly. "You seem to know a lot about it."

"Of course I do," replied Maurice, boisterously.

"From Durnovo?"

"Yes, he even offered to take me into partnership."

Jack turned on him in a flash.

"Did he indeed? On what conditions?"

And then, when it was too late, Maurice saw his mistake. It was not the first time that the exuberance of his nature had got him into a difficulty.

"Oh, I don't know," he replied, vaguely. "It's a long story. I'll tell you about it some day."

Jack would have left it there for the moment. Maurice Gordon had made his meaning quite clear by glancing significantly towards his sister. Her presence, he intimated, debarred further explanation.

But Jocelyn would not have it thus. She shrewdly suspected the nature of the bargain proposed by Durnovo, and a sudden desire possessed her to have it all out—to drag this skeleton forth and flaunt it in Jack Meredith's face. The shame of it all would have a certain sweetness behind its bitterness; because, forsooth, Jack Meredith alone was to witness the shame. She did not pause to define the feeling that rose suddenly in her heart. She did not know that it was merely the pride of her love—the desire that Jack Meredith, though he would never love her, should know once for all that such a man as Victor Durnovo could be nothing but repugnant to her.

"If you mean," she said, "that you cannot tell Mr. Meredith because I am here, you need not hesitate on that account."

Maurice laughed awkwardly, and muttered something about matters of business. He was not good at this sort of thing. Besides, there was the initial handicapping knowledge that Jocelyn was so much cleverer than himself.

"Whether it is a matter of business or not," she cried, with glittering eyes, "I want you to tell Mr. Meredith now. He has a right to know. Tell him upon what condition Mr. Durnovo proposed to admit you into the Simiacine."

Maurice still hesitated, bewildered, at a loss—such as men are when a seemingly secure secret is suddenly discovered to the world. He would still have tried to fend it off; but Jack Meredith, with his keener perception, saw that Jocelyn was determined—that further delay would only make the matter worse.

"If your sister wants it," he said, "you had better tell

me. I am not the sort of man to act rashly—on the impulse of the moment."

Still Maurice tried to find some means of evasion.

"Then," cried Jocelyn, with flaming cheeks, "*I* will tell you. You were to be admitted into the Simiacine scheme by Mr. Durnovo if you could persuade or force me to marry him."

None of them had foreseen this. It had come about so strangely, and yet so easily, in the midst of their first greetings.

"Yes," admitted Maurice, "that was it."

"And what answer did you give?" asked Jocelyn.

"Oh, I told him to go and hang himself—or words to that effect," was the reply, delivered with a deprecating laugh.

"Was that your final answer?" pursued Jocelyn, inexorable. Her persistence surprised Jack. Perhaps it surprised herself.

"Yes, I think so."

"Are you sure?"

"Well, he cut up rough and threatened to make things disagreeable; so I think I said that it was no good his asking me to do anything in the matter, as I didn't know your feelings."

"Well, you can tell him," cried Jocelyn, hotly, "that never, under any circumstances whatever, would I dream even of the possibility of marrying him."

And the two men were alone.

Maurice Gordon gazed blankly at the closed door.

"How was I to know she'd take it like that?" he asked, helplessly.

And for once the polished gentleman of the world forgot himself—carried away by a sudden unreasoning anger which surprised him almost as much as it did Maurice Gordon.

"Why, you damned fool," said Jack, "any idiot would

have known that she would take it like that. How could
she do otherwise? You, her brother, ought to know that
to a girl like Miss Gordon the idea of marrying such a low
brute as Durnovo could only be repugnant. Durnovo—
why, he is not good enough to sweep the floor that she has
stood upon! He's not fit to speak to her; and you go on
letting him come to the house, sickening her with his beastly attentions! You're not capable of looking after a lady!
I would have kicked Durnovo through that very window
myself, only"—he paused, recalling himself with a little
laugh—"only it was not my business."

Maurice Gordon sat down forlornly. He tapped his
boot with his cane.

"Oh, it's very well for you," he answered, "but I'm not
a free agent. *I* can't afford to make an enemy of Durnovo."

"You need not have made an enemy of him," said Jack,
and he saved Maurice Gordon by speaking quickly—saved
him from making a confession which could hardly have
failed to alter both their lives.

"It will not be very difficult," he went on; all she wants
is your passive resistance. She does not want you to help
him—do you see? She can do the rest. Girls can manage
these things better than we think, if they want to. The
difficulty usually arises from the fact that they are not always quite sure that they do want to. Go and beg her pardon. It will be all right."

So Maurice Gordon went away also, leaving Jack Meredith alone in the drawing-room with his own thoughts.

CHAPTER XXXII

AN ENVOY

> "What we love perfectly
> For its own sake we love . . .
> . . . That which is best for it is best for us."

"FEEL like gettin' up to breakfast, do you, sir?" said Joseph to his master a few days later. "Well, I am glad. Glad ain't quite the word, though!"

And he proceeded to perform the duties attendant on his master's wardrobe with a wise, deep-seated shake of the head. While setting the shaving necessaries in order on the dressing-table, he went further—he winked gravely at himself in the looking-glass.

"You've made wonderful progress the last few days, sir," he remarked. "I always told Missis Marie that it would do you a lot of good to have Mr. Gordon to heart you up with his cheery ways—and Miss Gordon too, sir."

"Yes, but they would not have been much good without all your care before they came. I had turned the corner a week ago—I felt it myself."

Joseph grinned—an honest, open grin of self-satisfaction. He was not one of those persons who like their praise bestowed with subtlety.

"Wonderful!" he repeated to himself, as he went to the well in the garden for his master's bath-water. "Wonderful! but I don't understand things—not bein' a marryin' man."

During the last few days Jack's progress had been rapid enough even to satisfy Joseph. The doctor expressed himself fully reassured, and even spoke of returning no more.

But he repeated his wish that Jack should leave for England without delay.

"He is quite strong enough to be moved now," he finished by saying. "There is no reason for further delay."

"No," answered Jocelyn, to whom the order was spoken. "No—none. We will see that he goes by the next boat."

The doctor paused. He was a young man who took a strong—perhaps too strong a personal interest in his patients. Jocelyn had walked with him as far as the gate, with only a parasol to protect her from the evening sun. They were old friends. The doctor's wife was one of Jocelyn's closest friends on the Coast.

"Do you know anything about Meredith's future movements?" he asked. "Does he intend to come out here again?"

"I could not tell you. I do not think they have settled yet. But I think that when he gets home he will probably stay there."

"Best thing he can do—best thing he can do. It will never do for him to risk getting another taste of malaria— tell him so, will you? Good-bye."

"Yes, I will tell him."

And Jocelyn Gordon walked slowly back to tell the man she loved that he must go away from her and never come back. The last few days had been days of complete happiness. There is no doubt that women have the power of enjoying the present to a greater degree than men. They can live in the bliss of the present moment with eyes continually averted from the curtain of the near future which falls across that bliss and cuts it off. Men allow the presence of the curtain to mar the brightness.

These days had been happier for Jocelyn than for Jack, because she was conscious of the fulness of every moment, while he was merely rejoicing in comfort after hardship, in pleasant society after loneliness. Even with the knowledge that it could not last, that beyond the near future lay a

whole lifetime of complete solitude and that greatest of all
miseries, the desire of an obvious impossibility—even with
this she was happier than he; because she loved him and
she saw him daily getting stronger; because their relative
positions brought out the best and the least romantic part
of a woman's love—the subtle maternity of it. There is a
fine romance in carrying our lady's kerchief in an inner
pocket, but there is something higher and greater and much
more durable in the darning of a sock; for within the hand-
kerchief there is chiefly gratified vanity, while within the
sock there is one of those small infantile boots which have
but little meaning for us.

Jocelyn entered the drawing-room with a smile.

"He is very pleased," she said. "He does not seem to
want to see you any more, and he told me to be inhospit-
able."

"As how?"

"He told me to turn you out. You are to leave by the
next steamer."

He felt a sudden unaccountable pang of disappointment
at her smiling eyes.

"This is no joking matter," he said, half seriously. "Am
I really as well as that?"

"Yes."

"The worst of it is that you seem rather pleased."

"I am—at the thought that you are so much better."
She paused and turned quite away, busying herself with a
pile of books and magazines. "The other," she went on
too indifferently, "was unfortunately to be foreseen. It is
the necessary drawback."

He rose suddenly and walked to the window.

"The grim old necessary drawback," he said, without
looking towards her.

There was a silence of some duration. Neither of them
seemed to be able to find a method of breaking it without
awkwardness. It was she who spoke at last.

" He also said," she observed in a practical way, " that you must not come out to Africa again."

He turned as if he had been stung.

" Did he make use of that particular word ?" he asked.

" Which particular word ?"

" Must."

Jocelyn had not foreseen the possibility that the doctor was merely repeating to her what he had told Jack on a previous visit.

" No," she answered. " I think he said, ' better not.' "

" And you make it into ' must.' "

She laughed, with a sudden light-heartedness which remained unexplained.

" Because I know you both," she answered. " For him ' better not ' stands for ' must.' With you ' better not ' means ' doesn't matter.' "

" ' Better not ' is so weak that if one pits duty against it it collapses. I cannot leave Oscard in the lurch, especially after his prompt action in coming to my relief."

" Yes," she replied, guardedly. " I like Mr. Oscard's way of doing things."

The matter of the telegram summoning Oscard had not yet been explained. She did not want to explain it at that moment; indeed, she hoped that the explanation would never be needed.

" However," she added, " you will see when you get home."

He laughed.

" The least pleasant part of it is," he said, " your evident desire to see the last of me. Could you not disguise that a little—just for the sake of my feelings ?"

" Book your passage by the next boat and I will promptly descend to the lowest depths of despair," she replied, lightly.

He shrugged his shoulders with a short laugh.

" This is hospitality indeed," he said, moving towards the door.

Then suddenly he turned and looked at her gravely.

"I wonder," he said, slowly, "if you are doing this for a purpose. You said that you met my father—"

"Your father is not the man to ask any one's assistance in his own domestic affairs, and anything I attempted to do could only be looked upon as the most unwarrantable interference."

"Yes," said Meredith, seriously. "I beg your pardon; you are right."

He went to his own room and summoned Joseph.

"When is the next boat home?" he asked.

"Boat on Thursday, sir."

Meredith nodded. After a little pause he pointed to a chair.

"Just sit down," he said; "I want to talk over this Simiacine business with you."

Joseph squared his shoulders, and sat down with a face indicative of the gravest attention. Sitting thus he was no longer a servant, but a partner in the Simiacine. He even indulged in a sidelong jerk of the head, as if requesting the attention of some absent friend in a humble sphere of life to this glorious state of affairs.

"You know," said Meredith, "Mr. Durnovo is more or less a blackguard."

Joseph drew in his feet, having previously drawn his trousers up at the knees.

"Yes, sir," he said, glancing up. "A blackguard — a damned blackguard," he added, unofficially under his breath.

"He wants continual watching and a special treatment. He requires some one constantly at his heels."

"Yes, sir," admitted Joseph, with some fervor.

"Now I am ordered home by the doctor," went on Meredith. "I must go by the next boat; but I don't like to go and leave Mr. Oscard in the lurch, with no one to fall back upon but Durnovo—you understand."

Joseph's face had assumed the habitual look of servitude;

he was no longer a partner, but a mere retainer, with a half-comic resignation in his eyes.

"Yes, sir," scratching the back of his neck. "I am afraid I understand. You want me to go back to that Platter—that God-forsaken Platter, as I may say."

"Yes," said Meredith; "that is about it. I would go myself—"

"God bless you! I know you would!" burst in Joseph. "You'd go like winkin'. There's no one knows that better nor me, sir; and what I says is, 'like master, like man.' Game, sir—game it is! I'll go. I'm not the man to turn my back on a pal—a—a partner, sir, so to speak."

"You see," said Meredith, with the deep insight into men that made command so easy to him—"you see there is no one else. There is not another man in Africa who could do it."

"That's true, sir."

"And I think that Mr. Oscard will be looking for you."

"And he won't need to look long, sir. But I should like to see you safe on board the boat; then I'm ready to go."

"Right. We can both leave by Thursday's boat, and we'll get the captain to drop you and your men at Lopez. We can get things ready by then, I think."

"Easy, sir."

The question thus settled, there seemed to be no necessity to prolong the interview. But Joseph did not move. Meredith waited patiently.

"I'll go up, sir, to the Platter," said the servant, at length, "and I'll place myself under Mr. Oscard's orders; but before I go I want to give you notice of resignation. I resigns my partnership in this 'ere Simiacine at six months from to-day. It's a bit too hot, sir, that's the truth. It's all very well for gentlemen like yourself and Mr. Oscard, with fortunes and fine houses, and, as sayin' goes, a wife apiece waiting for you at home—it's all very well for you to go

about iu this blamed country with yer life in yer hand, and
not a tight grip at that. But for a poor soldier-man like
myself, what has smelt the regulation-powder all 'is life, and
hasn't got nothing to love and no gal waiting for him at
home—well, it isn't good enough. That's what I say, sir,
with respects."

He added the last two words by way of apology for having banged a very solid fist on the table.

Meredith smiled.

"So you've had enough of it?" he said.

"Enough ain't quite the word, sir. Why, I'm wore to a
shadow with the trouble and anxiety of getting you down
here."

"Fairly substantial shadow," commented Meredith.

"Maybe, sir. But I've had enough of money - makin'.
It's too dear at the price. And if you'll let an old servant
speak his mind, it ain't fit for you, this 'ere kind of work.
It's good enough for black scum and for chocolate-birds like
Durnovo; but this country's not built for honest white men
—least of all for born and bred gentlemen."

"Yes; that's all very well in theory, Joseph, and I'm much
obliged to you for thinking of me; but you must remember
that we live in an age when money sanctifies everything.
Your hands can't get dirty if there is money inside them."

Joseph laughed aloud.

"Ah, that's your way of speaking, sir, that's all. And
I'm glad to hear it. You have not spoken like that for
two months and more."

"No; it is only my experience of the world."

"Well, sir, talkin' of experience, I've had about enough,
as I tell you, and I beg to place my resignation in your
hands. I shall do the same by Mr. Oscard if I reach that
Platter, God willin', as the sayin' is."

"All right, Joseph."

Still there was something left to say. Joseph paused and
scratched the back of his neck pensively with one finger.

" Will you be writin' to Mr. Oscard, sir, for me to take ?"
" Yes."

" Then I should be obliged if you would mention the fact
that I would rather not be left alone with that blackguard
Durnovo, either up at the Platter or travelling down. That
man's got on my nerves, sir, and I'm mortal afraid of doing
him a injury. He's got a long neck—you've noticed that,
perhaps. There was a little Gourkha man up in Cabul
taught me a trick; it's as easy as killing a chicken, but you
want a man wi' a long neck—just such a neck as Durnovo's."

" But what harm has the man done you," asked Meredith,
" that you think so affectionately of his neck ?"

" No harm, sir, but we're just like two cats on a wall,
watchin' each other and hating each other like blue poison.
There's more villany at that man's back than you think for
—mark my words."

Joseph moved away towards the door.

" Do you *know* anything about him — anything shady ?"
cried Meredith after him.

" No, sir. I don't *know* anything. But I suspects a
whole boxful. One of these days I'll find him out, and
if I catch him fair there'll be a rough-and-tumble. It'll
be a pretty fight, sir, for them that's sittin' in the front
row."

Joseph rubbed his hands slowly together and departed,
leaving his master to begin a long letter to Guy Oscard.

And at the other end of the passage, in her room with
the door looked, Jocelyn Gordon was sobbing in a wild
burst of grief, because she had probably saved the life of
Jack Meredith, and in doing so had only succeeded in sending him away from her.

CHAPTER XXXIII

"Only an honest man doing his duty."

WHEN Jack Meredith said that there was not another
man in Africa who could make his way from Loango to the
Simiacine Plateau he spoke no more than the truth. There
were only four men in all the world who knew the way,
and two of them were isolated on the summit of a lost
mountain in the interior. Meredith himself was unfit for
the journey. There remained Joseph.

True, there were several natives who had made the journey, but they were as dumb and driven animals, fighting as
they were told, carrying what they were given to carry,
walking as many miles as they were considered able to walk.
They hired themselves out like animals, and as the beasts of
the field they did their work — patiently, without intelligence. Half of them did not know where they were going
— what they were doing; the other half did not care. So
much work so much wage was their terse creed. They
neither noted their surroundings nor measured distance. At
the end of their journey they settled down to a life of ease
and leisure, which was to last until necessity drove them to
work again. Such is the African. Many of them came
from distant countries, a few were Zanzibaris, and went
home made men.

If any doubt the inability of such men to steer a course
through the wood, let him remember that three months'
growth in an African forest will obliterate the track left by
the passage of an army. If any hold that men are not

created so dense and unambitious as has just been represented, let him look nearer home in our own merchant service. The able-bodied seaman goes to sea all his life, but
he never gets any nearer navigating the ship—and he a
white man.

In coming down to Loango Joseph had had the recently-
made track of Oscard's rescuing party to guide him day by
day. He knew that this was now completely overgrown.
The Simiacine Plateau was once more lost to all human
knowledge.

And up there — alone amid the clouds — Guy Oscard
was, as he himself tersely put it, "sticking to it." He had
stuck to it to such good effect that the supply of fresh
young Simiacine was daily increasing in bulk. Again,
Victor Durnovo seemed to have regained his better self.
He was like a full-blooded horse—tractable enough if kept
hard at work. He was a different man up on the Plateau
to what he was down at Loango. There are some men who
deteriorate in the wilds, while others are better, stronger,
finer creatures away from the luxury of civilization and the
softening influence of female society. Of these latter was
Victor Durnovo.

Of one thing Guy Oscard soon became aware—namely,
that no one could make the men work as could Durnovo.
He had merely to walk to the door of his tent to make
every picker on the little plateau bend over his tree with
renewed attention. And while above all was eagerness and
hurry, below, in the valley, this man's name insured peace.

The trees were now beginning to show the good result
of pruning and a regular irrigation. Never had the leaves
been so vigorous, never had the Simiacine-trees borne such
a bushy, luxuriant growth since the dim, dark days of the
Flood.

Oscard relapsed into his old hunting ways. Day after
day he tranquilly shouldered his rifle, and alone, or followed
by one attendant only, he disappeared into the forest, only

to emerge therefrom at sunset. What he saw there he never spoke of. Sure it was that he must have seen strange things, for no prying white man had set foot in these wilds before him; no book has ever been written of that country that lies around the Simiacine Plateau.

He was not the man to worry himself over uncertainties. He had an enormous faith in the natural toughness of an Englishman, and while he crawled breathlessly in the track of the forest monsters he hardly gave a thought to Jack Meredith. Meredith, he argued to himself, had always risen to the occasion: why should he not rise to this? He was not the sort of man to die from want of staying power, which, after all, is the cause of more deaths than we dream of. And when he had recovered he would either return or send back Joseph with a letter containing those suggestions of his which were really orders.

Of Millicent Chyne he thought more often, with a certain tranquil sense of a good time to come. In her also he placed a perfect faith. A poet has found out that, if one places faith in a man, it is probable that the man will rise to trustworthiness — of woman he says nothing. But of these things Guy Oscard knew little. He went his own tranquilly strong way, content to buy his own experience.

He was thinking of Millicent Chyne one misty morning while he walked slowly backward and forward before his tent. His knowledge of the country told him that the mist was nothing but the night's accumulation of moisture round the summit of the mountain; that down in the valleys it was clear, and that half an hour's sunshine would disperse all. He was waiting for this result when he heard a rifle-shot far away in the haze beneath him; and he knew that it was Joseph — probably making one of those marvellous long shots of his which roused a sudden sigh of envy in the heart of this mighty hunter whenever he witnessed them.

Oscard immediately went to his tent and came out with

his short-barrelled, evil-looking rifle on his arm. He fired both barrels in quick succession and waited, standing gravely on the edge of the Plateau. After a short silence two answering reports rose up through the mist to his straining ears.

He turned and found Victor Durnovo standing at his side.

"What is that?" asked the half-breed.

"It must be Joseph," answered Guy, "or Meredith. It can be nobody else."

"Let us hope that it is Meredith," said Durnovo, with a forced laugh, "but I doubt it."

Oscard looked down in his sallow, powerful face. He was not quick at such things, but at that moment he felt strangely certain that Victor Durnovo was hoping that Meredith was dead.

"I hope it isn't," he answered, and without another word he strode away down the little pathway from the summit into the clouds, loading his rifle as he went.

Durnovo and his men, working among the Simiacine bushes, heard from time to time a signal shot as the two Englishmen groped their way towards each other through the everlasting night of the African forest.

It was mid-day before the new-comers were espied making their way painfully up the slope, and Joseph's welcome was not so much in Durnovo's hand-shake, in Guy Oscard's silent approval, as in the row of grinning, good-natured black faces behind Durnovo's back.

That night laughter was heard in the men's camp for the first time for many weeks—nay, several months. According to the account that Joseph gave to his dusky admirers, he had been on terms of the closest familiarity with the wives and families of all who had such at Loango or on the Coast. He knew the mother of one, had met the sweetheart of another, and confessed that it was only due to the fact that he was not "a marryin' man" that he had not stayed at

Loango for the rest of his life. It was somewhat singular that he had nothing but good news to give.

Durnovo heard the clatter of tongues, and Guy Oscard, smoking his contemplative pipe in a camp-chair before his hut door, noticed that the sound did not seem very welcome.

Joseph's arrival with ten new men seemed to give a fresh zest to the work, and the carefully packed cases of Simiacine began to fill Oscard's tent to some inconvenience. Thus things went on for two tranquil weeks.

"First," Oscard had said, "let us get the crop in, and then we can arrange what is to be done about the future."

So the crop received due attention; but the two leaders of the men—he who led by fear and he who commanded by love—were watching each other.

One evening, when the work was done, Oscard's meditations were disturbed by the sound of angry voices behind the native camp. He turned naturally towards Durnovo's tent, and saw that he was absent. The voices rose and fell; there was a singular accompanying roar of sound which Oscard never remembered having heard before. It was the protesting voice of a mass of men—and there is no sound like it — none so disquieting. Oscard listened attentively, and suddenly he was thrown upon his feet by a pistol-shot.

At the same moment Joseph emerged from behind the tents, dragging some one by the collar. The victim of Joseph's violence was off his feet, but still struggling and kicking.

Guy Oscard saw the flash of a second shot, apparently within a few inches of Joseph's face; but he came on, dragging the man with him, whom from his clothing Oscard saw to be Durnovo.

Joseph was spitting out wadding and burnt powder.

"Shoot *me*, would yer—yer damned skulking chocolate-bird? I'll teach you! I'll twist that. brown neck of yours."

He shook him as a terrier shakes a rat, and seemed to shake things off him—among others a revolver which described a circle in the air, and fell heavily on the ground, where the concussion discharged a cartridge.

"'Ere, sir," cried Joseph, literally throwing Durnovo down on the ground at Oscard's feet, "that man has just shot one o' them poor niggers, so 'elp me God!"

Durnovo rose slowly to his feet, as if the shaking had disturbed his faculties.

"And the man hadn't done 'im no harm at all. He's got a grudge against him. I've seen that this last week and more. It's a man as was kinder fond o' me, and we understood each other's lingo. That's it—he was afraid of my 'earing things that mightn't be wholesome for me to know. The man hadn't done no harm. And Durnovo comes up and begins abusing 'im, and then he strikes 'im, and he out with his revolver and shoots 'im down."

Durnovo gave an ugly laugh. He had readjusted his disordered dress and was brushing the dirt from his knees.

"Oh, don't make a fool of yourself," he said, in a hissing voice; "you don't understand these natives at all. The man raised his hand to me. He would have killed me if he had had the chance. Shooting was the only thing left to do. You can only hold these men by fear. They expect it."

"Of course they expect it," shouted Joseph in his face; "of course they expect it, Mr. Durnovo."

"Why?"

"Because they're *slaves*. Think I don't know that?"

He turned to Oscard.

"This man, Mr. Oscard," he said, "is a slave-owner. Them forty that joined at Msala was slaves. He's shot two of 'em now: this is his second. And what does he care? —they're his slaves. Oh, shame on yer!" turning again to Durnovo; "I wonder God lets yer stand there. I can only think that He doesn't want to dirty His hand by strikin' yer down."

Oscard had taken his pipe from his lips. He looked bigger, somehow, than ever. His brown face was turning to an ashen color, and there was a dull, steel-like gleam in his blue eyes. The terrible, slow - kindling anger of this Northerner made Durnovo catch his breath. It was so different from the sudden passion of his own countrymen.

"Is this true?" he asked.

"It's a lie, of course," answered Durnovo, with a shrug of the shoulders. He moved away as if he were going to his tent, but Oscard's arm reached out. His large brown hand fell heavily on the half-breed's shoulder.

"Stay," he said; "we are going to get to the bottom of this."

"Good," muttered Joseph, rubbing his hands slowly together; "this is prime."

"Go on," said Oscard to him.

"Where's the wages you and Mr. Meredith has paid him for those forty men?" pursued Joseph. "Where's the advance you made him for those men at Msala? Not one ha'penny of it have they fingered. And why? Cos they're slaves! Fifteen months at fifty pounds—let them as can reckon tot it up for theirselves. That's his first swindle— and there's others, sir! Oh, there's more behind. That man's just a stinkin' hot-bed o' crime. But this 'ere slave-owning is enough to settle his hash, I take it."

"Let us have these men here—we will hear what they have to say," said Oscard, in the same dull tone that frightened Victor Durnovo.

"Not you!" he went on, laying his hand on Durnovo's shoulder again; "Joseph will fetch them, thank you."

So the forty—or the thirty-seven survivors, for one had died on the journey up and two had been murdered—were brought. They were peaceful, timorous men, whose manhood seemed to have been crushed out of them; and slowly,

word by word, their grim story was got out of them.
Joseph knew a little of their language, and one of the head
fighting men knew a little more, and spoke a dialect known
to Oscard. They were slaves, they said at once, but only
on Oscard's promise that Durnovo should not be allowed to
shoot them. They had been brought from the north by a
victorious chief who in turn had handed them over to Victor
Durnovo in payment of an outstanding debt for ammunition supplied.

The great African moon rose in the heavens and shone
her yellow light upon this group of men. Overhead all was
peace; on earth there was no peace. And yet it was one
of Heaven's laws that Victor Durnovo had broken.

Guy Oscard went patiently through to the end of it. He
found out all that there was to find; and he found out something which surprised him. No one seemed to be horror-
struck. The free men stood stolidly looking on, as did the
slaves. And this was Africa—the heart of Africa, where,
as Victor Durnovo said, no one knows what is going on.
Oscard knew that he could apply no law to Victor Durnovo
except the great law of humanity. There was nothing to
be done; for one individual may not execute the laws of
humanity. All were assembled before him—the whole
of the great Simiacine Expedition except the leader,
whose influence lay over one and all only second to his
presence.

"I leave this place at sunrise to-morrow," said Guy Oscard to them all. "I never want to see it again. I will
not touch one penny of the money that has been made. I
speak for Mr. Meredith and myself—"

"Likewise me—damn it!" put in Joseph.

"I speak as Mr. Meredith himself would have spoken.
There is the Simiacine—you can have it. I won't touch it.
And now who is going with me—who leaves with me to-
morrow morning?"

He moved away from Durnovo.

"And who stays with me?" cried the half-breed, "to share and share alike in the Simiacine?"

Joseph followed Oscard, and with him a certain number of the blacks, but some stayed. Some went over to Durnovo and stood beside him. The slaves spoke among themselves, and then they all went over to Durnovo.

So that which the placid moon shone down upon was the break-up of the great Simiacine scheme. Victor Durnovo had not come off so badly. He had the larger half of the men by his side. He had all the finest crop the trees had yet yielded—but he had yet to reckon with high Heaven.

CHAPTER XXXIV

AMONG THORNS

"We shut our hearts up nowadays,
Like some old music-box that plays
Unfashionable airs."

SIR JOHN MEREDITH was sitting stiffly in a straight-backed chair by his library fire. In his young days men didn't loll in deep chairs, with their knees higher than their heads. There were no such chairs in this library, just as there was no afternoon tea except for ladies. Sir John Meredith was distressed to observe a great many signs of the degeneration of manhood—which he attributed to the indulgence in afternoon tea. Sir John had lately noticed another degeneration, namely, in the quality of the London gas. So serious was this falling off that he had taken to a lamp in the evening, which lamp stood on the table at his elbow.

Some months earlier—that is to say, about six months after Jack's departure—Sir John had called casually upon an optician. He stood upright by the counter, and frowned

down on a mild-looking man who wore the strongest spec
tacles made, as if in advertisement of his own wares.

"They tell me," he said, " that you opticians make glasses
now which are calculated to save the sight in old age."

"Yes, sir," replied the optician, with wriggling white
fingers. "We make a special study of that. We endeavor
to save the sight—to store it up, as it were, in—a middle
life, for use in old age. You see, sir, the pupil of the eye—"

Sir John held up a warning hand.

"The pupil of the eye is your business, as I understand
from the sign above your shop—at all events, it is not mine,"
he said. "Just give me some glasses to suit my sight, and
don't worry me with the pupil of the eye."

He turned towards the door, threw back his shoulders,
and waited.

"Spectacles, sir?" inquired the man, meekly.

"Spectacles, sir?" cried Sir John. "No, sir. Spectacles
be damned. I want a pair of eye-glasses."

And these eye-glasses were affixed to the bridge of Sir
John Meredith's nose, as he sat rather stiffly in the straight-
backed chair.

He was reading a scientific book which society had been
pleased to read, mark, and learn, without inwardly digest-
ing, as is the way of society with books. Sir John read a
good deal—he had read more lately, perhaps, since enter-
tainments and evening parties had fallen off so lamentably
—and he made a point of keeping up with the mental
progress of the age.

His eyebrows were drawn down, as if the process of stor-
ing up eyesight for his old age was somewhat laborious.
At times he turned and glanced over his shoulder impatiently at the lamp.

The room was very still in its solid, old-fashioned luxury.
Although it was June, a small wood-fire burned in the grate,
and the hiss of a piece of damp bark was the only sound
within the four walls. From without, through the thick

curtains, came at intervals the rumble of distant wheels. But it was just between times, and the fashionable world was at its dinner. Sir John had finished his, not because he dined earlier than the rest of the world—he could not have done that—but because a man dining by himself, with a butler and a footman to wait upon him, does not take very long over his meals.

He was in full evening dress, of course, built up by his tailor, bewigged, perfumed, and cunningly aided by toilet-table deceptions.

At times his weary old eyes wandered from the printed page to the smouldering fire, where a whole volume seemed to be written—it took so long to read. Then he would pull himself together, glance at the lamp, readjust the eye-glasses, and plunge resolutely into the book. He did not always read scientific books. He had a taste for travel and adventure—the Arctic regions, Asia, Siberia, and Africa—but Africa was all locked away in a lower drawer of the writing-table. He did not care for the servants to meddle with his books, he told himself. He did not tell anybody that he did not care to let the servants see him reading his books of travel in Africa.

There was nothing dismal or lonely about this old man, sitting in evening dress in a high-backed chair, stiffly reading a scientific book of the modern, cheap science tenor—not written for scientists, but to step in when the brain is weary of novels and afraid of communing with itself. Oh no! A gentleman need never be dull. He has his necessary occupations. If he is a man of intellect he need never be idle. It is an occupation to keep up with the times.

Sometimes after dinner, while drinking his perfectly-made black coffee, Sir John would idly turn over the invitation cards on the mantel-piece—the carriage was always in readiness—but of late the invitations had not proved very tempting. There was no doubt that society was not what it used to be. The summer was not what it used to be,

either. The evenings were so confoundedly cold. So he
often stayed at home and read a book.

He paused in the midst of a scientific definition, and
looked up with listening eyes. He had got into the way
of listening to the passing wheels. Lady Cantourne sometimes called for him on her way to a festivity, but it was
not that.

The wheels he heard had stopped—perhaps it was Lady
Cantourne. But he did not think so. She drove behind a
pair, and this was not a pair. It was wonderful how well he
could detect the difference, considering the age of his ears.

A few minutes later the butler silently threw open the
door, and Jack stood in the threshold. Sir John Meredith's
son had been given back to him from the gates of death.

The son, like the father, was in immaculate evening dress.
There was a very subtle cynicism in the thought of turning
aside on such a return as this to dress—to tie a careful
white tie and brush imperceptibly ruffled hair.

There was a little pause, and the two tall men stood,
half-bowing with a marvellous similarity of attitude, gazing
steadily into each other's eyes. And one cannot help wondering whether it was a mere accident that Jack Meredith
stood motionless on the threshold until his father said,

"Come in."

"Thomson," he continued to the butler, with that pride
of keeping up before all the world which was his, "bring
up coffee. You will take coffee?" to his son while they
shook hands.

"Thanks, yes."

The butler closed the door behind him. Sir John was
holding on to the back of his high chair in rather a con-
strained way—almost as if he were suffering pain. They
looked at each other again, and there was a resemblance in
the very manner of raising the eyelid. There was a stronger resemblance in the grim, waiting silence which neither
of them would break.

At last Jack spoke, approaching the fire and looking into it.

"You must excuse my taking you by surprise at this—unusual hour." He turned; saw the lamp, the book, and the eye-glasses—more especially the eye-glasses, which seemed to break the train of his thoughts. "I only landed at Liverpool this afternoon," he went on, with hopeless politeness. "I did not trouble you with a telegram, knowing that you object to them."

The old man bowed gravely.

"I am always glad to see you," he said, suavely. "Will you not sit down?"

And they had begun wrong. It is probable that neither of them had intended this. Both had probably dreamed of a very different meeting. But both alike had counted without that stubborn pride which will rise up at the wrong time and in the wrong place—the pride which Jack Meredith had inherited by blood and teaching from his father.

"I suppose you have dined," said Sir John, when they were seated, "or may I offer you something?"

"Thanks, I dined on the way up—in a twilit refreshment-room, with one waiter and a number of attendant black-beetles."

Things were going worse and worse.

Sir John smiled, and he was still smiling when the man brought in coffee.

"Yes," he said, conversationally, "for speed combined with discomfort I suppose we can hold up heads against any country. Seeing that you are dressed, I supposed that you had dined in town."

"No. I drove straight to my rooms, and kept the cab while I dressed."

What an important matter this dressing seemed to be! And there were fifteen months behind it—fifteen months which had aged one of them and sobered the other.

Jack was sitting forward in his chair with his immaculate

dress-shoes on the fender—his knees apart, his elbows resting on them, his eyes still fixed on the fire. Sir John looked keenly at him beneath his frowning, lashless lids. He saw the few gray hairs over Jack's ears, the suggested wrinkles, the drawn lines about his mouth.

"You have been ill?" he said.

Joseph's letter was locked away in the top drawer of his writing-table.

"Yes, I had rather a bad time — a serious illness. My man nursed me through it, however, with marked success; and —the Gordons, with whom I was staying, were very kind."

"I had the pleasure of meeting Miss Gordon."

Jack's face was steady—suavely impenetrable.

Sir John moved a little, and set his empty cup upon the table.

"A charming girl," he added.

"Yes."

There was a little pause.

"You are fortunate in that man of yours," Sir John said. "A first-class man."

"Yes—he saved my life."

Sir John blinked, and for the first time his fingers went to his mouth, as if his lips had suddenly got beyond his control.

"If I may suggest it," he said, rather indistinctly, "I think it would be well if we signified our appreciation of his devotion in some substantial way. We might well do something between us."

He paused and threw back his shoulders.

"I should like to give him some substantial token of my —gratitude."

Sir John was nothing if not just.

"Thank you," answered Jack, quietly. He turned his head a little, and glanced, not at his father, but in his direction. "He will appreciate it, I know."

"I should like to see him to-morrow."

Jack winced, as if he had made a mistake.

"He is not in England," he explained. "I left him behind me in Africa. He has gone back to the Simiacine Plateau."

The old man's face dropped rather piteously.

"I am sorry," he said, with one of the sudden relapses into old age that Lady Cantourne dreaded. "I may not have a chance of seeing him to thank him personally. A good servant is so rare nowadays. These modern democrats seem to think that it is a nobler thing to be a bad servant than a good one. As if we were not all servants!"

He was thirsting for details. There were a thousand questions in his heart, but not one on his lips.

"Will you have the kindness to remember my desire," he went on, suavely, "when you are settling up with your man?"

"Thank you," replied Jack, "I am much obliged to you."

"And in the meantime, as you are without a servant, you may as well make use of mine. One of my men—Henry—who is too stupid to get into mischief—a great recommendation by-the-way—understands his business. I will ring and have him sent over to your rooms at once."

He did so, and they sat in silence until the butler had come and gone.

"We have been very successful with the Simiacine—our scheme," said Jack, suddenly.

"Ah!"

"I have brought home a consignment valued at seventy thousand pounds."

Sir John's face never changed.

"And," he asked, with veiled sarcasm, "do you carry out the—er—commercial part of the scheme?"

"I shall begin to arrange for the sale of the consignment to-morrow. I shall have no difficulty—at least, I anticipate none. Yes, I do the commercial part—as well as the other.

I held the Plateau against two thousand natives for three months, with fifty-five men. But I do the commercial part as well."

As he was looking into the fire still, Sir John stole a long comprehensive glance at his son's face. His old eyes lighted up with pride and something else — possibly love. The clock on the mantel-piece struck eleven. Jack looked at it thoughtfully, then he rose.

"I must not keep you any longer," he said, somewhat stiffly.

Sir John rose also.

"I dare say you are tired; you need rest. In some ways you look stronger, in others you look fagged and pulled down."

"It is the result of my illness," said Jack. "I am really quite strong."

He paused, standing on the hearth-rug, then suddenly he held out his hand.

"Good-night," he said.

"Good-night."

Sir John allowed him to go to the door, to touch the handle, before he spoke.

"Then—" he said, and Jack paused. "Then we are no further on?"

"In what way?"

"In respect to the matter over which we unfortunately disagreed before you went away?"

Jack turned, with his hand on the door.

"I have not changed my mind in any respect," he said, gently. "Perhaps you are inclined to take my altered circumstances into consideration — to modify your views."

"I am getting rather old for modification," answered Sir John, suavely.

"And you see no reason for altering your decision?"

"None."

" Then I am afraid we are no further on," he paused.
"Good-night," he added, gently, as he opened the door.
"Good-night."

CHAPTER XXXV

ENGAGED

"Well, there's the game. I throw the stakes."

LADY CANTOURNE was sitting alone in her drawing-room,
and the expression of her usually bright and smiling face
betokened considerable perturbation.

Truth to tell, there were not many things in life that had
power to frighten her ladyship very much. Hers had been
a prosperous life as prosperity is reckoned. She had married a rich man who had retained his riches while he lived
and had left them to her when he died. And that was all
the world knew of Lady Cantourne. Like the majority of
us, she presented her character and not herself to her neighbors; and these held, as neighbors do, that the cheery,
capable little woman of the world whom they met everywhere was Lady Cantourne. Circumstances alter us less
than we think. If we are of a gay temperament—gay we
shall be through all. If sombre, no happiness can drive
that sombreness away. Lady Cantourne was meant for
happiness and a joyous motherhood. She had had neither;
but she went on being "meant" until the end—that is to
say, she was still cheery and capable. She had thrown an
open letter on the little table at her side—a letter from
Jack Meredith announcing his return to England, and his
natural desire to call and pay his respects in the course of
the afternoon.

"So," she had said before she laid the letter aside, "he
is home again—and he means to carry it through?"

Then she had settled down to think in her own comfortable chair (for if one may not be happy, comfort is at all
events within reach of some of us), and the troubled look
had supervened.

Each of our lives is like a book with one strong character
moving through its pages. The strong character in Lady
Cantourne's book had been Sir John Meredith. Her whole
life seemed to have been spent on the outskirts of his—
watching it. And what she had seen had not been con-
ducive to her own happiness.

She knew that the note she had just received meant a
great deal to Sir John Meredith. It meant that Jack had
come home with the full intention of fulfilling his engagement to Millicent Chyne. At first she had rather resented
Sir John's outspoken objection to her niece as his son's wife,
but during the last months she had gradually come round
to his way of thinking; not, perhaps, for the first time in
her life. She had watched Millicent. She had studied her
own niece dispassionately, as much from Sir John Meredith's point of view as was possible under the circumstances.
And she had made several discoveries. The first of these
had been precisely that discovery which one would expect
from a woman—namely, the state of Millicent's own feelings.

Lady Cantourne had known for the last twelve months—
almost as long as Sir John Meredith had known—that Millicent loved Jack. Upon this knowledge came the humiliation—the degradation—of one flirtation after another; and
not even after, but interlaced. Guy Oscard in particular,
and others in a minor degree had passed that way. It was
a shameless record of that which might have been good in
a man prostituted and trampled under foot by the vanity
of a woman. Lady Cantourne was of the world worldly;
and because of that, because the finest material has a seamy
side, and the highest walks in life have the hardiest weeds,
she knew what love should be. Here was a love—it may

be modern, advanced, *chic*, *fin-de-siècle*, up to date, or anything the coming generation may choose to call it—but it was eminently cheap and ephemeral because it could not make a little sacrifice of vanity. For the sake of the man she loved—mark that!—not only the man to whom she was engaged, but whom she loved—Millicent Chyne could not forbear pandering to her own vanity by the sacrifice of her own modesty and purity of thought. There was the sting for Lady Cantourne.

She was tolerant and eminently wise, this old lady who had made one huge mistake long ago, and she knew that the danger, the harm, the low vulgarity lay in the little fact that Millicent Chyne loved Jack Meredith according to her lights.

While she still sat there the bell rang, and quite suddenly she chased away the troubled look from her eyes, leaving there the keen, kindly gaze to which the world of London society was well accustomed. When Jack Meredith came into the room she rose to greet him with a smile of welcome.

"Before I shake hands," she said, "tell me if you have been to see your father."

"I went last night — almost straight from the station. The first person I spoke to in London, except a cabman."

So she shook hands.

"You know," she said, without looking at him—indeed, carefully avoiding doing so—"life is too short to quarrel with one's father. At least, it may prove too short to make it up again—that is the danger."

She sat down with a graceful swing of her silken skirt which was habitual with her—the remnant of a past day.

Jack Meredith winced. He had seen a difference in his father, and Lady Cantourne was corroborating it.

"The quarrel was not mine," he said. "I admit that I ought to have known him better. I ought to have spoken to him before asking Millicent. It was a mistake."

Lady Cantourne looked up suddenly.

" What was a mistake ?"

" Not asking his—opinion first."

She turned to the table where his letter lay, and fingered the paper pensively.

" I thought, perhaps, that you had found that the other was a mistake—the engagement."

" No," he answered.

Lady Cantourne's face betrayed nothing. There was no sigh, of relief or disappointment. She merely looked at the clock.

" Millicent will be in presently," she said; " she is out riding."

She did not think it necessary to add that her niece was riding with a very youthful officer in the Guards. Lady Cantourne never made mischief from a sense of duty, or any mistaken motive of that sort. Some people argue that there is very little that is worth keeping secret; to which one may reply that there is still less worth disclosing.

They talked of other things—of his life in Africa, of his success with the Simiacine, of which discovery the news-papers were not yet weary—until the bell was heard in the basement, and thereafter Millicent's voice in the hall.

Lady Cantourne rose deliberately and went down-stairs to tell her niece that he was in the drawing-room, leaving him there, waiting, alone.

Presently the door opened and Millicent hurried in. She threw her gloves and whip—anywhere—on the floor, and ran to him.

" Oh, Jack !" she cried.

It was very prettily done. In its way it was a poem. But while his arms were still round her she looked towards the window, wondering whether he had seen her ride up to the door accompanied by the very youthful officer in the Guards.

" And, Jack—do you know," she went on, " all the newspapers have been full of you. You are quite a celebrity. And are you really as rich as they say?"

Jack Meredith was conscious of a very slight check—it was not exactly a jar. His feeling was rather that of a man who thinks that he is swimming in deep water, and finds suddenly that he can touch the bottom.

"I think I can safely say that I am not," he answered.

And it was from that eminently practical point that they departed into the future—arranging that same, and filling up its blanks with all the wisdom of lovers and the rest of us.

Lady Cantourne left them there for nearly an hour, in which space of time she probably reflected they could build up as rosy a future as was good for them to contemplate. Then she returned to the drawing-room, followed by a full-sized footman bearing tea.

She was too discreet a woman—too deeply versed in the sudden changes of the human mind and heart—to say anything until one of them should give her a distinct lead. They were not shy and awkward children. Perhaps she reflected that the generation to which they belonged is not one heavily handicapped by too subtle a delicacy of feeling.

Jack Meredith gave her the lead before long.

"Millicent," he said, without a vestige of embarrassment, "has consented to be openly engaged now."

Lady Cantourne nodded comprehensively.

"I think she is very wise," she said.

There was a little pause.

"I *know* she is very wise," she added, turning and laying her hand on Jack's arm. The two phrases had quite a different meaning. "She will have a good husband."

"So you can tell *everybody* now," chimed in Millicent in her silvery way. She was blushing and looking very pretty with her hair blown about her ears by her last canter with the youthful officer, who was at that moment riding pensively home with a bunch of violets in his coat which had not been there when he started from the stable.

She had found out casually from Jack that Guy Oscard was exiled vaguely to the middle of Africa for an indefinite period. The rest—the youthful officer and the others—did not give her much anxiety. They, she argued to herself, had nothing to bring against her. They may have *thought* things—but who can prevent people from thinking things? Besides, " I thought " is always a poor position.

There were, it was true, a good many men whom she would rather not tell herself. But this difficulty was obviated by requesting Lady Cantourne to tell everybody. Everybody would tell everybody else, and would, of course, ask if these particular persons in question had been told; if not, they would have to be told at once. Indeed, there would be quite a competition to relieve Millicent of her little difficulty. Besides, she could not marry more than one person. Besides—besides—besides—the last word of Millicent and her kind.

Lady Cantourne was not very communicative during that refined little tea à *trois*, but she listened smilingly to Jack's optimistic views and Millicent's somewhat valueless comments.

" I am certain," said Millicent, at length boldly attacking the question that was in all their minds, " that Sir John will be all right now. Of course, it is only natural that he should not like Jack to—to get engaged yet. Especially before, when it would have made a difference to him—in money I mean. But now that Jack is independent—you know, auntie, that Jack is richer than Sir John—is it not nice ?"

" Very," answered Lady Cantourne, in a voice rather suggestive of humoring a child's admiration of a new toy; " very nice indeed."

" And all so quickly !" pursued Millicent. " Only a few months — not two years, you know. Of course, at first the time went horribly slowly; but afterwards, when one got accustomed to it, life became tolerable. You did not expect me to sit and mope all day, did you, Jack?"

"No, of course not," replied Jack; and quite suddenly, as in a flash, he saw his former self, and wondered vaguely whether he would get back to that self.

Lady Cantourne was rather thoughtful at that moment. She could not help coming back and back to Sir John.

"Of course," she said to Jack, "we must let your father know at once. The news must not reach him from an outside source."

Jack nodded.

"If it did," he said, "I do not think the 'outside source' would get much satisfaction out of him."

"Probably not; but I was not thinking of the 'outside source' or the outside effect. I was thinking of his feelings," replied Lady Cantourne, rather sharply. She had lately fallen into the habit of not sparing Millicent very much; and that young lady, bright and sweet and good-natured, had not failed to notice it. Indeed, she had spoken of it to several people — to partners at dances and others. She attributed it to approaching old age.

"1 will write and tell him," said Jack, quietly.

Lady Cantourne raised her eyebrows slightly, but made no spoken comment.

"I think," she said, after a little pause, "that Millicent ought to write, too."

Millicent shuddered prettily. She was dimly conscious that her handwriting—of an exaggerated size, executed with a special broad-pointed pen purchasable in only one shop in Regent Street—was not quite likely to meet with his approval. A letter written thus—two words to a line—on note-paper that would have been vulgar had it not been so very novel, was sure to incur prejudice before it was fully unfolded by a stuffy, old-fashioned person.

"I will try," she said; "but you know, auntie dear, I *cannot* write a long explanatory letter. There never seems

to be time, does there? Besides, I am afraid Sir John dis-
approves of me. I don't know why; I'm sure I have tried"
—which was perfectly true.

Even funerals and lovers must bow to meal-times, and
Jack Meredith was not the man to outstay his welcome.
He saw Lady Cantourne glance at the clock. Clever
as she was, she could not do it without being seen by
him.

So he took his leave, and Millicent went to the head of
the stairs with him.

He refused the pressing invitation of a hansom-cabman,
and proceeded to walk leisurely home to his rooms. Perhaps he was wondering why his heart was not brimming
over with joy. The human heart has a singular way of seeing further than its astute friend and coadjutor, the brain.
It sometimes refuses to be filled with glee when outward
circumstances most distinctly demand that state. And at
other times, when outward things are strong, not to say
opaque, the heart is joyful, and we know not why.

Jack Meredith knew that he was the luckiest man in London. He was rich, in good health, and he was engaged to
be married to Millicent Chyne, the acknowledged belle of
his circle. She had in no way changed. She was just as
pretty, as fascinating, as gay as ever; and something told
him that she loved him—something which had not been
there before he went away, something that had come when
the overweening vanity of youth went. And it was just
this knowledge to which he clung with a nervous mental
grip. He did not feel elated as he should; he was aware
of that, and he could not account for it. But Millicent
loved him, so it must be all right. He had always cared
for Millicent. Everything had been done in order that he
might marry her—the quarrel with his father, the finding
of the Simiacine, the determination to get well which had
saved his life—all this so that he might marry Millicent.
And now he was going to marry her, and it must be all

right. Perhaps, as men get older, the effervescent elation of youth leaves them; but they are none the less happy. That must be it.

CHAPTER XXXVI

NO COMPROMISE

"Where he fixed his heart he set his hand
To do the thing he willed."

"MY DEAR SIR JOHN,—It is useless my pretending to ignore your views respecting Jack's marriage to Millicent; and I therefore take up my pen with regret to inform you that the two young people have now decided to make public their engagement. Moreover, I imagine it is their intention to get married very soon. You and I have been friends through a longer spell of years than many lives and most friendships extend, and at the risk of being considered inconsequent I must pause to thank you—well—to thank you for having been so true a friend to me all through my life. If that life were given to me to begin again, I should like to retrace the years back to a point when— little more than a child—I yielded to influence and made a great mistake. I should like to begin my life over again from there. When you first signified your disapproval of Millicent as a wife for Jack, I confess I was a little nettled; but on the strength of the friendship to which I have referred I must ask you to believe that never from the moment that I learned your opinion have I by thought or action gone counter to it. This marriage is none of my doing. Jack is too good for her—I see that now. You are wiser than I—you always have been. If any word of mine can alleviate your distress at this unwelcome event, let it be that I am certain that Millicent has the right feeling for your boy; and from this knowledge I cannot but gather great hopes. All may yet come to your satisfaction. Millicent is young, and perhaps a little volatile, but Jack inherits your strength of character; he may mould her to better things than either you or I dream of. I hope sincerely that it may be so. If I have appeared passive in this matter it is not because I have been indifferent; but I know that my yea or nay could carry no weight.

"Your old friend,
"CAROLINE CANTOURNE."

This letter reached Sir John Meredith while he was waiting for the announcement that dinner was ready. The announcement arrived immediately afterwards, but he did not go down to dinner until he had read the letter. He fumbled for his newly-purchased eye-glasses, because Lady Cantourne's handwriting was somewhat thin and spidery, as behooved a lady of standing; also the gas was so damned bad. He used this expression somewhat freely, and usually put a "Sir" after it as his father had done before him.

His eyes grew rather fierce as he read; then they suddenly softened, and he threw back his shoulders as he had done a thousand times on the threshold of Lady Cantourne's drawing-room. He read the whole letter very carefully and gravely, as if all that the writer had to say was worthy of his most respectful attention. Then he folded the paper and placed it in the breast-pocket of his coat. He looked a little bowed and strangely old as he stood for a moment on the hearth-rug thinking. It was his practice to stand thus on the hearth-rug from the time that he entered the drawing-room, dressed, until the announcement of dinner; and the cook far below in the basement was conscious of the attitude of the master as the pointer of the clock approached the hour.

Of late Sir John had felt a singular desire to sit down whenever opportunity should offer; but he had always been found standing on the hearth-rug by the butler, and, hard old aristocrat that he was, he would not yield to the somewhat angular blandishments of the stiff-backed chair.

He stood for a few moments with his back to the smouldering fire, and, being quite alone, he perhaps forgot to stiffen his neck; for his head drooped, his lips were unsteady. He was a very old man.

A few minutes later, when he strode into the dining-room where butler and footman awaited him, he was erect, imperturbable, impenetrable.

At dinner it was evident that his keen brain was hard at

work. He forgot one or two of the formalities which were religiously observed at that solitary table. He hastened over his wine, and then he went to the library. There he wrote a telegram, slowly, in his firm, ornamental hand-writing.

It was addressed to "Gordon, Loango," and the gist of it was—"Wire whereabouts of Oscard—when he may be expected home."

The footman was despatched in a hansom-cab, with instructions to take the telegram to the head office of the Submarine Telegraph Company, and there to arrange pre-payment of the reply.

"I rather expect Mr. Meredith," said Sir John to the butler, who was trimming the library lamp while the foot-man received his instructions. "Do not bring coffee until he comes."

And Sir John was right. At half-past eight Jack arrived. Sir John was awaiting him in the library, grimly sitting in his high-backed chair, as carefully dressed as for a great reception.

He rose when his son entered the room, and they shook hands. There was a certain air of concentration about both, as if they each intended to say more than they had ever said before. The coffee was duly brought. This was a revival of an old custom. In by-gone days Jack had frequently come in thus, and they had taken coffee before going together in Sir John's carriage to one of the great social functions at which their presence was almost a necessity. Jack had always poured out the coffee—to-night he did not offer to do so.

"I came," he said, suddenly, "to give you a piece of news which I am afraid will not be very welcome."

Sir John bowed his head gravely.

"You need not temper it," he said, "to me."

"Millicent and I have decided to make our engagement known," retorted Jack at once.

Sir John bowed again. To any one but his son his suave acquiescence would have been maddening.

"I should have liked," continued Jack, "to have done it with your consent."

Sir John winced. He sat upright in his chair and threw back his shoulders. If Jack intended to continue in this way, there would be difficulties to face. Father and son were equally determined. Jack had proved too cunning a pupil. The old aristocrat's own lessons were being turned against him, and the younger man has, as it were, the light of the future shining upon his game in such a case as this, while the elder plays in the gathering gloom.

"You know," said Sir John, gravely, "that I am not much given to altering my opinions. I do not say that they are of any value; but, such as they are, I usually hold to them. When you did me the honor of mentioning this matter to me last year, I gave you my opinion."

"And it has in no way altered?"

"In no way. I have found no reason to alter it."

"Can you modify it?" asked Jack, gently.

"No."

"Not in any degree?"

Jack drew a deep breath.

"No."

He emitted the breath slowly, making an effort so that it did not take the form of a sigh.

"Will you, at all events, give me your reasons?" he asked. "I am not a child."

Sir John fumbled at his lips—he glanced sharply at his son.

"I think," he said, "that it would be advisable not to ask them."

"I should like to know why you object to my marrying Millicent," persisted Jack.

"Simply because I know a bad woman when I see her," retorted Sir John, deliberately.

Jack raised his eyebrows. He glanced towards the door, as if contemplating leaving the room without further ado. But he sat quite still. It was wonderful how little it hurt him. It was more—it was significant. Sir John, who was watching, saw the glance and guessed the meaning of it. An iron self-control had been the first thing he had taught Jack—years before, when he was in his first knickerbockers. The lesson had not been forgotten.

"I am sorry you have said that," said the son.

"Just," continued the father, "as I know a good one."

He paused, and they were both thinking of the same woman—Jocelyn Gordon.

Sir John had said his say about Millicent Chyne; and his son knew that that was the last word. She was a bad woman. From that point he would never move.

"I think," said Jack, "that it is useless discussing that point any longer."

"Quite. When do you intend getting married?"

"As soon as possible."

"A mere question for the dress-maker?" suggested Sir John, suavely.

"Yes."

Sir John nodded gravely.

"Well," he said, "you are, as you say, no longer a child: perhaps I forget that sometimes. If I do, I must ask you to forgive me. I will not attempt to dissuade you. You probably know your own affairs best—"

He paused, drawing his two hands slowly back on his knees, looking into the fire as if his life were written there.

"At all events," he continued, "it has the initial recommendation of a good motive. I imagine it is what is called a love - match. I don't know much about such matters. Your mother, my lamented wife, was an excellent woman—too excellent, I take it, to be able to inspire the feeling in a mere human being—perhaps the angels . . . she never inspired it in me, at all events. My own life has not been quite a success within this room; outside it has been brilliant, active, full of excitement. Engineers know of machines which will stay upright so long as the pace is kept up; some of us are like that. I am not complaining. I have had no worse a time than my neighbors, except that it has lasted longer."

He leaned back suddenly in his chair with a strange little laugh. Jack was leaning forward, listening with that respect which he always accorded to his father.

"I imagine," went on Sir John, "that the novelists and poets are not very far wrong. It seems that there is such a thing as a humdrum happiness in marriage. I have seen quite elderly people who seem still to take pleasure in each other's society. With the example of my own life before me, I wanted yours to be different. My motive was not entirely bad. But perhaps you know your own affairs best. What money have you?"

Jack moved uneasily in his chair.

"I have completed the sale of the last consignment of Simiacine," he began, categorically. "The demand for it has increased. We have now sold two hundred thousand pounds' worth in England and America. My share is about sixty thousand pounds. I have invested most of that sum, and my present income is a little over two thousand a year."

Sir John nodded gravely.

"I congratulate you," he said; "you have done wonderfully well. It is satisfactory in one way, in that it shows that if a gentleman chooses to go into these commercial affairs he can do as well as the *bourgeoisie*. It leads one to believe that English gentlemen are not degenerating so rapidly as I am told the evening Radical newspapers demonstrate for the trifling consideration of one half-penny. But"—he paused with an expressive gesture of the hand—"I should have preferred that this interesting truth had been proved by the son of some one else."

"I think," replied Jack, "that our speculation hardly

comes under the category of commerce. It was not money that was at risk, but our own lives."

Sir John's eyes hardened.

"Adventure," he suggested, rather indistinctly, "travel and adventure. There is a class of men one meets frequently who do a little exploring and a great deal of talking. *Faute de mieux*, they do not hesitate to interest one in the special pill to which they resort when indisposed, and they are not above advertising a soap. You are not going to write a book, I trust?"

"No. It would hardly serve our purpose to write a book."

"In what way?" inquired Sir John.

"Our purpose is to conceal the whereabouts of the Simiacine Plateau."

"But you are not going back there?" exclaimed Sir John, unguardedly.

"We certainly do not intend to abandon it."

Sir John leaned forward again, with his two hands open on his knees, thinking deeply.

"A married man," he said, "could hardly reconcile it with his conscience to undertake such a perilous expedition."

"No," replied Jack, with quiet significance.

Sir John gave a forced laugh.

"I see," he said, "that you have outwitted me. If I do not give my consent to your marriage without further delay, you will go back to Africa."

Jack bowed his head gravely.

There was a long silence, while the two men sat side by side, gazing into the fire.

"I cannot afford to do that," said the father, at length; "I am getting too old to indulge in the luxury of pride. I will attend your marriage. I will smile and say pretty things to the bridesmaids. Before the world I will consent under the condition that the ceremony does not take place before two months from this date."

" I agree to that," put in Jack.

Sir John rose and stood on the hearth-rug, looking down from his great height upon his son.

" But," he continued, " between us let it be understood that I move in no degree from my original position. I object to Millicent Chyne as your wife. But I bow to the force of circumstances. I admit that you have a perfect right to marry whom you choose—in two months' time."

So Jack took his leave.

" In two months' time," repeated Sir John, when he was alone, with one of his twisted, cynic smiles—"in two months' time—*qui vivra verra.*"

CHAPTER XXXVII

FOUL PLAY

"Oh, fairest of creation, last and best
Of all God's works !"

FOR one or two days after the public announcement of her engagement Millicent was not quite free from care. She rather dreaded the posts. It was not that she feared one letter in particular, but the postman's disquietingly urgent rap caused her a vague uneasiness many times a day.

Sir John's reply to her appealing little letter came short and sharp. She showed it to no one.

" MY DEAR MISS CHYNE,—I hasten to reply to your kind letter of to-day announcing your approaching marriage with my son. There are a certain number of trinkets which have always been handed on from generation to generation. I will at once have these cleaned by the jeweller, in order that they may be presented to you immediately after the ceremony. Allow me to urge upon you the advisability of drawing up and signing a pre-nuptial marriage settlement.
" Yours sincerely,   JOHN MEREDITH."

Millicent bit her pretty lip when she perused this note. She made two comments, at a considerable interval of time.

"Stupid old thing!" was the first; and then, after a pause, "I *hope* they are all diamonds."

Close upon the heels of this letter followed a host of others. There was the gushing, fervent letter of the friend whose joy was not marred by the knowledge that a wedding present must necessarily follow. Those among one's friends who are not called upon to offer a more substantial token of joy than a letter are always the most keenly pleased to hear the news of an engagement. There was the sober sheet (crossed) from the elderly relative living in the country, who, never having been married herself, takes the opportunity of giving four pages of advice to one about to enter that parlous state. There was the fatherly letter from the country rector who christened Millicent, and thinks that he may be asked to marry her in a fashionable London church —and so to a bishopric. On heavily-crested stationery follow the missives of the ladies whose daughters would make sweet bridesmaids. Also the hearty congratulations of the slight acquaintance, who is going to Egypt for the winter, and being desirous of letting her house without having to pay one of those horrid agents, "sees no harm in mentioning it." The house being most singularly suitable for a young married couple. Besides these, the thousand and one who wished to be invited to the wedding in order to taste cake and champagne at the time, and thereafter the sweeter glory of seeing their names in the fashionable news.

All these Millicent read with little interest, and answered in that conveniently large caligraphy which made three lines look like a note and magnified a note into a four-page letter. The dress-makers' circulars—the tradesmen's illustrated catalogues of things she could not possibly want, and the jewellers' delicate photographs interested her a thousand times more. But even these did not satisfy her. All these people were glad—most of them were delighted. Millicent wanted to hear from those who were not delighted, nor even pleased, but in despair. She wanted to hear more of the broken-hearts. But somehow the broken-hearts were silent. Could it be that they did not care? Could it be that *they* were only flirting? She dismissed these silly questions with the promptness which they deserved. It was useless to think of it in that way—more useless, perhaps, than she suspected; for she was not deep enough nor observant enough to know that the broken-hearts in question had been much more influenced by the suspicion that she cared for them than by the thought that they cared for her. She did not know the lamentable, vulgar fact that any woman can be a flirt if she only degrade her womanhood to flattery. Men do not want to love so much as to be loved. Such is, more-over, their sublime vanity that they are ready to believe any one who tells them, however subtly—mesdames, you cannot be too subtle for a man's vanity to find your meaning—that they are not as other men.

To the commonplace observer it would, therefore, appear (erroneously, no doubt) that the broken-hearts, having been practically assured that Millicent Chyne did not care for them, promptly made the discovery that the lack of feeling was reciprocal. But Millicent did not, of course, adopt this theory. She knew better. She only wondered why several young men did not communicate, and she was slightly un-easy lest in their anger they should do or say something indiscreet.

There was no reason why the young people should wait. And when there is no reason why the young people should wait, there is every reason why they should not do so. Thus it came about that in a week or so Millicent was en-gaged in the happiest pursuit of her life. She was buying clothes without a thought of money. The full joy of the trousseau was hers. The wives of her guardians having been morally bought, dirt cheap, at the price of an antici-patory invitation to the wedding, those elderly gentlemen were with little difficulty won over to a pretty little femininely vague scheme of withdrawing just a little of the capital—said capital to be spent in the purchase of a really *good* trousseau, you know. The word "good" emanating from such a source must, of course, be read as "novel," which in some circles means the same thing.

Millicent entered into the thing in the right spirit. Whatever the future might hold for her—and she trusted that it might be full of millinery—she was determined to enjoy the living present to its utmost. Her life at this time was a whirl of excitement — excitement of the keenest order— namely, trying on.

"You do not know what it is," she said, with a happy little sigh, to those among her friends who probably never would, "to stand the whole day long being pinned into linings by Madame Videpoche."

And, despite the sigh, she did it with an angelic sweetness of temper which quite touched the heart of Madame Videpoche, while making no difference in the bill.

Lady Cantourne would not have been human had she assumed the neutral in this important matter. She frankly enjoyed it all immensely.

"You know, Sir John," she said in confidence to him one day at Hurlingham, "I have always dressed Millicent."

"You need not tell me that," he interrupted, gracefully. "*On ne peut s'y tromper.*"

"And," she went on, almost apologetically, "whatever my own feelings on the subject may be, I cannot abandon her now. The world expects much from Millicent Chyne. I have taught it to do so. It will expect more from Millicent—Meredith."

The old gentleman bowed in his formal way.

"And the world must not be disappointed," he suggested, cynically.

"No," she answered, with an energetic little nod, "it must not. That is the way to manage the world. Give it what it expects; and just a little more, to keep its attention fixed."

Sir John tapped with his gloved finger pensively on the knob of his silver-mounted cane.

"And may I ask your ladyship," he inquired, suavely, "what the world expects of me?"

He knew her well enough to know that she never made use of the method epigrammatic without good reason.

"A diamond crescent," she answered, stoutly. "The fashion-papers must be able to write about the gift of the bridegroom's father."

"Ah—and they prefer a diamond crescent?"

"Yes," answered Lady Cantourne. "That always seems to satisfy them."

He bowed gravely, and continued to watch the polo with that marvellously youthful interest which was his.

"Does the world expect anything else?" he asked, presently.

"No, I think not," replied Lady Cantourne, with a bright little absent smile. "Not just now."

"Will you tell me if it does?"

He had risen; for there were other great ladies on the ground to whom he must pay his old-fashioned respects.

"Certainly," she answered, looking up at him.

"I should deem it a favor," he continued. "If the world does not get what it expects, I imagine it will begin to inquire why; and if it cannot find reasons it will make them."

In due course the diamond crescent arrived.

"It is rather nice of the old thing," was Millicent's comment. She held the jewel, at various angles in various lights. There was no doubt that this was the handsomest present she had received — sent direct from the jeweller's shop with an uncompromising card inside the case. She never saw the irony of it; but Sir John had probably not expected that she would. He enjoyed it alone—as he enjoyed or endured most things.

Lady Cantourne examined it with some curiosity.

"I have never seen such beautiful diamonds," she said, simply.

There were other presents to be opened and examined. For the invitations had not been sent out, and many were willing to pay handsomely for the privilege of being mentioned among the guests. It is, one finds, after the invitations have been issued that the presents begin to fall off.

But on this particular morning the other presents fell on barren ground. Millicent only half-heeded them. She could not lay the diamond crescent finally aside. Some people have the power of imparting a little piece of their individuality to their letters, and even to a commonplace gift. Sir John was beginning to have this power over Millicent. She was rapidly falling into a stupid habit of feeling uneasy whenever she thought of him. She was vaguely alarmed at his uncompromising adherence to the position he had assumed. She had never failed yet to work her will with men—young and old—by a pretty persistence, a steady flattery, a subtle pleading manner. But Sir John had met all her wiles with his adamantine smile. He would not openly declare himself an enemy—which she argued to herself would have been much nicer of him. He was merely a friend of her aunt's, and from that contemplative position he never stepped down. She could not quite make out what he was "driving at," as she herself put it. He never found fault, but she knew that his disapproval of her was the result of long and careful study. Perhaps in her heart —despite all her contradictory arguments—she knew that he was right.

"I wonder," she said, half aloud, taking up the crescent again, " why he sent it to me?"

Lady Cantourne, who was writing letters at a terrible rate, glanced sharply up. She was beginning to be aware of Millicent's unspoken fear of Sir John. Moreover, she was clever enough to connect it with her niece's daily in-

creasing love for the man who was soon to be her husband.

"Well," she answered, "I should be rather surprised if
he gave you nothing."

There was a little pause, only broken by the scratching
of Lady Cantourne's quill pen.

"Auntie!" exclaimed the girl, suddenly, "why does he
hate me? You have known him all your life—you must
know why he hates me so."

Lady Cantourne shrugged her shoulders.

"I suppose," went on Millicent, with singular heat, "that
some one has been telling him things about me—horrid
things—false things—that I am a flirt, or something like
that. I am sure I'm not."

Lady Cantourne was addressing an envelope, and did not
make any reply.

"Has he said anything to you, Aunt Caroline?" asked
Millicent, in an aggrieved voice.

Lady Cantourne laid aside her letter.

"No," she answered, slowly; "but I suppose there are
things which he does not understand."

"Things?"

Her ladyship looked up steadily.

"Guy Oscard, for instance," she said; "I don't quite understand Guy Oscard, Millicent."

The girl turned away impatiently. She was keenly alive
to the advantage of turning her face away. For in her
pocket she had at that moment a letter from Guy Oscard—
the last relic of the old excitement which was so dear to
her, and which she was already beginning to miss. Joseph
had posted this letter in Msala nearly two months before.
It had travelled down from the Simiacine Plateau with
others, in a parcel beneath the mattress of Jack Meredith's
litter. It was a letter written in good faith by an honest,
devoted man to the woman whom he looked upon already
as almost his wife—a letter which no man need have been

ashamed of writing, but which a woman ought not to have read unless she intended to be the writer's wife.

Millicent had read this letter more than once. She liked it because it was evidently sincere. The man's heart could be heard beating in every line of it. Moreover, she had made inquiries that very morning at the post-office about the African mail. She wanted the excitement of another letter like that.

"Oh, Guy Oscard!" she replied, innocently, to Lady Cantourne; "that was nothing."

Lady Cantourne kept silence, and presently she returned to her letters.

CHAPTER XXXVIII

THE ACCURSED CAMP

"Here—judge if hell, with all its power to damn,
Can add one curse to the foul thing I am."

THERE are some places in the world where a curse seems to brood in the atmosphere. Msala was one of these. Perhaps these places are accursed by the deeds that have been done there. Who can tell?

Could the trees—the two gigantic palms that stood by the river's edge—could these have spoken, they might perhaps have told the tale of this little inland station in that country where, as the founder of the hamlet was in the habit of saying, no one knows what is going on.

All went well with the retreating column until they were almost in sight of Msala, when the flotilla was attacked by no less than three hippopotamuses. One canoe was sunk, and four others were so badly damaged that they could not be kept afloat with their proper complement of men. There

was nothing for it but to establish a camp at Msala, and
wait there until the builders had repaired the damaged
canoes.

The walls of Durnovo's house were still standing, and
here Guy Oscard established himself with as much comfort
as circumstances allowed. He caused a temporary roof of
palm-leaves to be laid on the charred beams, and within
the principal room—the very room where the three organiz-
ers of the great Simiacine scheme had first laid their plans
—he set up his simple camp furniture.

Oscard was too great a traveller, too experienced a wanderer, to be put out of temper by this enforced rest. The
men had worked very well hitherto. It had, in its way,
been a great feat of generalship, this leading through a
wild country of men unprepared for travel, scantily pro-
visioned, disorganized by recent events. No accident had
happened, no serious delay had been incurred, although the
rate of progress had necessarily been very slow. Nearly six
weeks had elapsed since Oscard with his little following had
turned their backs forever on the Simiacine Plateau. But
now the period of acute danger had passed away. They
had almost reached civilization. Oscard was content.

When Oscard was content he smoked a slower pipe than
usual—watching each cloud of smoke vanish into thin air.
He was smoking very slowly, this, the third evening of
their encampment at Msala. There had been heavy rain
during the day, and the whole lifeless forest was dripping
with a continuous, ceaseless clatter of heavy drops on tropic
foliage, with an amalgamated sound like a wide-spread whisper.

Oscard was sitting in the windowless room without a
light, for a light only attracted a myriad of heavy-winged
moths. He was seated before the long French window,
which, since the sash had gone, had been used as a door.
Before him in the glimmering light of the mystic Southern
Cross the great river crept unctuously, silently to the sea.

It seemed to be stealing away surreptitiously while the forest whispered of it. In its surface the reflection of the great stars of the southern hemisphere ran into little streaks of silver, shimmering away into darkness.

All sound of human life was still. The natives were asleep. In the next room, Joseph in his hammock was just on the barrier between the waking and the sleeping life—as soldiers learn to be. Oscard would not have needed to raise his voice to call him to his side.

The leader of this hurried retreat had been sitting there for two hours. The slimy moving surface of the river had entered into his brain; the restless silence of the African forest alone kept him awake. He hardly realized that the sound momentarily gaining strength within his ears was that of a paddle — a single, weakly irregular paddle. It was not a sound to wake a sleeping man. It came so slowly, so gently through the whisper of the dripping leaves that it would enter into his slumbers and make itself part of them.

Guy Oscard only realized the meaning of that sound when a black shadow crept on to the smooth evenness of the river's breast. Oscard was eminently a man of action. In a moment he was on his feet, and in the darkness of the room there was the gleam of a rifle-barrel. He came back to the window—watching.

He saw the canoe approach the bank. He heard the thud of the paddle as it was thrown upon the ground. In the gloom, to which his eyes were accustomed, he saw a man step from the boat to the shore and draw the canoe up. The silent midnight visitor then turned and walked up towards the house. There was something familiar in the gait —the legs were slightly bowed. The man was walking with great difficulty, staggering a little at each step. He seemed to be in great pain.

Guy Oscard laid aside the rifle. He stepped forward to the open window.

"Is that you, Durnovo?" he said, without raising his voice.

"Yes," replied the other. His voice was muffled, as if his tongue were swollen, and there was a startling break in it.

Oscard stepped aside, and Durnovo passed into his own house.

"Got a light?" he said, in the same muffled way.

In the next room Joseph could be heard striking a match, and a moment later he entered the room, throwing a flood of light before him.

"*Good God!*" cried Guy Oscard. He stepped back as if he had been struck, with his hand shielding his eyes.

"Save us!" ejaculated Joseph in the same breath.

The thing that stood there—sickening their gaze—was not a human being at all. Take a man's eyelids away, leaving the round balls staring, blood-streaked; cut away his lips, leaving the grinning teeth and red gums; shear off his ears—that which is left is not a man at all. This had been done to Victor Durnovo. Truly the vengeance of man is crueller than the vengeance of God!

Could he have seen himself, Victor Durnovo would never have shown that face—or what remained of it—to a human being. He could only have killed himself. Who can tell what cruelties had been paid for, piece by piece, in this loathsome mutilation? The slaves had wreaked their terrible vengeance; but the greatest, the deepest, the most inhuman cruelty was in letting him go.

"They've made a pretty mess of me," said Durnovo, in a sickening, lifeless voice—and he stood there, with a terrible caricature of a grin.

Joseph set down the lamp with a groan, and went back into the dark room beyond, where he cast himself upon the ground and buried his face in his hands.

"O Lord!" he muttered. "O God in heaven—kill it, kill it!"

Guy Oscard never attempted to run away from it. He stood slowly gulping down his nauseating horror. His teeth were clinched; his face, through the sunburn, livid; the blue of his eyes seemed to have faded into an ashen gray. The sight he was looking on would have sent three men out of five into gibbering idiocy.

Then at last he moved forward. With averted eyes he took Durnovo by the arm.

"Come," he said, "lie down upon my bed. I will try and help you. Can you take some food?"

Durnovo threw himself down heavily on the bed. There was a punishment sufficient to expiate all his sins in the effort he saw that Guy Oscard had had to make before he touched him. He turned his face away.

"I haven't eaten anything for twenty-four hours," he said, with a whistling intonation.

"Joseph," said Oscard, returning to the door of the inner room—his voice sounded different, there was a metallic ring in it—"get something for Mr. Durnovo—some soup or something."

Joseph obeyed, shaking as if ague were in his bones.

Oscard administered the soup. He tended Durnovo with all the gentleness of a woman, and a fortitude that was above the fortitude of men. Despite himself his hands trembled—big and strong as they were; his whole being was contracted with horror and pain. Whatever Victor Durnovo had been, he was now an object of such pity that before it all possible human sins faded into spotlessness. There was no crime in all that human nature has found to commit for which such cruelty as this would be justly meted out in punishment.

Durnovo spoke from time to time, but he could see the effect that his hissing speech had upon his companion, and in time he gave it up. He told haltingly of the horrors of the Simiacine Plateau—of the last grim tragedy acted there —how at last, blinded with his blood, maimed, stupefied by agony, he had been hounded down the slope by a yelling, laughing horde of torturers.

There was not much to be done, and presently Guy Oscard moved away to his camp-chair, where he sat staring into the night. Sleep was impossible. Strong, hardened, weather-beaten man that he was, his nerves were all a-tingle, his flesh creeping and jumping with horror. Gradually he collected his faculties enough to begin to think about the future. What was he to do with this man? He could not take him to Loango. He could not risk that Jocelyn or even Maurice Gordon should look upon this horror.

Joseph had crept back into the inner room, where he had no light, and could be heard breathing hard, wide awake in his hammock.

Suddenly the silence was broken by a loud cry:

" Oscard! Oscard!"

In a moment Joseph and Oscard were at the bedside.

Durnovo was sitting up, and he grabbed at Oscard's arms.

" For God's sake!" he cried. "For God's sake, man, don't let me go to sleep!"

" What do you mean?" asked Oscard. They both thought that he had gone mad. Sleep had nothing more to do with Durnovo's eyes—protruding, staring, terrible to look at.

" Don't let me go to sleep," he repeated. "Don't! Don't!"

" All right," said Oscard, soothingly—"all right. We'll look after you."

He fell back on the bed. In the flickering light his eyeballs gleamed.

Then, quite suddenly, he rose to a sitting position again with a wild effort.

" I've got it! I've got it!" he cried.

"Got what?"

" The sleeping sickness!"

The two listeners knew of this strange disease. Oscard

had seen a whole village devastated by it, the habitants lying about their own doors, stricken down by a deadly sleep, from which they never woke. It is known on the West Coast of Africa, and the cure for it is unknown.

" Hold me !" cried Durnovo. " Don't let me sleep !"

His head fell forward even as he spoke, and the staring, wide-open eyes that could not sleep made a horror of him.

Oscard took him by the arms, and held him in a sitting position. Durnovo's fingers were clutching at his sleeve.

"Shake me ! God ! shake me !"

Then Oscard took him in his strong arms and set him on his feet. He shook him gently at first, but as the dread somnolence crept on he shook harder, until the mutilated inhuman head rolled upon the shoulders.

" It's a sin to let that man live," exclaimed Joseph, turning away in horror.

" It's a sin to let *any* man die," replied Oscard, and with his great strength he shook Durnovo like a garment.

And so Victor Durnovo died. His stained soul left his body in Guy Oscard's hands, and the big Englishman shook the corpse, trying to awake it from that sleep which knows no earthly waking.

So, after all, Heaven stepped in and laid its softening hand on the judgment of men. But there was a strange irony in the mode of death. It was strange that this man, who never could have closed his eyes again, should have been stricken down by the sleeping sickness.

They laid the body on the floor, and covered the face, which was less grewsome in death, for the pity of the eyes had given place to peace.

The morning light, bursting suddenly through the trees as it does in Equatorial Africa, showed the room set in order and Guy Oscard sleeping in his camp-chair. Behind him, on the floor, lay the form of Victor Durnovo. Joseph, less iron-nerved than the great big-game hunter, was awake and astir with the dawn. He, too, was calmer now. He had seen death face to face too often to be appalled by it in broad daylight.

So they buried Victor Durnovo between the two giant palms at Msala, with his feet turned towards the river which he had made his, as if ready to arise when the call comes and undertake one of those marvellous journeys of his which are yet a household word on the West Coast.

The cloth fluttered as they lowered him into his narrow resting-place, and the face they covered had a strange mystic grin, as if he saw something that they could not perceive. Perhaps he did. Perhaps he saw the Simiacine Plateau, and knew that, after all, he had won the last throw; for up there, far above the table-lands of Central Africa, there lay beneath high heaven a charnel-house. Hounded down the slope by his tormentors, he had left a memento behind him surer than their torturing knives, keener than their sharpest steel—he had left the sleeping sickness behind him.

His last journey had been worthy of his reputation. In twenty days he had covered the distance between the Plateau and Msala, stumbling on alone, blinded, wounded, sore-stricken, through a thousand daily valleys of death. With wonderful endurance he had paddled night and day down the sleek river without rest, with the dread microbe of the sleeping sickness slowly creeping through his veins.

He had lived in dread of this disease, as men do of a sickness which clutches them at last; but when it came he did not recognize it. He was so racked by pain that he never recognized the symptoms; he was so panic-stricken, so paralyzed by the nameless fear that lay behind him, that he could only think of pressing forward. In the night hours he would suddenly rise from his precarious bed under the shadow of a fallen tree and stagger on, haunted by a picture of his ruthless foes pressing through the jungle in pursuit. Thus he accomplished his wonderful journey alone through trackless forests; thus he fended off the sickness which gripped him the moment that he laid him down to rest.

He had left it—a grim legacy—to his torturers, and before he reached the river all was still on the Simiacine Plateau.

And so we leave Victor Durnovo. His sins are buried with him, and beneath the giant palms at Msala lies Maurice Gordon's secret.

And so we leave Msala, the accursed camp. Far up the Ogowe River, on the left bank, the giant palms still stand sentry, and beneath their shade the crumbling walls of a cursed house are slowly disappearing beneath luxuriant growths of grass and brushwood.

CHAPTER XXXIX

THE EXTENUATING CIRCUMSTANCE

"Yet I think at God's tribunal
Some large answer you shall hear."

In a dimly-lighted room in the bungalow at Loango two women had been astir all night. Now, as dawn approached, one of them, worn out with watching, wearied with that blessed fatigue of anxiety which dulls the senses, had laid her down on the curtain-covered bed to sleep.

While Marie slept Jocelyn Gordon walked softly backward and forward with Nestorius in her arms. Nestorius was probably dying. He lay in the Englishwoman's gentle arms—a little brown bundle of flexible limbs and cotton night-shirt. It was terribly hot. All day the rain had been pending; all night it had held off until the whole earth seemed to pulsate with the desire for relief. Jocelyn kept moving so that the changing air wafted over the little bare limbs might allay the fever. She was in evening dress, having, indeed, been called from the drawing-room by

Marie; and the child's woolly black head was pressed against her breast as if to seek relief from the inward pressure on the awakening brain.

A missionary possessing some small knowledge of medicine had been with them until midnight, and, having done his best, had gone away leaving the child to the two women. Maurice had been in twice, clumsily, on tiptoe, to look with ill-concealed awe at the child, and to whisper hopes to Marie which displayed a ludicrous, if lamentable, ignorance of what he was talking about.

"Little chap's better," he said; "I'm sure of it. See, Marie, his eyes are brighter. Devilish hot, though, isn't he —poor little soul?"

Then he stood about, awkwardly sympathetic.

"Anything I can do for you, Jocelyn?" he asked, and then departed, only too pleased to get away from the impending calamity.

Marie was not emotional. She seemed to have left all emotion behind, in some other phase of her life which was shut off from the present by a thick curtain. She was patient and calm, but she was not so clever with the child as was Jocelyn. Perhaps her greater experience acted as a handicap in her execution of those small offices to the sick which may be rendered useless at any moment. Perhaps she knew that Nestorius was wanted elsewhere. Or it may only have been that Jocelyn was able to soothe him sooner, because there is an unwritten law that those who love us best are not always the best nurses for us.

When, at last, sleep came to the child, it was in Jocelyn's arms that he lay with that utter abandonment of pose which makes a sleeping infant and a sleeping kitten more graceful than any living thing. Marie leaned over Nestorius until her dusky cheek almost touched Jocelyn's fair English one.

"He is asleep," she whispered.

And her great dark eyes probed Jocelyn's face as if

wondering whether her arms, bearing that burden, told her that this was the last sleep.

Jocelyn nodded gravely, and continued the gentle swaying motion affected by women under such circumstances.

Nestorius continued to sleep, and at last Marie, overcome by sleep herself, lay down on her bed.

Thus it came about that the dawn found Jocelyn moving softly in the room, with Nestorius asleep in her arms. A pink light came creeping through the trees, presently turning to a golden yellow, and, behold! it was light. It was a little cooler, for the sea-breeze had set in. The cool air from the surface of the water was rushing inland to supply the place of the heated atmosphere rising towards the sun. With the breeze came the increased murmur of the distant surf. The dull continuous sound seemed to live amid the summits of the trees far above the low-built house. It rose and fell with a long-drawn, rhythmic swing. Already the sounds of life were mingling with it — the low of a cow, the crowing of the cocks, the hum of the noisier daylight insect-life.

Jocelyn moved to the window, and her heart suddenly leaped to her throat.

On the brown turf in front of the house were two men, stretched side by side, as if other hands had laid them there dead. One man was much bigger than the other. He was of exceptional stature. Jocelyn recognized them almost immediately—Guy Oscard and Joseph. They had arrived during the night, and, not wishing to disturb the sleeping household, had lain them down in the front garden to sleep with a quiet conscience beneath the stars. The action was so startlingly characteristic, so suggestive of the primeval, simple man whom Oscard represented as one born out of time, that Jocelyn laughed suddenly.

While she was still at the window, Marie rose and came to her side. Nestorius was still sleeping. Following the direction of her mistress's eyes, Marie saw the two men. Joseph was sleeping on his face, after the manner of Thomas Atkins all the world over. Guy Oscard lay on his side, with his head on his arm.

"That is so like Guy Oscard," said Marie, with her pa- tient smile, "so like—so like. It could be no other man— to do a thing like that."

Jocelyn gave Nestorius back to his mother, and the two women stood for a moment looking out at the sleepers, little knowing what the advent of these two men brought with it for one of them. Then the Englishwoman went to change her dress, awaking her brother as she passed his room.

It was not long before Maurice Gordon had hospitably awakened the travellers and brought them in to change their torn and ragged clothes for something more presenta- ble. It would appear that Nestorius was not particular. He did not mind dying on the kitchen table if need were. His mother deposited him on this table on a pillow, while she prepared the breakfast with that patient resignation which seemed to emanate from having tasted of the worst that the world has to give.

Joseph was ready the first, and he promptly repaired to the kitchen, where he set to work to help Marie, with his customary energy.

It was Marie who first perceived a difference in Nestorius. His dusky little face was shining with a sudden, weakening perspiration, his limbs lay lifelessly, with a lack of their usual comfortable-looking grace.

"Go!" she said, quickly. "Fetch Miss Gordon!"

Jocelyn came, and Maurice and Guy Oscard; for they had been together in the dining-room when Joseph delivered Marie's message.

Nestorius was wide awake now. When he saw Oscard his small face suddenly expanded into a brilliant grin.

"Bad case!" he said.

It was rather startling, until Marie spoke.

"He thinks you are Mr. Meredith," she said. "Mr. Meredith taught him to say ' bad case.'"

Nestorius looked from one to the other with gravely speculative eyes, which presently closed.

"He is dying — yes!" said the mother, looking at Jocelyn.

Oscard knew more of this matter that any of them. He went forward and leaned over the table. Marie removed a piece of salted bacon that was lying on the table near to the pillow. With the unconsciousness of long habit she swept some crumbs away with her apron. Oscard was trying to find the pulse in the tiny wrist, but there was not much to find.

"I am afraid he is very ill," he said.

At this moment the kettle boiled over, and Marie had to turn away to attend to her duties.

When she came back Oscard was looking, not at Nestorius, but at her.

"We spent four days at Msala," he said, in a tone that meant that he had more to tell her.

"Yes?"

"The place is in ruins, as you know."

She nodded with a peculiar little twist of the lips as if he were hurting her.

"And I am afraid I have some bad news for you. Victor Durnovo, your master—"

"Yes—tell quickly!"

"He is dead. We buried him at Msala. He died — in my arms."

At this moment Joseph gave a little gasp and turned away to the window, where he stood with his broad back turned towards them. Maurice Gordon, as white as death, was leaning against the table. He quite forgot himself. His lips were apart, his jaw had dropped; he was hanging breathlessly on Guy Oscard's next word.

"He died of the sleeping sickness," said Oscard. "We

had come down to Msala before him — Joseph and I. I
broke up the partnership, and we left him in possession of
the Simiacine Plateau. But his men turned against him.
For some reason his authority over them failed. He was
obliged to make a dash for Msala, and he reached it, but
the sickness was upon him."

Maurice Gordon drew a sharp sigh of relief which was
almost a sob. Marie was standing with her two hands on
the pillow where Nestorius lay. Her deep eyes were fixed
on the Englishman's sunburnt, strongly gentle face.

"Did he send a message for me—yes?" she said, softly.

"No," answered Oscard. "He—there was no time."

Joseph at the window had turned half round.

"He was my husband," said Marie, in her clear, deep
tones : "the father of this little one, which you call Nestorius."

Oscard bowed his head without surprise. Jocelyn was
standing still as a statue, with her hand on the dying infant's cheek. No one dared to look at her.

"It is all right," said Marie, bluntly. "We were married
at Sierra Leone by the English chaplain. My father, who
is dead, kept a hotel at Sierra Leone, and he knew the ways
of the — half-castes. He said that the Protestant Church
at Sierra Leone was good enough for him, and we were
married there. And then Victor brought me away from
my people to this place and to Msala. Then he got tired
of me—he cared no more. He said I was ugly."

She pronounced it "ogly," and seemed to think that
the story finished there. At all events, she added nothing
to it. But Joseph thought fit to contribute a *post scriptum*.

"You'd better tell 'em, mistress," he said, "that he tried
to starve yer and them kids — that he wanted to leave yer
at Msala to be massacred by the tribes, only Mr. Oscard
sent yer down 'ere. You'd better tell 'em that."

"No," she replied, with a faint smile. "No, because he
was my husband."

Guy Oscard was looking very hard at Joseph, and, catching his eye, made a little gesture commanding silence. He did not want him to say too much.

Joseph turned away again to the window, and stood thus, apart, till the end.

"I have no doubt," said Oscard to Marie, "that he would have sent some message to you had he been able; but he was very ill — he was dying — when he reached Msala. It was wonderful that he got there at all. We did what we could for him, but it was hopeless."

Marie raised her shoulders with a pathetic gesture of resignation.

"The sleeping sickness," she said, "what will you? There is no remedy. He always said he would die of that. He feared it."

In the greater sorrow she seemed to have forgotten her child, who was staring open-eyed at the ceiling. The two others — the boy and girl — were playing on the door-step with some unconsidered trifles from the dust-heap — after the manner of children all the world over.

"He was not a good man," said Marie, turning to Jocelyn, as if she alone of all present would understand. "He was not a good husband, but"—she shrugged her shoulders with one of her patient, shadowy smiles — "it makes so little difference—yes?"

Jocelyn said nothing. None of them had aught to say to her; for each in that room could lay a separate sin at Victor Durnovo's door. He was gone beyond the reach of human justice to the Higher Court where the Extenuating Circumstance is fully understood. The generosity of that silence was infectious, and they told her nothing. Had they spoken she would perforce have believed them; but then, as she herself said, it would have made "so little difference." So Victor Durnovo leaves these pages, and all we can do is to remember the writing on the ground. Who among us dares to withhold the Extenuating Circumstance? Who is ready to leave this world without that crutch to lean upon? Given a mixed blood—evil black with evil white—and what can the result be but evil? Given the climate of Western Africa and the mental irritation thereof, added to a lack of education and the natural vice inherent in man, and you have—Victor Durnovo.

Nestorius—the shameless—stretched out his little bare limbs and turned half over on his side. He looked from one face to the other with the grave wonder that was his. He had never been taken much notice of. His short walk in life had been very near the ground, where trifles look very large, and from whence those larger stumbling-blocks which occupy our attention are quite invisible. He had been the third—the solitary third child who usually makes his own interest in life, and is left by or leaves the rest of his family.

It was not quite clear to him why he was the centre of so much attention. His mind did not run to the comprehension of the fact that he was the wearer of borrowed plumes—the sable plumes of King Death.

He had always wanted to get on to the kitchen-table—there was much there that interested him, and supplied him with food for thought. He had risked his life on more than one occasion in attempts to scale that height with the assistance of a saucepan that turned over and poured culinary delicacies on his toes, or perhaps a sleeping cat that got up and walked away much annoyed. And now that he was at last at this dizzy height, he was sorry to find that he was too tired to crawl about and explore the vast possibilities of it. He was rather too tired to convey his forefinger to his mouth, and was forced to work out mental problems without that aid to thought.

Presently his eyes fell on Guy Oscard's face, and again his own small features expanded into a smile.

"Bad case!" he said, and, turning over, he nestled down into the pillow, and he had the answer to the many questions that puzzled his small brain.

CHAPTER XL

" 'Tis better playing with a lion's whelp
Than with an old one dying."

As through an opera runs the rhythm of one dominant
air, so through men's lives there rings a dominant note, soft
in youth, strong in manhood, and soft again in old age.
But it is always there; and whether soft in the gentler periods, or strong amid the noise and clang of the perihelion,
it dominates always and gives its tone to the whole life.

The dominant tone of Sir John Meredith's existence had
been the high, clear note of battle. He had always found
something or some one to fight from the very beginning, and
now, in his old age, he was fighting still. His had never
been the din and crash of warfare by sword and cannon, but
the subtler, deeper combat of the pen. In his active days
he had got through a vast amount of work—that unchron-
icled work of the Foreign Office which never comes, through
the cheap newspapers, to the voracious maw of a chattering
public. His name was better known on the banks of the
Neva, the Seine, the Bosporus, or the swift-rolling Iser,
than by the Thames; and grim Sir John was content to
have it so.

His face had never been public property; the comic papers had never used his personality as a peg upon which to
hang their ever-changing political principles. But he had
always been " there," as he himself vaguely put it. That is
to say, he had always been at the back—one of those invisible powers of the stage by whose command the scene is
shifted, the lights are lowered for the tragedy, or the gay

music plays on the buffoon. Sir John had no sympathy
with a generation of men and women who would rather be
laughed at and despised than unnoticed. He belonged to
an age wherein it was held better to be a gentleman than
the object of a cheap and evanescent notoriety; and he was
at once the despair and the dread of newspaper interview-
ers, enterprising publishers, and tuft-hunters.

He was so little known out of his own select circle that
the porters in Euston Station asked each other in vain who
the old swell waiting for the four o'clock "up" from Liverpool could be. The four o'clock was, moreover, not the first
express which Sir John had met that day. His stately car-
riage-and-pair had pushed its way into the crowd of smaller
and humbler vehicular fry earlier in the afternoon, and on
that occasion also the old gentleman had indulged in a grave
promenade upon the platform.

He was walking up and down there now, with his hand
in the small of his back, where of late he had been aware of
a constant aching pain. He was very upright, however, and
supremely unconscious of the curiosity aroused by his presence in the mind of the station "canaille." His lips were
rather more troublesome than usual, and his keen eyes
twinkled with a suppressed excitement.

In former days there had been no one equal to him in
certain diplomatic crises, where it was a question of brow-
beating suavely the uppish representative of some foreign
State. No man could then rival him in the insolently aristocratic school of diplomacy which England has made her
own. But in his most dangerous crisis he had never been
restless, apprehensive, pessimistic, as he was at this moment.
And, after all, it was a very simple matter that had brought
him here. It was merely the question of meeting a man as
if by accident, and then afterwards making that man do certain things required of him. Moreover, the man was only
Guy Oscard—learned, if you will, in forest craft, but a mere
child in the hands of so old a diplomatist as Sir John Meredith.

That which made Sir John so uneasy was the abiding knowledge that Jack's wedding-day would dawn in twelve hours. The margin was much too small, through, however, no fault of Sir John's. The West African steamer had been delayed, unaccountably, two days. A third day lost in the Atlantic would have overthrown Sir John Meredith's plan. He had often cut things fine before, but somehow now—not that he was getting old, oh no!—but somehow the suspense was too much for his nerves. He soon became irritated and distrustful. Besides, the pain in his back wearied him and interfered with the clear sequence of his thoughts.

The owners of the West African steamer had telegraphed that the passengers had left for London in two separate trains. Guy Oscard was not in the first—there was no positive reason why he should be in the second. More depended upon his being in this second express than Sir John cared to contemplate.

The course of his peregrinations brought him into the vicinity of an inspector whose attitude betokened respect while his presence raised hope.

"Is there any reason to suppose that your train is coming?" he inquired of the official.

"Signalled now, my lord," replied the inspector, touching his cap.

"And what does that mean?" uncompromisingly ignorant of technical parlance.

"It will be in in one minute, my lord."

Sir John's hand was over his lips as he walked back to the carriage, casting as it were the commander's eye over the field.

"When the crowd is round the train you come and look for me," he said to the footman, who touched his cockaded hat in silence.

At that moment the train lumbered in, the engine wearing that inanely self-important air affected by locomotives

of the larger build.   From all quarters an army of porters
besieged the platform, and in a few seconds Sir John was
in the centre of an agitated crowd.   There was one other
calm man on that platform—another man with no parcels,
whom no one sought to embrace.   His brown face and
close-cropped head towered above a sea of agitated bonnets.
Sir John, whose walk in life had been through crowds, el-
bowed his way forward and deliberately walked against Guy
Oscard.

"Damn it!" he exclaimed, turning round.   "Ah!—Mr.
Oscard—how d'ye do?"

"How are you?" replied Guy Oscard, really glad to see
him.

"You are a good man for a crowd; I think I will follow
in your wake," said Sir John.   "A number of people—of
the baser sort.   Got my carriage here somewhere.   Fool of
a man looking for me in the wrong place, no doubt.   Where
are you going?   May I offer you a lift?   This way.   Here,
John, take Mr. Oscard's parcels."

He could not have done it better in his keenest day.
Guy Oscard was seated in the huge, roomy carriage before
he had realized what had happened to him.

"Your man will look after your traps, I suppose?" said
Sir John, hospitably drawing the fur rug from the opposite
seat.

"Yes," replied Guy, "although he is not my man.   He
is Jack's man Joseph."

"Ah, of course; excellent servant, too.   Jack told me he
had left him with you."

Sir John leaned out of the window and asked the footman whether he knew his colleague Joseph, and upon re-
ceiving an answer in the affirmative he gave orders—acting
as Guy's mouth-piece—that the luggage was to be conveyed
to Russell Square.   While these orders were being executed
the two men sat waiting in the carriage, and Sir John lost
no time.

"I am glad," he said, "to have this opportunity of thanking you for all your kindness to my son in this wild expedition of yours."

"Yes," replied Oscard, with a transparent reserve which rather puzzled Sir John.

"You must excuse me," said the old gentleman, sitting rather stiffly, "if I appear to take a somewhat limited interest in this great Simiacine discovery, of which there has been considerable talk in some circles. The limit to my interest is drawn by a lamentable ignorance. I am afraid the business details are rather unintelligible to me. My son has endeavored, somewhat cursorily perhaps, to explain the matter to me, but I have never mastered the—er—commercial technicalities. However, I understand that you have made quite a mint of money, which is the chief consideration—nowadays."

He drew the rug more closely round his knees and looked out of the window, deeply interested in a dispute between two cabmen.

"Yes — we have been very successful," said Oscard. "How is your son now? When I last saw him he was in a very bad way. Indeed, I hardly expected to see him again."

Sir John was still interested in the dispute which was not yet settled.

"He is well, thank you. You know that he is going to be married."

"He told me that he was engaged," replied Oscard; "but I did not know that anything definite was fixed."

"The most definite thing of all is fixed—the date. It is to-morrow."

"To-morrow?"

"Yes. You have not much time to prepare your wedding garments."

"Oh," replied Oscard, with a laugh, "I have not been bidden."

"I expect the invitation is awaiting you at your house

No doubt my son will want you to be present—they would both like you to be there no doubt. But come with me now: we will call and see Jack. I know where to find him. In fact, I have an appointment with him at a quarter to five."

It may seem strange that Guy Oscard should not have asked the name of his friend's prospective bride, but Sir John was ready for that. He gave his companion no time. Whenever he opened his lips Sir John turned Oscard's thoughts aside.

What he had told him was strictly true. He had an appointment with Jack—an appointment of his own making.

"Yes," he said, in pursuance of his policy of choking questions, "he is wonderfully well, as you will see for yourself."

Oscard submitted silently to this high-handed arrangement. He had not known Sir John well. Indeed, all his intercourse with him has been noted in these pages. He was rather surprised to find him so talkative and so very friendly. But Guy Oscard was not a very deep person. He was sublimely indifferent to the Longdrawn Motive. He presumed that Sir John made friends of his son's friends; and in his straightforward acceptance of facts he was perfectly well aware that by his timely rescue he had saved Jack Meredith from the hands of the tribes. The presumption was that Sir John knew of this, and it was only natural that he should be somewhat exceptionally gracious to the man who had saved his son's life.

It would seem that Sir John divined these thoughts, for he presently spoke of them.

"Owing to an unfortunate difference of opinion with my son we have not been very communicative lately," he said, with that deliberation which he knew how to assume when he desired to be heard without interruption. "I am therefore almost entirely ignorant of your African affairs, but I imagine Jack owes more to your pluck and promptness than has yet transpired. I gathered as much from one or two conversations I had with Miss Gordon when she was in England. I am one of Miss Gordon's many admirers."

"And I am another," said Oscard, frankly.

"Ah! Then you are happy enough to be the object of a reciprocal feeling which for myself I could scarcely expect. She spoke of you in no measured language. I gathered from her that if you had not acted with great promptitude the—er—happy event of to-morrow could not have taken place."

The old man paused, and Guy Oscard, who looked somewhat distressed and distinctly uncomfortable, could find no graceful way of changing the conversation.

"In a word," went on Sir John, in a very severe tone, "I owe you a great debt. You saved my boy's life."

"Yes, but you see," argued Oscard, finding his tongue at last, "out there things like that don't count for so much."

"Oh — don't they?" There was the suggestion of a smile beneath Sir John's grim eyebrows.

"No," returned Oscard, rather lamely, "it is a sort of thing that happens every day out there."

Sir John turned suddenly, and with the courtliness that was ever his he indulged in a rare exhibition of feeling. He laid his hand on Guy Oscard's stalwart knee.

"My dear Oscard," he said, and when he chose he could render his voice very soft and affectionate, "none of those arguments apply to me because I am not out there. I like you for trying to make little of your exploit. Such conduct is worthy of you—worthy of a gentleman—but you cannot disguise the fact that Jack owes his life to you and I owe you the same, which, between you and me I may mention, is more valuable to me than my own. I want you to remember always that I am your debtor, and if—if circumstances should ever seem to indicate that the feeling I have for you is anything but friendly and kind, do me the honor of disbelieving those indications—you understand?"

" Yes," replied Oscard, untruthfully.

" Here we are at Lady Cantourne's," continued Sir John, " where, as it happens, I expect to meet Jack. Her lady-ship is naturally interested in the affair of to-morrow, and has kindly undertaken to keep us up to date in our be-havior. You will come in with me?"

Oscard remembered afterwards that he was rather puzzled —that there was perhaps in his simple mind the faintest tinge of a suspicion. At the moment, however, there was no time to do anything but follow. The man had already rung the bell, and Lady Cantourne's butler was holding the door open. There was something in his attitude vaguely suggestive of expectation. He never took his eyes from Sir John Meredith's face, as if on the alert for an unspoken order.

Guy Oscard followed his companion into the hall, and the very scent of the house—for each house speaks to more senses than one—made his heart leap in his broad breast. It seemed as if Millicent's presence was in the very air. This was more than he could have hoped. He had not in-tended to call this afternoon, although the visit was only to have been postponed for twenty-four hours.

Sir John Meredith's face was a marvel to see. It was quite steady. He was upright and alert, with all the in-trepidity of his mind up in arms. There was a light in his eyes—a gleam of light from other days, not yet burned out.

He laid aside his gold-headed cane and threw back his shoulders.

" Is Mr. Meredith up-stairs?" he said to the butler.

" Yes—sir."

The man moved towards the stairs.

" You need not come!" said Sir John, holding up his hand.

The butler stood aside and Sir John led the way up to the drawing-room.

At the door he paused for a moment. Guy Oscard was

at his heels. Then he opened the door rather slowly, and motioned gracefully with his left hand to Oscard to pass in before him.

Oscard stepped forward. When he had crossed the threshold Sir John closed the door sharply behind him and turned to go down-stairs.

CHAPTER XLI

À TROIS

"Men serve women kneeling: when they get on their feet they go away."

Guy Oscard stood for a moment on the threshold. He heard the door closed behind him, and he took two steps farther forward.

Jack Meredith and Millicent were at the fireplace. There was a heap of disordered paper and string upon the table, and a few wedding presents standing in the midst of their packing.

Millicent's pretty face was quite white. She looked from Meredith to Oscard with a sudden horror in her eyes. For the first time in her life she was at a loss—quite taken aback.

"Oh—h!" she whispered, and that was all.

The silence that followed was tense, as if something in the atmosphere was about to snap; and in the midst of it the wheels of Sir John's retreating carriage came to the ears of the three persons in the drawing-room.

It was only for a moment, but in that moment the two men saw clearly. It was as if the veil from the girl's mind had fallen — leaving her thoughts confessed, bare before them. In the same instant they both saw—they both sped

back in thought to their first meeting, to the hundred links
of the chain that brought them to the present moment—
they *knew;* and Millicent felt that they knew.

"Are *you* going to be married to-morrow?" asked Guy
Oscard, deliberately. He never was a man to whom a successful appeal for the slightest mitigation of justice could
have been made. His dealings had ever been with men,
from whom he had exacted as scrupulous an honor as he
had given. He did not know that women are different—
that honor is not their strong point.

Millicent did not answer. She looked to Meredith to
answer for her; but Meredith was looking at Oscard, and
in his lazy eyes there glowed the singular affection and admiration which he had bestowed long time before on this
simple gentleman—his mental inferior.

"Are *you* going to be married to-morrow?" repeated Oscard, standing quite still, with a calmness that frightened her.

"Yes," she answered, rather feebly.

She knew that she could explain it all. She could have
explained it to either of them separately, but to both together, somehow it was difficult. Her mind was filled with
clamoring arguments and explanations and plausible excuses; but she did not know which to select first. None
of them seemed quite equal to this occasion. These men
required something deeper, and stronger, and simpler than
she had to offer them.

Moreover, she was paralyzed by a feeling that was quite
new to her—a horrid feeling that something had gone from
her. She had lost her strongest, her single arm : her beauty.
This seemed to have fallen from her. It seemed to count
for nothing at this time. There is a time that comes as
surely as death will come in the life of every beautiful
woman—a time wherein she suddenly realizes how trivial a
thing her beauty is — how limited, how useless, how in-
effectual!

Millicent Chyne made a little appealing movement tow-

ards Meredith, who relentlessly stepped back. It was the
magic of the love that filled his heart for Oscard. Had
she wronged any man in the world but Guy Oscard, that
little movement—full of love and tenderness and sweet con-
trition—might have saved her. But it was Oscard's heart
that she had broken; for broken they both knew it to be,
and Jack Meredith stepped back from her touch as from
pollution. His superficial, imagined love for her had been
killed at a single blow. Her beauty was no more to him
at that moment than the beauty of a picture.

"Oh, Jack!" she gasped; and had there been another
woman in the room that woman would have known that
Millicent loved him with the love that comes once only.
But men are not very acute in such matters—they either
read wrong or not at all.

"It is all a mistake," she said, breathlessly, looking from
one to the other.

"A most awkward mistake," suggested Meredith, with a
cruel smile that made her wince.

"Mr. Oscard must have mistaken me altogether," the
girl went on, volubly addressing herself to Meredith—she
wanted nothing from Oscard. "I may have been silly, perhaps, or merely ignorant and blind. How was I to know
that he meant what he said?"

"How, indeed?" agreed Meredith, with a grave bow.

"Besides, he has no business to come here bringing false
accusations against me. He has no right—it is cruel and
ungentlemanly. He cannot prove anything; he cannot say
that I ever distinctly gave him to understand—er, anything
—that I ever promised to be engaged, or anything like that."

She turned upon Oscard, whose demeanor was stolid, almost dense. He looked very large and somewhat difficult
to move.

"He has not attempted to do so yet," suggested Jack,
suavely, looking at his friend.

"I do not see that it is quite a question of proofs," said

Oscard quietly, in a voice that did not sound like his at all. " We are not in a court of justice, where ladies like to settle these questions now. If we were I could challenge you to produce my letters. There is no doubt of my meaning in them."

"There are also my poor contributions to—your collection," chimed in Jack Meredith. "A comparison must have been interesting to you, by the same mail presumably, under the same postmark."

"I made no comparison," the girl cried, defiantly ; "there was no question of comparison."

She said it shamelessly, and it hurt Meredith more than it hurt Guy Oscard, for whom the sting was intended.

"Comparison or no comparison," said Jack Meredith, quickly, with the keenness of a good fencer who has been touched, "there can be no doubt of the fact that you were engaged to us both at the same time. You told us both to go out and make a fortune wherewith to buy—your affections. One can only presume that the highest bidder—the owner of the largest fortune—was to be the happy man. Unfortunately we became partners, and—such was the power of your fascination—we made the fortune, but we share and share alike in that. We are equal, so far as the—price is concerned. The situation is interesting and rather—amusing. It is your turn to move. We await your further instructions in considerable suspense."

She stared at him with bloodless lips. She did not seem to understand what he was saying. At last she spoke, ignoring Guy Oscard's presence altogether.

"Considering that we are to be married to-morrow, I do not think that you should speak to me like that," she said, with a strange, concentrated eagerness.

"Pardon me, we are not going to be married to-morrow."

Her brilliant teeth closed on her lower lip with a snap, and she stood looking at him, breathing so hard that the sound was almost a sob.

"What do you mean ?" she whispered, hoarsely.

He raised his shoulders in polite surprise at her dulness of comprehension.

"In the unfortunate circumstances in which you are placed," he explained, "it seems to me that the least one can do is to offer every assistance in one's power. Please consider me *hors de concours*. In a word—I scratch."

She gasped like a swimmer swimming for life. She was fighting for that which some deem dearer than life—namely, her love. For it is not only the good women who love, though these understand it best and see further into it.

"Then you can never have cared for me," she cried; "all that you have told me"—and her eyes flashed triumphantly across Oscard—"all that you promised and vowed was utterly false, if you turn against me at the first word of a man who was carried away by his own vanity into thinking things that he had no business to think."

If Guy Oscard was no great adept at wordy warfare, he was at all events strong in his reception of punishment. He stood upright and quiescent, betraying by neither sign nor movement that her words could hurt him.

"I beg to suggest again," said Jack, composedly, "that Oscard has not yet brought any accusations against you. You have brought them all yourself."

"You are both cruel and cowardly," she exclaimed, suddenly descending to vituperation. "Two to one. Two men—*gentlemen*—against one defenceless girl. Of course I am not able to argue with you. Of course you can get the best of me. It is so easy to be sarcastic."

"I do not imagine," retorted Jack, "that anything that we can say or do will have much permanent power of hurting you. For the last two years you have been engaged in an — intrigue such as a thin-skinned or sensitive person would hardly of her own free will undertake. You may be able to explain it to yourself—no doubt you are—but to our more limited comprehensions it must remain inexplicable. We can only judge from appearances."

" And, of course, appearances go against me—they always do against a woman," she cried, rather brokenly.

"You would have been wise to have taken that peculiarity into consideration sooner," replied Jack Meredith, coldly. "I admit that I am puzzled; I cannot quite get at your motive. Presumably it is one of those—*sweet* feminine inconsistencies which are so charming in books."

There was a little pause. Jack Meredith waited politely to hear if she had anything further to say. His clean-cut face was quite pallid ; the suppressed anger in his eyes was perhaps more difficult to meet than open fury. The man who never forgets himself before a woman is likely to be an absolute master of women.

" I think," he added, "that there is nothing more to be said."

There was a dead silence. Millicent Chyne glanced towards Guy Oscard. He could have saved her yet—by a simple lie. Had he been an impossibly magnanimous man, such as one meets in books only, he could have explained that the mistake was all his, that she was quite right, that his own vanity had blinded him into a great and unwarranted presumption. But, unfortunately, he was only a human being—a man who was ready to give as full a measure as he exacted. The unfortunate mistake to which he clung was that the same sense of justice, the same code of honor, must serve for men and women alike. So Millicent Chyne looked in vain for that indulgence which is so inconsistently offered to women, merely because they are women—the indulgence which is sometimes given and sometimes withheld, according to the softness of the masculine heart and the beauty of the suppliant feminine form. Guy Oscard was quite sure of his own impressions. This girl had allowed him to begin loving her, had encouraged him to go on, had led him to believe that his love was returned. And in his simple ignorance of the world he did not see why these matters should be locked up in his own breast from a mistaken sense of chivalry to be accorded where no chivalry was due.

"No," he answered. "There is nothing more to be said."

Without looking towards her, Jack Meredith made a few steps towards the door—quietly, self-composedly, with that perfect *savoir faire* of the social expert that made him different from other men. Millicent Chyne felt a sudden plebeian desire to scream. It was all so heartlessly well-bred. He turned on his heel with a little half-cynical bow.

"I leave my name with you," he said. "It is probable that you will be put to some inconvenience. I can only regret that this—*dénouement* did not come some months ago. You are likely to suffer more than I, because I do not care what the world thinks of me. Therefore you may tell the world what you choose about me — that I drink, that I gamble, that I am lacking in—honor! Anything that suggests itself to you, in fact. You need not go away; *I* will do that."

She listened with compressed lips and heaving shoulders; and the bitterest drop in her cup was the knowledge that he despised her. During the last few minutes he had said and done nothing that lowered him in her estimation—that touched in any way her love for him. He had not lowered himself in any way, but he had suavely trodden her under foot. His last words—the inexorable intention of going away—sapped her last lingering hope. She could never regain even a tithe of his affection.

"I think," he went on, "that you will agree with me in thinking that Guy Oscard's name must be kept out of this entirely. I give you *carte blanche* except that."

With a slight inclination of the head he walked to the door. It was characteristic of him that although he walked slowly he never turned his head nor paused.

Oscard followed him with the patient apathy of the large and mystified.

And so they left her — amid the disorder of the half-

unpacked wedding presents—amid the ruin of her own
life. Perhaps, after all, she was not wholly bad. Few
people are; they are only bad enough to be wholly unsatisfactory and quite incomprehensible. She must have
known the risk she was running, and yet she could not
stay her hand. She must have known long before that she
really loved Jack Meredith, and that she was playing fast
and loose with the happiness of her whole life. She knew
that hundreds of girls around her were doing the same, and,
with all shame be it mentioned, not a few married women.
But they seemed to be able to carry it through without accident or hinderance. And illogically, thoughtlessly, she
blamed her own ill-fortune.

She stood looking blankly at the door which had closed
behind three men—one old and two young—and perhaps
she realized the fact that such creatures may be led blindly,
helplessly, with a single hair, but that that hair may snap
at any moment.

She was not thinking of Guy Oscard. Him she had
never loved. He had only been one of her experiments,
and by his very simplicity—above all, by his uncompromising honesty—he had outwitted her.

It was characteristic of her that at that moment she
scarcely knew the weight of her own remorse. It sat lightly on her shoulders then, and it was only later on, when
her beauty began to fade, when years came and brought no
joy for the middle-aged unmarried woman, that she began
to realize what it was that she had to carry through life
with her. At that moment a thousand other thoughts filled
her mind—such thoughts as one would expect to find there.
How was the world to be deceived? The guests would
have to be put off—the wedding countermanded—the presents returned. And the world—her world—would laugh
in its sleeve; there lay the sting.

CHAPTER XLII

A STRONG FRIENDSHIP

"Still must the man move sadlier for the dreams
That mocked the boy"

" WHERE are you going?" asked Meredith, when they were in the street.

" Home."

They walked on a few paces together.

" May I come with you?" asked Meredith, again.

" Certainly ; I have a good deal to tell you."

They called a cab, and singularly enough they drove all the way to Russell Square without speaking. These two men had worked together for many months, and men who have a daily task in common usually learn to perform it without much interchange of observation. When one man gets to know the mind of another, conversation assumes a place of secondary importance. These two had been through more incidents together than usually fall to the lot of man—each knew how the other would act and think under given circumstances ; each knew what the other was thinking now.

The house in Russell Square, the quiet house in the corner where the cabs do not pass, was lighted up and astir when they reached it. The old butler held open the door with a smile of welcome and a faint aroma of whiskey. The luggage had been discreetly removed. Joseph had gone to Mr. Meredith's chambers. Guy Oscard led the way to the smoking-room at the back of the house—the room wherein the eccentric Oscard had written his great history

—the room in which Victor Durnov had first suggested the Simiacine scheme to the historian's son.

The two survivors of the originating trio passed into this room together, and closed the door behind them.

"The worst of one's own private tragedies is that they are usually only comedies in disguise," said Jack Meredith, oracularly.

Guy Oscard grunted. He was looking for his pipe.

"If we heard this of any two fellows except ourselves we should think it an excellent joke," went on Meredith.

Oscard nodded. He lighted his pipe, and still he said nothing.

"Hang it!" exclaimed Jack Meredith, suddenly throwing himself back in his chair, "it *is* a good joke."

He laughed softly, and all the while his eyes, watchful, wise, anxious, were studying Guy Oscard's face.

"He is harder hit than I am," he was reflecting. "Poor old Oscard!"

The habit of self-suppression was so strong upon him—acquired as a mere social duty—that it was only natural for him to think less of himself than of the expediency of the moment. The social discipline is as powerful an agent as that military discipline that makes a man throw away his own life for the good of the many.

Oscard laughed, too, in a strangely staccato manner.

"It is rather a sudden change," observed Meredith; "and all brought about by your coming into that room at that particular moment—by accident."

"Not by accident," corrected Oscard, speaking at last. "I was brought there and pushed into the room."

"By whom?"

"By your father."

Jack Meredith sat upright. He drew his curved hand slowly down over his face—keen and delicate as was his mind—his eyes deep with thought.

"The guv'nor," he said, slowly. "The guv'nor—by God!"

He reflected for some seconds.

"Tell me how he did it," he said, curtly.

Oscard told him, rather incoherently, between the puffs. He did not attempt to make a story of it, but merely related the facts as they had happened to him. It is probable that to him the act was veiled which Jack saw quite distinctly.

"That is the sort of thing," was Meredith's comment when the story was finished, "that takes the conceit out of a fellow. I suppose I have more than my share. I suppose it is good for me to find that I am not so clever as I thought I was — that there are plenty of cleverer fellows about, and that one of them is an old man of seventy-nine. The worst of it is that he was right all along. He saw clearly where you and I were—damnably blind."

He rubbed his slim brown hands together, and looked across at his companion with a smile wherein the youthful self-confidence was less discernible than of yore. The smile faded as he looked at Oscard. He was thinking that he looked older and graver—more of a middle-aged man who has left something behind him in life—and the sights reminded him of the few gray hairs that were above his own temples.

"Come," he said, more cheerfully, "tell me your news. Let us change the subject. Let us throw aside light dalliance and return to questions of money. More important—much more satisfactory. I suppose you have left Durnovo in charge? Has Joseph come home with you?"

"Yes, Joseph has come home with me. Durnovo is dead."

"Dead!"

Guy Oscard took his pipe from his lips.

"He died at Msala of the sleeping sickness. He was a bigger blackguard than we thought. He was a slave-dealer and a slave-owner. Those forty men we picked up at Msala were slaves belonging to him."

"Ach!" It was a strange exclamation, as if he had burned his fingers. "Who knows of this?" he asked, immediately. The expediency of the moment had presented itself to his mind again.

"Only ourselves," returned Oscard. "You, Joseph, and I."

"That is all right, and the sooner we forget that the better. It would be a dangerous story to tell."

"So I concluded," said Oscard, in his slow, thoughtful way. "Joseph swears he won't breathe a word of it."

Jack Meredith nodded. He looked rather pale beneath the light of the gas.

"Joseph is all right," he said. "Go on."

"It was Joseph who found it out," continued Oscard, "up at the Plateau. I paraded the whole crowd, told them what I had found out, and chucked up the whole concern in your name and mine. Next morning I abandoned the Plateau with such men as cared to come. Nearly half of them stayed with Durnovo. I thought it was in order that they might share in the Simiacine—I told them they could have the whole confounded lot of the stuff. But it was not that; they tricked Durnovo there. They wanted to get him to themselves. In going down the river we had an accident with two of the boats, which necessitated staying at Msala. While we were waiting there, one night after ten o'clock the poor devil came, alone, in a canoe. They had simply cut him in slices—a most beastly sight. I wake up sometimes even now dreaming of it, and I am not a fanciful sort of fellow. Joseph went into his room and was simply sick; I didn't know that you could be made sick by anything you saw. The sleeping sickness was on Durnovo then; he had brought it with him from the Plateau. He died before morning."

Oscard ceased speaking and returned to his pipe. Jack Meredith, looking haggard and worn, was leaning back in his chair.

"Poor devil!" he exclaimed. "There was always something tragic about Durnovo. I did hate that man, Oscard! I hated him and all his works."

" Well, he's gone to his account now.

" Yes, but that does not make him any better a man while he was alive. Don't let us cant about him now. The man was an unmitigated scoundrel — perhaps he deserved all he got.

"Perhaps he did. He was Marie's husband."

"The devil he was!"

Meredith fell into a long reverie. He was thinking of Jocelyn and her dislike for Durnovo, of the scene in the drawing-room, of the bungalow at Loango; of a thousand incidents all connected with Jocelyn.

"How I hate that man!" he exclaimed, at length. "Thank God—he is dead—because I should have killed him."

Guy Oscard looked at him with a slow, pensive wonder. Perhaps he knew more than Jack Meredith knew himself of the thoughts that conceived those words—so out of place in that quiet room from those suave and courtly lips.

All the emotions of his life seemed to be concentrated into this one day of Jack Meredith's existence. Oscard's presence was a comfort to him—the presence of a calm, strong man is better than many words.

"So this," he said, "is the end of the Simiacine. It did not look like a tragedy when we went into it."

"So far as I am concerned," replied Oscard, with quiet determination, " it certainly is the end of the Simiacine! I have had enough of it. I, for one, am not going to look for that Plateau again."

"Nor I. I suppose it will be started as a limited liability company by a German in six months. Some of the natives will leave landmarks as they come down so as to find their way back."

" I don't think so!"

" Why ?"

Oscard took his pipe from his lips,

"When Durnovo came down to Msala," he explained, "he had the sleeping sickness on him. Where did he get it from?"

"By God!" ejaculated Jack Meredith, "I never thought of that. He got it up at the Plateau. He left it behind him. They have got it up there now."

"Not now—"

"What do you mean, Oscard?"

"Merely that all those fellows up there are dead. There is ninety thousand pounds' worth of Simiacine packed ready for carrying to the coast, standing in a pile on the Plateau, and there are thirty-four dead men keeping watch over it."

"Is it as infectious as that?"

"When it first shows itself, infectious is not the word. It is nothing but a plague. Not one of those fellows can have escaped."

Jack Meredith sat forward and rubbed his two hands pensively over his knees.

"So," he said, "only you and I and Joseph know where the Simiacine Plateau is."

"That is so," answered Oscard.

"And Joseph won't go back?"

"Not if you were to give him that ninety thousand pounds' worth of stuff."

"And you will not go back?"

"Not for nine hundred thousand pounds. There is a curse on that place."

"I believe there is," said Meredith.

And such was the end of the great Simiacine Scheme—the wonder of a few seasons. Some day, when the Great Sahara is turned into an inland sea, when steamers shall ply where sand now flies before the desert wind, the Plateau may be found again. Some day, when Africa is cut from east to west by a railway line, some adventurous soul will scale the height of one of many mountains, one that seems no different from the rest and yet is held in awe by the phantom-haunted denizens of the gloomy forest, and there he will find a pyramid of wooden cases surrounded by bleached and scattered bones where vultures have fed.

In the meantime the precious drug will grow scarcer day by day, and the human race will be poorer by the loss of one of those half-matured discoveries which have more than once in the world's history been on the point of raising the animal called man to a higher, stronger, finer development of brain and muscle than we can conceive of under existing circumstances. Who can tell? Perhaps the strange, solitary bush may be found growing elsewhere—in some other continent across the ocean. The ways of Nature are past comprehension, and no man can say who sows the seed that crops up in strange places. The wind bloweth where it listeth and none can tell what germs it bears. It seems hardly credible that the Plateau, no bigger than a cricket field, far away in the waste-land of Central Africa, can be the only spot on this planet where the magic leaf grows in sufficient profusion to supply suffering humanity with an alleviating drug, unrivalled —a strength-giving herb, unapproached in power. But as yet no other Simiacine has been found and the Plateau is lost.

And the end of it was two men who had gone to look for it two years before—young and hearty—returning from the search successful beyond their highest hopes, with a shadow in their eyes and gray upon their heads.

They sat for nearly two hours in that room in the quiet house in Russell Square, where the cabs do not pass, and their conversation was of money. They sat until they had closed the Simiacine account, never to be reopened. They discussed the question of renouncement, and, after due consideration, concluded that the gain was rightly theirs seeing that the risk had all been theirs. Slaves and slave-owner had both taken their cause to a Higher Court, where the defendant has no worry and the plaintiff is at rest. They were beyond the reach of money — beyond the glitter of gold—far from the cry of anguish. A fortune was set aside for Marie Durnovo, to be held in trust for the children of the man who had found the Simiacine Plateau ; another was apportioned to Joseph.

"Seventy-seven thousand one hundred and four pounds for you," said Jack Meredith, at length, laying aside his pen, "seventy-seven thousand one hundred and four pounds for me. And," he added, after a little pause, "it was not worth it."

Guy Oscard smoked his pipe and shook his head.

"Now," said Jack Meredith, "I must go. I must be out of London by to-morrow morning. I shall go abroad— America or somewhere."

He rose as he spoke, and Oscard made no attempt to restrain him.

They went out into the passage together. Oscard opened the door and followed his companion to the step.

"I suppose," said Meredith, "we shall meet some time— somewhere ?"

"Yes."

They shook hands.

Jack Meredith went down the steps almost reluctantly. At the foot of the short flight he turned and looked up at the strong, peaceful form of his friend.

"What will you do ?" he said.

"I shall go back to my big game," replied Guy Oscard. "I am best at that. But I shall not go to Africa."

CHAPTER XLIII

"The life unlived, the deed undone, the tear
Unshed."

"I RATHER expect—Lady Cantourne," said Sir John to his servants when he returned home, "any time between now and ten o'clock."

The butler, having a vivid recollection of an occasion when Lady Cantourne was shown into a drawing-room where there were no flowers, made his preparations accordingly. The flowers were set out with that masculine ignorance of such matters which brings a smile—not wholly of mirth—to a woman's face. The little-used drawing-room was brought under the notice of the house-keeper for that woman's touch which makes a drawing-room what it is. It was always ready—this room, though Sir John never sat in it. But for Lady Cantourne it was always more than ready.

Sir John went to the library and sat rather wearily down in the stiff-backed chair before the fire. He began by taking up the evening newspaper, but failed to find his eyeglasses, which had twisted up in some aggravating manner with his necktie. So he laid aside the journal and gave way to the weakness of looking into the fire.

Once or twice his head dropped forward rather suddenly so that his clean-shaven chin touched his tie-pin, and this without a feeling of sleepiness warranting the relaxation of the spinal column. He sat up suddenly on each occasion and threw back his shoulders.

"Almost seems," he muttered once, "as if I were getting to be an old man."

After that he remembered nothing until the butler, coming in with the lamp, said that Lady Cantourne was in the drawing-room. The man busied himself with the curtains, carefully avoiding a glance in his master's direction. No one had ever found Sir John asleep in a chair during the hours that other people watch, and this faithful old servant was not going to begin to do so now.

" Ah," said Sir John, surreptitiously composing his collar and voluminous necktie, " thank you."

He rose and glanced at the clock. It was nearly seven. He had slept through the most miserable hour of Millicent Chyne's life.

At the head of the spacious staircase he paused in front of the mirror, half hidden behind exotics, and pressed down his wig behind either ear. Then he went into the drawing-room.

Lady Cantourne was standing impatiently on the hearth-rug, and scarcely responded to his bow.

" Has Jack been here?" she asked.

" No."

She stamped a foot, still neat despite its long journey over a road that had never been very smooth. Her manner was that of a commander-in-chief, competent but unfortunate in the midst of a great reverse.

" He has not been here this afternoon?"

" No," answered Sir John, closing the door behind him.

" And you have not heard anything from him?"

" Not a word. As you know, I am not fortunate enough to be fully in his confidence."

Lady Cantourne glanced round the room as if looking for some object upon which to fix her attention. It was a characteristic movement which he knew, although he had only seen it once or twice before. It indicated that if there was an end to Lady Cantourne's wit, she had almost reached that undesirable bourne.

" He has broken off his engagement," she said, looking

her companion very straight in the face, "*now*—at the eleventh hour. Do you know anything about it?"

She came closer to him, looking up from her compact little five-feet-two with discerning eyes.

"John!" she exclaimed.

She came still nearer and laid her gloved hands upon his sleeve.

"John! you know something about this."

"I should like to know more," he said, suavely. "I am afraid—Millicent will be inconvenienced."

Lady Cantourne looked keenly at him for a moment. Physically she almost stood on tiptoe, mentally she did it without disguise. Then she turned away and sat on a chair which had always been set apart for her.

"It is a question," she said, gravely, "whether any one has a right to punish a woman so severely."

The corner of Sir John's mouth twitched.

"I would rather punish her than have Jack punished for the rest of his life."

"*Et moi?*" she snapped, impatiently.

"Ah!" with a gesture learned in some foreign court, "I can only ask your forgiveness. I can only remind you that she is not your daughter—if she were she would be a different woman—while he *is* my son.

Lady Cantourne nodded as if to indicate that he need explain no more.

"How did you do it?" she asked, quietly.

"I did not do it. I merely suggested to Guy Oscard that he should call on you. Millicent and her *fiancé*—the other—were alone in the drawing-room when we arrived. Thinking that I might be *de trop*, I withdrew, and left the young people to settle it among themselves, which they have apparently done! I am, like yourself, a great advocate for allowing young people to settle things among themselves. They are also welcome to their enjoyment of the consequences so far as I am concerned."

" But Millicent was never engaged to Guy Oscard."

" Did she tell you so ?" asked Sir John, with a queer smile.

" Yes."

" And you believed her ?"

" Of course—and you ?"

Sir John smiled his courtliest smile.

" I always believe a lady," he answered, " before her face. Mr. Guy Oscard gave it out in Africa that he was engaged to be married, and he even declared that he was returning home to be married. Jack did the same in every respect. Unfortunately, there was only one fond heart waiting for the couple of them at home. That is why I thought it expedient to give the young people an opportunity of settling it between themselves."

The smile left his worn old face. He moved uneasily and walked to the fireplace, where he stood with his unsteady hands moving idly, almost nervously, among the ornaments on the mantel-piece. He committed the rare discourtesy of almost turning his back upon a lady.

" I must ask you to believe," he said, looking anywhere but at her, " that I did not forget you in the matter. I may seem to have acted with an utter disregard for your feelings—"

He broke off suddenly, and, turning, he stood on the hearth-rug with his feet apart, his hands clasped behind his back, his head slightly bowed.

" I drew on the reserve of an old friendship," he said. " You were kind enough to say the other day that you were indebted to me to some extent. You are indebted to me to a larger extent than you perhaps realize. You owe me fifty years of happiness—fifty years of a life that might have been happy had you decided differently when—when we were younger. I do not blame you now—I never blamed you. But the debt is there—you know my life, you know almost every day of it—you cannot deny the debt. I drew upon that."

And the white-haired woman raised her hand.

"Don't," she said, gently, "please don't say any more. I know all that your life has been, and why. You did quite right. What is a little trouble to me, a little passing inconvenience, the tattle of a few idle tongues, compared with what Jack's life is to you? I see now that I ought to have opposed it strongly instead of letting it take its course. You were right—you always have been right, John. There is a sort of consolation in the thought. I like it. I like to think that you were always right and that it was I who was wrong. It confirms my respect for you. We shall get over this somehow."

"The young lady," suggested Sir John, "will get over it after the manner of her kind. She will marry some one else, let us hope, before her wedding-dress goes out of fashion."

"Millicent will have to get over it as she may. Her feelings need scarcely be taken into consideration."

Lady Cantourne made a little movement towards the door. There was much to see to—much of that women's work which makes weddings the wild, confused ceremonies that they are.

"I am afraid," said Sir John, "that I never thought of taking them into consideration. As you know, I hardly considered yours. I hope I have not overdrawn that reserve."

He had crossed the room as he spoke to open the door for her. His fingers were on the handle, but he did not turn it, awaiting her answer. She did not look at him, but passed him towards the shaded lamp, with that desire to fix her attention upon some inanimate object which he knew of old.

"The reserve," she answered, "will stand more than that. It has accumulated—with compound interest. But I deny the debt of which you spoke just now. There is no debt. I have paid it, year by year, day by day. For each one of those fifty years of unhappiness I have paid a year—of regret."

He opened the door and she passed out into the brilliantly lighted passage and down the stairs, where the servants were waiting to open the door and help her to her carriage.

Sir John did not go down-stairs with her.

Later on he dined in his usual solitary grandeur. He was as carefully dressed as ever. The discipline of his household—like the discipline under which he held himself —was unrelaxed.

"What wine is this?" he asked, when he had tasted the port.

"Yellow seal, sir," replied the butler, confidentially.

Sir John sipped again.

"It is a new bin," he said.

"Yes, sir. First bottle of the lower bin, sir."

Sir John nodded with an air of self-satisfaction. He was pleased to have proved to himself and to the "damned butler," who had caught him napping in the library, that he was still a young man in himself, with senses and taste unimpaired. But his hand was at the small of his back as he returned to the library.

He was not at all sure about Jack—did not know whether to expect him or not. Jack did not always do what one might have expected him to do under given circumstances. And Sir John rather liked him for it. Perhaps it was that small taint of heredity which was in blood, and makes it thicker than water.

"Nothing like blood, sir," he was in the habit of saying, "in horses, dogs, and men." And thereafter he usually threw back his shoulders.

The good blood that ran in his veins was astir to-night. The incidents of the day had aroused him from the peacefulness that lies under a weight of years (we have to lift the years one by one and lay them aside before we find it), and Sir John Meredith would have sat very upright in his chair were it not for that carping pain in his back.

He waited for an hour with his eyes almost continually on the clock, but Jack never came. Then he rang the bell. "Coffee," he said. "I like punctuality, if you please."

"Thought Mr. Meredith might be expected, sir," murmured the butler, humbly.

Sir John was reading the evening paper, or appearing to read it, although he had not his glasses.

"Oblige me by refraining from thought," he said, urbanely.

So the coffee was brought, and Sir John consumed it in silent majesty. While he was pouring out his second cup —of a diminutive size—the bell rang. He set down the silver coffee-pot with a plebeian clatter, as if his nerves were not quite so good as they used to be.

It was not Jack, but a note from him.

" MY DEAR FATHER,—Circumstances have necessitated the breaking off of my engagement at the last moment. To-morrow's ceremony will not take place. As the above-named circumstances were partly under your control, I need hardly offer an explanation. I leave town and probably England to-night.
"I am, your affectionate son,   JOHN MEREDITH."

There were no signs of haste or discomposure. The letter was neatly written in the somewhat large caligraphy, firm, bold, ornate, which Sir John had insisted on Jack's learning. The stationery bore a club crest. It was an eminently gentlemanly communication. Sir John read it and gravely tore it up, throwing it into the fire, where he watched it burn.

Nothing was further from his mind than sentiment. He was not much given to sentiment, this hard-hearted old sire of an ancient stock. He never thought of the apocryphal day when he, being laid in his grave, should at last win the gratitude of his son.

"When I am dead and gone you may be sorry for it" were not the words that any man should hear from his lips.

More than once during their lives Lady Cantourne had
said :

"You never change your mind, John," referring to one
thing or another. And he had invariably answered :

"No, I am not the sort of man to change."

He had always known his own mind. When he had
been in a position to rule he had done so with a rod of
iron. His purpose had ever been inflexible. Jack had been
the only person who had ever openly opposed his desire.
In this, as in other matters, his indomitable will had carried
the day, and in the moment of triumph it is only the weak
who repine. Success should have no disappointment for
the man who has striven for it if his will be strong.

Sir John rather liked the letter. It could only have been
written by a son of his—admitting nothing, not even defeat.
But he was disappointed. He had hoped that Jack would
come—that some sort of a reconciliation would be patched
up. And somehow the disappointment affected him physically. It attacked him in the back, and intensified the
pain there. It made him feel weak and unlike himself.
He rang the bell.

"Go round," he said to the butler, " to Dr. Damer, and
ask him to call in during the evening if he has time."

The butler busied himself with the coffee-tray, hesitating,
desirous of gaining time.

"Anything wrong, sir? I hope you are not feeling ill,"
he said, nervously.

"Ill, sir!" cried Sir John. "Damn it, no; do I look ill?
Just obey my orders, if you please."

CHAPTER XLIV

MADE UP

"My faith is large in Time,
And that which shapes it to some perfect end."

"MY DEAR JACK,—At the risk of being considered an interfering old woman, I write to ask you whether you are not soon coming to England again. As you are aware, your father and I knew each other as children. We have known each other ever since—we are now almost the only survivors of our generation. My reason for troubling you with this communication is that during the last six months I have noticed a very painful change in your father. He is getting very old — he has no one but servants about him. You know his manner—it is difficult for any one to approach him, even for me. If you could come home—by accident—I think that you will never regret it in after-life. I need not suggest discretion as to this letter.

"Your affectionate friend,
"CAROLINE CANTOURNE."

Jack Meredith read this letter in the coffee-room of the Hotel of the Four Seasons at Wiesbaden. .It was a lovely morning — the sun shone down through the trees of the Friedrichstrasse upon that spotless pavement, of which the stricken wot; the fresh breeze came bowling down from the Taunus mountains all balsamic and invigorating—it picked up the odors of the seringa and flowering currant in the Kurgarten, and threw itself in at the open window of the coffee-room of the Hotel of the Four Seasons.

Jack Meredith was restless. Such odors as are borne on the morning breeze are apt to make those men restless who have not all that they want. And is not their name legion? The morning breeze is to the strong the moonlight of the

328 WITH EDGED TOOLS

sentimental. That which makes one vaguely yearn incites the other to get up and take.

By the train leaving Wiesbaden for Cologne, "over Mainz," as the guide-book hath it, Jack Meredith left for England, in which country he had not set foot for fifteen months. Guy Oscard was in Cashmere; the Simiacine was almost forgotten as a nine days' wonder except by those who live by the ills of mankind. Millicent Chyne had degenerated into a restless society "hack." With great skill she had posed as a martyr. She had allowed it to be understood that she, having remained faithful to Jack Meredith through his time of adversity, had been heartlessly thrown over when fortune smiled upon him and there was a chance of his making a more brilliant match. With a chivalry which was not without a keen shaft of irony father and son allowed this story to pass uncontradicted. Perhaps a few believed it; perhaps they had foreseen the future. It may have been that they knew that Millicent Chyne, surrounded by the halo of whatever story she might invent, would be treated with a certain careless nonchalance by the older men, with a respectful avoidance by the younger. Truly women have the deepest punishment for their sins here on earth; for sooner or later the time will come— after the brilliancy of the first triumph, after the less pure satisfaction of the skilled siren — the time will come when all that they want is an enduring, honest love. And it is written that an enduring love cannot, with the best will in the world, be bestowed on an unworthy object. If a woman wishes to be loved purely she must have a pure heart, and *no past*, ready for the reception of that love. This is a *sine quâ non*. The woman with a past has no future.

The short March day was closing in over London with that murky suggestion of hopelessness affected by metropolitan even-tide when Jack Meredith presented himself at the door of his father's house.

In his reception by the servants there was a subtle sug-

gestion of expectation which was not lost on his keen
mind.   There is no patience like that of expectation in an
old heart.   Jack Meredith felt vaguely that he had been expected thus, daily, for many months past.

He was shown into the library, and the tall form standing there on the hearth-rug had not the outline for which
he had looked.   The battle between old age and a stubborn
will is long.   But old age wins.   It never raises the siege.
It starves the garrison out.   Sir John Meredith's head
seemed to have shrunk.   The wig did not fit at the back.
His clothes, always bearing the suggestion of emptiness,
seemed to hang on ancient - given lines as if the creases
were well established.   The clothes were old.   The fateful
doctrine of not-worth-while had set in.

Father and son shook hands, and Sir John walked feebly
to the stiff-backed chair, where he sat down in shamefaced
silence.   He was ashamed of his infirmities.   His was the
instinct of the dog that goes away into some hidden corner
to die.

"I am glad to see you," he said, using his two hands to
push himself farther back in his chair.

There was a little pause.   The fire was getting low.   It
fell together with a feeble, crumbling sound.

"Shall I put some coals on?" asked Jack.

A simple question—if you will.   But it was asked by
the son in such a tone of quiet, filial submission, that a
whole volume could not contain all that it said to the old
man's proud, unbending heart.

"Yes, my boy, do."

And the last six years were wiped away like evil writing
from a slate.

There was no explanation.   These two men were not of
those who explain themselves, and in the warmth of explanation say things which they do not fully mean.   The
opinions that each had held during the years they had left
behind had perhaps been modified on both sides, but neither

sought details of the modification. They knew each other
now, and each respected the indomitable will of the other.

They inquired after each other's health. They spoke of
events of a common interest. Trifles of every-day occurrence seemed to contain absorbing details. But it is the
every-day occurrence that makes the life. It was the putting on of the coals that reconciled these two men.

"Let me see," said Sir John, "you gave up your rooms
before you left England, did you not?"

"Yes."

Jack drew forward his chair and put his feet out towards
the fire. It was marvellous how thoroughly at home he
seemed to be.

"Then," continued Sir John, "where is your luggage?"

"I left it at the club."

"Send along for it. Your room is—er, quite ready for
you. I shall be glad if you will make use of it as long as
you like. You will be free to come and go as if you were
in your own house."

Jack nodded with a strange, twisted little smile, as if he
were suffering from cramp in the legs. It was cramp—at
the heart.

"Thanks," he said, "I should like nothing better. Shall
I ring?"

"If you please."

Jack rang and they waited in the fading daylight without speaking. At times Sir John moved his limbs, his
hand on the arm of the chair and his feet on the hearth-rug,
with the jerky, half-restless energy of the aged which is not
pleasant to see.

When the servant came it was Jack who gave the orders,
and the butler listened to them with a sort of enthusiasm.
When he had closed the door behind him he pulled down
his waistcoat with a jerk, and as he walked down-stairs he
muttered "Thank 'eaven!" twice, and wiped away a tear
from his bibulous eye.

"What have you been doing with yourself since—I saw you?" inquired Sir John, conversationally, when the door was closed.

"I have been out to India—merely for the voyage. I went with Oscard, who is out there still, after big game."

Sir John Meredith nodded.

"I like that man," he said; "he is tough. I like tough men. He wrote me a letter before he went away. It was the letter of—one gentleman to another. Is he going to spend the rest of his life 'after big game?'"

Jack laughed.

"It seems rather like it. He is cut out for that sort of life. He is too big for narrow streets and cramped houses."

"And matrimony?"

"Yes—and matrimony."

Sir John was leaning forward in his chair, his two withered hands clasped on his knees.

"You know," he said, slowly, blinking at the fire, "he cared for that girl—more than you did, my boy."

"Yes," answered Jack, softly.

Sir John looked towards him, but he said nothing. His attitude was interrogatory. There were a thousand questions in the turn of his head, questions which one gentleman could not ask another.

Jack met his gaze. They were still wonderfully alike, these two men, though one was in his prime while the other was infirm. On each face there was the stamp of a long-drawn silent pride; each was a type of those haughty conquerors who stepped, mail-clad, on our shore eight hundred years ago. Form and feature, mind and heart, had been handed down from father to son, as great types are.

"One may have the right feeling and bestow it by mistake on the wrong person," said Jack.

Sir John's fingers were at his lips.

"Yes," he said, rather indistinctly, "while the right person is waiting for it."

Jack looked up sharply, as if he either had not heard or did not understand.

" While the right person is waiting for it," repeated Sir John, deliberately.

" The right person—"

" Jocelyn Gordon," explained Sir John, "is the right person."

Jack shrugged his shoulders and leaned back so that the firelight did not shine upon his face. "So I found out eighteen months ago," he said, " when it was too late."

"There is no such thing as too late for that," said Sir John, in his great wisdom. " Even if you were both quite old it would not be too late. I have known it longer than you. I found it out two years ago."

Jack looked across the room into the keen, worldly-wise old face.

" How ?" he inquired.

" From her. I found it out the moment she mentioned your name. I conducted the conversation in such a manner that she had frequently to say it, and whenever your name crossed her lips she—gave herself away."

Jack shook his head with an incredulous smile.

" Moreover," continued Sir John, "I maintain that it is not too late."

There followed a silence; both men seemed to be wrapped in thought, the same thoughts with a difference of forty years of life in the method of thinking them.

" I could not go to her with a lame story like that," said Jack. " I told her all about Millicent."

"It is just a lame story like that that women understand," answered Sir John. "When I was younger I thought as you do. I thought that a man must needs bring a clean slate to the woman he asks to be his wife. It is only his hands that must be clean. Women see deeper into these mistakes of ours than we do; they see the good of them where we only see the wound to our vanity. Sometimes one would almost be inclined to think that they prefer a few mistakes in the past because it makes the present surer. Their romance is a different thing from ours—it is a better thing, deeper and less selfish. They can wipe the slate clean and never look at it again. And the best of them—rather like the task."

Jack made no reply. Sir John Meredith's chin was resting on his vast necktie. He was looking with failing eyes into the fire. He spoke like one who was sure of himself —confident in his slowly accumulated store of that knowledge which is not written in books.

"Will you oblige me?" he asked.

Jack moved in his chair, but he made no answer. Sir John did not indeed expect it. He knew his son too well.

"Will you," he continued, "go out to Africa and take your lame story to Jocelyn—just as it is?"

There was a long silence. The old worn-out clock on the mantel-piece wheezed and struck six.

"Yes," answered Jack, at length, "I will go."

Sir John nodded his head with a sigh of relief. All, indeed, comes to him who waits.

"I have seen a good deal of life," he said, suddenly, arousing himself and sitting upright in the stiff-backed chair, "here and there in the world; and I have found that the happiest people are those who began by thinking that it was too late. The romance of youth is only fit to write about in books. It is too delicate a fabric for every-day use. It soon wears out or gets torn."

Jack did not seem to be listening.

"But," continued Sir John, "you must not waste time. If I may suggest it, you will do well to go at once."

"Yes," answered Jack, "I will go in a month or so. I should like to see you in a better state of health before I leave you."

Sir John pulled himself together. He threw back his shoulders and stiffened his neck.

"My health is excellent," he replied, sturdily. "Of course

I am beginning to feel my years a little; but one must expect to do that after—eh—er—sixty. *C'est la vie.*"

He made a little movement of the hands.

"No," he went on, "the sooner you go the better."

"I do not like leaving you," persisted Jack.

Sir John laughed rather testily.

"That is rather absurd," he said; "I am accustomed to being left. I have always lived alone. You will do me a favor if you will go now and take your passage out to Africa."

"Now—this evening?"

"Yes—at once. The offices close about half-past six, I believe. You will just have time to do it before dinner."

Jack rose and went towards the door. He went slowly, almost reluctantly.

"Do not trouble about me," said Sir John; "I am accustomed to being left."

He repeated it when the door had closed behind his son.

The fire was low again—it was almost dying. The daylight was fading every moment. The cinders fell together with a crumbling sound, and a grayness crept into their glowing depths. The old man sitting there made no attempt to add fresh fuel.

"I am accustomed," he said, with a half-cynical smile, "to being left."

CHAPTER XLV

THE TELEGRAM

"How could it end in any other way?
You called me, and I came home to your heart."

"THEY tell me, sir, that Missis Marie — that is, Missis Durnovo—has gone back to her people at Sierra Leone."

Thus spoke Joseph to his master one afternoon in March, not so many years ago. They were on board the steamer

Bogamayo, which good vessel was pounding down the West Coast of Africa at her best speed. The captain reckoned that he would be anchored at Loango by half-past seven or eight o'clock that evening. There were only seven passengers on board, and dinner had been ordered an hour earlier for the convenience of all concerned. Joseph was packing his master's clothes in the spacious cabin allotted to him. The owners of the steamer had thought it worth their while to make the finder of the Simiacine as comfortable as circumstances allowed. The noise of that great drug had directed towards the West Coast of Africa that floating scum of ne'er-do-welldom which is ever on the alert for some new land of promise.

"Who told you that?" asked Jack, drying his hands on a towel.

"One of the stewards, sir — a man that was laid up at Sierra Leone in the hospital."

Jack Meredith paused for a moment before going on deck. He looked out through the open port-hole towards the blue shadow on the horizon which was Africa — a country that he had never seen three years before, and which had all along been destined to influence his whole life.

"It was the best thing she could do," he said. "It is to be hoped that she will be happy."

"Yes, sir, it is. She deserves it, if that goes for anything in the heavenly reckonin'. She's a fine woman — a good woman that, sir."

"Yes."

Joseph was folding a shirt very carefully.

"A bit dusky," he said, smoothing out the linen folds reflectively; "but I shouldn't have minded that if I had been a marryin' man—but I'm not."

He laid the shirt in the portmanteau and looked up. Jack Meredith had gone on deck.

While Maurice and Jocelyn Gordon was still at dinner that same evening a messenger came announcing the arrival

of the *Bogamayo* in the roads.   This news had the effect of
curtailing the meal.   Maurice Gordon was liable to be called
away at any moment thus by the arrival of a steamer.   It
was not long before he rose from the table and lighted a
cigar preparatory to going down to his office, where the captain of the steamer was by this time probably awaiting him.
It was a full moon, and the glorious golden light of the
equatorial night shone through the high trees like a new
dawn.   Hardly a star was visible ; even those of the Southern Hemisphere pale beside the Southern moon.

Maurice Gordon crossed the open space of cultivated
garden and plunged into the black shadow of the forest.
His footsteps were inaudible.   Suddenly he ran almost into
the arms of a man.

" Who the devil is that ?" he cried.

" Meredith," answered a voice.

" Meredith—Jack Meredith, is that you ?"

" Yes."

" Well, I'm blowed !" exclaimed Maurice Gordon, shaking
hands—" likewise glad. What brought you out here again ?"

" Oh, pleasure !" replied Jack, with his face in the shade.

" Pleasure ! you've come to the wrong place for that.
However, I'll let you find that out for yourself.   Go on to
the bungalow; I'll be back in less than an hour.   You'll
find Jocelyn in the veranda."

When Maurice left her, Jocelyn went out into the veranda.   It was the beginning of the hot season.   At mid-
day the sun on his journey northward no longer cast a
shadow.   Jocelyn could not go out in the daytime at this
period of the year.   For fresh air she had to rely upon a
long, dreamy evening in the veranda.

She sat down in her usual chair while the moonlight, red
and glowing, made a pattern on the floor and on her white
dress with the shadows of the creepers.   The sea was very
loud that night, rising and falling like the breath of some
huge sleeping creature.

Jocelyn Gordon fell into a reverie. Life was very dull at Loango. There was too much time for thought and too little to think about. This girl only had the past, and her past was all comprised in a few months—the few months still known at Loango as the Simiacine year. She had lapsed into a bad habit of thinking that her life was over, that the daylight of it had waned, and that there was nothing left now but the gray remainder of the evening. She was wondering now why it had all come—why there had been any daylight at all. Above these thoughts she wondered why the feeling was still in her heart that Jack Meredith had not gone out of her life forever. There was no reason why she should ever meet him again. He was, so far as she knew, married to Millicent Chyne more than a year ago, although she had never seen the announcement of the wedding. He had drifted into Loango and into her life by the merest accident; and now that the Simiacine Plateau had been finally abandoned, there was no reason why any of the original finders should come to Loango again.

And the creepers were pushed aside by one who knew the method of their growth. A silver glory of moonlight fell on the veranda floor, and the man of whom she was thinking stood before her.

" You !" she exclaimed.

"Yes."

She rose, and they shook hands. They stood looking at each other for a few moments, and a thousand things that had never been said seemed to be understood between them.

" Why have you come?" she asked, abruptly.

" To tell you a story."

She looked up with a sort of half-smile, as if she suspected some pleasantry of which she had not yet detected the drift.

" A long story," he explained, " which has not even the merit of being amusing. Please sit down again."

She obeyed him.

The curtain of hanging leaves and flowers had fallen into place again; the shadowed tracery was on her dress and on the floor once more.

He stood in front of her and told her his story, as Sir John had suggested. He threw no romance into it—attempted no extenuation—but related the plain, simple facts of the last few years with the semi-cynical suggestion of humor that was sometimes his. And the cloak of pride that had fallen upon his shoulders made him hide much that was good, while he dragged forward his own shortcomings. She listened in silence. At times there hovered round her lips a smile. It usually came when he represented himself in a bad light, and there was a suggestion of superior wisdom in it as if she knew something of which he was ignorant.

He was never humble. It was not a confession. It was not even an explanation, but only a story—a very lame story indeed—which gained nothing by the telling. And he was not the hero of it.

And all came about as wise old Sir John Meredith had predicted. It is not our business to record what Jocelyn said. Women — the best of them — have some things in their hearts which can only be said once to one person. Men cannot write them down; printers cannot print them.

The lame story was told to the end, and at the end it was accepted. When Sir John's name was mentioned— when the interview in the library of the great London house was briefly touched upon—Jack saw the flutter of a small lace pocket-handkerchief, and at no other time. The slate was wiped clean, and it almost seemed that Jocelyn preferred it thus with the scratches upon it where the writing had been.

Maurice Gordon did not come back in an hour. It was nearly ten o'clock before they heard his footstep on the gravel. By that time Jocelyn had heard the whole story.

She had asked one or two questions which somehow cast a different light upon the narrative, and she had listened to the answers with a grave, judicial little smile—the smile of a judge whose verdict was preordained, whose knowledge had nothing to gain from evidence.

Because she loved him she took his story and twisted it and turned it to a shape of her own liking. Those items which he had considered important she passed over as trifles; the trifles she magnified into the corner-stones upon which the edifice was built. She set the lame story upon its legs, and it stood upright. She believed what he had never told, and much that he related she chose to discredit —because she loved him. She perceived motives where he assured her there were none; she recognized the force of circumstance where he took the blame to himself—because she loved him. She maintained that the past was good, that he could not have acted differently, that she would not have had it otherwise—because she loved him.

And who shall say that she was wrong?

Jack went out to meet Maurice Gordon when they heard his footsteps, and as they walked back to the house he told him. Gordon was quite honest about it.

"I hoped," he said, "when I ran against you in the wood, that that was why you had come back. Nothing could have given me greater happiness. Hang it, I *am* glad, old chap!"

They sat far into the night arranging their lives. Jack was nervously anxious to get back to England. He could not rid his mind of the picture he had seen as he left his father's presence to go and take his passage to Africa—the picture of an old man sitting in a stiff-backed chair before a dying fire. Moreover, he was afraid of Africa; the Irritability of Africa had laid its hand upon him almost as soon as he had set his foot upon its torrid strand. He was afraid of the climate for Jocelyn; he was afraid of it for himself. The happiness that comes late must be firmly held to; nothing must be forgotten to secure it, or else it may slip between the fingers at the last moment.

Those who have snatched happiness late in life can tell of a thousand details carefully attended to—a whole existence laid out in preparation for it, of health fostered, small pleasures relinquished, days carefully spent.

Jack Meredith was nervously apprehensive that his happiness might even now slip through his fingers. Truly, climatic influence is a strange and wonderful thing. It was Africa that had done this, and he was conscious of it. He remembered Victor Durnovo's strange outburst on their first meeting a few miles below Msala on the Ogowe River, and the remembrance only made him the more anxious that Jocelyn and he should turn their backs upon the accursed West Coast forever.

Before they went to bed that night it was all arranged. Jack Meredith had carried his point. Maurice and Jocelyn were to sail with him for England by the first boat. Jocelyn and he compiled a telegram to be sent off first thing by a native boat to St. Paul de Loanda. It was addressed to Sir John Meredith, London, and signed " Meredith, Loango." The text of it was:

"I bring Jocelyn home by first boat."

And the last words, like the first, must be of an old man in London. We found him in the midst of a brilliant assembly; we leave him alone. We leave him lying stiffly on his solemn four-post bed, with his keen, proud face turned fearlessly towards his Maker. His lips are still; they wear a smile which even in death is slightly cynical. On the table at his bedside lies a submarine telegram from Africa. It is unopened.

THE END

www.ingramcontent.com/pod-product-compliance
Lightning Source LLC
Chambersburg PA
CBHW021803110726
47902CB00006B/1629